Daisy Buchanan is an award-winning journalist, author and broadcaster. She has written for every major newspaper and magazine in the UK, from the *Guardian* to *Grazia*. She hosts the chart-topping podcast, *You're Booked*, where she interviews legendary writers from all over the world about how their reading habits shape their work. Her previous books include *How To Be A Grown Up* and *The Sisterhood*. *Insatiable* is her first novel.

DAISY BUCHANAN

insatiable

sphere

SPHERE

First published in Great Britain in 2021 by Sphere

1 3 5 7 9 10 8 6 4 2

A CIP catalogue record for this book
is available from the British Library.

ISBN 978-0-7515-8018-1

Typeset in Sabon by M Rules
Printed and bound in Great Britain by Clays Ltd, Elcograf S.p.A.

Papers used by Sphere are from well-managed forests
and other responsible sources.

Sphere
An imprint of
Little, Brown Book Group
Carmelite House
50 Victoria Embankment
London EC4Y 0DZ

An Hachette UK Company
www.hachette.co.uk

www.littlebrown.co.uk

For Dale, my happy beginning

A twosome is a fragile structure that
an intruder can slip into, but a triangle
is a closed figure sufficient unto itself.

BIANCA LAMBLIN,
A Disgraceful Affair
Translated by Julie Plovnick

Chapter One

I don't want to be at this party.

Quite honestly, I suspect the party does not want me either. I am about six miles from my flat, and sixty million miles outside my comfort zone. For every guest, there seems to be three waiters, carrying pyramid-stacked platters of lobster rolls. No one is acknowledging the waiters, let alone saying 'No, thank you'. This is not my world, this is very much my boss's natural habitat but, unusually, the invitation wasn't addressed to her.

It's my job to open all the 'nobody' post, and the Susan Miller app had mentioned something about 'bravely seizing opportunities instead of expecting them to arrive' and 'being rewarded by courageously forging new connections with influential VIPs'. Anyway, it wasn't as though Connie was there to ask. Something to do with it being 'simply *impossible* to re-mortgage when you're in the middle of a basement conversion', which is her justification for coming into the office four times in three weeks. In order to get Connie to listen to anything, you have to ad lib random bits of property and interiors information. (For example, 'Rich from Sotheby's rang, can you call him back? And then I'll tell you about the Jonathan Adler cushions I saw in TK Maxx on Kensington High Street!') So here I am. Bravely not talking to anyone. Courageously staring at the ceiling, pretending to be fascinated by a disco ball that is shaped like a Rubik's cube.

I'm waiting for a reply from Handsome Dan, thirty-two, who is, according to his Bumble bio, 'Not here for a good time. Here for a long time.' Semi-stealing the invite was a transparent attempt to impress him. I thought, 'Do you fancy this gallery opening? There's a free bar' sounded more appealing than, 'Do you want to come and have sex with me in my shabby ex-council flat?'

According to the internet, Dan works in publishing, Dan vaguely knows someone I was at university with, and Dan is capable of composing the kind of brief, concise, erudite filth that would leave me, against my better judgement, wanking at work, feet up against the cubicle door of the disabled loo, thumb on my clit, index finger working its way into the slipperiest part of myself until I'd come, shuddering and gasping silently. I've cried in that toilet. I've eaten supermarket sushi in that toilet. Now, thanks to Dan, I've achieved more satisfaction in that toilet than I've known in any other area of the workplace.

My exciting new single life has not been *quite* the thrilling, giddy, zipless fuckfest that I was hoping for. My best friend Nadia says that Tinder should change their advertising slogan to 'The odds are good. But the goods are odd'. Oh. Ex best friend, I guess. For half a second I remember all over again, and feel as though I've dropped my heart down a well. Still, I'm yet to meet someone who proves her wrong. The best by far was Luca, sweet, Italian, twenty-two. He spoke barely any English, but he knew 'beautiful' and 'hot', and he brought me a bottle of Fanta Limon afterwards. It was just a bit … boring. He took so long to come that I could feel myself getting cystitis. By the time he had finished, I'd plotted an elaborate route home that took me a mile out of my way via several 24-hour chemists. Still, I didn't actually get cystitis that time. I shudder. I'll always regret Andrew, who I had sex with because I felt incredibly guilty about judging him for having such bad BO. I feel my face flame and flare, as I remember him sweatily pulling out and saying, 'I'm sorry, this isn't going to work, I usually go for girls who are a bit skinny … ah, taller than you.'

But Dan seemed different, perhaps as a result of the deeply underrated erotic power of omission. I honestly didn't know what half my turn-offs were before I saw a load of men in their twenties and thirties going online and boasting about them. Unlike most of his peers, Dan, to the best of my knowledge, has never claimed to have competed in Tough Mudder or the Marathon de Sables, or forced his mates to sponsor him in order to leap from a plane and land in a field just outside Luton. Dan does not consider himself to be a legend. Dan, as far as I am aware, has not been to Asia and paid money to pose with a sedated tiger.

Dan seemed clever, cool and quick witted. For the first time in ages, I had a proper crush. I had sent him my best jokes, my most thoughtful, political commentary – well, screenshots of *New Yorker* cartoons – and nudes. Obviously. He got sent the moodiest, sexiest selfies, my home-made Helmut Newton jobs that took an hour and three separate filter apps. For him, for the pictures, I'd worn

3

the instant thrush knickers and demi-cup bras that left welts on my skin, licking, rubbing, pulling, pouting, posing, displaying everything I had to show. When I messaged Dan, I dreamed up scenarios so explicit I shocked myself. There were moments when I worried that these images could disappear into the internet ether and come back to haunt me, photos where I was so soaked, swollen and exposed that I had almost turned myself inside out. But in the moment, with one hand working the tender space inside myself and the other on the send button, I did not care.

He might still come. The idea that he has stood me up makes me feel hot with shame, so I push it away. I can't bring myself to give up hope just yet.

I am eating my eighth lobster roll. If no one else wants them, I might as well eat them all. My left hand is full of balled up, thick, sticky napkins. They feel thicker and more luxurious than any sheet I have ever slept on, but they have not absorbed any canapé grease. Eventually, I know, I'll absent-mindedly wipe a hand on my dress. I think I've gone off this dress anyway. This morning, the reflection in my bedroom mirror looked OK, good even. I'd give myself a cautious seven out of ten. Still, as always, by the time I checked myself out in the loos at work I felt quite depressed. Even allowing for the fact that the lighting in there is always set to 'morgue', I knew my outfit had turned on me.

On the website, and on the first couple of occasions that I wore it, the dress looked great. It's black, with a bold, red, splodgy print, and fluttery elbow-length sleeves, fitted at the waist, and calf length. It was made to be worn with a vintage, distressed leather jacket and a pair of Grenson Nanettes. It does not look as good with a three-year-old black coat from

H&M, and distressed white Converse. (Distressed in the sense of 'having witnessed trauma', after walking past too many crime scenes in Streatham's kebab district.) Anyway, I washed the stupid dress because I couldn't afford to have it dry cleaned. I can barely afford to get the Tube to work in the week before payday. The sleeves no longer flutter, the hem is now asymmetric and the overall effect is essentially 'spinster matron of honour'. I suppose it's my best dress.

The dress is fine, really, but in this room, it sets me apart. And *not* in a 'and there she was', Hollywood starlet, somebody-please-discover-me way. It looks really, really cheap. I feel cheap. There's a loose thread trailing from the hem. I bend to snap it off and sigh, as the crappy fabric puckers into a ladder. Not for the first time, I decide that I am haunted by a sort of spiritual shabbiness. If my soul has fingernails, they are ragged, and the polish is chipped.

This room is filled with people who live frictionless lives. Everyone here looks as though they have been dry cleaned alongside their outfits. These people never get stood up. They are not eating, partly because they have trained their bodies and minds into such perfect, graceful submission that they are beyond hunger, and partly because the phrase 'free food' is no more exciting to them than 'ring road' or 'assembly instructions'. I'm overwhelmed with a longing so acute that I feel drunk. Will I ever be a real, glossy grown-up? Will I ever go to a party like this and feel as though I belong? Will I ever get to a point in my life where I don't see a canapé, panic and rush to position myself by the kitchen door? Peering at the partygoers, I search for clues. If I stare for long enough, perhaps the secrets of sophistication will reveal themselves, like a Magic Eye puzzle for failing adults.

I gaze at a slender, blonde woman who might be twenty-five, or forty-five. She is wearing a sleek, velvet sealskin suit, it's not quite blue or black. It's the colour of a countryside sky at night, the sort of shade that you stop being able to summon from memory when you've moved to a city and you're always within six feet of an illuminated Tesco Metro. I reach for another lobster roll.

She is standing in front of an enormous mural of a smiling dolphin who is anally penetrating a suited man with a Coke bottle. I should be taking a picture of this picture. I should be posting this to Instagram. 'Urgent. Prescient. Contemporary. Necessary.' This is, technically, a work event. I should be taking a mental inventory and working out whether any of the organisations that we work with are naive or insane enough to put this in their lobbies. But, even on my fourth glass of Veuve, I'm struggling to summon any enthusiasm for conceptual dolphin rapists. Shuddering, I remember an Erica Jong novel that featured a character who could only reach orgasm when penetrated with a bottle of a particular brand of champagne. I'm not sexually evolved enough to think about this without also thinking about how you'd explain yourself in A&E.

Looking at my phone again feels like an admission of failure, but I can't stop myself. This is the part I hate the most. Single girls are supposed to behave as though we don't care. We need to pretend to be bored by the boys in order to make them want us. Our passion, I'm learning, is a passion killer.

Now that I reek of lobster, there is a slightly stronger chance that Dan will appear, but it's half past eight, he said seven, and if I'm deeply honest with myself, 'I'll probably stop by, be nice to see you' and a winking face does not constitute a considered romantic gesture. I don't understand what I've done wrong. Is this because I sent him a heart by accident, because my thumbs are clumsy? I should give up and go home. Maybe I'll find that man with the honey mustard sausages and *then* give up and go home.

Someone vaguely familiar is getting very agitated about a Jeff Koons-esque balloon model avocado – oh, is that Rod Stewart? No. Against my better judgement, I press my smeary phone screen one more time. According to WhatsApp, Dan was last seen today at 7.28 p.m. Fuck you, Dan. I hope you're out with another girl right now, and you marry her, and she has your babies, all nineteen of them, and then you discover that she says 'yourself' when she means 'you' and it's *too late*.

Then I see her.

She's surrounded by noisy, gesticulating guests, but in a sea of shrieks and flying limbs, she's an island of stillness and silence. For a moment, I wonder whether she's medi-tating. Her smirk gives her away – this isn't a moment of deep spiritual peace, this is a woman remembering a private joke. I want to know what's making her smile, and who cuts her hair.

Where my hair is flyaway, frizzy, falling across my face, she has a perfect blunt, glossy fringe that stops just above her eye line. It has an effect on her gaze: she's coy, yet shrewd, part Cinéma Vérité ingénue and part Dame Judi Dench. She's two or three inches taller than me, but she's carrying herself as though the difference were two or three feet. She gives the impression of slimness rather than thinness. Words from decade-old gossip magazines float, unbidden, into my head. I think *trainer* and *Pilates* and *Gwyneth* and *Tracy Anderson* and *is ashtanga yoga still something people do?* As my brain makes me apologise to the people who have practised yoga for spiritual reasons for tens of thousands of years, it realises that she is wearing the £350 original Rixo version of my Topshop frock. I look beyond the hem. The Nanettes. Of course. She's the glossiest person I've ever seen in real life. She's everything I have spent my adult life desperately trying and failing to be.

I often feel as though I'm constantly, anxiously, making an effort, even though failure is inevitable. I'm the human version of a smudged, crumpled maths exam paper. The result is never quite right, but at least I'm showing my working. This woman is a walking right answer. She looks as though she's never made a mistake in her life. I'm not sure that she has ever *sweated*. She's a beautiful, stylish person in a room filled with beautiful stylish people, but it's her confidence that is captivating. Even my mother would grudgingly say 'she holds herself very well'. Somehow, I don't think she learned this with a book balanced on her head. It's as though she's standing properly because she knows she owes it to her bones. Her feet are hip width apart, her weight spread evenly across them. I become aware of my own body, the way I'm slouching to the left, with my right foot grinding a smear of mayonnaise into the parquet floor. Immediately, I stop and stand as if called to attention.

This is someone who is in charge of both of her feet, at all times. Even in a room full of power players, she has a noticeable aura. She has reached the next level of self-possession.

She sees me staring, and smiles. Then, she gestures towards the picture she's looking at, and rolls her eyes. It's an enormous, shocking pink collage – maybe three metres square. In the centre, about a hundred non-applicator tampons have been arranged into the shape of a spurting penis. I drain my glass and walk towards her, not knowing what I'll say when I get there.

It turns out to be, 'I think they should have used Mooncups for the balls.'

Her eyes crinkle up and disappear under her fringe, and she laughs – it's not polite and tinkly, it's a proper honk.

'Christ, it's all a bit … I mean, I thought we were post cock. I'm feeling a bit post cock to be honest. It's put me right off the little sausages.'

'Did you see the dolphin?' I ask her. 'It just looks like a cry for help.'

'Or a cry from someone who is going to keep making these monstrosities until he's allowed to access his trust fund,' she says, drily. 'I'm Lottie.'

'Violet,' I reply, taking the hand she offers in my own, before remembering that it's covered in bits of pastry and butter.

'Are you here to buy?'

This idea is so preposterous that I start laughing hard enough to choke on my own tongue. I see a small scrap of lobster shoot out of the back of my mouth, and land on Lottie's dry-clean-only dress. My eyes could burn a hole through the fabric, but Lottie pretends not to notice. She carries on talking while I get my breath back.

'I'm really gutted, actually. When I got the invite I hoped there would be some really fresh, new pieces here, but I'm bored. Always the way, isn't it? When you're window shopping, everything looks good, but when you actually have money to spend, you're over it.'

'Are you a collector?' I'm supposed to be meeting collectors! I'm networking! I'm making a valuable business contact! I've regurgitated my dinner onto the valuable business contact!

Lottie smiles and explains that she and her husband have dabbled for a while. They met when they were both working in galleries in New York after they graduated, he ended up in auctioneering, they came back to London and she does a tiny bit of dealing on the side 'but really only between friends, it's *very* low-key. It's a bit like buying coke – no one wants to get into the grubby bit, the entire supply chain seems to begin and end with a bloke in a stripy shirt called Jeremy.'

I laugh, as though I know what she's talking about, momentarily basking in the warmth of her world, and imagining what it's like to be equally blasé about cocaine and million-dollar paintings.

'Are you attached to a gallery at the moment?' I ask, stalling for time. If I keep asking her questions, I've got time to invent an impressive new life to dazzle her with. At least, I can work out a way of hiding the fact that I've just been stood up, I came for the free food and I don't earn enough in a year to buy a tenth of the cheapest piece on display.

'I have a few that I've worked with, but at the moment I'm concentrating on this start-up I'm launching with my husband. Jesus, I hate saying "launching a start-up" out loud, I feel like my mother when she calls it "the online web internet".'

'What sort of start-up?'

'There's an auction element, but it's mainly a business that guides people through their early art purchases. We really want to start encouraging people to invest in art, and to educate themselves about what's going on in the art world now. As I'm sure you know, it's such an elitist space. You'd think it would be the one industry that wasn't entirely dominated by white men in their fifties, and yet ... Anyway, we think there's room for us to do something really exciting.'

'That sounds great! I work for a company called Acquire, we're doing something not dissimilar. Do you know it?'

Acquire is supposed to be an app that links everyone important in the art world – dealers, collectors and emerging artists – but beyond that, no one really seems to know what it's for, or why. It's owned by a 23-year-old called Jasper who has left it in the care of a management team in order to pursue a career in reality TV. It's supposed to do for art 'what property tech has done for estate agents', although I fail to see how that could be a good thing. Bafflingly, people keep investing in us, even though I have no idea how we make money. In fact, I strongly suspect we don't, and won't. I send terrible emails about why Acquire is great, and why everyone should sign up to it, even though I'm still not sure what it is. I keep a database of 'key contacts' and once a month someone shouts at me for failing to get an email address for Jeremy Deller. Every so often I ask if I can write some short artist profiles for the newsletter or write a guide to under-the-radar galleries in Basel and Miami or fire out a glowing two hundred word review of an exhibition we'd like to be involved with – and I get told to sod off. The only time I have ever been praised for using my initiative was when I worked out why the fridge was leaking. Someone (and I have a list of suspects) kept turning it off at the socket before leaving the office.

Lottie rolls her eyes and takes a deep breath. I can tell she's about to try to be tactful.

'I think that what we're doing is a bit different, there's more of a focus on education and alternative investments. I was under the impression that Acquire was a bit more, ah, for the *Made in Chelsea* set?'

Lottie is right. About a month ago, I had a painful meeting with a Natasha or a Natalya who had expressed an interest in being a brand ambassador. Natasha or Natalya spent two tearful hours WhatsApping her friends and telling me about who had betrayed her by sleeping with her ex. I tried to find out about her connection with the art world, and the work she loved, and she gave me a very long and detailed account of what happens in *The Da Vinci Code*. She brought her dachshund with her and it shat all over the breakout room. Connie was supposed to take that meeting, but she had an *armoire* that was stuck in Venetian customs.

I want Lottie to like me. And I want her to know that I *love* art. Not this art, not the dicks and dolphins, but that before I knew better, I wanted to work at Acquire because I believed it meant that I could surround myself with beauty all day long. I want to explain that pictures move me in ways I struggle to articulate, that living in my own head can feel intense and claustrophobic and untenable, but when I look at a Cindy Sherman, or an Edward Hopper, or a Fragonard, it's as if someone has opened a trap door inside me, and I can escape myself and head towards the light. I want to tell her that I went to the Robert Rauschenberg exhibition at the Tate and I wept all the way around, because it humbled me and broke my heart to learn that he was making the boldest, bravest, wall-sized collages at a time when the critical world was telling him that he was bad at art and shouldn't bother. But I don't want her to think I'm mad, so I try to be tactful too.

'I guess it's not always exactly what I signed up for, but what job is? They keep telling us that this is part of start-up culture, and we're supposed to "pivot" and "be responsive"!' Urghhh, why am I making air quotes with my fingers? 'What you're doing sounds like what I hoped my job might be. I know it's probably not a political move, and I don't even know if you're hiring but I'd really love to talk to you about it properly.'

In all honesty, I thought that working for a start-up sounded quite cool, and quite sexy. I didn't really understand that sometimes it means working for people whose 'business acumen' might well have been picked up while watching *The Apprentice* with the sound off. I didn't know that it meant I might have to wait days, or once, horribly, three weeks, after our official pay day to get my monthly money, because of 'cash flow' – an excuse, presented with an airy frequency, by senior management, who suspiciously seemed to acquire brand new Macbooks at the same time. I didn't realise that while the words were all new and thrilling – passion and synergy, energy and commitment – the meaning was the same. You work late, you eat at your desk, and you won't let anyone's stapler get empty.

But – and I have nothing concrete to base this on – I would work for Lottie's start-up. I would join her cult. If

Lottie were to ask me to leave the party and stand by the barriers at Green Park Tube station, trying to get strangers to listen to the more alarming sections of the Old Testament, I'd step out into the chilly evening air without hesitating or stopping to pick up my stuff from the cloakroom. If I were to just do what she says, forever, I don't think I would ever feel lost again. She's digging around in her bag – Céline, I think, oxblood coloured – and she hands me a thick card. The word 'Intuition' is printed in copper cursive. In the same font-breath, she is described as its founder and COO.

'Let's get a coffee. It's early days, and we've got to get through some funding rounds, but I have a very good feeling about you. It sounds silly, I know – but I have a weird knack for finding my hires. It's like falling in love.' She pauses, like a comedian waiting for their audience to catch up, and then supplies her own gun-rattle laugh.

Even through her Jeanne Damas fringe, her gaze is very direct. Her eyes won't leave mine, and they're mesmeric – the shades keep shifting, I see everything from emerald to moss. I still can't work out how old she is. She could be five years older than me, or fifteen. When she smiles, which is often, it's possible to make out the most delicate cobweb of crow's feet around her eyes, but her skin is fresh and plump. I think of very clean, white pillows in an expensive hotel. Then, for half a second, I can imagine her wrapped in rumpled sheets, naked, tousled, sexily smudged. Where did that come from?

I smile, promise to email her and excuse myself – because if I don't go now, I'll burp or fall over or do something to ruin Lottie's very good feeling. After collecting my coat and peeking inside the obligatory attendance prize tote bag – a gin miniature, a small bar of chocolate that purports to have a 98 per cent cocoa content and actual Mayan gold, and a coupon for 'discreet aesthetic enhancements: spend £7500 on Botox and get £500 off your next treatment' – I skip out onto the street.

It's my favourite time of year, that point at the start of September when summer isn't fully finished, but autumn crispness is creeping in, and the world is starting to feel clean again, bright and new. It's the true beginning of the year, and I'm ready to start over.

In the more rarefied parts of London, the street lighting seems to be arranged for theatrical impact, rather than better visibility. The street lights are all shining directly onto turning leaves, burnishing the orange and brown. Mayfair is a mood, and I feel rich. I am wallowing in the 'what if'. I glow like the leaves, burnished by Lottie's attention. She belongs. Maybe this is the moment when I start to belong, too. I walk a little further, dream a little longer and deliberately miss the first bus back to Streatham. I'm not quite ready to turn into a pumpkin yet.

Chapter Two

I'm in bed, with one eye open, carefully scrolling through Lottie's Instagram. It's important to be careful because this is a high-risk activity. It would be very easy to accidentally like a post and reveal myself for what I am – a desperate, twitchy, covetous stalker who is up at four o'clock in the morning, thinking obsessively about a woman she met eight hours ago. I'm in quite deep now, too. I've travelled back in time by almost two years, a distant January in Miami, at Art Basel. Lottie has about eight thousand followers, but she doesn't appear to be courting the likes. These are mostly photos of Cy Twombly pictures that she hasn't even bothered to write a caption for. A stunning pink sunset with a simple #basic underneath, then one of Lottie looking over her shoulder in a low-backed, black swimsuit, wearing a giant white straw hat, with 'Thanks @ellenvonunwerth' – *seriously*? Then Lottie with, gosh, a Chapman brother I think, on one side of her, and a Gandy-handsome, six-foot-something, stubbled Adonis on the other, captioned 'Men of my dreams'.

The Adonis is, I decide, as I screenshot the picture in

order to pull it up and apart with my fingers, hyper-real. He seems to exist in a fifth dimension, a back cover perfume ad that makes everyone and everything else look as though they're a pre-digital presence in an HD world. I'm staring at his crotch, struggling to understand why I don't see a giant bottle of Hugo Boss. He's wearing the blackest suit and the whitest shirt, top button undone, and he's gazing down at Lottie – his chin grazes the top of her head – as though she is the miracle that generations of his family have been praying for. It's the way that I imagine Chris Martin looked at hamburgers after the conscious uncoupling. No man has ever looked at me that way before. Not even Mark, my ex fiancé, who would sometimes stare at me in wonder – but the baffled sort, rather than in tender adoration. Lottie is far, far too cool to tag her clothes but I'd bet my bank account – all minus £2093.82 of it – that she's wearing a Vampire's Wife dress. It's a dark, carnal green, the colour of money and secrets. The colour of her eyes. Tiredness overtakes me, my hand starts to droop, and I find myself imagining my life as her employee, and as her friend.

'God, this, I've not worn it for years! It would look amazing on you! Take it!'

'Of course you must come to Miami with us! And don't let me forget to book your flights to Venice!'

I wonder what she would pay me. Letting my flight of fancy mutate into delusion, I think about storming out of Acquire – *no*, having a very calm and mature talk with Connie and saying, 'I simply can't miss out on this opportunity, they really recognise my potential,' and Connie saying, 'Whatever they're offering, we'll double it! I'll be *your* assistant!' Nadia would see me posting pictures taken all over the world, in my shiny new clothes, with my shiny new best friend, and she would feel something heavy and poisonous filling her veins, she would feel nauseous and weepy and short of breath, and she'd accidentally hit a heart in the middle of the night and I'd *know* that I still existed in her imagination, that I can haunt her as hard as she haunts me, still. I'm not going to look again. I'm not. I'm going back to sleep.

Muscle memory takes over, and I'm typing N, A. She has nearly ten thousand followers now. She's way, way ahead of me – well, I never post or comment any more, so I suppose I can't get too upset about that. There she is, hugging some girl I don't recognise, a smile splitting her face in two, brown abs gleaming, glistening, sweaty but sexy. Oh, GOD, she's made something called Paleo Pie. Apparently she's knocked nearly three minutes off her PB – it takes me a moment to realise what that means – and she's wearing a #gifted Stella McCartney for Adidas sports bra. If I didn't know this was Nadia, my Nadia, I wouldn't recognise her. We spent the first half of our twenties constantly complaining about our jobs, our bodies, our lives. Now she's done something about it all, and I feel betrayed. She looks *happy*.

I can feel the poison, the heaviness, tracing tendrils across my chest, and I scroll back, back, back. The two of us, uncontoured, unformed, hugging each other in our dressing gowns. Nadia trying to write my name with a sparkler. Nadia doubled over laughing at a burned, blackened tray containing my home-made lasagne. Nadia kissing me on the cheek as I gurn for the camera, touching my nose with my tongue. If I concentrate hard, I can smell her. I had to stop using Tesco's own-brand fabric conditioner, it was too evocative of shared clothes and shared secrets. Sometimes I sneakily sniff it when I'm buying washing-up liquid. Last Sunday I ended up weeping into the freezer compartments, and had to pretend to a kind, concerned assistant that I was simply struggling to find the broccoli florets. If I'd married Mark, Nadia might still be my best friend. If I'd been able to live the life that everyone else wanted for me, if I hadn't been so selfish, if I'd been stronger and braver, if I hadn't allowed myself to be crushed by the constant sense of a heavy weight pushing against my chest.

The only real answer to 'Will you marry me?' is 'Yes!' just as the only answer to 'How are you?' is 'Fine thanks, you?' I'd learned that life became very difficult very quickly if Mark heard the word no. I'd made so many excuses for him. It was important that everyone thought he was perfect, because that might make them believe that I was perfect too. I left it too late to admit that I'd made a huge mistake, when deposits were non-refundable, when T-shirts had been printed, when twenty busy hens had cleared a weekend over the course of thousands of passive-aggressive WhatsApp messages, when Mum and Dad had written a giant cheque to the Parish Heating Fund in order to fudge the fact that Mark and I had been Living In Sin.

'Perhaps this wouldn't have happened if you'd, you know, kept yourself to yourself,' sighed Mum, as I sobbed and hyperventilated down the phone.

The one thing we have in common is our overactive imaginations. In Mum's mind, I hadn't just broken off an engagement, but walked out on a devoted husband and a gaggle of fantasy ghost children. Even through my weeping wall of sound, I knew it was only a matter of time before my mother brought up Princess Diana.

'Look at the Princess of Wales. Look what she brought upon herself.'

Even though I'd shaken off most of my mother's weird, warped, Catholic values, I could never quite escape the itchy residue of guilt. Mum has a very strange moral scale. It's not her place to speak out against paedophiliac priests, but she'll attack a wide range of strangers from the comfort of her Debenhams sofa. Don't you dare show up on prime-time television on a Saturday night if you're a young, attractive, female celebrity who has appeared in the *Daily Mail* in a low-cut dress or given a heart-rending exclusive to the *Telegraph* about a devastating abortion.

Of course, I always knew my parents were strict, and maybe a little strange – but I don't think I realised just how strange until I got to university. I was shocked by Nadia's closeness to both her parents, but it soon became apparent that she was normal, and I was not. Everyone on my course seemed to be a product of pride – a solid human return on a substantial investment of money and love. It wasn't just the trust funds, the inherited jewellery, the cars on seventeenth birthdays – but the fact that these things were given freely. I had only been allowed to pick History of Art because strict conditions were attached – mainly that I never asked them for money, because I shouldn't be studying something so 'bloody pointless' (thanks Dad) in the first place.

My wedding was the only plan I've ever made that my parents have approved of. I know this because it was the first time my parents gave me anything since they were legally obliged to clothe and feed me. If I'd married Mark, like I was supposed to, I guess my life would look exactly how it is supposed to, at least to my mother, my family and the group of friends who shelled out for the cottage in the Cotswolds that was booked for the hen do.

Everyone's life has a self-destruct button. Surely we've all walked over a bridge, or looked through a window, or just crossed a road and thought, Shall I fuck it up? I could ruin everything, forever! Usually, the moment passes, the mood fades, we resist temptation like ex-smokers turning down cigarettes, bolstering a resolve that has been softened by a second glass of wine. But the second you start to touch the button, once you have traced its outline with your finger-tips, imagined the weight of the click, the feeling of release, and imagined letting go of everything, surrendering all your power and letting your life spin entirely out of control as you walk away from it ... that's when you become a kid in the cockpit, frozen to the spot as your plane falls out of the sky.

Three months ago, I pressed the button. The wedding was meant to be taking place at the end of October, but we'd almost chosen a July date that had become available due to a cancellation. I kept thinking I'd had a 'lucky escape', before realising, over a course of panic attacks, that I hadn't escaped at all, I was just living on borrowed time.

I couldn't think. I ran. I left it to Nadia to break the news, which was a shitty thing to do, and gives her the right to be furious with me – and I blocked all of my calls. The wedding WhatsApp was abuzz, and I deleted every single message. Every so often, someone still tries to get in touch. I don't know if they want to shout at me or check up on me, but what would I say? I used up every single ounce of energy and agency I had, walking away from my fate. Now, I'm hiding. It's the only thing I know how to do.

Perhaps ironically, the only person who truly understands my decision not to marry Mark is Mark. Still, I choose freedom. I choose to never again spend a Saturday looking at the more expensive suits in the M&S menswear department, watching Mark preening in front of a mirror and asking, 'But does it come in a three piece?' I will never, ever have to hear the phrase 'estimated projections' when someone new asks Mark about his job during dinner. Best of all, I will *never again* climb into a company Audi containing Mark's colleagues and hear the man I thought I loved shout the words, 'All aboard the banter bus!'

But sometimes, when I come home to my new life and new flat, and scurry up the stairwell, past the boys on bikes, the basslines, the washing lines, the piss and crisp packets and cans and screaming and sadness, praying that my housemates won't be in, and the hell outside won't have got inside, I think about how and why the banter bus brought me here. Maybe my life would be a little bit more bearable if I hadn't got off several stops too early.

In many ways, the fact that my parents are barely speaking to me is the only good thing to come out of the situation. But sometimes I think that I would turn back time, and spend a literal lifetime staring at Mark's stupid Union Jack clock, where the minutes passed like hours, if I could be friends with Nadia again.

Chapter Three

On the bus the next morning, I write and delete nine emails to Lottie. Her card is already starting to look dog-eared at the corners, I've spent so much time touching it and gazing at it. If I look for long enough, it might tell me my fortune. I've dressed up for her, even though she will never see this outfit. It's too chilly to come out without a proper coat, but I'm wearing a pleather biker jacket. It's a bit thin, and sits just below my waist, giving me a tent-like silhouette. There's no question that I wouldn't be wearing this if it hadn't been twenty quid and on the New Look sale rail. I'm wearing my tights back to front because the ankles are so bobbly and fluffy, and I have to take tiny, wind-up doll steps, otherwise my knickers are pulled down and you can see a slightly stubbly glimpse of pubes through my skirt buttons. My shirt is covered in tiny zebras. When I left my flat, I loved the zebras. Now I am furious with the twee, stripy fuckers. I'm going to burn this shirt. The bus lurches, I stumble and almost press send, which would be *death*. Much too desperate to email Lottie before lunchtime.

Shockingly, Connie is in the office. She's standing at her desk with her coat on, and her hands on her hips, in a state of fury and bafflement, channelling Kirstie Allsopp confronting an avocado bathroom suite. In fairness, it is full of my dirty mugs, my Post-its ('URGENT! Email meeting details for Wed!' Email who? What meeting?), my crumpled copies of *Metro* and Connie's copies of *Town And Country*, which are no longer in an organised pile, and now slightly sticky to the touch. The top one is open at a feature called MEET THE DUKES WITH DARK SEX SECRETS. In lieu of a bookmark, there is a trail of Hobnob crumbs that leads directly to an empty packet on my desk.

'Sorry, I'll sort that,' I mumble. 'Lovely to see you!'

'Yes, I expect it is. Look, I just came in to tell you to watch out for my knobs.'

'Pardon?'

'My knobs! KNOBS. They're coming from Kenya and I had to do a complicated Bitcoin thing, something about the wood being technically illegal now, it's all rather ...' Connie taps her nose and raises her eyebrows at me. I'm at a loss. Does she have an allergy? 'The main thing is that the courier has been instructed to come *straight to my desk*, if they go to the post room I'll never see them again, and obviously that means it's curtains for the chest of drawers.'

Sometimes I wonder whether Terence Rattigan is still alive and in Connie's head, writing her dialogue.

'Anyway, going for acupuncture, ciao. I'll see you next Tuesday – oh, no I won't, I've got to go to Bath and inspect that dado.'

Solemnly, I look at her, and press my right hand to my heart.

'I will watch out for your knobs. And let me know how acupuncture goes, I've always been curious!'

Connie rolls her eyes so hard that I swear time actually slows.

'It's not for me, you *idiot!* I'm taking the dog.'

It's always relaxing to start the day with a big burst of Connie, because you know you're guaranteed hours, days, possibly weeks, of freedom. I sign for the knobs. I drink off-brand Nespresso and eat Hobnob crumbs off my desk in lieu of breakfast. I read the anonymous sex diary of a New York spinning instructor who picks clients up at work. I get a message from Dan and feel a jolt of adrenaline. *Can't wait for tonight. Send me a preview?* and then, less than a second later, *Sorry wasnt meant 4u.*

It occurs to me that if I'd not received the second message, I'd be in the disabled loos unbuttoning my stupid zebra shirt. Deep breaths. I'm single, I live in London, I work for 'the hottest concept to disrupt the art scene since Cubism', and the career gods appear to be smiling down on me right now. This is the first day of the rest of my life. I can send a fucking email.

'Dear Lottie, great to meet you last night. Intuition sounds ...' Fantastic? No. Great. NO. Lovely? Urghhh. '... intriguing, and I'd love to hear more. Are you free for a coffee next week?' I cannot work out whether to put 'love' or 'yours' or 'kind regards' because every single one makes me cringe so hard that I think my body is about to invert, so I settle for 'Violet x'. Shit, I sent it from my work email.

Leaving my phone on my desk, because it causes me nothing but heartbreak, I go for lunch and embark upon my daily series of depressing maths questions. *Technically,* I can't afford food at all, but I'll never, ever get out of my overdraft. What's another fiver? I want a Pret meatball wrap and a cookie, a luscious molten praline cookie that snaps before yielding and releasing hot chocolate sauce all over my ... stop that. I can't have one, because I know from experience that I will need another nine. Apparently, Nico from The Velvet Underground would post herself heroin when she was on tour, making sure it was waiting for her at her next hotel. If I was her, I would have been posting myself cookies. Anyway, I have a nagging feeling that Dan might have turned up last night if I hadn't been caning the biscuits, so I buy two clammy boiled eggs, surrounded by spinach leaves that look and taste like cheap, green paper towels in public toilets.

After I arrive back at my desk with my depressing lunch, I snatch my phone up, looking for the notification that tells me that Kim Kardashian has sent me a friend request, or that I've won £500,000 in a raffle. Nobody loves me, everybody hates me ... oh, but Lottie has replied!

Violet! SO great to meet you last night, funny girl! Highlight of a very dull party! I've told Simon all about you, and we'd love to have a chat. Super short notice but could you do lunch on Friday? Rovi? Our treat, obvs. Hope you don't mind, I mentioned you to Alan – we go back ages! He's a big fan, bet your ears were burning this morning. Then, fire emoji, ear emoji, fire emoji, before the sign-off, *Bisous L (and S!) XXX*

Of course Lottie is mates with Alan. I think it's in *The Art Of War* – 'know your enemy'. Alan is too much of a spod to be convincing as anybody's enemy, but Lottie is too smart and savvy to ignore a business competitor, even when that competitor is slightly less charismatic than a recorded phone message asking whether you've been in an accident that wasn't your fault.

Alan is one of the big bosses at Acquire, and I still can't get over the fact that he's a self-made millionaire who has put all of his money into an art dealing start-up when he wears suits from Burtons. Bought in 1995. (I saw the label and recognised it from my charity shop foraging.) When I came in for my interview, I met Gregor, Alan's assistant, assumed he was in charge (serious architect specs, charcoal grey cashmere polo) and started a nerdy, nervous spiel about emerging sculptors in South America. Gregor still looks stricken if he sees me in the lift. Crueller people than me – OK, me – have said that the only vaguely artistic thing about Alan is that he looks like what would happen if Gilbert ate George. Alan has a penchant for pinstripes and long, indulgent lunches. Alan favours a white shirt, unbuttoned past the point of 'ageing rocker' all the way down to 'sex criminal', and he loves a heavy, almost industrial chain. More than one staffer has said that they struggle during one-to-ones with Alan because they can't look at him without wondering whether they remembered to lock their bike up properly.

Alan is also away on Friday. He's going to grotty Lanzarote to play golf. He even walked past my desk yesterday and said, 'Oooh, you naughty girl! No biscotti before Lanzarote!' before helping himself to two of my Hobnobs and patting his paunch.

I reply to Lottie. *Didn't know you knew Alan, he's fab! Rovi on Friday sounds good. I'm free from 1pm if that works? X*

I'm entirely available from the moment I wake up, actually, but Lottie doesn't need to know that.

Simon must be the husband. Instinctively I'm imagining another Alan, a money man with straining shirt buttons and wandering hands, someone slug-like but powerful, who can bankroll the art, the hair, the dresses. Because surely no one can be as perfect as Lottie without a little pain and suffering. Is Princess Leia really Princess Leia unless she's been chained to Jabba the Hutt?

Later that night, in bed, on Instagram, I do a little more stalking. I think Simon might be the David Gandy lookalike from the pictures.

Chapter Four

On Friday, I wake up at 5 a.m. There are three dresses balanced on my wardrobe door, and I hate them all. There's the Zara leopard print that was meant to be a 'forever staple' – Connie saw it and said, almost sympathetically, 'The trouble with leopard print is that when you go cheap, it looks *really* cheap.' There's the insane, funnel-necked, woollen checked dress that I panic ordered from ASOS straight after getting Lottie's confirmation email. It's *quite* flattering, but I've put it on and taken it off three times now, thinking I was going to die from heatstroke. There's a Primark maxi that's slightly too summery. I've tried it with a cardigan and I somehow looked like an amalgamation of every single septuagenarian woman that my parents know from church. Obviously I can't wear the red and black dress because Lottie will definitely remember it. (Because I assume everyone makes records of what I wear at all times, and they expect me to bin every outfit and make sure I'm wearing something new each time I see them. This is a totally normal thing to think.)

The leopard is slightly less offensive with a slouchy black

jumper. I tug at my hair and wonder whether I can get away with being a little bit grungy, slightly low-key. It is very important that I do not seem needy. I'm trying to channel Lottie and be the sort of woman who does what she wants, with whoever she wants, and has not googled the Rovi menu and then googled every dish listed. (I now know that *furikake* is a Japanese rice seasoning and *not* pronounced 'furry cake'. I was picturing a Mr Kipling Bakewell tart that had gone a bit mouldy.) I have been worrying so obsessively about how to look like a Real Art Girl that I've forgotten to bone up on any actual art. Maybe I can do that on the bus. Perhaps I can nick the copy of *Aesthetica* from the lobby, and leave it hanging out of my bag, so that I look accidentally and yet quite conspicuously cool.

It's a good thing that I'm the only person in the office, because I spend most of the morning on the toilet, taking deep breaths. I allow an hour for the fifteen-minute journey to Charlotte Street, just in case the Tube breaks, or the traffic is bad, or a stretch of pavement between Piccadilly and Soho is suddenly swallowed by a sinkhole.

Rovi is not what I was expecting. It's bright and blonde, and the vibe is strangely focused, purposefully casual. Surely I haven't been here before? It seems weirdly familiar. Ah, yes, it looks like the place where I went sofa shopping with Mark. I'm seated at a table for four, and I decide it's a good omen. If they're bringing a bonus colleague, they must be seriously thinking about offering me a job. Unless it's Alan, and this is an elaborate, expensive way of firing me. I bite my nails, I put on more lipstick, I wipe it off with a napkin. I look down and realise that I've neatly shredded the paper specials menu, without noticing, and I hide it in my bag. And then, Kansas becomes Oz, and Lottie and Simon enter the restaurant.

They are perfect people. Together, they look like an advert for the act of having lunch. Her skin is glowing, her hair is mirror shiny, her soft leather boots look so immaculate that she must have bought them today, put them on in a taxi and then been carried through the door. He is so handsome that it's hard not to look straight through him. Billboard hot. The sort of perfect that I've become so accustomed to seeing on posters that it doesn't quite register. I wonder what he looks like with his shirt off ... He's coming towards me and puts his lips to my cheek.

'Violet? Simon. Thanks so much for coming.'

I think he is wearing Dior Homme – a scent that has always smelled, to me, of expensive sex. I once accidentally followed a man off the bus, two stops early, because he was wearing Dior Homme, and I was drawn to him like a cartoon character smelling a pie on a window ledge.

'It's really lovely to meet you. Are we waiting for someone else?' How am I squeaking, yet bellowing? Is my next line, 'A *handbag?*'

Lottie leans to give me a hug, just as I start to stand to greet her. I headbutt her on the chin, mussing her fringe. It instantly falls back into place.

'Just the three of us – but if you book a table for three you always get a crappy table for two with an extra chair shoved on the end. This is a bit more comfortable.' She sits down beside me.

Simon waits for us to settle ourselves before sitting next to Lottie. He orders a bottle of white wine and starts to tell me about Intuition. The trouble is that I'm too hypnotised by the way his mouth moves to really take in any of the information coming out of it.

Lottie chips in.

'We're really impressed by the work you're doing at Acquire, we understand you're spearheading the social strategy. I think that what we had in mind for you would be less sales based, not so focused on finding new users, but about creating really meaningful content for them, instead. It's hard to find people who genuinely understand the scene *and* get the digital side – plus a lot of our backers really want us to go after the twenty-something user. You'd be *perfect* for us. But obviously, we'd be poaching you. And we're very aware that Alan recognises your talent.'

Does he? Alan only knows who I am because I once, in a misguided fit of new girl enthusiasm, brought in a huge, expensive box of brownies and offered them all over the office. *All* over. Accounts, sales, the lot. Now, every time Alan sees me in a corridor, he points and says 'Brought any brownies for us?' or just 'Brownies!' I smile and say 'Ahahahahahahahaha!' and resolve to dig out my CV and get a job where I get taken seriously by always wearing black and not talking to anyone, which might actually result in promotions or bonuses.

Throughout the love bombing, I have been taking rapid whisper-sips of Chablis and smiling so hard that my eye sockets have started to ache. I'm too nervous to use my fork (provided, but presumably, in a Japanese fusion situation, frowned upon) but I'm tempted to stab myself in the hand with it, just to check I'm awake and this is real.

No one has ever called me a 'talent' before. I'm a 'life-saver', a 'tea queen', a 'busy bee' and 'the office saviour' (after I spent my lunchtime buying Alan a shirt and tie set from TK Maxx after a pigeon shat on him. He's still not signed off my expenses receipt.) Simon and Lottie are talking about travel, expense accounts, about how they are hoping to hire a junior to work alongside me and 'do the boring bits', and I'm starting to feel like a competition winner.

The detail that surprises and delights me is that they are both, clearly, crazy in love with each other. Simon listens to Lottie talking about the company as though she's giving a TED talk, even though he must know that spiel in his sleep. I catch him sneaking shy glances at her, as she speaks to the waiter. The chemistry is intoxicating. Which is why I don't immediately react when I feel a soft hand on my knee. Lottie's. She must be reaching for Simon, out of habit. She's so passionate, so enthusiastic, so inclusive that for a few seconds I let myself enjoy being touched. Simon's kiss and Lottie's hug comprise the most tender physical contact I've had with anyone in ages. Nadia was a hugger, a snuggler. We used to have afternoon naps in front of *Coast Or Country* and *Come Dine With Me,* lying on her bed in an L-shape, my head in her lap. I'm lost in thought, *aching* for a Nadia cuddle, when I notice that Lottie is now stroking my knee with her thumb, tracing patterns with it.

This is the woman who wants to offer me a job. It's weird. Or rather, it *should* be weird. But it's quite comforting. It's making me feel dreamy and expansive, and there's a new sensation I can't quite put my finger on – a yearning for something I didn't know I wanted.

My wine glass is empty, for the second time. I've eaten a single piece of tuna. I must just be drunk and confused.

This can't be what I think it is. Surely these perfect people wouldn't want *me*?

Lottie is still stroking. As soon as her touch starts to feel cosy and familiar, she moves her hand a little higher.

'God, all we've done is talk boring business. I don't think we've asked you a single question. Tell me, if you had ten billion pounds, which pieces would you buy with it? What's your favourite gallery? If you could commission anyone, living or dead, to do your portrait, who would you choose?'

Lottie is a very active listener, murmuring and nodding throughout, but Simon is thrillingly focused. His gaze is intense, but strangely reassuring – it's as though he's reaching inside me and turning the lights on. I talk about a documentary about Basquiat, and get so passionate and carried away that I knock over a glass of water. No one minds, or notices. The topic of dating comes up, and warmed by wine, I start to talk about my Bumble exploits.

Lottie widens her eyes in fake shock.

'Violet, have you been sexting half of London? Oh God, do they even call it that any more? I'm so old.'

'Well . . . ' I pause, trying to imply that I'm part of a wild, thrilling sexual underworld. They don't need to know that Solomon, my favourite message partner, lives in Wembley and refuses to cross the river for me. 'It's a creative outlet. Inventing scenarios, dressing up and posing for pictures, playing with the lighting, as well as . . . ' I'm bold enough, or drunk enough, to catch Simon's eye for this second pause. His pupils dilate, and I look down, blushing. Shit! I must not forget this is a work meeting. I think it's still a work meeting.

34

It's OK. Simon is definitely pissed.

'I can, ah, see the appeal,' he says, smirking slightly. 'And it makes sense that you approach it creatively, it's clearly such a big part of your personality. You know, you have a lot of charisma.'

Ouch. I fake a laugh.

'Oh God, is that the same thing as being bubbly?'

Simon rolls his eyes.

'Take the damn compliment, woman! No, it's more like an aura . . . do you remember those early campaigns Sophie Dahl did?'

Lottie squeezes her eyes shut, as though she's trying to conjure up the image and project it onto a back wall.

'Oh my God, the Opium ad. Pure, pre-Raphaelite babe. Absolutely that. And – don't take this the wrong way – a young Babs Windsor.'

I laugh like Sid James.

Lottie continues.

'When she did those Ealing films, she was beautiful. Spirited, you know?'

By this point, Lottie's hand has migrated to my inner thigh. For the last twenty minutes, I have been desperate for the loo, but I can't bear to leave and break the spell. I don't want her to stop touching me. I'm dazzled by them, and even more dazzled by the Violet I see reflected in their eyes. Right now, we are the only three people in the world, it's just us, wine and possibility. This feels like the beginning of an exceptionally good sex dream.

Still, Lottie is definitely giving me signals. She's so confident and sure in her touch that I'm certain she's been with women before. And I've certainly thought about it and fantasised about it before. I'm *curious*. In fact, fuck the job. I've spent my twenties working and trying and going nowhere. I want time off for good behaviour. Time off *from* good behaviour. No one cares where I am right now. No one is checking up on me. Right now, beside Lottie, I feel as though I'm living – not just barely existing.

I wonder what would happen if I kissed her? Her mouth is broad and bare, she's eaten and drunk all of her lipstick away. The mouth she kisses Simon with. The mouth that has, presumably, had Simon's dick in it. For a moment, I imagine them together, the sounds he might make as she kneels in front of him. Does he breathe in and inhale the scent of her hair, her skin? Did he buy her that perfume? She smells like hot asphalt in the rain, basil and bonfires.

I blink, and for the fraction of a second that my eyes are closed, I'm shocked, almost sobered, by an adrenaline shot of pure lust. I notice the watch on Lottie's wandering hands and snap back into consciousness.

'Shit! It's nearly six! How did that happen?'

Oh, God, I'll be sacked.

Simon looks amused.

'Oh dear. Will the Acquire people be coming to our office with pitchforks and flaming torches?'

Is it my imagination or does he look as though he's trying not to laugh at me?

I had thought of this.

'Actually, I'm usually the only one around on a Friday afternoon anyway, but as far as anyone knows, you're the emergency dentist.'

And I'm hoping that you're going to make me say 'ahhhhhhhh'.

'There's no point going back now, maybe we could get another drink somewhere?' I plead.

Will Simon suggest some more cocktails, a club, Soho House? (I'm desperate to have one drink in there, one day, even though everyone at work constantly bitches about how terrible it is. Connie says it's completely over, and she'd buy furniture from Argos before she'd be seen dead in there. Rumour has it that this is because she's been banned after she went to the Shoreditch branch and ate them out of free pick 'n' mix.)

Lottie asks, 'So where to?' and Simon says something that sounds like 'Not yet.'

I don't think I can have heard him properly. I need a glass of water.

'The night is young!' I gabble, sounding slightly desperate. *The night is young?* Shut up, Violet.

Simon smiles, looking almost relieved.

'The two of us have a lot on tomorrow, so we'd better call it a day. This has been great, thank you so much for seeing us. Do think about the job, we know you'd be a perfect fit, but it's a little while before we can move forward while we wait for funding rounds. I know you've got other commitments, a notice period. And, if it's not weird, I think we'd both love to see you again ... socially.'

If we were sober, and if Simon looked like most of the men in my office, this would be a creepy end to a creepy meeting. Is this really so different? Is my new boss hitting on me? Is it insane to think that someone who looks like Simon would ever hit on me?

The bill is settled – my card is waved away, *thank goodness* – and after being reunited with my coat, I'm standing on the pavement, the cool air soothing my flushed face.

'Lottie will be in touch with you. Have a great weekend!' Simon kisses me. He might have been aiming for my cheek, but his mouth lands right next to mine, catching the corner of my bottom lip. He feels smooth, but solid. My face begins to burn again. He turns to the road, looking for taxis.

Lottie says, 'We'll see you soon, yeah?' and pulls me in for a hug. She kisses me full on the mouth, opening her lips slightly, as though she's smiling, and then I'm aware of her tongue. I close my eyes and kiss her back, while the rest of the world blurs around us. Did she moan? Did I? Was that traffic noise? The sensation between my legs becomes so intense that I struggle to stand.

Lottie breaks away from me, cries 'Taxi's here!', jumps in a car and disappears from view.

I'm crushed. I don't even know what I wanted from them, but they didn't give it to me. They have abandoned me. This isn't the way a business meeting is supposed to feel – it reminds me of being a 'third best friend' at school.

Experimentally, I prod my mouth, which has become so swollen and sensitive that it seems wrong to touch it in the middle of the street. Socially. *See you socially.* What does that mean? All I want to do is follow them home, into bed. I exhale, trying to sober up and think of something else.

I can't.

I pick up my phone and start swiping, scrolling, searching for someone or something to take the edge off. Then, I see the messages from Dan.

You're quiet!

Where r u?

Are you pissed off with me?

Then, a weeping face and three fax machines.

Six minutes later, I'm climbing into the back seat of a stranger's Prius, wondering whether there's a German word for regretting what you're about to do just before you've done it.

Chapter Five

A weekend comes and goes. In order to stop myself from texting Lottie with a 'casual' hi, I hide my phone in my knicker drawer, in an old shoe box containing months of unopened credit card bills. In the moments between sleeping and waking, I stroke myself into wetness, letting my sub-conscious conjure various completely implausible scenarios. I've always been able to come up with outrageous sexual fantasies – even when I lived with Mark, I'd silently invent filthy, faceless encounters while he snored beside me. At the time, I was liberated by impossibility. My secret, erotic self could be wild and outrageous because I had no real space to act out. It didn't make any sense, even to me. When Mark objectified me, I was angry and resentful. Yet, when it came to imaginary sex with non-existent strangers, I pictured myself being treated like a porn star, or blow-up doll.

Even by my standards, my imagination is out of control at the moment. And the boundary between fantasy and reality is dissolving. I want this to happen. I think about straddling Simon while Lottie pinches my nipples – for some reason we're all trapped in a lift in that one. Or Lottie, discovering me in flagrante with Simon, and spanking me hard before going down on me.

My encounter with Dan was disappointing, of course. He was already pissed, I was already pissed, we had another bottle of rough red wine in a terrible bar in Old Street, one of those places where no surface is unadorned with a plastic neon chandelier or uncovered by a grubby zebra print rug.

There was no chemistry because it's impossible to establish any in a venue where no one can have a conversation over the looped hard house remixes of 'It's Raining Men'. Still, we went back to Hainault – which Dan claimed was 'really close to Stratford' – HA! Dan couldn't stay hard, I had to ask him nicely to please stop choking me, we had an exhausting discussion about twenty-first century feminism, then he talked obsessively and at length about a female colleague who was moving to Australia. The best part was when I found Hainault Tube in the early hours of the morning with four per cent battery on my phone, which died, just as I was going through the barriers. The usual.

At the time, I almost didn't mind. It felt like the last day of term, the hell before the happy ending. Lottie would be in touch soon, I thought, and then … and then … *something* will happen, and I'll never have to bother with this nonsense again. But it's been three days since she kissed me on the pavement. Three days of waking up in squalor, in Streatham, and wondering what her morning routine is like. I don't know where she lives. My brain is firing up its own version of Zoopla, considering the beautiful, unattainable possibilities. If it's not making proper porn for me, it's making property porn.

They're arty, so *maybe* it's a cavernous Hoxton

warehouse, flooded with white light, and poured resin floors – or what I imagine poured resin floors to be. Perhaps it's a Docklands penthouse, up in the sky with the bankers. But then I think about where I'd live if I wasn't so broke, and I picture Lottie and Simon in a townhouse in Hampstead or Highbury. White towels, white duvets, wooden floors. No clutter. A proper coffee machine in the kitchen. A velvet sofa. A place where you can walk around in bare feet without constantly having to dust away the grit and hair. A fridge from a Waitrose advert, filled with verdant vegetables, velvety hummus, Prestat chocolates. A Narnia fridge – if you go to the back you fall straight through and find yourself in the middle of Liberty. If I lived in Lottie's world, I wouldn't be the sort of girl who can eat an entire box of chocolates in less than ten minutes, and then the tub of hummus, with a teaspoon, as a chaser.

The memory of the lunch is sustaining me. I keep thinking about her hand on my thigh, and the compliments that made me feel dizzy, high even. I'm in the middle of a dirty daydream when Lottie calls me. I'm at my desk, with my eyes shut, replaying the kiss, wondering what would have happened if I'd followed her home. I'm thinking about her lips on my neck, my nipples, the insides of my thighs, and then she gets out of my dreams and into my phone. I grab it frantically and nearly drop it with shock when I process her name on the caller ID.

I say 'Helloooooooooo! I mean, hel-*lo*', trying to sound slightly more like Nigella and less like Keith Lemon. But it's Simon, not Lottie, on the other end.

'Violet, hi. This is really short notice, but we've been seeing investors all day and one of them really wants to meet you. I don't suppose you could come by at six? We're at the Zetter, the Farringdon one.'

He sounds exhausted, and quietly furious. This is a man who is already having a terrible day. If I say no, I'm going to ruin it completely.

Hold on. He hasn't even hired me yet. He can't just use me as investor bait. For all he knows, I have exciting plans tonight. He can't expect me to drop everything and run to him.

Although surely this is good news, really. I did not fuck it up over lunch. I impressed them. They were worried about investment, and now they want me to be part of the pitch. This is how their world works – they are people who make things happen. This is a chance for me to show passion, loyalty, commitment and all of those other synonyms for desperate that appear in bold at the top of my CV.

Still, isn't it a bit weird that they want to meet after work, in a hotel? Simon's breath sounds heavy, slightly laboured. Impatient. Kind of creepy. But then I remember the way he looked at me across the table, as though I was at the centre of his world. I remember the way Lottie touched me, the moan she made, the kiss.

Maybe I want it to get weird.

While my brain works overtime, my mouth fumbles for words.

'Simon, I, ah, *sure*! Let me think – I'm just about to go into a meeting but as long as that finishes when it's sup-posed to, I should be able to get out of here just before six, so hopefully I can be with you for about quarter past. This is all very exciting, how's it going?'

And then, it's as if a huge black cloud has drifted away,

and I can feel the sun's warmth beaming directly into my ear. The adult man is not going to have a temper tantrum. All is well.

'Ah, thank Christ for that! Lottie has been losing her mind, it's been a bit of a stressful one. This guy has a *lot* of money, but he's kept us on our toes.'

I get the impression that there is a lot more Simon would like to say, but he fears being overheard.

'We mentioned that we had this hugely talented person who might be joining us from Acquire, we were singing your praises and the guy says, "Great! Let's get her in!" and it turns out he means *now.*' He lowers his voice. 'He made a waitress cry. And I think Lottie might be next.'

I'm no business guru but I'm not sure Simon should be so keen to take money from assholes. Still, I brush that concern to one side.

'Tell Lottie not to worry, I'll be there as quick as I can.'

'We *really* appreciate this. I knew we were right about you.'

This is a strange thing for Simon to say, but I let it go, choosing to bask in the gratitude I hear in his voice. I've saved an extremely handsome man's day! The part of my chest that always feels tense and tight becomes warm, almost liquid. It's good to be part of the solution, not part of the problem. Usually I feel like the whole problem.

As always, the trouble is that I'm not wearing the right clothes.

Today is a Mistake Outfit Day. I'm in a charity shop special, a stonewashed denim button-down pinafore that gapes around the chest. I've tried all kinds of unbuttoning tricks and combinations, but no matter what I do, my tits look octagonal. This 'directional look' has been 'teamed' with a grey ribbed polo neck that has been washed three times and Febreezed under the armpits but remains haunted by the ghost of the owner's BO. It always seems fine in the morning, then spookily, at exactly midday, I am enveloped by a smell that makes me think someone has stubbed out a cigarette on an expired packet of ham. I like to put this together with scuffed ankle boots and bobbly tights that have been washed with a bit of tissue, for some classic day to night glamour.

Obviously, this is an emergency and I *have* to go shopping.

Fortunately, no one even looks up as I bundle my coat over my arm, walking with real purpose. I imagine my credit card glowing green, plutonium in my pocket. I feel drunk on irresponsibility, on *possibility*. For the first time since my student days, I feel giddy.

Sometimes, when we were getting ready to go out, Nadia would clutch me and say, with mock solemnity, 'You are going to be *discovered* in that dress. If anyone is going to see you and make you a star, tonight's the night.'

We both believed in clothes – dresses, especially – with a religious fervour. Some day we would find The One – the second skin, the dress that would allow us to make sense of ourselves and match our insides to our outsides. We spent hours in changing rooms together, trapped and squealing, our arms encased in scratchy fabric trapped above our heads, never giving up on our search for total transformation. I miss her so much. I hate missing her. I hate that at least once a day something will make me forget what happened, and then I have to remember it all over again. The shock is worse than the sadness. It's violent.

She's not here. I have nothing to lose, any more. So why not gamble on a life-changing dress? I'm betting everything on red. (Appropriate, because I'm already quite far in the red.) I'm not going to bother with my usual high street spots. I won't even glance at a sale rail. My lizard brain has taken over. I'm so dizzy with thoughts of dresses that I briefly forget where I am, and find myself coming to between Oxford Circus and Bond Street. It looks like I'm going to Selfridges.

When I left the office, the idea of blowing a hundred pounds on a brand new dress felt like the height of decadence, the epitome of indulgence. Now that I am on the sweaty, spotlit shop floor, I realise that the dresses of my dreams cost five times as much as that. It's so depressing that I'm tempted to call Simon and cancel. I stand in front of a rack and frown furiously as tears start to prickle my eyelids.

I'm tempted to let rip, and angrily blow my nose on £1500 of Roland Mouret when I'm nearly knocked over. Two giggling, blonde women (both wearing fur jackets that are *exactly* the same colour as their hair) rush past and push me into a wobbly pirouette, causing me to crash into a row of dresses. I clutch one for support, as I contemplate chasing after them with a coat hanger, and I realise it has a giant red tag. It has been reduced from £250 to £80, because there is a small hole at the back, on the hem. It's made from soft, matte, black silk, and it's dotted with tiny white stars. The bodice is slightly ruched, and low, and there is a suggestion of puff at the top of the sleeves. *Are you the one?* My heart is pounding as I examine it for further flaws and discover that it's my size. No *fucking* way.

I pay without trying it on, which is an act of faith, or an act of madness – and then, telling myself that I probably need tights too, I find myself looking at the lingerie. For a second, I indulge a daydream. It's a year from now, I work for Simon and Lottie, and I'm being paid ... lots. Enough to live in my own flat, enough to spend my weekends in Selfridges, buying beautiful lingerie for myself, for fun. That £500 whisper of apple blossom satin, trimmed with eyelash lace, would replace my current nightie, a coffee-stained Guerrilla Girls shirt.

I hazily remember something I once read about erotic capital, the notion – I *think* – that sexuality can be used as a sort of professional power. You're not supposed to actually have sex at work, but if you're confident of your own sexual charisma, you can command respect and get things done. I'm not quite sure about it, as a theory, but I would pay any amount of money for a pair of pants that stopped the interns from asking me to go down to the post room to collect their ASOS deliveries.

Among the stacks of rose and lilac lace, I spot something in dark blue. The colour is not quite navy, but deeper – as luminous and liquid as ink. The knickers have an old-fashioned cut, wide at the hips and narrow at the waist, proper showgirl hot pants. They are made from a dense lace with an abstract floral pattern, which is surprisingly soft to the touch. The matching bra is equally simple. The only unusual details are the thickness of the straps, and the band that sits under the breasts. This is proper, adult lingerie, I realise, designed to reveal by concealing. If I were to get changed in a phone box and unveil my secret super-hero identity, this is what I would come out wearing. For

47

a moment, I mentally flash on the image of Lottie gasping with lust at my lace, as I drop my dress to the floor. This makes me long to be looked at. I make my way back to the tills.

Chapter Six

By the time I emerge from the exit at Farringdon station, sweaty and edgy, it's just after six o'clock. Silently, hopefully, I have a thought that's something between a prayer and a wish, and I get lucky. Pret is still open. I buy a bottle of fizzy water, apologising in my head to the dolphins and David Attenborough, which gives me the secret password – the magic code that will grant me access to my dressing room for the evening *if* I can manage to tap it out on the impossibly tiny keys. Breathing through my mouth, almost laddering my new hold-ups on the sanitary towel bin, I transform myself.

Frankly it's a miracle of luck over logistics, but my hair is shiny and stays where I brush it. It's difficult to see much of anything else in the tiny mirror, but the outfit *feels* good. I'm smoothing lace over my stomach and noticing with relief that the new bra looks right under the new dress. The dress itself seems to hit my waist at the perfect point, clinging to it and then skimming my hips. I even have a single piece of chewing gum left at the bottom of my bag.

It's 6.11 exactly. My heart rate slows, from *Psycho* strings to Beethoven. And I walk away from the stinky toilet, away from Pret and the chaos and clamour of the Tube, from a life of grey skies and grubby pavements, of cereal for dinner and tights with tiny holes in the toe, up Clerkenwell Road and into the Zetter, where the lights shine amber through smoked glass and everyone looks pleased to see me. It even *smells* better than real life in here, of grapefruit and vetiver and, although it's crass to think it, money. I mention Simon's name to the woman behind the reception desk, and she directs me to a suite on the top floor.

Simon is waiting at the door.

'We can't thank you enough for this, and at such short notice, too.'

He has a way of weighing out his words which make them seem as precious as a rare scrap of Pinter dialogue. My own mother has never said that she is glad to see me and meant it. When Simon says it, I believe it. He moves to hug me, and I flinch slightly – I want him to touch me, but it feels as though he's breaking through the fourth wall, one of the posters on my old bedroom wall coming to life. Most men, I have noticed, start to unravel after about four o'clock in the afternoon. They start to smell of themselves – not unpleasantly, but there's that miasma of humanity, the scent of skin and lunch and shirts that are closer to their next laundering than their most recent one. Simon seems to have showered within the hour.

He pushes the door open, and I find myself in Anna Karenina's drawing room. I see velvet and brocade in clashing shades of begonia and bracken, and Lottie is in the centre of it all, the jewel in the crown. It's as if she rang the hotel and said, 'Do you have any rooms that go with . . . me?'

50

She's sitting on the edge of a chaise as though she's about to have her photo taken, her posture perfect and her legs crossed at an angle. Her full-sleeved, low-cut silk dress is the colour of a bruise, of a red wine stain that won't quite come out of the carpet, but its muted strangeness throws the brilliance of her hair and the shine of her eyes into sharp relief.

Standing beside her and looking almost protective is a man I have not seen before. He looks as though he could be Simon's brother – no, not quite. Their faces are very different, but they have the same stance, the same solid, very certain energy. *Of course, they're both white boys who went to private schools,* my brain silently snarks. This man might be a little younger than Simon, he's shorter and more densely compact, but still very attractive. If I were a casting agent, I'd get him auditions to be the bad boyfriend in a network teen drama.

He steps towards me.

'Violet? I'm Richard. Pleasure to meet you.'

He extends his hand and grabs mine, up-down-up. A Thunderbird handshake. Surely this can't be the man who made a waitress cry?

Ah, no, I think that must be the man with his back to me, fussing with the 'mini bar' – a narrow table with full-sized bottles of gin, vodka and whisky. I can tell that this man is in a bad mood just from the way that his back fat is exploding out of the sides of his trousers. Worryingly, I can see a large damp patch on his shirt, just above his kidneys.

Richard calls him over.

'Robert, come and meet Violet. She's going to be the next addition to the team, and she's a real tech expert, she's seriously impressive. Lottie says she's quite the young hotshot, she knows all about the Snapchat and so on ...'

For fuck's sake, Richard. As if you don't know what Snapchat is. As if you don't understand social media. As if I wouldn't find you on Tinder if I were to open my phone right now, bombarding women with indiscriminate aubergines. I reckon Richard is fifteen years older than me at most. I do not find it endearing when Gen X-ers pretend that their understanding of technology begins and ends with the Sony Walkman.

Robert lumbers towards me.

'Violet, hello.'

For a horrible moment I have a very bad feeling that he's about to kiss my hand, but he shakes too. Predictably, he's damp to the touch.

'I said that if they can bring me a girl or two, I'd definitely get on board. Heh, heh, heh.'

Most people laugh through their nose, their belly or their shoulders. Robert laughs entirely through his mouth, his liver sausage lips trembling. They are almost pendulous. For half a second I am absent, remembering Mark, a dinner party, a panna cotta that did not set properly. One look at Robert is enough to put me off pudding for life.

'So,' he asks my breasts, 'why don't you show us your credentials?'

Am I being *pimped*? Did I spend a hundred pounds on these nice new knickers for *Robert*? I think I've got this horribly, horribly wrong. I'm frozen with fear, shame, embarrassment – and anger, too. Lottie and Simon seem seedy, next to Robert. They're not the golden gods I remember. What does Simon have to do with any of this? How much does he know? At home, alone, at night, I'd probably fantasise about being dominated and exploited, taken advantage of during a 'job interview'. It's just casting couch porn, after all. But now that it might be real, I'm panicking. Maybe there is no job, and deep down, I knew it all along. They have made a fool of me, and I've let them.

I think Lottie has seen the whites of my eyes, because she says, gently, 'Robert has to leave in a bit, but he really wanted to meet you. I've told him that you'll be a key part of our team. I know he'd love to hear about the skills you'll be bringing from Acquire.'

'Robert! It's great to meet you!' If there is a real job, I want it. 'So, my focus at the moment is very much on social, but I'm really excited about the fact that there are so many opportunities to explore when it comes to education and research . . . '

If I keep talking, Robert will eventually go away. Because I'm frustrated and fed up, I don't attempt to be modest or likeable. For once, I'm not dumbing myself down. As the words fall out of my mouth, I realise that I don't need to be fake or front it out – I have genuine evidence that I'm good at my job. I talk about content engagement and audience growth, listing numbers and statistics I didn't realise I knew.

After a while, Robert's (glazed) gaze moves from my breasts.

'Very, um, impressive. I've got to get on, I'm late for parents' evening, actually, but it was very good to meet you. Simon, Lottie, Richard, you'll be hearing from me early next week but I think it's all looking good from my end. Thanks for today, you all really know your stuff. Um, ciao.'

Robert finds his jacket – I think he knows Alan's

tailor – and waddles out of the room, a walrus leaving Wonderland. Simon closes the door behind him, and for ten seconds, we are all motionless. I daren't fully exhale.

I breathe sharply through my mouth – I'm feeling a little faint – and then Lottie whoops.

'I think we've got the fucker! Thank Christ!'

Everyone cheers as she stands up and high fives me, and I find myself gathered into a giant hug. Even Simon touches his fingertips to his temple in a gesture of relief.

Richard untangles himself first.

'Violet, you did *so* well. I'm sorry we had to push you in at the deep end like that, Robert is a … challenge … '

'He's an arse!' calls Lottie from the bar, minesweeping Robert's whisky.

'Yes, but he's a rich arse.'

They say it's wise to avoid asking a question when you might not want to know the answer, but my mouth gets free of my brain. I can't help myself.

'Just to, ah, check, with Robert … look, I'm not sure I'm comfortable … I don't want to be here as a token girl. Woman. I mean, woman.'

So much for my erotic capital. Simon and Richard start to murmur their incredulity, but in their chorus of 'Of course not!', Lottie narrows her eyes.

'Yeah, it sucks. But you can make a feminist protest about it *or* you can make your peace with the fact that this is how the Roberts of the world work, and depressing as it sounds, the Roberts make the world work.'

I must look downcast, because Simon says, 'Violet, there is no way you'd be here if you weren't exceptionally able.

We want you because we know you're talented. But Robert is such a tricky bastard, and you're ... '

Richard smiles at me while interrupting Simon.

'... clearly a Velma in Daphne's clothing. And look at Lottie. She has a giant brain, but that's not why Robert is desperate to work with her.'

Lottie laughs.

'I must say, old Bobby was on extra pervy form today. Shall I call down for some champagne?'

Richard shakes his head.

'I would love that but I'm late for picking up the kids. But I understand we'll be celebrating properly next week?'

He looks at me quizzically, in a way that I struggle to read. He embraces Lottie and Simon before hugging me.

'Lovely to meet you, Violet. I'll be seeing you again *very* soon.' I move to kiss his cheek and he turns his face imperceptibly, so I just catch the corner of his lips, which are surprisingly smooth and firm.

Simon picks up a pile of glossy brochures and puts them away in a briefcase, and I feel a sharp, disorientating pang of pain. It's over. Time to go home. I'm not entirely sure what I came here for, but it wasn't this. I've been dizzy with the fizz of possibility, the idea that there might be ... more here for me. I want more. But perhaps I've misread the signals and got it all wrong, as usual? Maybe Lottie gives everyone a goodbye snog? The international art world might be much more tactile than I realised. If they knew what I'd been thinking about, they would probably find it hysterical. Little old me, with my Groupon highlights, maxing out my credit card on new underwear hoping to have sex with a living, breathing Peroni advert? It would be funny if it wasn't quite so tragic.

A strange sound escapes from my mouth, a sigh heavy enough to rattle a windowpane. Why do I feel tearful? I blink very hard and start fumbling for my bags, when Lottie says, 'But Violet, you'll stay and have some champagne with us? It's really thanks to you that we have something to celebrate!' And she's picking up a heavy-looking telephone and I hear the words 'two bottles' and Simon is putting the briefcase beside the door and undoing his top button while pushing his shiny hair away from his unshiny forehead. And I'm putting my bags beside Simon's, and sitting on Lottie's chaise, and kicking my boots off and curling up, tucking my feet under my torso, and pushing my almost shiny hair away from my very shiny face, remembering just in time to 'artfully muss' it instead of going for a full scalp scratch.

The champagne seems to arrive almost as soon as Lottie has put the phone down, because we're in Simon and Lottie land. Simon opens the bottle in another single, fluid movement, with a pop so perfect that it could be pre-recorded. Simon is probably more experienced with champagne bottles than with toasters – and not just because he has the lean, sculpted look of the terminally carb phobic.

Clutching the cool glass stem in my hand, I take a sip, resisting the urge to down the flute in one. Counting seconds, I hold the champagne in my mouth for as long as I can. This is what happy tastes like, and I want to stretch it out for as long as possible. For three seconds, nothing bad can touch me. Not even Nadia. Well, maybe. I swallow sharply.

'Cheers!' Lottie clinks forcefully, knocking half the contents of my glass onto my new dress without spilling a drop of hers. 'Honestly, it was so good of you to come today. Robert has been holding out on us because he needed to see that we can get a great team in place – he doesn't seem to understand that we can't hire people until he signs some cheques.'

As she refills my glass, I ask, 'What about that other man, Richard? He seemed nice.'

Simon smiles.

'He's a very old friend, he really knows his art, but his background is in finance – he's a great negotiator. We've been talking about doing this together for ages, and there's never been a good time. He got divorced a couple of years ago, two young kids, life happened. But he's got this terrifying new girlfriend, she works in the social sector, she's seriously impressive, and he felt he was ready to do something different.'

Lottie laughs softly, and smirks.

'I've always thought that was a very sexy quality, the search for meaning. When Richard was just a boring old banker, he could be hard work, but now he has a purpose. There's something about him . . .'

She makes full, steady eye contact with me. It should be strange and awkward, but I hold her gaze. I'm aware of something fizzing and unfurling.

Taking another sip, I say, 'I've always thought the sexiest quality was curiosity. Trying something new just to see what might happen.'

What has got into me? Who is writing my dialogue?

I know this is stupid. I know this is dangerous. But I remember the way I felt in the restaurant, reckless and bold. I could press the button right now.

Leaning forward, I kiss Lottie on the lips softly before pulling away, shocked by my own audacity.

For a second, I'm scared that I've got this very, very wrong, until I hear the smile in Lottie's voice. 'Let's see what might happen.'

Her right hand grazes my left thigh as she twists her body towards me, kissing me back. Her lips are parted slightly. For a second we're both coy, waiting for a signal from each other, but then her tongue is in my mouth and I'm closing my eyes, oblivious to everything but the heat of her, the weight of her body against mine and the silk of her hair, the curve of the back of her head against the palm of my hand.

She moans, forcing her body harder against mine. I'm aware of a hand in the front of my dress, reaching for a nipple through thick lace. Grinding against me, she pushes me down along the length of the chaise while feeling for the hem of my dress. It's up and over my head and I gasp, momentarily panicking that she might have ripped it, or seen the 'reduced to clear' hole, or both. I don't know how many times I've imagined doing this with another woman, but now that it's really happening, I feel excited, and terrified. What if it's bad? What if *I'm* bad?

The fabric of Lottie's dress feels good against my exposed skin, and I writhe and squirm. Simon, I realise, is probably watching us intently, and the idea thrills me. Shifting my hips so that one of Lottie's thighs is pushed up against my crotch, I intertwine my legs with hers, rubbing myself against her, still kissing her deeply. This feels so good it barely seems real – an out of body experience, but I've never been more *in* my body. For once, it's my mind that I am escaping.

This is dreamlike, a perfect teenage make out. I could stay on the chaise, in my bra and knickers, kissing Lottie forever, but she pulls away.

'Get up,' she commands, taking both my hands in hers, a tender gesture that belies the low menace in her voice.

She tears down my hold-ups – I'm thrilled by her impatience, and a little annoyed that she has clearly *never* needed to be careful about snags and ladders – and pulls my bra off over my head, immediately seeming to understand that there is no back clasp. She hooks her thumbs into the sides of my knickers and tugs. When they fall straight to my ankles, I step out of them and kick them aside, a lacy puddle of lust. The crotch seems to be stained a slightly darker blue than the rest of the fabric. I'm embarrassed, but a little turned on.

Lottie stands in front of me, and I feel completely exposed. This is exactly what I thought I wanted – but what do I want next? My breathing becomes heavy and rapid as I notice that Lottie still has her boots on. My forehead could touch her chin. I want her to take the lead. I don't care what she does, but I need her to do something.

From the corner of the room, I can feel the weight of Simon's stare. Lottie grabs my hips, awkwardly, hesitantly, and for a moment I feel disappointed. She doesn't know what she's doing. This is over before it's really started. I knew it was too good to be true.

Then she takes her right hand and places it between my legs, where I'm pulsing and bubbling with heat.

'Stand with your legs apart.'

She sounds so sure of what she wants from me. It's thrilling. Right now, in this moment, I want to surrender.

I want to stop thinking. I'm turned on just by being told what to do.

Following her instructions, my eyes flutter shut, and I press my body against the palm of her hand. Her teeth graze the soft space behind my ear, then there is a short, sharp bite on my left nipple. I stumble, and Lottie grabs my hips again to steady me, before her hand moves again. She's stroking my lips at their lowest point, she's almost at my asshole and I yearn for her to touch it, to push her finger all the way inside and make me gasp with pain, but she just traces it before trailing her fingers through the wetness of my pussy, circling my clit before starting again. I'm not sure how I'm still standing, every bit of blood in my body is between my legs.

Lottie wipes her wet fingers on the lowest part of my belly. Normally I would feel self-conscious (but what is 'normally'? This is not normal) but it's sexy, I feel sexy, I'm all softness and curvature, every part of me is sensitive to touch. Is it my move now? I cannot let her know that I'm totally out of my depth, so I grab at her dress, looking for an opening. She pulls my hand away and starts to lead me to the corner of the room where Simon is standing beside another chaise, a scratchy looking tweed one with a button back.

Simon is staring at my body, and I can't quite identify the look in his eyes. I'm searching for disappointment or disapproval before I realise he is openly leering at me. It reminds me of the way he looked at me during our lunch, magnified by the power of ten. My self-consciousness melts away and I preen. In this moment, I can see what Simon is seeing, I can experience my body through a lens of filthy delight and pure anticipation. Simon is looking at me in the way I've seen dirty old men look at the *Daily Star* on the bus. I'm ashamed but not surprised to discover that I love it.

He undresses Lottie, instantly finding the zip at the back of her silky dress, which immediately falls to the floor. Of course it does. Simon looks over at me, to make sure I'm looking at Lottie. In my fantasies, she has been wearing wisps of crimson silk, or uncompromising black corsetry. So I'm startled to see that she's in pale pink. It's distracting enough to shock me into thinking about how weird this is. Just for a second, I resent Lottie. I'm supposed to be the innocent, corruptible one here. I don't want to see her in lingerie that emphasises her youth, her girlishness.

I feel shy of her beauty, too. The colour matches her creamy skin so closely that she'd look naked if it wasn't for the sky blue velvet straps that sit on her shoulders and encircle her torso. Then I try to allow myself to look at her the way Simon looked at me. I'm startled and then thrilled to notice that the silk of her underwear, already almost translucent, is twisted at the crotch and soaked to a dark, rose colour. Something flips and contracts in the very lowest part of me. I want to touch her. Simon is rough, pulling her breasts out of their cups, pinching her nipples hard, watching my face. Searching for my reaction. I'm thrilled to realise that they're both performing for me. My breath is quickening, I'm impatient for more. I've relaxed into the role of voyeur.

Simon turns Lottie around, so that she is facing away from him. I notice that her knickers have no back, the strange straps that loop around her waist criss-cross over her buttocks. Simon tugs a strap and Lottie is entirely exposed. She bends over the hard, rolled arm of the chaise, and Simon seems to pull her whole body apart, spreading her wide with his fingers. I've never seen this much of another woman. I have never seen this much of my own body, and I can't quite believe that I'm allowed to look.

Lottie is luscious, like the inside of a foxglove. The skin inside her seems to have its own pulse, and she's so wet that she glitters in the lamplight. There's a line about an inch above the place where her pubes begin. It looks as though it might be an indentation from her underwear, but it doesn't extend beyond her crotch. I didn't know pubes could look like this, wiry and gold. They put me in mind of pre-Raphaelite paintings. There is something exotic about Lottie's pubes, they seem so *deliberate*. When I watch porn, I rarely see bodies like mine. There's a neatness and cleanness to the onscreen women that I just don't recognise in myself. I always suspect that I'm dirtier, sweatier, messier than most women. Lottie's body is probably, in a conventional sense, closer to 'perfect' than mine. She's more sculpted, less fleshy, more magazine ready. Yet, the realness of her naked body, the scattering of freckles on her shoulders, the slight slope of her breasts as her chest rises and falls, is the hottest thing I've ever seen in my life. She *isn't* perfect, but she is beautiful. And that makes me believe that I could be beautiful, too.

Simon plunges most of his right hand inside her, and Lottie gasps. Her buttocks clamp together and grind against the chaise as if she's trying to pull his whole body inside her.

'Don't stop, DON'T STOP,' she grunts, and hearing her voice sound so rough and unmodulated is so powerful that I moan with frustration. If someone doesn't touch me soon, I'll have to start touching myself.

Simon pulls his hand out of Lottie – impatiently, I count the beats, it takes a LONG five seconds – and then holds his fingers to my mouth. I lick his fingers, is that what he wants me to do? Then oh, oh, oh, he pushes them against my soaking lips and slowly, slowly, works his fingers up inside me, and I think he wants to control me, torment me, slow me down but it's too late, I'm coming, I'm using my every single muscle in my lower body to force his hand further in, I'm soaking from the inside of my thighs all the way down to my knees, and I appear to be trying to say 'oh God' and 'so good' and 'fuck' all at once. I feel dizzy and sick and I need to do it all over again immediately.

Simon kisses me in a way that seems sharp, almost per-functory – it's full, but short, and I'm distracted by the way his breath seems slightly minty, in spite of the champagne. I think of smug girls in adverts biting into apples while white coated dentists beam their approval, and I have to resist the urge to count his teeth with my tongue.

'Kneel,' he says, pointing at the area in front of Lottie.

Calm down, Christian Grey, snarks my brain, and I kneel, feeling the heat of Lottie's breath against my pussy, and then the wetness of her lips against mine as Simon drives into her. I close my eyes and arch my back, trying to guide Lottie into my most sensitive spot. Logistically, coming suddenly seems tricky but I want to, I *need* to.

When Lottie's hands reach out to cup my breasts, I lose control. A strange sound is dragged from my body, not a porno groan but a death rattle that vibrates in my clit, my toes, my heels, the top of my ears. A great tsunami of tension gathers and breaks, and I feel inexplicably giggly. I bite the side of my cheek, hard, and notice Lottie and Simon have also reached the point of no return. Her 'Ohhhhhhh' is melodic, his 'Ahhhhhh' harmonic.

Lottie blinks, grins and, looking up, kisses me on the lips.

'Now *that's* how you celebrate good news. Poor Robert, I bet he would have *loved* to join us.'

Simon is standing up, studying me. Unexpectedly, he looks slightly worried.

'Violet, was that all . . . OK? I just want to make sure that was something we all wanted to do?'

As he speaks, he puts his underpants back on, which makes me feel extra naked, and suddenly self-conscious.

I'm touched by his concern, but still a little bit too shy of him to tell him just how much I wanted to do it. In fact, I'm struggling to process the urge myself. Shame starts to gather, a cloud of sand kicked into a clear sea. Was this a terrible mistake? Has this cost me my dream job? Or is this proof of a long-held, private, paranoid conviction – has everyone else been having this kind of wild, secret fun without me all along? Maybe there are thousands of people who have threesomes with their colleagues all the time, and I'm the prude for wondering whether it's odd. I've spent so much of my life being good, worrying and questioning every single desire I've had. Perhaps other people go off and explore these great, strange, voluptuous bloomings, and then go home and wash their faces and go to sleep and go to work and manage to keep everything wholly discrete.

'Simon, shut up! She's not signed anything yet, we don't even have an HR department for her to complain to!' says Lottie sniffily.

The joke doesn't quite land, and I feel a little wrong-footed, so I force a laugh.

'It was definitely my best ever meeting. I don't even have to throw out leftover sandwiches!'

'As long as you're completely comfortable, that's all that matters,' says Simon. 'If you're happy, we're happy. Do you want to get dinner or anything? We could stay here, or there are loads of places nearby . . .'

Weirdly, I don't. I want to be back in my own bed with a disgusting takeaway, letting this all sink in. I'm ravenous too. I can't politely eat tiny portions of fancy food. I smile, regretfully, attempting to look enigmatic.

'Sadly, I've got to be on the other side of town, otherwise I'd love to.'

Always imply you might have a better offer, even when there are no other offers at all. It's the one useful thing Tinder taught me. It might be my imagination, but Lottie looks a little relieved too. She's reaching for her phone, squinting at something. Is she ordering a pizza, an Uber, another girl?

'Violet, before I forget, are you around on Friday? Not for a work thing, just a sort of . . . gathering, a few friends, very intimate, very informal. Nothing to be nervous about. Richard will be there. We're looking for someone else to join us, I think you'd enjoy it. Remind me, whereabouts do you live?'

'South London.' Which could mean anything, really – rarefied Chelsea, leafy Tulse Hill or the shithole I inhabit beyond Streatham.

'We're just off Upper Street, so it's a bit of a way for you to come, but you're very welcome to stay over, if you like. I'll text the address, but come at seven on Friday?'

Faffing about with my bags, trying to retrieve my nice

new underwear from whence it fell, I murmur my assent, doing my very best to hide how giddily thrilled I am. A third date! I guess.

It's only when my head is resting against the fogged up window of the 133 do I realise there was something strange about the way she phrased the invitation. 'A gathering.' Obviously this is an orgy. It *has* to be. What else could she mean?

Chapter Seven

It is 6.54 p.m. and I'm in Wetherspoons, crouched in the toilets, trying to attach a stocking to a suspender belt. The stocking had survived the journey from Zone 4 but instigated a quickie divorce from the belt when I was dashing up the first set of Angel escalators. I could lengthen the strap and make the connection easier, but then I would end up with a stocking top at knee rather than thigh level and look less wanton, and more like an escapee from an Oompa band. I trap the material in the hoop, push it into place, edge it up my leg – and immediately notice a ladder growing out of the back of my heel. I can't tell whether I feel excited, or slightly sick. Right now, I feel silly and squeaky in my scuffed smart shoes and sweatshop lingerie. My entire outfit cost less than fifty quid. I bet Lottie wouldn't use soap that cost less than fifty quid.

Simply because I could, I looked up their house with the details that Lottie sent me, and I know that they bought it four years ago, for £2.8 million pounds. Four bedrooms, garden, within walking distance of several excellent 'independent' day schools. Do they have children? I suppose they might have a small army of secret nannies and au pairs looking after a precocious, adorable, art-loving toddler, but it seems unlikely. Unless they're Victorian throwbacks who never actually spend time with their children, Lottie and Simon seem too hard and polished for parenthood.

In spite of all my Instagram stalking – sorry, *research* – parts of Lottie's life seem unknowable. This hasn't stopped me from imagining them, and I've been layering clichés all week. Does she leap out of bed at 5 a.m. for Pilates and a blow-dry? Does she do the school run, driving for half a mile in a vast, cuboid car that sits two metres off the ground? I imagine her in severe, Scandinavian suits, spending her days taking meetings in the city, making millions of pounds before lunchtime, racking up lines on lavatory cisterns and insisting that her limitless energy comes from green juice laced with matcha powder. At one point I realise that the elements of their life that I've been picturing are parts of the plot of *Scarface*, with Lottie as a Pacino-Pfeiffer hybrid.

I'm late. While I suspect that orgies aren't like plays, and you are not refused entry if you arrive ten minutes after the start time, I'm already feeling guilty. Is it definitely an orgy? Could it be an elaborate prank? Will I knock on the door and discover my parents in the hall, Alan standing between them, all saying, 'We're completely disgusted and horrified with your behaviour'? As I walk up the stairs and out of the pub, I'm tempted to turn tail, sit down and work my way through a £9 bottle of Merlot instead.

But I'm walking, walking, walking, past the shopping centre, past the bar where Nadia had her twenty-fifth birthday party, past another bar where Mark once got thrown out for being sick behind a 'Who Wants To Be A

Millionaire?' quiz machine, and past a shop filled with pastel, marble stone vases and plump velvet cushions, a shop that looks exactly like the way I hope and imagine the interior of Lottie's house will be.

I turn right, past another row of shops. Should I stop and buy wine? There's no time. This is not the sort of party where you can bring a bottle that's on special offer in Sainsbury's anyway. These people probably only drink wine that is ordered specially, by the crate, from those leaflets that fall out of *The Sunday Times*. I'm so lost in thought, so busy second-guessing myself, that I'm surprised to look up and find myself at the right address. Stone steps, brass knocker, bright blue door. It's quarter past seven. Lifting the knocker and letting it fall, I decide that it's too late to turn back. I don't know what I'm doing, but I'm doing it. Down the rabbit hole I go.

Lottie opens the door, looking exactly how I would love to if I could work out how. Her hair is luscious – no longer straight, but wavy, shiny and lightly mussed, as if she showered late and spent fifteen minutes upside down with a Parlux. She is glowing, definitely wearing a lot of make-up in order to look like she's wearing no make-up at all. But her eyes are bright and unlined, and I feel self-conscious about mine, smoky and heavily lashed, my paint-by-numbers Kardashian contouring. We're both wearing black dresses. Hers is a heavy slip, falling to mid shin. Her breasts are clearly outlined by the clinging fabric. Nervous of staring, I attempt to redirect my gaze. It's the contrast between the black material and her pale, satin skin that makes me breathe more heavily. I am reminded of something I read about white satin, and how it's one of the very few things that is beautiful on its own, without being a simile for something found in nature. It is not attempting to imitate a superior whiteness. Lottie is holding two glasses of what is almost certainly proper champagne.

'Violet! Come in! I'm so glad you're here! It's so good to see you!'

I'm being squeezed, then holding a glass, then my coat is off (and Lottie does not wrinkle her nose at the label) and I'm staring at my own feet.

'Shall I take them off, or ... ?'

'Whatever makes you feel comfortable! Although I can't imagine you'll be keeping them on for long. I think a few of us like feet, although I don't think anyone is into shoes.'

How many is a few? Am I going to follow Lottie into a room filled with two hundred naked people, sucking each other's toes? We go down a staircase, dark wood with a worn, pale red and orange carpet runner in the centre. Why downstairs? Is it a dungeon? The wall is the same grey-blue as an August storm cloud, unwelcome at a picnic but mandatory, I suspect, in this postcode.

I look for pictures on the wall. It takes me a second to recognise a photograph of Lottie and Simon, in white shirts and blue jeans, so bright and light that they might have come with the frame. I see a chubby toddler, perhaps two years old, smiling adorably in a dinosaur jumper, and assume he's a godchild or nephew. I just can't imagine children in this house. It's impossible to picture piles of colourful plastic tidied into cupboards, or ground-up biscuit being vacuumed out of the carpet.

There's a Hilma Af Klint picture I recognise, intricate, looping pastel shapes (do they look more phallic than I

70

remember or is it just a sign of where my head is right now?) and a dreary Bruce Klein, a Rothko rip-off that I do not like. I take a sip (definitely proper champagne) and decide that in the unlikely event that I see a framed slogan that tells me what to do and how to feel about it, I'm going back to Streatham. I can deal with a dungeon, but not a sign to 'Keep calm and carry on spanking'.

The idea of a dungeon is intriguing, simply because I'm curious about how Lottie would decorate it. She'd never go for red walls and pleather couches. Perhaps an artisanal rack, made from reclaimed wood, with tiny rose gold hooks? Diptyque candle wax? Brass and rattan paddles? A French tickler shaped like a palm tree? Bloody hell, I have to stop watching so much bad spanking porn. Or at least give up sneakily leafing through Connie's copies of *Livingetc*.

It's not a dungeon, it's a wet dream of bohemian good taste, a bit mid-century, a bit Morocco. Two long, low, chartreuse velvet sofas form a right angle, sitting under a bay window and along a wall that is all bookshelf. (Why is there a window in a basement? I assume it's a window, but I suppose Lottie might have hung those velvet curtains over the wall for a little trompe l'oeil cosiness.) One of the walls is lined with reassuringly battered books, orange Penguin classics and heavy, glossy Phaidons. I see a copy of the David Wojnarowicz biography I have under my bed.

I really do feel as though I'm among friends, now. These stories have been read. There's a sudden sense of intimacy which is unexpectedly welcome, while making me feel a little raw. It's jarring, reconciling my memories and fantasies with real life. This is a fascinating insight into Lottie

71

and Simon's lives, but I'm not sure I want to see it. Now that I've seen the way Simon's face looks when he comes, I feel a bit weird when I imagine him reading that dog-eared edition of Adrian Mole.

As real life interrupts, I think about the job offer and wince. I've been looking forward to this for days, replaying the last meeting over and over again in my head. But every so often I worry that I've unwittingly made a bad choice. I'm irresponsible. I've blown it. The thought stings, and I tense myself against it, pushing it away.

Although I was expecting a crowd, there's just one other person in the room. A man is sitting on the sofa under the window. He is large and grey, and I do not fancy him. Lottie stands between us.

'Max, I want you to meet Violet.' She gestures for me to join him on the sofa. He looks at me appraisingly. I feel like livestock, being judged in a farming competition. Worse, I feel like I'm twelve and at school, when a different Max decided to tell me exactly what was wrong with my breasts.

This Max seems just as bad.

'Lottie and Simon said you were fascinating,' he says incredulously, as I wait for the 'but'. 'And you work for . . . some sort of art app?'

'I've been at Acquire for just over two years. It's challenging, but I really love my job.'

They say that the best way to lie convincingly is to keep your lie consistent. I've been telling that lie for . . . well, just over two years.

Then Max does something unexpected. He takes my chin in his hands and says, dispassionately, 'A hundred years ago, you would have been a muse, you know. You have the most curious face. Plump, and yet the planes are surprisingly angular. You could have been Rembrandt's Juno.'

I do my awful, ringing, nervous laugh, for the first time that day.

'Gosh, you're very kind, I don't know about that!'

I know that painting. It's not a flattering painting. This reminds me of an incident that happened a few years ago, just after an argument with Mark. I was in the Tesco car park crying behind a big bin and a strange man walked up to me and asked for my autograph because he thought I was the woman in the Weight Watchers ad.

Max shakes his head.

'I'm not kind. Have you read *Delta of Venus*?'

'A long time ago.'

I never finished it because I honestly had to stop and masturbate after every two pages. I'm hopeless. In the right, or wrong, sort of mood, I could probably find something to wank about during the *Today* programme.

'You remember the story, "Artists and Models"? That is such a potent relationship.' Max rests his hand on my stockinged left knee, and starts to slide it up my thigh, so slowly that the movement is barely perceptible. This should feel all wrong, I should be smacking his hand away, clamping my knees together, shutting this down, running out of the door and into the night. But I don't really want him to stop. There is something about his bulk, his arrogance, his *certainty* that makes me more than willing to offer myself as his prey.

Closing my eyes for a moment, I think about the bad date I could be on right now, making small talk with another stranger with glazed eyes and a limp dick, and I remember how good it feels to be *desired*. Max sees me – no, that's not quite right, he leads me to see a fake, titillating version of myself, thrillingly young, willingly seducible, naive yet complicit. *Bad feminist*, murmurs my brain, but the rest of my body can only consider the wandering hand.

Max continues.

'I think that's such a fascinating time. Because, many of these women were prostitutes ... '

Sex workers, I correct him, in my head, realising that his hand is now at the very top of my stocking, his thumb kneading the bare inner flesh of my thigh.

' ... but I think there's a romance to it too. The mistake people make is that they think the artist has all the power. Ultimately it's an erotic collaboration.'

His hand is now under my black, plasticky satin knickers. I'm frozen to the spot, wanting to be outraged but, in spite of myself, hopelessly aroused. His thumb is hooked under the underwear, resting on my slightly sticky, freshly waxed skin. With his fingers, he strokes the front of my underwear, barely missing my lips, my clit, me. Exquisite torture. Is Max inept, or does he know exactly what he's doing? I can feel myself start to swell and trickle. Momentarily, I fear for Lottie's lovely sofa.

'I wish I could paint you. But I'm just a collector.' His middle finger is now inside me, and he's pushing against my wet pussy with the heel of his hand. Automatically, I grind my hips and moan. With his other hand, he puts a finger to my lips. The ones on my face.

'Shhh. Technically, we're not supposed to be starting yet. Why don't you tell me about the art you like?'

And I mumble something about Hockney and Man Ray

and a painting with ice skaters I saw in the Tate a long time ago, while Max makes near unblinking eye contact and dips his fingers in and out and in, fast and slow, until I come, gushing and gasping. He does not smile.

'Let me get you another drink.'

As Max departs, I realise how big the room is. I see him lift a bottle from an ice bucket, which has been placed on a heavy-looking teak bar cart. A crystal decanter catches the light, I see a shining brass ice bucket and, improbably, a bottle of Bailey's. I'm ravenous. Standing up, I pretend to examine the books and vintage vinyl when I'm really on a search-and-destroy mission for food. Surely Lottie would have left out a dish of olives, salty Parma ham, hummus scooped from an M&S tub and dolloped into a tiny terra-cotta bowl?

As I'm peering disappointedly into a dish that contains scented crystals – at least there's no pot pourri for me to accidentally eat – Lottie opens the door again. It's Richard, with a woman. Is this his girlfriend? Irrationally, I bristle. There is something about the presence of a brand new person that seems slightly intrusive. I know I'm being ridiculous; after all, what did I expect? Yet, suddenly the atmosphere seems less cosy and dreamlike, and more charged. I shiver slightly.

Perhaps because Richard seemed quite robust, and a little less cerebral than Simon, I'd imagined he had a type, and pictured his terrifying, clever girlfriend accordingly, assuming blondness and blowsiness. Terrifying in the 'keeping troublemakers out of the Queen Vic' sense. Yet this woman – if she's his partner – proves me wrong. Like Lottie, she's tall and pale, but unlike Lottie there's no hint of peach within the cream skin, instead she seems smooth and cool. I seem to have developed a temporary sort of synaesthesia. I look at her and I can taste mint imperials.

Her hair is at once jolly and severe, dark and centre parted, it alters its course abruptly just below her ears, where there's a controlled explosion of regimented curls. Her nose seems to start above the space between her eyes, an isosceles triangle that draws me to her broad, raspberry jam mouth. Bitchily, competitively, I note that her slim figure seems to have few clear points of delineation, and that her dress is strangely dated – knee length, shiny, severe, khaki taffeta with a sharp V that ends before her breasts begin. Lottie seems to inhabit her clothes with a sense of pleasure, as though they might taste delicious, but this woman seems to resent her own outfit, like an angry teenage pageboy.

It seems that Lottie has already told her who I am, and she introduces herself.

'Violet? Sasha.'

She indicates her status, and what I assume to be disapproval, by saying my name as if it contains no separate syllables. I can't calculate her age – from a distance, she seemed older than Richard, there was a seniority implied by the straightness of her spine, the tilt of her chin. But her skin is youthfully plump – there is a fullness to her face that throws everyone else's cosmetic enhancements into sharp relief, a blooming flower in a roomful of balloons. I can't decide whether she's beautiful, or simply a bitch.

Richard is warmer, and envelops me in a slightly sexy hug, kissing the patch of skin just below my left ear.

'Hello! You smell amazing! So great to see you again!'

He is a little too familiar, but after Sasha's chilliness, I'll take it. In fact, right now, I love Richard. Especially because I think he's wearing the suit he had on when I last saw him, which makes me feel much less self-conscious about my limited wardrobe.

Lottie is laughing.

'You all meet at last!' she says, smiling, when she's interrupted by a clear, ringing voice, which seems to be coming from the staircase.

'Sorry, sorry, I know, sorry! Fucking Arabs.'

I suspect my horror manifests itself immediately on my face, because Max, who has returned with my drink, immediately starts laughing at me.

'That's my partner, Mimi! She's not a horrible racist, as far as I know. She works in a gallery. She's spent the whole week with some very wealthy private collectors from the UAE. They have fifteen million pounds to spend, but they don't know what they want. And they've made her take them to tea at Fortnum's every day this week, while they quiz her about artists the gallery doesn't represent. I think she's on the brink of throwing a scone at someone. Darling!' he says, as Mimi enters, and then embraces her, tips her backwards and kisses her for a full ten seconds.

Mimi is immediately friendly.

'Violet! Our new girl!' she says, giving me the sort of brisk, tender hug that Nadia gives me. Used to give me. (Before I felt obliged to put myself in social purdah.)

Mimi might be the most classically beautiful person I've ever seen in my life. I'm curious about her ethnicity, and also absolutely sure it would be impolite to ask. She's taller than me, taller than Max, the tallest person in the room.

She looks as though she's standing in a beam of direct sunlight, like she's never known a windowless room or a Tube carriage or a scratchy jumper. Everything about her body seems full, and high up. She's wearing cream, brass logoed Tory Burch flats, a coral coloured shift, possibly in some kind of matte silk. She smells of jasmine and tobacco. (Purposeful, perfumed tobacco, not 'I've just had a quick Silk Cut behind a tree.')

'Can I have a drink? The fucking week I've had. Where's Simon?' asks Mimi. 'Oh, Lottie's gone again.'

'Heeeeere he is!' trills a returning Lottie, trailed by Simon, who, beside Mimi, seems to have lost his lustre. For a walking aftershave advert, he is looking a little bit too much like a Prime Minister on holiday, for my liking. Very new jeans that might seem subversive in The Ned but that would get him beaten up if he were in my local chicken shop. A pale blue linen shirt with three? – four! – buttons undone, worn untucked, but with a slight sense of anxiety, as if it's a new puppy that Simon has let off a lead against his better judgement, while believing it would be better for everyone if it was brought under control and shoved back into his underpants. Is that a puppy in your underpants, Simon, or are you just pleased to ... no. Stop that. He's wearing blue deck shoes, too.

My horny, licentious buzziness recedes. Simon's shoes have an effect on me that is not incomparable to being halfway down a relaxing glass of white wine and then discovering that your bank has just left you a voicemail. He has done something to his hair that I can't quite describe, but I'm confident that it shouldn't be attempted by any man who is over twenty-three.

'Right. We must sort out drinks,' says Lottie, sounding surprisingly head-girlish. 'Mimi, you fabulous woman, I've been looking forward to seeing you all week, what will it be? Sasha, champagne, of course. Did you sort out that thing with Olu? Someone said they saw you on *Newsnight*, I must watch it online. Max, you need to tell me about the Saatchi. And Violet!'

I'm staring at the corner of a tasselled rug, and Simon catches me off guard. I look up and he holds my gaze for several uncomfortable seconds.

'I've been having some very disturbing thoughts about you this week.'

He kisses me softly and briefly on the mouth, and I start to forgive him for the jeans. He makes me feel a little bit like I've won a prize and a little bit like I've come to school without any knickers on.

Mimi slots an arm through mine and guides me to the sofa by the bookshelves, saying, conversationally, 'Simon says you're filthy!'

Have I heard that right? Because she's using the same sort of tone that she might if she were saying 'Simon says you've just got back from Crete!'

I smile at her, wondering if I can fascinate her even a hundredth as much as she is fascinating me. Don't be suburban! Think art! I used up all of my art chat when her boyfriend was fingering me. Deep breath.

'Max says that you have a challenging job. It sounds exciting! Do you, um, do you ah, buy the art yourself? Or just ... curate it?'

What fucking kind of stupid question even is that? I am ashamed of myself.

79

Mimi is very kind.

'I'm lucky, it's a fairly independent gallery, so while I'm not officially someone who has any say in the artists that we represent, I do tend to work closely with the owners, and if I love someone, they really listen to what I like.'

Another sip, another deep breath.

'How did you get into it?'

Mimi looks genuinely thrilled to be asked.

'I started my career in banking, but I've always loved art. To be honest, I've only been in the industry for a couple of years. I was ready for a career change. The world of finance gets a bit mindless – there's lots of pressure, lots of money, but you burn out fast. I spoke to a career coach, and I got out, and found this job through a friend of a friend. I was a thirty-nine-year-old intern, which is ridiculous, but I loved it. Then I sold a few paintings.'

I interrupt her.

'Your own paintings? That you painted?'

Mimi laughs, a throaty bass chuckle that could generate a reading on the lower end of the Richter scale.

'Oh, God no! Imagine! I couldn't draw ... you know, a stick man! Once, at school, I tried to draw a horse, and my teacher thought it was an anteater, because the mouth looked a lot like a snout. She kept saying, "How clever, to draw an animal that comes from where your family is from!" and I didn't understand, and I actually thought, for a long time, that there were anteaters in Forest Hill. I looked for them in Brockley Park.'

'Oh God, that's awful! I'm sorry! Although I kind of wish there were anteaters in Brockley Park. Sorry, anyway, you sold some paintings ...'

'Yeah, for the gallery, for the ticket price, which was the biggest shock. I didn't know that most people negotiate a deal, and I was all, "No, we can't possibly go lower!" so I earned them this fat commission, and now I'm in charge of sales. To be honest, I think they thought I was going to be an idiot, you know, Max's bimbo. But actually, what I'm doing now is very similar to what I was doing in my old job. But I get to travel more, I get – hee hee! – a sort of staff discount, and I get to do what I love the most and find new art!'

Mimi pulls out her phone and continues speaking.

'Last weekend I went to Dover, and I found some stunners. There's this kid on the harbour, barely out of his teens, doing these landscapes in this really restricted primary palette, with a portrait element, a figure picked out.' She shows me the images. 'Turner meets a sort of painty Martin Parr, I thought. And this man who is perhaps nearly ninety doing these batshit glass sculptures.' She shows me another image and I make an approving noise. 'Apparently, it's one of those man and boy, his father, his father's father, industries – for years, the family has been doing loads of tourist tat and interior commissions and doing OK. But late in life, this man's gone fully Jeff Koons!' Mimi grins.

I like her enormously. I want to be her friend.

She sips her champagne.

'What about you? I hear you're in a trendy tech start-up, and Simon and Lottie are trying to poach you for their trendy start-up?'

My heart sings with relief. If this is how Lottie and Simon have explained me to Mimi, that must mean there *is* a job. It's going to be OK. For a moment, I consider telling Mimi how miserable and frustrating Acquire is, and how desperate I am to move, leave, go absolutely *anywhere else*. Just in time, I realise that might bring the mood down. After all, job hunting is a lot like dating. Putting out straight away is not necessarily a deal breaker, but trash talking.

I smile and try to summon the most tactful words I know.

'Lottie and Simon's idea is so exciting, I can't wait for them to tell me more. It seems a bit up in the air at the moment, but I'm ready to move. Right now, I don't really feel as though I'm doing the job I was hired for. But I think that's part of being in your twenties. There are aspects of the work I love, but lots of details I'd like to change.'

I'm expecting her to nod politely, but she seems genuinely interested.

'How do you mean?'

'Well, I interned everywhere I could, for ages, just to get any experience at all in the art world. Money was always a bit of a worry – I did a lot of temping, between gigs. I was in the same position as lots of my uni mates, but lots of them have family in London who will pay their way while they do work experience stints. I was on the brink of giving up when I started at Acquire, as a temp. At first, I was a receptionist slash general dogsbody. For about six months, I really did love it, I was so happy to be in the building. Then I got promoted and made permanent, but it doesn't feel like a promotion. I'm arranging meetings I don't get to go to. Or ringing around every nice restaurant near Covent Garden to get a price per head for a thirty-person private dinner with champagne reception, when I know that I have just enough cash at the bottom of my bag for a Diet Coke as long as I go to the dodgy shop that illegally splits the multipacks.'

Mimi laughs, and I remember that I need to put a positive spin on my misery.

'Still, millions of people would love to work in this world, at all. And if it's led me to Lottie and Simon, I'm sure it will have been worth it.'

Mimi puts an arm around my shoulders.

'It's so important, to do a job that excites you, something where you feel you're making a difference, and getting paid properly. I had a shitty time in my twenties, partly because back then, there weren't many other girls in the City and men could shout, "Show us your wabs!" if you got up to go to the loo, and they wouldn't get fired for it.'

I laugh nervously.

'That's awful.'

'I put up with so much utter bollocks, purely because I felt that I had to prove myself and get taken seriously. There comes a point when you think, fuck that noise, and start to realise that it's you who needs to take yourself seriously. I really, really wish that I'd believed in myself a bit more, when I was in my twenties, especially at work. That I'd found the confidence to put myself first and be less of a doormat.'

I smile, and nod. I feel my eyes prickle at her kindness.

She continues.

'But one thing is that I was earning plenty of money, and while that comes with its own set of problems, it does make it easier to walk away. But I know the margins are getting narrower, especially when you come in at the start of something new. You're on ten grand less than you would have been in a similar job five years ago. And London being London, you might as well be on a hundred grand less.'

With a pang of sadness, I realise that even if I earned a hundred grand a year, I couldn't afford this house. I don't know that there would ever be enough for this much wood and velvet. I'm not sure that I will *ever* be in a position to entertain three couples, not sexually, but in terms of sheer space. My imagination is tempered by a lack of hope, a fundamental feeling that I will never move through the world easily. I watch Max topping up Sasha's champagne, and carelessly kicking about three hundred pounds of shoe off his foot, saying to Richard, 'I keep telling you to convert your Avios! You can probably both go to Sydney and back in club!'

In spite of Mimi's compassion, I will never understand these people, and they could not begin to understand me. They were built for brightness, and the world will always work for them. Maybe I belong in a chicken shop.

Mimi gets up to go to the loo, and Lottie descends on me.

'Glad you're getting on. Is everything all right? You look a bit stricken. Did Max freak you out earlier? He can be a bit intense!'

I choose my words carefully.

'No, we had a nice chat. And I'm in love with Mimi, she's brilliant. Is there a plan, or do we just hang out and see what happens?'

Lottie looks at me indulgently.

'Well, we don't usually eat anything too heavy beforehand, so I'm doing a mezze thing for dinner. Someone usually ends up ordering a Domino's before midnight. But just follow our lead – we'll include you in any way that makes you feel comfortable. Or maybe I should say uncomfortable.'

She looks at me and grins. I suspect she'd like to raise her eyebrows, although I notice that there is extremely little movement in her forehead.

'I cannot imagine, for one second, that you're not going to have a good time. Just relax.'

She winks at me. That, she can do.

Simon, Richard and Max are talking intently and seem to have no interest in moving. Sasha stands on the outside, interjecting with 'Yes!' and 'Well . . .' and 'Exactly' but is largely ignored. Mimi gets up and smiles at me, so I follow her out of the room and into another, a longer space that has been divided into two sections, with a large, brightly lit kitchen at one end and a long, rough wooden picnic bench at the other. The bench is covered in fat, white dripping church candles. I sit at one end, and Mimi sits next to me. Lottie looks at her pointedly, and she rolls her eyes.

'You're not going to make us sit boy-girl, are you? Are we having port at the end as well?' Lottie looks as if she's going to say something, but leaves the room, presumably to fetch the others.

Mimi smirks.

'Lottie may look as if she's full of boho bollocks, but she has a real Oxbridge stick up her arse.'

I'm curious.

'Oxford or Cambridge? What degree did she do?'

Mimi looks at the door.

'Oxford Brookes, I think she had some sort of breakdown during her A levels. It's where she met Simon, he was in Brasenose. I've been at parties where she tells people she was at Oxford. Technically, it's true. But she gets caught out

85

when people say "Which college?" and "Oh, so you would have been there at the same time as Rosamund Pike?" I mean, it's not exactly held her ba—'

She stops abruptly as Lottie re-enters with the missing four.

Damn. I feel horribly disloyal, but I was really enjoying Mimi's gossip.

Simon sits on a chair at the head of the bench, on my right. Richard sits opposite me. Max sits next to him, opposite Mimi. Sasha slides next to Max, looking put out. Lottie asks Simon to organise some wine, as she walks back and forth from the kitchen area, carrying a series of pretty, mismatched dishes.

'Oooh, I love that,' says Mimi, pointing to a deep, shell-pink bowl speckled with gold, filled with a pomegranate salad. 'Anthropologie?'

Lottie laughs.

'You know it!'

Sasha smirks and says, 'It's a bit plain for you. Did they not do one that was covered with tiny gold L's, or came in the shape of an owl?'

Daringly, I meet Lottie's eyes and flick my gaze ceiling-ward. Gratifyingly, she smiles, and I glow pink with approval.

Even though I'm suspicious of Sasha, I'm also sensing that she doesn't like me – which makes me desperate to win her over. So I try too hard.

'Lottie mentioned that you were on *Newsnight*, that's exciting! What were you talking about?'

Sasha sniffs.

'Hardly, I'm usually on about once a month, it's pretty dull really. I'm the director of a charity that supports vulnerable women, and I work with the government quite a lot with regards to policy development and changes in the law.'

I'm not quite sure how to reply. I can't really say 'And do you enjoy it?'

Blunderingly, awkwardly, I ask, 'How did you get into it? What did you study at uni?'

Sasha narrows her eyes, and speaks brusquely.

'I'm actually a trained barrister, I worked at the bar for years. This is the problem I'm having at the moment, we've hired too many kids who have come straight out of university, and they don't have a clue. I was in my early thirties before I could even begin to think about doing this work.'

Am I going mad, or is she being actively, purposefully *rude*?

I'm open mouthed. It occurs to me that everyone else, in their own way, has done everything they can to put me at my ease. Admittedly, Mimi's technique is a little more straightforward than Max's, but in a strange, yet recognisable way, everyone has been kind. This Sasha is downright hostile. Still, the rule of any group gathering is that one person will always end up being a bit of a dick. Hopefully, her meanness will blunt the edge of my awkwardness.

I blunder on.

'How did you all meet?'

Max smiles at me.

'Mutual friends, mostly. I met Simon and Lottie through an old college mate. Oh, that reminds me, did you hear that Aika and Jamie are having a baby?'

Mimi claps her hands together.

'You didn't tell me! That's fab! That's really good news!

I know they've been trying for ages. Lottie, have you thought abou— '

The words die on her lips. Max shoots her a look that I can't quite interpret. He continues. 'Sorry, got side-tracked. Anyway, I graduated a couple of years before they did.'

Simon raises his eyebrows and says, 'A *couple*?' and Max laughs and puts up his palms in mock surrender.

'OK, five years! Mimi, I had a colossal office crush on, and then made my move at a Christmas party, right at the start of our respective break ups.'

Mimi chuckles.

'Let's be real. I was actually single, and you were still at the "my wife doesn't understand me!" stage. Richard, you were working with Simon for a bit, weren't you? And I think that Richard and Sasha got together . . . ' Sasha looks murderous and Richard interrupts quickly. 'At a party.'

Richard pours more champagne into my glass and fixes my gaze.

'Violet, we're all dying to know. You're, what? Twenty-two? Twenty-three.'

I swallow.

'Twenty-six.'

'Right, right. So tell us. What's it like being young and gorgeous and on Tinder? Are you having wild sex every night? Is it crazy?'

Max interjects.

'There's a chap in the office who's about your age, and he says that it's demented. Sometimes he hooks up with more than one girl in a night.'

All eyes are on me, and I feel immense pressure to deliver something. Where do I begin?

88

'There was this guy called Dan who I wasted hours of my life messaging, only to meet him and discover that he couldn't maintain an erection'?

Or, 'There was this very flirty boy that I was very into, until my manager pointed out that his profile picture was an old photo of the actor who played Adam Barton in Emmerdale.'

I suppose I could tell them that the other month, some guy asked for sexy photos, and I spent forty minutes editing and filtering a full-frontal mirror shot, only for him to reply, *Not really into big tits. Soz :(*

I blink, I swallow, and I take my life into my own hands.

'Well, there was this guy called Dan, and the messaging got super hot. He was seriously well endowed,' (although now I think of it, there wasn't anything else in the picture for scale) 'and kept sending me these filthy messages. And one afternoon, I was bored at work,' (true) 'and there was barely anyone in the office,' (also true) 'so I got him to come over,' (LIE) 'and ... you know!'

Mimi is agog!

'Tell us, tell us, tell us! How did you get him in the building? Did you say, "Ah, Mr Dan, here for my meeting?" and then take him to a room and fuck his brains out?'

Ah, to lie with convincing logistics. This has never been my forte.

'Um, he brought round a package.'

'I bet he did!' cackles Mimi.

Oh, God.

'So, I said I'd go to reception to sign for it, and he said, "My boss wanted me to see you checking the contents, but obviously the documents are confidential."'

I've hit my stride, I'm warming to my theme.

'There's this basement meeting room that nobody uses, and I lead him downstairs from reception, pretending to be very professional. Not that anyone cares. And we get to the room, and shut the door, and he says, "I suppose I better check these contents then" and starts to undress me.'

'What were you wearing?' breathes Lottie, who is leaning forward and breathing through her mouth quite heavily.

What was I wearing, in Imaginary Land?

'Um, a dress that zips all the way down the back. He just pulls the zip all the way down, and the dress falls to the floor. I start to unhook my bra, but he says, "No, let me" and pushes my hands away. He takes it off, and he pulls my knickers down, and puts them in his pocket. And I'm standing in my, um, shoes, and hold-ups.'

'Go on,' says Mimi. '*Please*, go on.'

I shut my eyes and I'm there, fully reliving what never was.

'He runs – ran a finger from the base of my neck to the base of my spine, and then he pulled my arse cheeks apart. And he's got his finger, sort of between my pussy and my arsehole.' Urghhh, I hate saying 'pussy' out loud.

'You mean, your perineum?' corrects Sasha.

I ignore her.

'And he's got a finger inside me, but he keeps stroking . . . the outside part, and I know I'm about to come, but then he stops – stopped – really abruptly, and smacked me, really hard, there was this cracking noise. And he said, "Not yet, not now," and repeated it a few times. And then he said, "If you're a good girl, and suck me really hard, I'll fuck you." Then I . . . took him all the way into my mouth.'

This is turning *me* on. I'm so bloody suggestible. I open my eyes and I'm delighted to see that Simon is staring at me.

'As soon as he got close, he pulled out, and bent me over. I don't know how many times I came.'

'Where did he come?' asks Richard, agog.

In Neverland, duh!

'All over my arse.'

Predictably, Sasha is unmoved.

'Well, I can't wait to see exactly what it says on your P45.'

My career fear raises its head again. How does this woman know exactly where my weak spots are?

Richard shushes her.

'Shall we go to the other room? Violet, I want to see if your dress unzips all the way.' Suddenly, everyone is getting up. No one loiters. Poor Lottie's dinner remains uneaten. I can't resist picking a pomegranate seed from the pink bowl and putting it in my mouth. Persephone, descending to the Underworld.

Adorably, Mimi takes my hand, and Richard waits for us by the door. I wonder whether this means I'm expected to go with them first, and whether configuration has been planned. Has Lottie put us into groups, as though we're in the World Cup? First to come gets Max in the final? I try to imagine what is happening on the other side of the wall. I can see Sasha and Lottie together, but will the boys be playing with each other? Somehow, it seems unlikely. Max might be the most aggressively heterosexual man I've ever met – and Mark's friends defined themselves by their prolific womanising. While Mimi, Lottie and even Sasha all carry an air of curiosity and fluidity, the men seem oddly rigid. So far, the vibe has been curiously old-fashioned for an orgy.

91

As soon as we're in the sitting room, Lottie lifts her slip above her head. In the lamplight, I notice the slightly convex silhouette of her belly. She sits on the window sofa, and I'm shocked to see that it's Sasha, still dressed, who buries her head between Lottie's legs. I can't look for long as Mimi has started kissing me, while Richard hunts for my zip. Mimi's lips are soft, she wraps her tongue around mine, she has her hands on my waist and she smells like the beach – no, she smells like a picture of a deserted beach at sunset, in Hawaii. She catches my lips with her tongue, pulls me deeper, makes my mouth feel new.

Richard moves around us and suddenly we're both standing in our underwear, still kissing, and kissing, and kissing. Richard whispers something to Mimi, who giggles, and motions for me *to lie* on the floor. I'm drunk and find my way to the rug slightly more quickly than I was expecting. Once I'm on the floor, I feel relaxed, unselfconscious – and impatient.

Mimi crouches down next to me, pulls off my knickers and, agonisingly briefly, licks the lowest part of my pussy, pushing her tongue inside me for a second – like a traditional French kiss. She shimmies out of her knickers (lilac, silky) and, unlike me, she's not wearing a bra or any sort of hosiery. Her breasts are smaller than I'd expected, teacup sized, with tiny nipples. Mimi lies on top of me, which is a bit of a shock. She's so tall that I have to adjust my head and peer out from behind her neck, and I get a mouthful of synthetic hair. She's lying so our torsos are aligned, her hips are directly on top of my hips, and Richard kneels between our splayed legs and starts to lick us. It feels amazing, but frustrating, he's not really creating any kind of momentum. Still, Mimi seems

92

to be having a lovely time, bucking and groaning. Suddenly, Mimi's weight *shifts* on my pelvis and I'm there, I'm so, so close, and Richard's swirling tongue catches the very edge of my outer lips, and I'm back in the room and coming like I'm high. I can only make strange sounds. I just want to come, and keep coming, and I don't care who makes it happen. Even Sasha can have a go, if she likes.

Richard stands up, and Mimi rolls off me. She leans into my ear and whispers, 'I want you to make me come. I want you to make me this wet,' while stroking me between my legs for four unbearably pleasurable seconds. She lies down, again, and I kneel.

'Get down there,' hisses Richard, gripping my hips and pushing me forward, so that my face is in Mimi and my arse is in the air. I start to lick, suck and rub, aware that someone, Richard I assume, is now inside me. I can hear Mimi screaming. I can feel Richard's short, scratchy nails catching the flesh of my arse, using it for purchase. I'm moaning into Mimi, she's moaning back, Richard is fucking me so furiously that I can't tell whether or not I'm actually in pain, he's thrusting, and I'm coming, and I want his nails to draw blood, and I want Mimi to squirt all over my face, but Richard says 'Oh, fuck,' in a slightly exasperated way and pulls out of me the moment before he starts to come, as Mimi says 'Ahhh, yeah, so good,' and sits up again.

I open my eyes. I feel horribly disorientated, as though I've just woken up in the cinema during the final credits of the film.

'Anyone want a drink?' asks Lottie cheerily, still naked, with her fringe sticking up.

Sasha replies first.

'We should probably be heading back. We've got the plumber in the morning. Richard?' He's already tugging his trousers on, even though I can see his boxers under a cushion. Max looks slightly put out, although that may just be the way his face looks in repose. I have no idea what he and Simon have been doing. Did they join Sasha and Lottie? Did they talk about box sets? Did they give each other hand jobs? Once again, I feel disorientated, as I try to reconcile what just happened with reality as I know it – the room, the rugs, the lives these people lead.

'Mimi, did you want to stay for longer?' asks Max, frowning slightly. 'You know your mum's coming in the morning.'

Mimi screws up her face.

'Shit, I'd forgotten. We should probably make a move.'

How can everyone be leaving? No one actually had any dinner! Do I have to get the night bus? I'm starting to feel as though I might have made a horrible mistake. Even though I don't know what I really wanted from these people, I thought there would be ... more. For some reason, I thought tonight might change my life – I don't understand where I got this from, and I feel like an idiot for thinking it. And it makes me sad that everyone is going back to their own homes, to comfort and security and reality, now that I've got nothing else to offer them. I start to dress.

Lottie notices.

'Violet, you're not going, are you? We assumed you'd stay over!'

I feel as though I'm on the verge of tears, and I can't fully understand or articulate why.

'No, honestly, that's so kind of you but the night bus is actually really easy, and ...'

I want to get out, run away, go back to my normal life and never think about any of this, ever again. I've had enough sex for a lifetime. I'll move back home and change my name and pretend that all of this happened to someone else.

Lottie talks over me.

'Please. Simon and I would really love to have you here. We can run you home in the morning, but don't go. You've not eaten! We'll get a pizza!'

Lottie's voice cracks slightly, and I'm overwhelmed by an emotion that runs perilously close to self-pity.

'We don't need pizza! You made all of that lovely salad.'

Lottie laughs.

'You're too polite for your own good. Are you seriously telling me you want to eat my attempt at Ottolenghi, which is getting warm and wilting as we speak, when we could get a stuffed crust barbecue pepperoni feast?'

The woman has a point. I start awkwardly dressing and trying to gather glasses at the same time.

'Simon, make her stop that!' shouts Lottie. 'Violet, why don't you have a nice hot shower? Up the stairs to where you came in, and it's the second door on the left in the hall. Help yourself to anything, clean towels are in the cabinet, there are loads of robes on the hook on the door. Everyone, say "Goodnight Violet!"'

'Goodnight Violet!' I reply, facetiously, and I run up the stairs.

It isn't possible to overestimate the healing powers of hot water. Especially when you're showering in a show room. Simon and Violet's bathroom is everything I dreamed it would be. I see cliché upon glorious middle class cliché, and I have never been gladder. The bath has a roll top. The shower cubicle takes up over two square metres, with two different chrome heads and jets that pin me to the glass wall. There's an almost full bottle of Pomegranate Noir, and I attack it greedily. I lift up the detachable shower head and blast myself between my legs, and I feel light and clean again. I think about trying to make myself come and decide that I feel too tired, and strangely sated. Almost relieved.

Out of the shower, I wrap myself in a fat, fluffy, White Company bath sheet and anoint myself with more Pomegranate Noir, finding the matching body butter in a cylindrical glass jar. I want to brush my teeth, but I can only find an electric toothbrush base and two heads. Pinching a manual toothbrush seems OK in an emergency but for some reason, using someone's electric toothbrush is a bit invasive. I did bring my own, but I can't remember where I left my bag.

Warm, dry, and luxuriously scented, I choose the biggest robe – which is essentially a tailored version of the bath towel – and shroud my body within it. After giving myself a tiny, tight hug, I head downstairs.

All of the other guests have left. Simon, who is picking up corks and dirty glasses, sees me and smiles.

'Ah, you naughty girl, you've pinched my robe! You look so cosy, it suits you! I'm nearly done here, why don't you go to the den and get the telly on. Lottie is changing, and the pizza is on the way. It's back upstairs, I'm afraid, if you're standing with the front door behind you, it's the first one on the right.'

I follow his instructions, and find a slightly chilly, dark room. I switch on the overhead light, and see a squashy looking grey corner sofa, the palest pink walls, and a shockingly big telly. I switch on a softer, pink glass lamp on a table, turn the big light off and try to find some suitable post-orgy viewing, while sitting on the edge of the middle sofa cushion. Gratifyingly, I notice that someone has recorded over twenty episodes of *The Real Housewives of Atlanta*.

Lottie enters, wearing a robe that matches mine. She has pulled her hair into a loose, low bun. It's perfect, and it obviously took her less than ten seconds. She switches on another lamp, a black, cast iron star studded with bulbs. Reaching behind her, she pulls at a soft, white wool blanket that has been folded and draped over the back of the sofa.

'Let's get comfy. You lie down, and put your head here,' she says, touching her lap.

I love it when she tells me what to do. As I move into position, she throws the blanket over us.

'Simon will join us in a bit, he's on pizza watch. You did very well tonight, everyone loved you.'

It's a strange, and slightly condescending, compliment but it leaves me beaming all the same. She flicks channels until she finds a programme about Americans who are hiring detectives to follow their unfaithful partners. I snuggle into her lap, and she strokes my hair. Everything feels so strange and unexpected, yet so safe. For the first time I can remember, I get to not think and eat melted cheese and watch stupid TV, while being stroked, cuddled, *loved*.

Chapter Eight

It takes me a moment to remember where I am when I wake up. I stretch my legs and wiggle my toes, trying to feel for the edge of infinity while never wanting to touch the sides of this enormous, endless bed. I try to retrace yesterday's steps, and remember Simon wrapping a furry blanket around my feet, and how he stroked them distractedly as he laughed at an old episode of *South Park*. I remember Lottie kissing my hair and saying 'Bedtime!', while I yawned and said I'd sleep on the sofa. Lottie's retort, 'You will in your arse, this room gets Baltic!' and how she took both of my hands in hers and pulled me up, and Simon said 'Come on girls!' and led us both up another set of stairs, to a third floor. And I remember Lottie saying, 'There's no rush to get up tomorrow, sleep in, it's Saturday!' and the sound of them both giggling and disappearing, and how I tried to look for something to read, and an old T-shirt or something to sleep in, and wondered where my phone was, and now it's morning.

At the time, I was so sleepy and overwhelmed that I didn't question the fact that I'd been put in the spare room. Yet right now, as I replay the end of the evening, something jars.

Is it strange that I didn't sleep in their bed, with them? Oh, I don't know what the rules are. When I am included, and when I can expect them to shut me out. Still, right now, being on my own is blissful. I'm gorging on the feeling of comfort and calmness.

Everything is so beautifully and blindingly white, I feel as though I've woken up, flung the curtains open and discovered banks upon banks of snow. This is the nicest place I've woken up since Mark and I stayed in a country hotel when one of his school friends got married in Berkshire. At the time, I failed to fully appreciate it because I was horribly hungover, we missed the hotel breakfast and I ended up having a very dry, sugar-free blueberry muffin in the Costa at Chieveley services. Just for fun, I roll over, twice, before coming to the end of the mattress. Experimentally, I rub my nipple with the thick fabric of the duvet cover. Right now, I feel reborn. It's as though the luxury bedding has permeated my skin, and I'm a couple of steps closer to a shiny future filled with crisp, clean cotton.

I wonder what Lottie and Simon have planned for today. They will probably have toast and coffee – well, maybe just coffee, if Lottie is still Dukan-ing, although she did make some serious inroads into that pizza. They'll make coffee with a gleaming, bean grinding machine, no nonsense pods for them, and they'll read *The Times* and the *Guardian,* and they'll know what the columnists are going to say in advance because they're all friends, or friends-of-friends, and probably live over the road. Then perhaps they'll potter about locally, they'll look at shops like Fired Earth and they'll see a battered old armchair and talk about whether it's worth buying it and having it recovered, and would it do for the den, and is there really room for it anywhere else?

Then they'll go somewhere smart for salad and cold white wine, or perhaps that nice pub with the fireplace, where they will immediately get a good table and no one will accidentally put their elbow in a half-squeezed packet of ketchup. Then they'll walk to the Heath, or maybe get on a bus and go to the gallery, and it will be a bright red bus with passengers who could have walked out of a Richard Curtis casting, fellow professionals in soft leather boots and hundred pound scarves, and no one will play Skepta from their phones at them, or ask if they want saving by Christ Jesus, or tell them that they're cunts cunts cunts.

There is part of me that would love to spend the rest of the weekend here, but I'm terrified of outstaying my welcome. All I know is that I'm simply desperate not to go home. Because when I shower at home, the water doesn't blast me clean, but trickles lukewarm onto my head, some-how making me dirtier than I was when I got in. I won't have a warm, dry, fluffy towel to swaddle myself in, but a crispy, greasy, hard one that smells as old and damp as it feels. When I eat dinner tonight, there won't be a table to sit up at, and I'll have to perch at the end of my bed again, using piled up magazines as a tray. If I make a lot of effort, and hang my clothes up, and turn on the fairy lights that I hung over the mirror, and light a couple of candles (Muji ones – I have the smallest Diptyque Feu Du Bois that money can buy, and I'd only light it if I knew that I had a week to live), my sad little room has an almost romantic quality – I can pretend that I'm in a turn of the century hovel, instead of a twenty-first-century one. It's especially effective when I've been crying. It looks a lot more bearable when your eyes are puffy, and your vision is blurred.

Still, there is nothing I can do about the fact that every square centimetre of the flat feels gritty underfoot, no matter how many times I run the crappy vacuum cleaner over it. Or the fact that I have no real idea who my house-mates are, beyond knowing they are nocturnal, furious door slammers. (The only thing I like about the flat is that they seem to go out for weeks at a time.) When hungover, I've spent enough time contemplating the toilet bowl to realise that not even a controlled explosion could shift the grey and brown stains. It's impossible for me to shake the mounting dread that starts at the back of my throat when I get off the bus, and spreads into my stomach, across my shoulders and down my back as I wonder if the post has come, and whether today is the day that the unopened white envelopes turn scary and brown, and if I will ever be able to cross my own threshold without comparing the sensation to leaping over a pit of especially venomous snakes.

Still, the longer I leave it, the more anxious I'll get. I need to leave, brave my bus, the 133, check for terrifying post, wash my hair, chuck my sexy outfit in the wash and get on with my day. With my life.

It takes me a little while to find the bathroom. I forget where I am within the layout of the house, and I try to open what appears to be a locked cupboard door before I realise I need to go downstairs.

My clothes are still on the floor and I dress quickly, with-out bothering to shower. I look for some deodorant, but I can't open the door of the mirrored cabinet. It might just be a mirror, and if I try any harder to find out I might take if off the wall. In the hall, I'm reassured to see my handbag hanging next to my coat, and I'm delighted to discover that my battery is still at 79 per cent. The house sounds still, and I decide to go downstairs and leave a note in the kitchen, but Lottie is up, sitting on a stool, drinking coffee, sloppy grey cashmere sliding off one bare shoulder.

'Violet!' she says huskily. 'Want a coffee? Simon's gone, he likes to get his lengths in on a Saturday morning.'

I look behind her and see a jar of Nescafé with its lid off. I sense that she would resentfully make me a proper coffee, and I would have to spend twenty minutes thinking of small talk while she muttered and sighed, and then at least another ten minutes thinking of more small talk while I drank it. I think on my feet.

'That's really kind of you, but actually, I completely forgot, this morning I have a . . .'

Oh, what could I have? Doctor's appointment? Not on a Saturday. Lunch with a friend? Just thinking about the impossibility of this makes me feel a bit depressed.

'A haircut! In . . . Clapham! At eleven o'clock! And I thought I'd better go home and change before I go out again.'

'Is he any good?' asks Lottie, thoughtfully. 'Lord knows, I'm always looking for backup, my guy is great, but he can get a bit erratic. And he gets booked up so quickly! Christmas is a nightmare!'

Ah, yes, the lesser known Nightmare Before Christmas, when the heroine fails to find the terrifying portal to another world because she can't see out of her own fringe.

'I'll . . . put you in touch! But I really must be going!' I cry wildly.

Should I mention the job, before I go? Or is it one of those things where I need to wait for her to bring it up?

Lottie puts down her coffee and gives me a three second, squeezy, unsexy hug.

'Do come and see us again soon, yes? I'll text when I know what the plan is, it's always tricky to find a night where everyone is free. By the way, would you like to come on holiday with us?'

What?

'What?'

'We go to this villa in Ibiza at the end of October, friend of a friend's place, it's in the quiet bit, really beautiful. You might not fancy it, you probably go to San Antonio, foam parties and things, and it's really just us, hanging out and reading and drinking. It's a bit, well, I should check with the others, but I think they'd be thrilled to have you there.'

I can't stop myself.

'Even Sasha?'

Oh, I wish I'd bitten my tongue, I didn't mean to say that. Lottie looks slightly apologetic.

'Sasha's not great with new people, I forget that she's got such a dry sense of humour and it doesn't make people feel very welcome. But it's worth getting to know her, I promise. And she's going to love you. Anyway, think about it, I'll send you the details.'

'It's so nice of you to ask, but I'm not sure I can afford . . .'

'Oh, no no no, you'd be our guest, absolutely, we'll organise your plane tickets and everything.'

I hug Lottie again, promise to think about it, and run down Upper Street to get to my imaginary haircut, my sinking spirits bobbing at Lottie's failure to mention my shiny new job, then rising again at the euphoric prospect of a free holiday.

I've just tapped through the Tube barrier when my phone rings, and panicking, I grab it without checking the caller ID.

'Hello darling, we've not heard from you for a while.'

Ah, Mum.

'Hello, Mum, I'm actually just about to get on a Tube. Can I call you back?'

'Surely you've got time for a catch up? Did you see, on Facebook, we're doing this International Women's fete, at church? I thought it was up your alley, with your feminism and things. The theme is Baking for Self-Sufficiency.'

'Mmmm . . .'

'Your father thinks it's nonsense, of course. How's your little job going? Have they promoted you yet?'

'Ahahahaha! Well, an interesting opportunity might be coming up at a similar company, I think there would be much more room for development . . .'

'Not another one of those, what are they called, beginner companies? Starters? We do worry, you know, especially because it's going to be so much harder for you to get on the property ladder now, after everything, on your own. You are saving, aren't you?'

Of course I'm saving. Just the other day I saved one pound fifty by walking home in the rain, for two miles, instead of getting the bus. Maybe I should do that today!

'Yes, of course, Mum.'

'I mean, if you got really stuck we might be able to help you out, I suppose, but obviously we're quite strapped

104

ourselves, losing all of those deposits. There was something in the paper about how your generation is so reliant on the Bank of Mum and Dad. I think that's where the country is going wrong, really.'

I know exactly how this conversation will go, and I cannot bear to have it again.

'What's that Mum? Sorry, my signal's bad, my battery's going, I'll call you back!'

I feel angry tears beginning to prickle. I hang up, dig out my earbuds, and listen to the loudest, sweariest hip hop I can find on Spotify as I run down the stairs. I get on a southbound train, find a precious unoccupied end seat, and sit slumped against the Perspex panel. Why can't I have a mum like other mums? Why can't she just love me?

I wonder what Mum would make of Lottie, her licentiousness, her generosity, her sense of ease and abundance. I think of what Lottie would say to a lost, lonely daughter, the offers of decadent dinners, the house deposits, this imaginary girl who lives in their loft in Zone 1, who went to a smart school, and might be allowed to smoke weed at the dinner table and take an art foundation course in the middle of her twenties, who doesn't know what it feels like to have her bank card declined. Rebelliously, I resolve to waste as much money as I can afford and seek out the most expensive coffee I can find as soon as I get to Stockwell.

Chapter Nine

In the last few months, I've noticed something that I used to be shamefully oblivious to. The world – or rather my corner of it – is built for couples. It's as though everyone was brought here on an ark. There's the pair I sometimes see on my bus route. He looks like Mark, or rather, he doesn't *not* look like him – he's a thirty-something corporate type who clearly stopped playing sport after graduation but kept up with his drinking habits. She looks like my diametric opposite, my shiny nemesis. She has a very precise, brunette bob, a taupe tote with a big brass Michael Kors logo, and revolving range of jewel-toned shift dresses. There is something in her eyes that makes me think she might have stalked out of a few Karen Millen sample sales, swinging cord-handled bags dripping with blood that wasn't her own. Even when I'm trying not to look at her, with him, I can hear them kissing. She looks as though she'd barely disturb the surface of the water in a bath, but when she kisses him, she sounds like a water mill. She moans, she slurps, she sucks, and I have to breathe through my mouth until the nausea passes because it's hard to take before breakfast. I hate her. That way, it's easier for me to hate Mark too.

But at the weekends, when the world is paired up, when everyone I see has a 'we', but me, I *miss* Mark. I imagine an alternative reality where I didn't run away. In my dreams, I become my Bus Nemesis, passionate yet precise. I see my old life, our old flat, and remember a time when I could turn on a tap and take the flow of hot water for granted.

On a Saturday morning, Mark would sing in the shower. It was endearing – he would honk along to anything that came on the radio, and his strangely squeaky Katy Perry impression sometimes reduced me to hysterical tears. It was a sign that he was in a good mood, and I loved feeling responsible for that good mood. No matter how hungover Mark was on a Saturday morning, and I don't remember a single Saturday that did not begin with him cursing the invention of beer, the bar staff at Inferno's or the weakness of Nurofen, he always wanted to have sex. I learned, quite quickly, that it was better to capitulate than to protest. I was usually quite hungover myself, and under the circumstances, a brief bout of motion sickness was easier to endure than half an hour of, 'Please? Go on! See how hard I am for you!'

Mark's body was – and as far as I know, still is – appealingly bearish. Slightly stocky and densely hairy, he was comfortingly, reassuringly masculine. Sometimes, when we were having sex, I'd fantasise that I was a fairy-tale heroine who had passed up the prince for Mr Tumnus, that instead of heading for the castle, I'd found a surprisingly appealing troll and we'd shacked up under a bridge. That reflects badly on me, but it was Mark's more princely qualities that

I struggled with. On those Saturday mornings, I felt close to him, glad to be crushed by the weight of his body, proof of his want.

I think it all started to go wrong at the farmers' market.

From the start, Mark and I cast each other in awkward caricatures, exaggerated roles – and then contorted ourselves to complement this distorted version of The Other, bending and twisting into shapes that bounced between our wrongly reflected selves, a haunted hall of mirrors. I suggested that we go to the farmers' market because I thought I wanted to be the sort of woman who was prepared to spend several of her precious weekend hours deciding whether or not to spend thirty pounds on a jar of honey. Mark, I think, liked the legitimacy of it. To him, it seemed to symbolise the start of our transition into true adulthood. When we were among other couples, market chat was the secret password that established our right to be part of a gathering. All we had to say was, 'I've heard rumours that there's a new one in Battersea with a great vegan frittata place' and we were *in,* we were part of the Clapham crowd, wholesome as a yoghurt advert, legitimate as John Lewis, forever concealing the fact that Mark sometimes farted himself awake and I only noticed because I'd been staring out into the dark for hours, worrying about my Visa bill.

The trouble was that we actually had to *go* to the sodding markets. We'd shag, we'd shower, we'd drink coffee and dress in our weekend drag, fresh and photogenic as Maria and Captain von Trapp. (In my memory, I was always in a white cotton dress, carrying a straw basket, and Mark was in a striped blazer. In reality, I was always in tights I'd retrieved from the laundry basket and Mark was in a

T-shirt that identified him as a 'beer monster'.) Within three hours I would be holding a bushel of anaemic, muddy carrots and having an existential crisis.

'We don't have to get dinner stuff here. Why don't we just get a Chinese tonight?' Mark would plead.

'You don't understand!' I'd wail, when what I really meant was '*I* don't understand'.

I don't understand how I've convinced myself that your perfect woman is someone who is happy to have a public, theatrical breakdown about the quality of organic vegetables. I don't understand why we aren't still in bed. I don't understand how I could feel so close to you an hour ago, yet so far away from myself.

Still, if I'd have known about what was waiting for me on the other side, maybe I would have learned to endure and even adore the farmers' market.

Certainly, I could have been a lot nicer when he surprised me with a set of cushions adorned with pugs wearing appliquéd diamanté crowns, as a way of making amends after he ordered a vast, hideous, black leather sofa. ('It's like a giant poisonous mushroom pretending to be the very worst kind of Liquorice Allsort,' was my uncharitable review.) I could have lived with the ampersand mugs and Union Jack tea towels forced upon us by his generous, tasteless family. His mother once gave me a melamine tray decorated with the Mona Lisa 'because you're arty'.

Mark frequently tried to give me the room and the space to bring my own aesthetic ideas to bear.

'You're good at this sort of stuff,' he'd say encouragingly, passing me Dulux charts, or pointing at creepy fake Degas dancing dolls in junk shops.

The trouble with studying art was that I didn't *know* art – I just knew what I didn't like. I felt like a sulky teenager, turning my nose up at everything, and I didn't know how to bring my vision into our flat without screaming, 'Everything you like is terrible!' Sometimes, I'd lie on that sofa, with my head in Mark's lap, and the room would start to spin. I'd search the walls for anything that might anchor me in the present moment, and I'd feel dizzy from disassociation. There I was, all over the walls, here a champagne flute, there a feather in my hair, smiling and posing, a girl who was pleased with her lot, proud of her man, ready to be bound forever by an invisible ampersand. She knows that there's a 'we' in 'weekend', and she knows those forty-eight hours will be slow and painful if you refuse to march into them, two by two. I think I lost her at the farmers' market. Sometimes it's enough to know I'll never have to lie on the leather sofa again. Sometimes I think I'd do it for a whole year, just for the comfort of one more minute of Mark's bear weight on top of me.

Chapter Ten

I spend the next couple of days dreaming of Ibiza, sun cream smells, lobster and Simon's inevitable selection of linen trousers. However, I'm starting to get scared. What if Lottie only confirms it the day before they go, and it's impossible for me to get the time off work? Would she change her mind, and decide not to give me a job at Intuition because she thinks I'm flaky? What if Sasha blackballs my entry, and I never see these people again? These thoughts are interrupted by flashes of disturbing, semi-welcome erotic memories: Richard's gasping face, Max's fingers moving inside me, the way that Mimi tasted, which I can recall as immediately and sharply as Coca-Cola from a glass bottle on a summer holiday.

Even though reluctant to break the surface of my recollections, curiosity gets the better of me by the afternoon. I'd love to become proper friends with Mimi, but it's difficult to find her without any other details. I search for her artists, glasswork, Kent, and I find mention of a Maria Thompson, which might be her – but again, what Google yields is too dense and confusing to make sense of. Burned out and exhausted, I finally find eight different videos of Sasha, mostly hectoring Evan Davis. She has a Wikipedia entry which does not mention Richard. When my mouth is dry, and my eyes are itchy, I shut my laptop and curl up next to it.

On Monday morning, I wake up in the middle of a dream in which Max is asking me who won the Turner Prize in 2015 and Sasha, who is delivering stinging, vicious cunnilingus, is threatening to bite if I don't get the answer right.

My flat isn't so bad in the mornings, especially at the moment, as I haven't seen either of my housemates in weeks. When I moved in, the landlady described them as 'nice young professionals – they keep themselves to themselves'. I was briefly introduced to a psychotically surly Australian man, who seemed to be halfway through unknotting his own tie, and a sweet-faced Irish man with pale, improbably fluffy facial hair, who put me in mind of Yoda.

Yoda, the nicest of the two, explained that he was on secondment in Mumbai and he'd be home once a month or so. There was no sign of Surly during my first week, and I hoped he was in Mumbai too. But on the seventh day, he returned in the early hours of the morning with what sounded like a torch-wielding mob. On the eighth day, my peanut butter was all gone.

Still, I limit any human contact by spending the briefest amount of time in any communal areas, barely getting damp in the 'wet room' – the sad, mouldy cubicle filled with relics of housemates past, a shrine to various discontinued varieties of Herbal Essences shampoo.

I avoid the kitchen – a small cupboard filled with slightly

smaller cupboards – because I don't eat breakfast before I leave the house. (Even then, I usually only eat breakfast the week after payday. If you're a normal person, with a normal relationship with your appetite, it's the most important meal of the day. If you're me, it's the opening of the food floodgates, the agitation of a craving and a preoccupation that won't release me from its clutches until it's bedtime again.) To be honest, even bedtime isn't entirely safe. I have been known to make it through the day on minimal rations and then leave the house at 10 p.m., returning to binge on 'Reduced To Clear' birthday cakes.

To be honest, I don't even make coffee in the morning any more after I found a strange man face down in the sink. He had a tribal tattoo on his neck, and the leaky tap was dripping on his baseball cap. I screamed, then he screamed, and I emailed the lettings agent to ask if they could notify the landlady and get her to talk to the other tenants about overnight guests. They replied to say that this wasn't really their area to get involved in, and if I *did* want to move out, I still had to pay the next three months' rent and I wouldn't get my deposit back until a suitable replacement was found. But if I was interested, there was a studio flat available that cost the same as my monthly take home pay.

I shower hastily, apply as much make-up as I can in four minutes, sigh over the fact that my dress is sagging and I look like an especially timid supply teacher, and board the bus. I hold the pole, sway and squint at my phone and see an email in my work account that has been sent from simorton_22@gmail.com:

Sending from gmail for obvious reasons, we're waiting for final investor sign off but still v keen to move forward with new role at Intuition. Got a hectic week, could you do 12.30 today, Itsu on the Strand, with me and Richard? Will take you out properly soonest but this all on the DL right now. SXX

I'm not expecting good news, and I think this is good news. I can hear my brain clicking to assimilate it, the joy is tessellating into place. And even though it's Monday, and I'm still slightly wet and cold and cross, and I know that I'm going to spend the first two hours of the day pasting numbers into an Excel spreadsheet, I feel light and bright and excited. I'm a girl in a movie, caught in an updraft of optimism. Maybe I'll look back on this moment as the real beginning of my career, the moment when everything finally changed, and I was allowed to dare to hope. Drifting off, I'm hazily imagine myself recounting this moment whilst on a stage, collecting some sort of award – God knows what the award is, but I know I'm wearing mainline Preen – when a disembodied voice interrupts my daydream. Ah, the bus is terminating half a mile away from its destination and I'm going to be very late. Still hopeful, though.

Once I'm at my desk, I reply to Simon with a curt *Sounds good, see you there, V.* It's going to be a little strange seeing Richard, after Friday, but perhaps his presence is a good sign on the work front. Simon didn't mention Lottie, but surely she'll be there too? It might be a little nerve-wracking without her. It's easy to tune into Impressive Professional

114

Me with Lottie, but Simon on his own *still* makes me feel a little bit gauche, a kid on work experience.

It's time to start my distracting daily morning ritual based around activities of Things That Sort Of Count As Work, But Are Not Really Work. Deleting emails. Googling news about our competitors. I actually have a document saved as 'Research into marketing behaviour' which is really a constantly evolving stream of consciousness, with a shopping list at the bottom. Connie asks after my weekend, and I tell her that I didn't do much because my hair appointment got cancelled, and I feel oddly proud of myself for covering my tracks so consistently, even though she can barely be bothered to listen to my reply. She's hardly going to track Lottie down and compare notes.

By ten past twelve I've escaped, and I'm bouncing along the Embankment, looking up at the last leaves, imagining my future. What salary would they offer me? Could I *move*?

Richard is waiting at the counter and gives me a hug.

'It's great to see you! I'm sorry that this isn't a very glamorous lunch – we had to choose a place where neither of us were going to bump into anyone, and for me, this is handy for the City but not *too* handy, if that makes sense. Simon wanted to take you to Bob Bob Ricard, but one of the sales reps is meeting a dealer there and he's got to keep this project quiet until the money is signed off. What would you like? Simon has grabbed a table, I'll pay and see you there.'

I panic and ask for some chicken noodle thing, wistfully clocking the glossy sashimi as I go. It's OK, I'll have the meeting, pick at my chicken, wait for them to leave and buy some California rolls. I think about California rolls *a lot*. I like to eat them whole, without stopping, drenched in sticky hoisin sauce, but only in deserted restaurant basements where no one else is looking.

Simon is sitting on a stool at a blonde wooden counter, looking too big for his surroundings and his own suit. He gets up to hug me, and I worry that he won't be able to sit down and balance again.

No Lottie. Maybe she's late, or in the loo?

'Lovely to see you so soon after the weekend,' says Simon. 'We're just waiting for one big backer to sign off on the next investment round – the numbers are Richard's department, really – but we need to know your timings.'

'Right!' I force a smile, doing my best to look him in the eye, not his distracting, dazzling white mouth. 'Sounds good! Is, er, Lottie on her way?'

Simon shakes his head.

'She's not joining us today, she's not really part of the cash flow part. Richard is keeping an eye on the figures, har har.'

Did he really just glance at my tits? Surely, he couldn't be that crude? Maybe I'm being silly and oversensitive, and when your prospective new boss has hosted you at an orgy he can look anywhere he likes, even when you're fully clothed and it's Monday lunchtime.

He continues.

'The thing is, it's got to be super small to begin with, and most of our budget will be diverted away from talent acquisition.'

My mind alights on this phrase and I turn it over, realising it's a red flag that my brain is too slow to translate. Ah. They don't want to pay me much money. Does Lottie know about this? Would she fight for some more cash for me, if she were here? Has she avoided this conversation because she doesn't want to think about the fact that my proposed annual salary is what she spends on haircuts?

I zone back in and hear Simon saying something about 'young talent that can come in on the ground floor'.

I'm not sure I want the ground floor, I want someone who will strap a rocket to me and lift me up, up and away. There's something slightly off about the way Simon is speaking, he's a little too loud and too fast. I get the sense that he's not sure how to be alone with me. He keeps glancing around and looking up whenever someone new walks through the door. Maybe this is as weird for him as it is for me.

I want to ask him about Richard. I want to know how this came to pass, how they went from their student boyhood to business, via several sex parties. I'm wondering whether they have brought any other girls here – into the group, not to Itsu. A tiny part of me is thinking that perhaps I've slipped through the net. This might just be the way the world works for the people who run it, and I'm silly and small minded and parochial for thinking that there might be something strange at play.

'Where exactly do you see me fitting in?' I ask, wincing at the mental picture this evokes, and wishing I had a drink to sip. Surely Richard can't *still* be queuing?

'Well, we don't want to get too hung up on defining roles. You'll know from Acquire that during the first few years of a start-up, everyone mucks in everywhere.'

Ah, tea making, then.

'But obviously you're valuable to us because you have such a strong understanding of digital and the, ah, twenty-something market.'

Simon reaches out and puts a hand on my knee, a distance that is slightly too far to be comfortable for him. We look at each other in the same second, and hold each other's gaze for a little too long. I see him, and I can't see him. Who is this man, this tender, ravenous, simple man, building a screen of syllables, talking in words I understand, but put together in an order that makes me wonder whether English is in fact his second or third language?

Richard arrives, my face flushes and I look away.

'Thank you, this looks lovely,' I say with harsh brightness, as if I've just been presented with a home-made casserole and not a tub of MSG and hot water.

Then Richard starts to speak, quietly. I think he sounds slightly nervous. Focusing on his food, he explains that he has always loved art, but ended up in banking, and found that the better he got at his job, the further away it took him from the career he really wanted. It's eerily, depressingly similar to my conversation with Mimi – Richard is caught between defending his high-paying job and apologising for it. But I'm starting to think that I'm the one who has got things wrong. I worked so hard to find a job in my dream industry, and it's made me miserable and broke. An unwelcome little voice pipes up inside my brain. *If you'd worked in banking, Violet, you might be miserable, but you wouldn't be broke. You would never have had to move in with Mark. You would never have got engaged to someone you didn't really love because you didn't think you had any other options.*

Richard has not noticed that I've zoned out. 'To be honest, Violet, I'm a tiny bit terrified about all of this. I think the timing is great. As Simon has probably told you, the traditional organisations are starting to struggle, and it's a great moment to be the little guy. I can't quite believe that soon, if it all goes to plan, I'll get to choose what my job is and how I'll do it. But I've never walked away from anything regular and secure before. My ex is not dealing with it especially well. We're having a *lot* of tense conversations about school fees.'

Does Richard want me to feel sorry for him? I'm not going to make sympathetic noises about job security and the cost of private education when he's not the one who might get fired for being out for more than an hour at lunchtime. Right now, I'm in danger of losing my current job while I hang about waiting for this mythical new one.

'Listen, I'd love to talk about this more, but I really need to get back to the office,' I say.

Simon looks slightly affronted.

'Well, we both made space in our schedules in order to discuss this opportunity we're offering you ...'

It's as if I'm the one who summoned him for sushi with a couple of hours' notice, and he's put himself out for me, not the other way around. In that moment, Simon reminds me of Mark, my dad, almost every man I've known. As soon as I try to assert myself, a mask slips. I've made the world less easy and less safe for them, and suddenly I'm clambering up steep, slippery rocks, frantically attempting a kind of conversational orienteering in order to restore their happiness.

Richard's smile is a grimace. I get the fleeting sense that Simon often makes him feel as though he's up against the cliff face too.

'We're maybe three months away from being able to make formal offers, but we are serious about this, and we need to be sure that you are, too.'

Not trusting myself to speak, I nod. Again, I feel a little underwhelmed, as though I've opened a small, eau de nil jewellery box and pulled out a plastic key ring. I promise to think about it and start to put my coat on.

Simon stands up.

'Violet, I'm going in your direction. I'll walk with you.'

The gesture feels consolatory, and I fight the urge to tell him to leave me alone and let me go, because I'm in a rush. The air hits me, toothpaste fresh on my hot, cross face. I turn right and right again, down to the river. Simon catches up with me, he gently pushes me back against the brick wall of the corner building. He's wearing a heavy, navy cashmere coat and his buttons clash against mine.

'Oh, *Violet*. I'm sorry, I know this is strange, but I haven't been able to stop thinking about you. I tried to avoid you when we were, you know, at the party. I didn't want to come on too strong, this is all so overwhelming. I don't want this to get in the way of work, it's complicated, but *CHRIST*, I want you, Violet, Violet, Violet,' he mumbles.

It's the way he says my name, as though it were the last prayer of a cursed man, that melts my resolve to resist. I'd wanted to kick him on the shins, but I've turned to liquid, his mouth is on mine and I close my eyes and I'm kissing him back, he's kissing me like the world is ending and he's going to war, and maybe it is, and maybe he is.

His hands are under my coat, he's searching for an entrance, an opening, and I feel weak and whimpery and he says, 'Oh God, we can't, not now.' He takes a breath, composes himself. 'Listen. I have to go to Bristol. Can you come to Bristol?'

'When?'

Also *what?* And WHY? With Lottie? Will she come too?

'Tomorrow, I think ... no hold on, it's Monday today so ... Wednesday? Get the train after work, I'll meet you at the station. *Please.*'

His neediness is surprising, and appealing. Being the entire focus of Simon's attention is akin to being caught in the full beam of a stadium spotlight. I'm starting to understand why lunch felt so strained and sad, and why he couldn't look directly at me. He's so *much.* I'm not sure whether I'm thrilled or frightened. This reminds me of meeting Lottie for the very first time – and finally realising how it feels to be in the presence of genuine charisma. This is a man who has enough appeal to head up a large, successful cult. I can imagine him addressing a captivated crowd of thousands. Being the direct recipient of Full Simon is dizzying, it's a drug that's pure enough to kill you.

'OK.' Anxious of betraying myself, I daren't say any more. I go limp, shrug off his embrace, and start walking. I do not look back, because I need him to be watching me. I could not bear it if he had already returned to Richard, the restaurant, his rapidly cooling noodles.

Chapter Eleven

Bristol will require An Outfit, and I have no idea how Simon wants me to look. Because I'm an idiot, I start to imagine myself stepping onto the platform, through a cloud of steam, in some sort of enormous wide brimmed hat, which would be entirely achievable if we were going to have sex in 1928. I wonder whether I ought to go for some sort of Lottie look, even though I know I could never pull it off. I'd be a budget MILF in man-made fibres. Then I wonder whether I should be emphasising my youth and otherness. I'm quite close to buying a black vinyl skirt, and then I get a grip and remember that Simon has asked me there in order to take my clothes off, and he's really in no position to judge, ask not who casts the first deck shoe, etc.

I remember that I have a Date Dress, something I bought in the French Connection sale the week after breaking up with Mark, thinking of it as a bright flag to raise up on my mast and salute my future. Ironically, Mark would have loved it. Mark was one of those misguided men who cast themselves as 'curve-loving' ambassadors for body positivity. If anyone mentioned feminism in his presence, he would deliver a ten-minute panegyric on the body of Christina Hendricks.

The dress is royal blue, capped sleeves, nipped in at the waist with a tight pencil skirt. It's very, 'Take a letter, Miss Smith. And while you're at it, you can take my penis too.' Mark described himself as a retrosexual, and claimed to love my body because of its unfashionable in-and-out shape. He saw himself as being dominant, red-blooded, hyper masculine, but what started with some occasional spanking ended up becoming tedious and tiresome. He'd ask me to make him a sandwich, or do his ironing, and it took me a little while to realise he wasn't joking. He'd give me marks out of ten for my 'wife-ing' and I'd laugh along because I knew he meant it sweetly, even though I didn't feel as though I was in on the joke. I *was* the joke. It was intrusive, and I resented it. Mark knew that someone else had already nicknamed me 'wifey'. Nadia. She made up so many silly permutations and combinations of the nickname that sometimes I'd meet people who thought I was German and my name was pronounced 'Wiolet'.

The trouble is that my body does look quite wife-like, in a retro way. I've got the hips for an apron. There are infinite ways for our bodies to betray us, and mine does it through false advertising. I am the red rag, and the bull is a 'tit man'. The blue dress might have been designed to deliver me into the arms of Mark II. Still, I don't think that description applies to Simon. He's just offered me a job, sort of. He hasn't ruined a perfectly nice lunch with a discussion about why I might stop working when I have his children 'because when we start a family, you won't *need* to work, will you? Being a mum will be your job.'

Mark was generous – he paid most of our rent, and I'd begged to be allowed to pay anything at all. But our Clapham attic was his castle, a benign dictatorship where life could be very easy for me as long as I didn't ask difficult questions or let down my hair in the wrong way. The rules were unspoken, but unbreakable. Remain in the tower. Do not look directly at Camelot.

I'm convinced that Simon will change his mind and cancel the trip. However, he emails again the next day, with the details of a return train ticket, and a sweet, slightly condescending explanation of how to retrieve it from the machine at Paddington, an assurance that it won't charge my own bank card. It is thoughtful, and I'm touched. I reply from my personal address, more for Simon's sake than mine. I've already erased all trace of him from my professional inbox, an instinctive act of self-preservation. With a day and a night to go, I am on the brink of giddy madness. There are moments when my excitement turns into dread. Should I cancel? It was weird being alone with Simon for ten minutes in a sushi restaurant. A whole night might be impossible! And what about Lottie? This *has* to be part of their arrangement. Presumably, she's absolutely fine with it. In fact, she'll probably be there too! Still, I remember Simon's intensity and anxiety, and queasily acknowledge this might be a convenient lie that I'm telling myself.

Working my worry into knots, I consider cancelling until I remember the kiss, and then I'm desperate to see him again. Coughing experimentally, I wonder whether I should lay the groundwork for a skive, buying myself a few extra hours of preparation and panicking. Still, being in the office actually forces me into a kind of calm normality that would be impossible to achieve if I were home and alone. I compromise and book a lunch time blow-dry I can't really afford, especially because it ends up costing £45, not the advertised £30. (I would have had a wax, but everything is too short and stubbly to bother with, so I use a whole can of Nivea gel and two different Bic razors, attempting to depilate my entire body in my stupid, narrow, badly lit shower cubicle.)

Finally, finally, it is fourteen minutes past eight on Wednesday, and I am three minutes away from Bristol Temple Meads. Will Simon be standing on the platform, scanning the train windows for my face, embracing me with his left arm while his right, outstretched, clasps cellophane containing a dozen red roses? Ah, he has sent me a message! It has the address of a hotel in it, a chain I recognise. I am to meet him at the bar.

In the taxi, I agitatedly take off the top of my right fingernail, almost to the quick, just the slenderest crescent of white remains. I bury the evidence between the seats, gross and guilty. Should I go to reception? Will I be told off for ruining the lovely hotel with my sordid sexing? I notice a streetlight shining gold on a tree of yellow leaves and remember the text. Simon said the bar.

He's in there, scanning the room for me, his torso twisted at a forty-five-degree angle. An advert for smart casual, he's in tailored navy trousers, but jacket and tie-less. The top two buttons of his shirt are undone. He really is shockingly handsome, I'd forgotten, I'd been so consumed by thoughts of what was to come that his face had faded in my memory.

There's a faint suggestion of tiredness around his eyes. It makes him seem more vulnerable, and I wonder about the work and worry that brought him here. I have to make this worth his while, I must show him a good time.

'Violet! Oh, lovely, you made it! I was going to ask you to meet me in the room, but it's called Merlot or Margaux or something, and there's no lift, and it might have been a bugger to find. Would you like a drink here or shall we go upstairs, and you can get rid of your ... things.'

He eyes my meagre overnight kit: clean knickers, deodorant, a toothbrush and a make-up bag, which I've squashed into a grubby cotton Tate tote.

Simon still seems like a stranger in real, vertical life. I'm filled with an urge to rush past this wincing awkwardness, to get straight to the point where I know him best, soft, hard, warm, pliant. Daringly, I take his hand.

'Let's go upstairs.'

He wasn't exaggerating. We walk across a carpeted corridor, up more stairs and through a swinging door. I could not find my way back to the bar unaided. Simon pats his pockets and pulls out a silver key, which has been attached to a large, plastic keyring bearing the room's name, which does not begin with M. It's surprising. It seems vast, the lighting is low and luxurious, but the TV looks cheap and small on its stand. The heavily embossed paper that covers a single wall seems dark and dated. I remember the splendour of the Zetter and feel a little disappointed.

Simon is slightly apprehensive. It's not a word I ever thought I'd use about him, but it's as though he's shy of me. He starts to take a step and then pivots, as if he can't remember why he came into the room, as if he's forgotten something.

'A drink? Red wine? Something cold from the mini bar?'
I smile.

'Oooh, red wine would be lovely.'

This feels awkward. He seems nervous, and I'm forcing cheer, attempting to put him at his ease and trying to make everything seem more normal. Our usual roles are reversed, we've got this the wrong way around. Maybe Lottie is coming, and he'll relax when she arrives? I had been shamefully excited about the prospect of having Simon all to myself, but I'm starting to wish she was here.

Simon's tense demeanour is affecting my posture. I clasp my hands more tightly and lean forward, trying to squash myself down. Simon is built along lean, spare lines, and I'm horribly aware of taking up too much space. The bed is enormous and yet I'm so far near the end I might fall off. Simon is fumbling with the corkscrew, a waiter's friend, failing to remove the foil from the bottle.

'It's not your friend is it! Ha! Oh ...' My stupid joke hangs in the air for a moment.

Then Simon smiles tightly.

'I should have the hang of this, I'll have you know that I was a waiter in my gap year!'

'Oooh, I didn't know you went travelling, where did you go?'
Simon looks slightly abashed.

'Well, I did the usual South East Asia, and came home when I ran out of money, but I couldn't quite face reality, so I did a ski season. I did a few, actually, in the vacs and things, Val d'Isère mainly. I wasn't exactly a "sommelier"' – he drags the word out for an extra couple of syllables, using a pantomime French accent, and I giggle – 'I mainly poured tequila shots. Do you ski?'

I think about telling a lie, and realise, at this stage, I might as well be honest, I don't have anything to lose.

'Not really. Well, not at all, I've never been. It's always struck me as the sort of thing where you have to grow up going, and I never fancied the school trips because I was never one of the sporty girls. I love the idea of the snow, you know, boozy hot chocolate in log cabins – but I'm so clumsy that I don't think I could ski. I suspect that if I were to try, every travel insurance company in the world would say, "No, we've heard about you, we've got a picture of you up in our office with a big red cross through it."'

Simon, safe in the knowledge that his bluff will never be called, is optimistic for me.

'I could teach you! Honestly, you'd love it, you really feel like you're careening off the end of the world. All-powerful and completely powerless at the same time. And then we'd have hot chocolate, and there would be a fire, and we'd both sit by the window, and watch the snow fall ...'

'Exactly like the "Last Christmas" video!' I cry, but Simon has already sat down beside me, and he's kissing my neck, and saying my name. There's a slowness, a gentleness, a quality that seems more deliberate than urgent. He finds my zip, but doesn't pull it all the way down, just enough to expose my right shoulder, which he barely kisses, resting his mouth on my flesh.

He inhales.

'Oh Violet, when I smell your skin I can't ... I don't ... it's just too much, I don't know what to do with myself, I want time to stop.'

I want time to stop too, I want to get my phone out, make him say it again, record it, I need permanent proof that someone has felt that way about me, even if only for a moment. If I could I'd scratch his words into my skin with my fingernails.

It seems right to face him and kiss him, to open his mouth with mine and feel his warmth, his yielding softness. I kiss faster, kiss harder, but he slows me down. It's awkward, kissing like this, so I wrap my arms around him and we roll backwards onto the bed. I love feeling the warmth of his back through the thin cotton of his shirt. And I slide a palm under the shirt and feel his smooth skin, muscle and down, and I love that even more. I stop to unbutton him, just as he makes an unfocused attempt to grab my zip, pull it further down.

'Let me,' I say, looking him in the eyes and smiling.

I kneel up on the bed, and still facing him, with my right arm behind the back, I find the zip. When it's halfway down my back, I reach for the hem and pull my dress up and over my head. It has to be done in one fluid movement, if it gets stuck on my head, I will look ridiculous. But the gesture goes my way. For once, life has a cinematic quality and I manage to make it slick, maybe even seductive.

Simon sees my breasts spilling out of their polyester cups and groans. Looking down, I feel like groaning too. They are so dramatic that they're almost corny. I feel illusory, like a burlesque sketch. There is something deeply arousing about objectifying myself – I can see what Simon sees, and it gives me respite from the constant noise in my head. It is liberating to let myself become two dimensional for a moment, albeit with tits that are indisputably 3D.

Simon pulls down both bra straps, so they cup my upper arms. He swiftly unclasps the bra, his earlier maladroit moment forgotten.

'Oh, oh God, oh!' he moans, as he lowers his mouth to my right nipple, kissing, sucking, touching. Between my legs, I'm burning, I feel wild with impatience, I want to be touched so much I feel angry. Hooking my thumbs into my knickers, I'm about to yank them down, when Simon says 'Let me.'

I have to lie down, so that he can slide them over my ankles and off my feet, and he does. He gazes at me for minutes, at my face, my stupid face, while I'm horizontal, throbbing and furious. Finally, his right thumb grazes the soft flesh of the inside of my left thigh and he starts to roll down my stocking, getting slower and slower, as though he's taking a panoramic photo on his phone and wants to be extra careful to stop the picture warping. I yelp.

'Simon, please, now!'

I still have one stocking on, and I sit up, I need his fly, I'm going to break the zip if I'm not careful. He pushes me away. I've undone his trousers, but they're still at hip height, and I've felt his dick and I've felt exactly how badly he wants me.

'Violet! Not. Yet.'

Just make me come. Please. Please. I make an odd noise, I sound like I'm about to cry, maybe I am, and thank God, he moves his mouth between my legs, using my hips for leverage. He licks me at the very lowest, most sensitive part of my lips, at first lapping at me, savouring me, which is infuriating, and then really kissing me properly, tender and sure. He slides a single finger inside me, and I cry out. Something feels different, I'm going to come, I think I'm going to wet myself, and I need to stop, I need to regain control and I can't, it's too much, this is an explosion. I make an unappealing, guttural noise, which seems to be coming from far away.

Simon pulls away, looks up at me and giggles. I've seen him smirk, but I didn't know he was a giggler.

I flush, I'm suddenly self-conscious.

'I didn't know you could do that,' he says.

'Do what?'

I'm confused, and then I notice his face is sticky and shiny, and I get it. He strokes back the hair that has fallen across my forehead.

'Oh, Violet, I don't think I can last any longer,' he says, and he wiggles out of his suit trousers and his boxers, which are, I notice, unexpectedly stripy, and with his unbuttoned shirt still flapping around his body, he leans on his elbows and slides his dick inside me, and I squeeze him in my muscles, as hard as I can, because I want to feel him as much as I can, and he says 'Oh God, don't' and comes before I can come again.

We both giggle, hysterically, for a few seconds, and then I kiss his lips, and he kisses my nose, and I want to stay pressed up against his warm body but scuttle off to the loo because no man is charismatic enough to force me to surrender any battle in the ongoing Cystitis Wars.

I sit forward, feet planted firmly on the cold white tiles, idly pinching one of the nipples that was just in his mouth. The toiletries are all made by a brand I love but cannot afford to buy, and the scent of the soap is fresh and green. I'm pretending. Right now, life is too precious and perfect to completely believe in. One wrong move and I'll shatter the surface.

Simon has climbed into bed, he's wearing a robe, he's still giggling.

'Let's get room service!' he says, cheerily. 'I'm hungry for something that comes in a silver dome!'

I get in beside him, and we order huge burgers, onion rings, extra cheese on our chips. We drink more wine, find *The Simpsons* on TV and I rest my head on his chest while he rubs the middle of the back of my neck. When he gets up to sign for the room service, I childishly hide in the bed, holding a pillow over my face until he says, 'The coast is clear.' We eat, and he tells me off for dropping chips in the bed.

I'm longing to quiz him about Intuition. I'm starting to feel as though I'm in a toxic relationship with this future job, and with my own ambition. But I can't tell him that I'm feeling insecure and vulnerable, because those are not qualities you want in your new hire. I still need to make him think that I'm fending off job offers and bonuses, not brown envelopes and scary phone calls. I cannot let the real world inside the bed. But what *can* I ask him about?

'So, Mimi mentioned that you met Lottie when you were at uni. What did you study?' Halfway through the sentence, I realise mentioning Lottie was a mistake. In fact, this might all be a mistake. A powerful wave of nausea breaks, deep in the pit of my stomach.

Simon doesn't blanch at his wife's name.

'The optics, mostly. I read history.'

'Are you all friends because you're art fans?' I gulp, trying to ignore what my body is telling me. I will never, ever do anything bad again if I can just pretend that reality is suspended in this one room. Bloody hotels. They make you feel safe enough to be dangerous. They trick you into believing that nothing you do inside them could possibly count outside, afterwards.

'Violet, you can't be a fan of "art". I'm not going to ask

you if you're a "fan" of music. "Hey, Violet, do you enjoy the concept of noise and sound?"'

I feel embarrassed, and my cheeks are hot. Talking into his chest, I mutter, 'I just want to find out more about you, that's all.'

Simon distractedly pats my head.

'It's been a long day, you don't want my boring biography. Now, be a good girl and shut up, or I'll put the golf on.'

We watch a programme where a couple are building a glass coastal castle, while living in a caravan, and laugh at the presenter who won't stop pointing out what a terrible time they're having, and keeps counting how many thousands, or hundreds of thousands, of pounds that they've exceeded their budget by. Even though I'm longing for the programme to end so that we can have a proper talk, I drift off to sleep, and sleep heavily until I'm woken by Simon coming out of the shower the next morning.

'I've got meetings, but do stay for breakfast, they've got my credit card so don't worry about that when you check out, everything's taken care of. Listen,' he pauses, and rubs his back vigorously with a towel before resuming. 'Let's not tell Lottie about last night.'

Even though I had a horrible sense that this was a secret, I still feel as though I've just been punched. Part of me is thrilled to be conspiring with Simon, to have a secret with this addictive man. But I don't want to leave Lottie out in the cold. It feels like an abuse of power. It would feel different, I think, if I'd snuck off with Lottie for a sexy city break, a sleepover that got out of hand. I wouldn't care about lying to Simon. But this? I'm shuddering with shame. I feel as though I've broken the rules without understanding what

133

they really were. I was genuinely clinging on to the hope that Lottie was so cool and so secure that she'd send her hot husband off for a West Country shag with her blessing.

'I didn't realise! I assumed she knew! I won't tell her, but maybe we shouldn't ... do this again.'

Simon kisses the top of my head.

'I'm a bad man, and I couldn't resist. Still, what Lottie doesn't know won't hurt her, eh?'

Oh God. I feel a bit sick. I already have too many secrets for any normal person to successfully keep.

I had dreamily imagined sharing a cosy train ride back to London with Simon. He'd buy me a vast plastic beaker full of coffee, and he'd be impressed that I drink black Americanos, not maple syrup and marshmallow lattes. We'd complete the *Times* crossword together, even though I usually struggle to answer a single clue.

The Simon-in-my-head is evolving to be entirely different from Simon-in-real-life, Simon-who-penetrated-me-in-the-Zetter. This morning, as I dozed, imaginary Simon took me to Tuscany and fed me spaghetti vongole. (Imaginary Violet can put away a *lot* of pasta without bloating.) Meanwhile, Real Simon snored beside me, forcing me to question the rules I'd made for myself about men who wear vests. Surely it counted as a T-shirt. A very thin T-shirt, with no sleeves.

In real life, I'm squashed into the corner of a table seat, feeling entirely alone. Or as alone as a person can be when surrounded by three harrumphing, spluttering, newspaper-shaking middle-aged men. One has just picked his nose, examined his forefinger, raised his eyes to heaven and made an outraged 'PAH!' noise, before flicking the contents behind him. I feel the bile rising in my throat, and I have to swallow hard.

Why didn't Simon tell Lottie about what we were doing? Admittedly, a wicked part of me loves the idea of us having our own special connection, of Simon and I having some kind of private relationship, something I can hug to myself and cherish. Imaginary Simon could say, 'Violet, live with me and be my love,' and I'd feel so thrilled, so *chosen*, I'd be on someone's team again. Yet Real Life Simon makes me feel slightly strange, and grubby. He won't give me anything of himself. I can't pin him down. I think of Mark, trying to remember what it's like to be with someone who doesn't have any boundaries, his refusal to shut bathroom doors, his insistence on sharing the mundanity of his day, without analysis or evaluation, in real time. Better to lie awake next to a snoring, secretive man in a vest than to be woken up by a man in a vest who is watching porn on your laptop.

It's weird to think that wasn't the first time I had sex with Simon, but it was the only time we've spent the night together, alone. Maybe I will refuse to do it again. I'll be a wild, wanton party participant, and I'll offer up my body while refusing him any kind of glimpse into my mind, my soul. And maybe *then* I'll make him fall in love with me, and Lottie will get jealous of him, and she'll fight for me, and ... oh, shut up, Violet.

Thinking about sex makes me feel self-conscious, and I gaze out of the window at the speeding countryside, trying to relive every orgasm while cutting the middle-aged men from my peripheral vision. What will happen next? If Lottie finds out about what just happened, will I be banned from the group? In some ways, it might be a relief. I wasn't built to tell so many lies, I don't think I have the metabolism for it. I prod the underside of my jaw, noticing a small, painful cluster of lumpy spots that have sprouted over the last few hours – the first thing my body produces in the throes of stress. My heart can take an emotional pounding, but my skin is not game.

Still, I can't bear the idea of returning to reality – to normality. I'm very invested in my new job and new life. What if this promised trip materialises? I think of lying topless, face down on a lounger, Lottie oiling the sun-warmed skin of my bare back, her hands running up the inside of my thighs, the inside of my bikini. I try to distract myself with the thought until I can't ignore the fact that my bladder is full of coffee, and have to climb over one of the middle-aged men and find the terrible train toilet with its terrible poem printed on the seat and breathe through my mouth and accidentally open the door instead of locking it by pressing the wrong flashing button, and sit with the seat down and drop last night's knickers to my ankles and read the stupid poem about things you can't flush down the toilet. The train company is too coy to mention condoms. Oh God. Condoms.

A memory floats into my brain, unbidden. Ms Smythwick, the sweet, wild-haired teacher whose main responsibility was geography, shouting, 'There is no excuse for having sex without a condom! Never, ever! It's the riskiest thing you can do!' At the time, my classmates and I were eleven, and our experience of risky behaviour was limited to finishing homework in the morning before the register was taken and leaving chocolate bars in unattended cloakroom bags, because Ben Bowden had an 'impulse control problem' and would regularly walk into his weekly counselling sessions munching someone else's stolen Snickers. Ms Smythwick definitely meant well.

Years later, I filled in the gaps that she left between her anecdotes and explanations and realised that someone very close to her had died of an HIV-related illness. But before I fully understood what sex was, I knew that it could kill you. Then, at home and at church, it was heavily hinted that having sex would ensure that you immediately went to hell. So, the punishments for having sex started in this life and continued, endlessly, in the next.

When I was fourteen, I went on the Pill, because I suffered from cramps. This is the word my mother used for the four or five days a month when disgusting lumps of blood, heavy like liver and sticky like blackcurrant jelly, fell out of me. I thought of myself as a beach in a storm, waves of pain breaking ceaselessly. The cramps made me feel hopeless, as though the sky could never be still. I'd lie upside down, my head at the bottom of the stairs and my feet on the landing, sobbing as quietly as I could, because it was the only position in which I could process the pain. When I lay flat in bed, the agony had nowhere to go. At least this way I could imagine it pouring out of the top of my head, away from my body. Dad would shake his head and say, 'Most women can put up with this, why can't you?' Mum had three arguments with the GP about putting me on the Pill, initially insisting on painkillers that made me slur and crash into furniture.

I still remember sitting in the surgery, on the cold, hard chair, a slightly scaled up version of the tiny stools we used in primary school, while Mum and Dr Asher faced me, somewhere between an interview and an interrogation. Dr Asher was gentle.

'Now, Violet, it's best to think of this as a medication to help with your menstruation. The Pill is a contraceptive, but I *must* stress that you're below the legal age of consent, and I want you to tell me that you understand that it's against the law for you to have sex.'

Mum interrupted before I could reply.

'You hear her, Violet? I'm only doing this as a last resort. You're not to tell anyone, no one must know there are contraceptives in my house. If anyone finds out, we'll all have to stop going to church.'

Good, I thought, *I hate church.* But I didn't want to say anything out loud, that might make Mum change her mind, and stop this sweet relief. The Pill didn't stop the pain, but it did ease it. It was a secret I was happy to keep. According to locker gossip, Emily Hill, in the year above, had turned into a complete slut when she went on it. Apparently, she'd had sex with someone's cousin from another school and let a different boy finger her at the same party. It was only at a sixth form party, before she went to university, that Emily, white wine drunk and desperate to offload on a relative stranger, told me that she was actually a virgin. She'd almost had sex with a boy who had been so disappointed to discover that her reputation was false that he refused to have anything to do with her, and abandoned her at a party, crying on someone else's parents' bed.

Emily asked me if I'd ever had sex. I was drunk too, and I wanted to be more than honest. I wanted to honour her honesty, and demonstrate the same level of vulnerability that she had shown me. For a second, I questioned the wisdom of what I was about to tell her, and then I ploughed ahead.

'I've never had sex with anyone else. But sometimes, I make myself come.'

The moment the words were out of my mouth I sobered up, regretting everything.

She looked horrified.

'Why would you do that? Urghhhh!'

Immediately, I knew I'd gone too far. My response was panicky and inadequate.

'Um, it feels nice. Forget it. Don't tell anyone. Please.'

Poor Slutty Emily could never shake off her reputation, but she could leave a bitter legacy. For my final year of school, among certain circles, I was known as Violet Fingers Herself.

Unlike Emily, I didn't have the grounds to sue for slander. I'd started to discover the benefits of my body by accident, at different points of puberty. As I turned into a teenager, I'd take long, hot baths, and notice that it felt strange and good when my nipples were submerged in water. Experimentally, I'd lie on my stomach and press myself against the bath's buoyancy, aware of the frustrating, almost maddeningly pleasurable sensation of the surface of the water lapping the lips between my legs. I'd stroke and rub and pinch almost instinctively, knowing something was happening while being entirely clueless about how to make it happen more. If people had sex on TV, and I was watching with my parents, I had to leave the room. I'd pretend it was because I was embarrassed, but my emotions weren't quite so straightforward. When I watched those scenes, I longed to be naked with someone, anyone, and my longing felt so

139

violent and ferocious that I burned with it. I was worried that my desires were so intense that they might as well have been written with black ink on my forehead, and that as soon as my parents noticed, they would have me sent away to a home for wicked, wayward teenagers.

Then, a few months before my sixteenth birthday, another girl, Jasmine Riley, changed my life. We were supposed to be revising for a mock exam. Her parents were at work and her brother was on a school trip. We had the house to ourselves.

'I have to show you this, I caught my brother watching it, it's *disgusting*!' she said, gleefully.

I hovered awkwardly in the doorway of this weird room, with its musty, unfamiliar smell, skateboarders rendered in black and white on the wall, the tangle of dusty leads and wires piled up in each corner. Jasmine went to his computer and clicked open a video. It was a grainy shot, taking up a full screen, of a room containing no furniture but a black leather sofa and a low wooden table, with a potted green cactus on the top.

On the sofa was a man, naked, shaven-headed, with thick linear tattoos that extended all the way down both arms. He had his penis in his right hand and was rubbing it vigorously. It was the first time I'd seen a man's penis, and I was appalled and aroused.

'It gets *worse*!' squealed Jasmine, as two slender, naked girls approached the man. A blonde and a brunette, long, glossy hair cascading down their backs. They didn't look much older than us, but they had enormous, identical, solid-looking breasts. The blonde sat on the man's knee and started to moan and rock. The brunette faced her, and the blonde licked her between the legs as she had sex with the man. Everyone seemed to be having constant, simultaneous orgasms. The two girls swapped places, and finally the man stood up as they knelt down, breasts to breasts, kissing each other and licking his penis until something pumped and gushed all over their bodies and faces.

Jasmine wrinkled her nose.

'Men are pigs. And what kind of *slut* would let a man do something like that to her? I can't believe anyone watches this. So, so gross.'

I smiled weakly.

'I wish you'd never shown me, that was the worst thing I've ever seen. You're such a bitch.'

As soon as I got home that night, I told my parents that I wanted to go to bed early and get ahead with some extra reading for English. Under the covers I mentally replayed everything I'd seen, imagining myself sitting on that man's enormous penis, licking those women, being licked by those women. I found my clitoris and rubbed it, discovering it felt better if I licked my finger first, and that it felt better still if I pushed another finger inside myself. When I came, I thought I would burst, from both the sensation and from the effort of trying to do so silently. What I was doing felt very wrong, fleshy and creepy and shameful. I couldn't imagine anyone I knew experimenting with their body, or having these thoughts. But it was completely addictive. As long as I was doing it alone, I felt relatively safe. I thought about Jasmine's brother's video every night for months. Then I started to find my own videos, always getting more pleasure from the mental replay than the initial viewing, when I'd be overwhelmed with terror about being discovered as I watched.

Eventually, when I was a student, I started to see that I had nothing to be ashamed of. I made new friends, feminists who told me that masturbating was nothing to feel guilty about, even though my choice of material made me a tool of the patriarchy. We all went vibrator shopping and I didn't leave my room for a week. I still watched too much porn, but I was starting to unlearn shame and undo all of that Catholic bad magic. A couple of times, I'd get a boy back to my room and then one of us would get nervous.

'I'm sorry, I think it's all the Pro Plus,' said one – Rich? Steve? – after his promises that he was going to get so hard for me failed to materialise. 'I've got an essay due for my quantum mechanics module, I've not slept for two days.'

And I'd be disappointed, but slightly relieved, that I wasn't about to try to force some pleasure from Rich-or-Steve, who said 'haitch', not 'aitch', and had a spotty back. We'd make a midnight snack of gluey penne and jarred pasta sauce and talk about the pretend sexual conquests we'd had on imaginary holidays and gap years.

Then I met Mark.

It was an inauspicious start. Towards the end of my first year I'd gone out on some bar crawl, dressed, for spurious reasons, as a cheerleader.

'Be careful,' warned Nadia. 'You don't want to come home pissed with some rugby player.'

Mark was a rugby player. One of the biggest, and loudest. I noticed him throughout the night, singing, shouting, always the most obnoxious in a particularly obnoxious group of friends. All night, I heard him bragging about

142

women, what his plans were, what he was going to do to them with his enormous penis. I found him repellent. Yet, after midnight, when he bought me a drink while putting his hand up my skirt and discovering the tops of my socks ('Thigh highs are my *favourite*,' he confided, as if I'd just got him the Christmas present he didn't know he wanted), I decided that I wanted to have a go at having sex with him.

What sold Mark to me was his shocking confidence. He knew exactly what he wanted, and who I was – 'a dirty girl' who 'really wants it'. His technique was paint-by-numbers porn, complete with a narrative of exactly how he was objectifying my body at each moment in time. I *loved* it. It was, I imagined, the sexual equivalent of Disneyland. You go in knowing it's fake, and possibly offensive, wrong and ridiculous on a thousand levels, but if you suspend your disbelief and allow yourself to be in character, while being taken in by characters, you will have a brilliant time.

I left Mark's that morning, whistling, abandoning my silly socks as a souvenir for him. He was graduating, I never needed to see him again, and I was finally, in my own eyes, a grown-up. For the first time, I felt sated. My cravings were satisfied, and the day was mine. I could have a bath, a fried egg sandwich, a nap.

Nadia was drinking a peppermint tea in the kitchen when I skipped in. She noticed my smudged twelve-hour-old make-up, my mis-buttoned shirt, my hair, which, according to a car's wing mirror, had become hilarious – one bunch perpendicular to my left ear, the other sprouting up from the centre of my skull. She sighed, theatrically.

'What did you do? What did I tell you?'

Attempting to make a contrite face, I failed and giggled.

'I know. But Rugby Mark! Who knew?'

Nadia rolled her eyes at me.

'So, he's being a gentleman, yes? Dinner tonight at Café Rouge? He's picking you up at seven?'

We laughed, and I told her, affectionately, to piss off.

'This, Nads, is the beauty part. Holidays start next week. He's got less than seven days to tell everyone about what a slag I am, and then he buggers off forever to work at Wankerhouse bank, or wherever it is he's going, and I am free! I begin my summer as a strong, sexually confident woman! Hooray!'

'Whatever,' she replied, sipping her tea. 'Don't forget to pack your rabbit.'

The next day, when Nadia and I were in the pub, one of Mark's acolytes solemnly walked over to where I was sitting, bearing a Jäger-bomb. He placed it in front of me as though he were a billionaire, and he was presenting me with a cheque for matching four numbers on the Lottery.

'This is for you. Mark needs your number.'

I snorted.

'Mark can ask me himself. Thank you for the drink, though.'

It was five o'clock in the afternoon, and far too early for Jägermeister – but far too late in the term to turn down free alcohol. Nadia was laughing so hard she was on the brink of tears.

'That was magnificent! Well done!'

She was still laughing when Mark turned up.

'Would you give us some privacy?' he asked Nadia, a courteous question cut with a note of chilly pomposity. His voice sounded different from the night before, less husky and needy, but low and clipped, even though he spoke as if he could barely be bothered to move his lips.

I sighed.

'Mark, this is Nadia and it's really rude to ask her to leave. Let's go outside.'

The moment we reached the smoking area, Mark started kissing me, softly, but forcefully. I felt myself tingle and yield, and start to kiss back, before pulling away and drawing myself up to my full height. Mark, I thought, probably made most of his conquests by kissing them with such assurance and *droit de seigneur* that they felt they had no choice but to continue until they were pregnant and on the brink of raising his child alone in a studio flat.

'Mark, are you drunk? It's the afternoon!'

Mark was drunk. Slowly, he pulled one black thigh-high sock out of one of his jeans pockets, and then the other, like a goth magician.

'I wanted to return these.'

'Oh, it's fine, I don't want them. Give them to some other girl. Throw them away.'

He looked petulant. It was an expression I was about to become very familiar with.

'I want you to come on a date with me. Tonight.'

'I'm busy. And you're leaving. After this week we'll never see each other again.'

'But!' He took my hands in his, squeezing them so hard that for a second, I thought he might fracture my little fingers. I realised 'no' was a new word for him, one he had not heard often, and I felt furious. Yet I loved that my hands felt tiny in his, the idea that maybe I could be the girl and he could be the lion. I looked up at him, at his narrowed eyes and huge forehead, and said no again.

The next day, a card arrived in my pigeonhole informing me that the porter had taken delivery of twelve red roses on my behalf. Another card was attached to the roses with a time, a date, the name of a hotel and the word 'Please'.

Over time, Mark became a habit. I fully expected him to get bored and go off with someone who fitted with his graduate status, his glossy London life. But he kept turning up at weekends, generously buying booze for house parties, unbothered by the shared bathroom – and by the time my own graduation rolled around, I was glad – well, relieved – to know one bit of my future seemed certain. Mark made me feel safe.

Chapter Twelve

When the train pulls into Paddington, I've had a big cry and a little look on my phone, and I've found a drop-in clinic near work. It's not impossible that anyone in the group has HIV, but now that I've calmed down, I'd say it's unlikely. If I do have gonorrhoea or chlamydia or syphilis, I'll just have to take all of the antibiotics and never have sex again. And I've accompanied enough terrified friends to the GUM clinic to know that it's probably going to be OK. For comfort, I think about the time Nadia had 'herpes', a condition that lasted for two hours until an understandably grumpy nurse explained that it was just a particularly itchy, dramatic reaction to Immac. In fact, that was one of our very first bonding experiences – a very early outing that marked our transition from new friends to soulmates.

All of the best romances have an excellent origin story, and I always liked mine and Nadia's more than mine and Mark's. When I spoke to Nadia for the first time, she was in the middle of doing an impression of me.

I'd seen her around campus, a full head taller than nearly everyone else in any given room. I'd noticed her in netball gear, striding along the pavement, looking like a woman who was going places, figuratively and literally. I was usually skulking, hungover in a hoodie. Once she smiled invitingly, as if she was on the brink of asking me to join in, and I scuttled away. I cannot talk to you, I thought, for I am a fat dwarf.

Nadia was – is – spectacular, a dead ringer for the French actress, Stéfi Celma. Her Afro was a glorious golden bonfire, and she moved as though she had helium, not blood, in her veins. In fact, I'd convinced myself she *was* Stéfi Celma, so I was taken aback when I heard her at the union bar, yelling for a triple vodka in a broad Liverpudlian accent.

It was usually hard to get near to Nadia, because most of the time she was surrounded by an equally fabulous gang of women. One of her friends was in my seminar group, but I didn't talk to her. I didn't really talk to anyone because I didn't know what to say. When I started uni, I'd fantasised about reinventing myself. I wasn't going to be the nerd who always put her hand up before the teacher had finished asking the question. I wasn't going to be the breathless, enthusiastic, chubby, mockable girl any more. I could be enigmatic, sophisticated, restrained. The trouble was that I'd always been a little bit too much to compensate for my crippling shyness. Shutting up didn't make me feel sexy or mysterious – it only served to reinforce my awkwardness.

Unfortunately, Nadia and her mates didn't think I was sophisticated or shy. They assumed I was simply stuck-up. I was queuing in the canteen for coffee one day and I heard Grace, Nadia's pal, say something about 'all of these awful stuck-up southern bitches in my class' (Grace was from Leeds) and I heard Nadia, in a voice that was pure Chelsea embankment via the River Mersey, say, 'I'm Violet, and I don't talk to other humans, they are too common for me! I only speak to my horse!'

I turned around. She looked me in the eyes, and her mouth fell open in slow motion. I burst out laughing. I couldn't stop, I was doubled over. I spilled my coffee while I was paying for it.

I walked over to their table, and introduced myself, trying to use the voice Nadia had invented for me.

'I'm Violet, and I can't ride because I have been scared of horses ever since one bit me on the ear on a school trip!'

Gratifyingly, Grace cackled, and Nadia, beautiful, perfect, six foot tall supermodel Nadia, laughed so hard that she hooted like an owl.

She bought me another coffee. I bought a bottle of wine. And that was that.

We were more or less inseparable. By the end of the first term, we'd pretty much moved into each other's rooms. We shared everything. Sometimes we'd even go to each other's lectures. She was very fond of a tutor of mine who sometimes started a session with the sentence, 'Picasso was a twat.'

Nadia dressed unapologetically, and for attention. She loved showing her body off – partly because she was often on a weird diet and she wanted to display the results. She'd eat only apples for a week in order to fit into the prized sample-size Herve Leger frock she'd found in the Barnardo's in Alderley Edge. Or she'd start a 'cleanse'. We'd share an extra large Domino's and she'd spend the next three days consuming nothing but lemon juice in hot water. I told Nadia almost everything, but I couldn't share the details of

149

my own cleansing methods – puking the Domino's straight back up again, sometimes first thing in the morning if I'd eaten the leftover slices for breakfast. Her method seemed much more sophisticated. I'd seen it in magazines.

It also seemed much more effective. Nadia was so slim, but no amount of bingeing, purging and starving seemed to make my hips any smaller. I had grown up believing that a female body was a problem to be solved. I had to emphasise its most narrow points and conceal the widest ones. Gaping black holes would open in the earth's crust and consume me, by way of punishment, if I picked up a crop top on a hanger in H&M. A horizontal stripe would lead to the declaration of a national state of emergency. I envied Nadia's wardrobe. The most conservative item in it was a shrunken leopard print cardigan, cut to stop just below her nipples. She'd wear it with nothing underneath – in fact, she was wearing it when she admonished me for my lack of sartorial flair.

'Vi, you know I'd kill for your curves. Why do you hide away in your clothes? You always dress as though you're about to be interviewed for the *Daily Mail*. Where do you even buy these cashmere cardigans?'

'Primark, as you well know. They're not actual cashmere.'

'Well, this ends here. We're going shopping.'

So at the start of every term, when our loans came in, we'd go out and blow the borrowed money on dressing-up clothes. Nadia was a gifted vintage shopper and had a deep fondness for anything beaded and backless. She made me give my V-neck collared jumpers to the nearest charity shop ('and I'm genuinely conflicted about this, because if you give them away, some other poor sod is going to end up wearing these aberrations').

Nadia was the first naked woman that I ever saw in real life. Her mum had been a model in the eighties – her dad was a very sweet, round, shipping millionaire who had gone bust in the nineties – and Nadia claimed this was why she spent as much time nude as dressed.

'Mum reckons that for 90 per cent of her working life, she wore nothing but heels and hairspray. When I was a kid, she'd make me try on clothes in the middle of the shop if there was a queue for the changing room – I just got used to it.'

The first time I met Kim, Nadia's mum, she was in her knickers, smoking at the kitchen table. She got up to give me a hug without even mentioning the fact that her nipples were up against my pyjamas. That's when I understood Nadia. The only way we could have been brought up any differently from each other was if one of us had lived underground in the woods as the human child of a pair of badgers. But meeting Nadia always seemed like a *coup de foudre*. We both had boyfriends but for a long time, she was the real love of my life.

Even though I don't think Nadia ever really liked Mark, she's the one I feel the guiltiest about – the one that I feel I let down the worst. More than my parents. More than Mark. Nadia has always seemed so sure of her actions and opinions. That's why it stung so badly when she called me a coward – and when she told me I was 'throwing away' my future. I didn't know how cold the world could feel until I realised she wasn't in my corner any more. I tried to tell her that I wasn't just weak, I was disintegrating, and everything that lay before me seemed as treacherous as quicksand, sucking me under.

I wonder what Nadia would tell me to do. I'm not even sure that I need advice right now. Just some perspective on what this is, on why I'm here. I'd want Nadia to tell me that this is weird and thrilling. If she said I should stop, I don't think I'd want to listen.

Because the Phlegm Express brought me back to London shortly after dawn, I'm in the office before 9 a.m. for the first time in a year. Bizarrely, Connie is already at her desk, pointy of shoe and demeanour, and extremely agitated about something. She's bristling with prickly energy, a tweed Venus flytrap on the brink of Hulking out of her skirt suit. Oh, God. My heart sinks. I was relying on having at least half an hour to myself and a restorative nap, or at least a relaxing period of dicking about on the internet.

'Morning, Connie? Would you like a cup of coffee?' I trill, wincing at the sound of my own voice.

'Violet, goodness me, you're early. How unusual. I'm actually glad you're here, it's time we had a bit of a chat.'

I'm about to get fired, aren't I? Shall I just run away? I'm panicking so hard and so sweatily that I can feel my clothes gluing themselves to my skin.

'Of course!' I beam, as Connie motions for me to sit down.

'We all think you've been dropping the ball lately,' she says, pursing her lips.

'Pardon me?' I blink and widen my eyes, feigning innocence. Even I realise that I just look mentally disturbed.

'There have been long lunches, unexplained absences, lateness ...'

This, from a woman who comes in once every three weeks! As I feel the heat rising to my cheeks, I take a deep breath. Mustn't get angry, it won't look good. Anyway, I *definitely* explained most of my absences, what was my lie again?

'I was at ... the dentist? I've been having some root canal work, it's been awful, actually. Really painful. He found this infection, and ...'

Mercifully Connie cuts in and stops me from embellishing my made-up story. Frowning meaningfully at the crumbs on my desk, then at my thighs, she says, 'You really do eat *far too much* sugar for someone who is having problems with her teeth. Anyway, this isn't a formal warning yet, but you can't just go sloping off whenever you feel like it. If your dental ... *issues* are so serious and time consuming, you need to look at arranging appointments outside office hours.'

Nodding mutely, I try to arrange my face into an expression of contrition. Still, I'm *fuming*. It might be true, but coming from Connie, this seems seriously unfair. She continues.

'Look, we all did our best to be very understanding about the business with whatsit ... Matthew? Luke? *Mark,* that was the fellow. Heaven knows, if I'd suffered the indignity of a broken engagement I'd probably be far too ashamed to leave the house. It happened to my sister, actually, but it was because *she* was having an affair with a vicar. God, it was awful, we couldn't go to Glyndebourne that year. Anyway, everyone here made a *lot* of allowances for you.'

Have they? I think back to the recent past. A couple of days in bed with fake flu, then turning up at work with a grey face, with everyone trying to avoid meeting my eyes. The grace period lasted almost a week. If I'd actually married Mark and divorced him, perhaps it would have stretched to a fortnight.

Connie has more to say.

'I know you Millennials expect your personal lives to take precedence, it's all mental health and duvet days. But this is a place of work and it's your job to do . . . ' She pauses for a second, while she tries to remember what I'm actually supposed to do. 'It's your job to do your job. You've had enough time to deal with your problems. We've all done our bit for you, and frankly you're looking rather ungrateful. Anyway, your teeth look *fine* to me.'

Where do I begin? Punching Connie in the face is my preferred option. It's also tempting to simply vomit out the truth. I'm desperate to confide in *someone,* and although my manager is the last person on earth that I want to share this with, she's also one of the last people who is still speaking to me. Alternatively, I could look her in the eye and tell her that I'm being courted for a thrilling new job with some of the hottest names in the art world, and she'll have to find some other chump to take her messages about antique armoires and mother of pearl inlay. Still, I fear the jinx. Flouncing never pays, and I know how to speak Connie. Taking a breath and trying to steady the tremor in my voice, I apologise.

'I'm sorry about the dentist, it won't happen again. Really, I appreciate everything you've done for me, and I don't want to let you down. That's why I came in early today,' because another little lie can't hurt, 'I wanted to catch up and really focus on the, erm, the database.'

Connie sniffs, but I can tell she's bought it.

'Well, as long as you appreciate how lenient we've all

been, and as you say, it won't happen again, will it?' She chuckles to herself, a sound that always makes me picture someone being startled by an air horn and dropping a mug. 'To be honest, if I didn't know better, I'd think that you were having a thrilling affair or that you were after a new job! But,' she gestures at me dismissively, 'I couldn't think which was less likely! Now, I'll have that coffee, but then I've got to go for a breakfast meeting with my upholsterer. I'll need you to stay by my phone, I'm waiting to hear from the man who's repointing my alcove.'

Making Connie's coffee, I resolve to get a little bit better at compartmentalising. While she is *the worst*, I need to be careful about how I conduct myself. Hopefully I'll be out of here very soon, but I simply can't get ahead of myself. I feel like I'm gambling, and I'm scared that if I throw everything into the idea of this new job and new life, I might end up with no jobs at all. I have become emotionally incontinent, and what I *really* need is a condom for my heart. All day long, I make myself promises. I am going to focus when I'm in the office and stop getting distracted, simply for the sake of my sanity. My resolve lasts until 5.38 p.m., when my phone lights up. Hoping for Simon, my heart sinks when I see Lottie's name. Oh, help. Does she know? She must know. It's over, I can't catch my breath, I'm falling, falling, falling.

Max and Mimi are hosting a week on Fri. You in? X

No. Yes! Absolutely not. Maybe? Is it me, or is she being more abrupt than usual? But then surely, she wouldn't still invite me if she knew? I stare dumbly at the screen for nearly half an hour before typing *Sure x*.

Chapter Thirteen

I have been counting down the days to Max and Mimi's party, and time is passing very slowly. Since sending the message, Lottie has been silent, which is unnerving. Is she punishing me, or is she just busy? I've been rereading every single scrap of communication I've had with her, memorising them, searching for patterns and clues. She hasn't been using Instagram – or rather, she hasn't been *posting* on it, which isn't necessarily proof that she isn't looking. Every day, I type out a text suggesting a coffee, an 'Intuition catch-up', and every day I delete the words before I can press send. The quietness feels like a form of torture. Why can't I just ask about what's going on? Is it because I'm too scared to hear the answer?

I haven't heard from Simon, either, which doesn't upset me as much as it should. Is it a sign of his bad manners, or a sign that we're busted? When I close my eyes and try to remember exactly what happened in the hotel room, I almost draw a blank – I can see it all, but I can't remember how I felt. It's the memory of the way he said my name that makes me shudder and tingle. To Connie's shock, the only way to get through all this has been for me to actually do some work. She's even been making references to me 'holding down the fort' while she disappears to source vintage bedpans in Twickenham.

Still, I don't think I can pass up the invitation. I need this release. Also, I am very keen to see where Max and Mimi live.

Deciding that I deserve a treat, I have booked a day off work, and I've spent more money I don't have on a dress on the internet. It's dark green and diaphanous, sleeved, flouncy chiffon over a tight satin slip. In the slip alone, I look like a schoolboy's drawing, or a blow-up doll – it barely covers my nipples and buttocks. I've been fantasising about wearing it while straddling Simon, as Lottie pulls at the straps and grabs at my tits. But the cover makes me respectable and should allow me to wear it to smart dinners, in the unlikely event that I'll ever be invited to any. Most importantly, I should be able to travel across London unhampered, without anyone on the Northern line giving me an unsolicited review of my breasts if I dare to unbutton my coat. I worry about my choice of underwear, and eventually decided not to bother with any, just hold up stockings.

Max and Mimi live in Shad Thames. There's a chance that they're in a bleak ex-council place, like mine – albeit knocked through and fabulised within. However, based on Lottie's description and directions, I'm thinking and hoping that they live in one of those glassy, glittering riverside flats. I'm so excited that I've turned up early, knickerless and eager, and had my hair blow-dried into soft, glossy waves.

Well, I asked the lady to make me look 'sort of sexy and elegantly dishevelled', which was a euphemism for 'please do my hair so I look as though I'm in the middle of wild movie star coitus.' What she has done, I now realise, is spray me and tong me until I look a bit like the Duchess of Cambridge about to visit a hospital. As I watch the other women in the other chairs, I realise that nearly everyone here has been given Duchess of Cambridge hair. Still, it could be worse. One client appears to be blinking back tears from under a 1985 Fergie fringe.

The salon is ten minutes away from Max and Mimi's. I set off, wearing my coat unbuttoned and over my head, in a pointless attempt to protect my Duchess hair from the mizzle. This door doesn't look right, it must be an office. I see smoked grey glass, an empty reception desk, a cheap looking red sofa. I follow Lottie's complicated keypad instructions – hashtag first, star last – and open the door. I take the lift to the top floor, the eighteenth. Taking a deep breath, I knock on the only door I can find, wooden, with a gleaming golden '18' on it.

Mimi answers, her body wrapped in a pristine white towel, her hair wrapped in a slightly grubby-looking blue one. She hugs me tightly and unselfconsciously. She feels damp and smells of, I think, Jo Malone Orange Blossom.

'Violet! You look UH-MAZE-ING! Did you get your hair cut? Sorry, sorry, I'm running late, utterly, bloody Max should be on door duty but he's pissing about with his – MAX! COME THE FUCK ON!'

Max appears, and he's – I blink and check that I'm not hallucinating this and dressing him with the Photoshop of the mind – he's actually wearing a dark blue velvet smoking jacket. No pipe, though, that was my invention. He's beaming.

'I just found my Thelonious Monk! It's a record I bought back in, it must have been '89, from that little shop just off Denmark Street. Violet, hello! You look sensational!'

I grin. Suddenly I feel like The Girl In The Sexy Dress, not The Girl Who Smells Of Desperation And Elnett. Their welcome is as potent as a large glass of wine, and I feel confidence and ease spiralling up from my stomach and blooming throughout my body. Like a plant shoot, I've just broken through the ground and they are radiating warmth and sunlight. Max takes my coat and looks me up and down.

'Are you still allowed to wear dresses like that in Zone One? It must be Sodom and Gomorrah out there! Did you leave a trail of braying, priapic men in your wake?'

'Something like that. I was given a police caution and told that if they caught me again I'd get a fifty pound fine for every coat button I'd left undone.'

It's easy to be quick and sassy with Max, maybe because I fancy him the least.

Mimi excuses herself to get dressed, and Max leads me in. Everything is wooden and well lit. I find myself in an enormous room, a plate glass window delivering a floor to ceiling cityscape. London glitters and gleams like an open chocolate box. It's as if Harry Winston has emptied his entire jewellery box and scattered it over green baize. I squint and look for landmarks, but I can see lights, trees, cars. Everything is moving. Everything is too much. Gosh, is that my flat?

'Is that, er, Brockwell Park?' I ask Max, searching for a pin to put in the map.

He laughs.

'What, near Ally Pally?'

'Sorry, my sense of direction is awful.'

Max is gentle.

'Being up here for the first time is pretty disorientating. When I moved here, it must be fifteen years ago now, I was horrified to realise how little I knew London. I had to teach myself where everything was. I'd been living in one of those mad Dubai skyscrapers, and it's the desert. Nothing but shopping malls and the ocean. London is harder, but it's more interesting.'

'In geography terms, or generally?'

'Both. It was a very good place to be to make money. It was chock-full of billionaires and their favourite kind of art was expensive art. They couldn't tell you what they loved about a particular picture, but they'd fall over themselves to tell you what they were prepared to pay for it.'

'That sounds miserable.' And it makes me angry. I can barely afford to buy decent prints and posters – imagine selling beautiful things to people who just want to look at the walls and see their money looking back at them.

He looks at me indulgently.

'It could be, but it's also addictive. At first, my plan was to stick it out for a year or two, make a pile and come home. But it was a bit like being a hitman, or a drug dealer. There's always one more big score. I'd spend six months desperately courting someone, getting them what they needed, and think, This is awful, I'm leaving as soon as I'm done. Then a brand new billionaire comes to town, and everyone is fighting to be their art guy, and you think, It would be mad not to pursue this, he could be worth millions, one more go, and I'll walk away.'

It feels a bit like being on a film set, the view, the flat the size of the ground floor of a provincial department store, Max saying million and billion as zeros and lines fill my head as rapidly as a computer running binary code.

Max opens a bottle of champagne and pours me a glass, without asking me what I'd like to drink.

'Money makes people monstrous. To be honest, I see it a bit in everyone I know, that air of calculation, that entitlement, that assumption that the world has to run their way. You're refreshing. It's so nice to be around someone with more questions than answers, someone who isn't dead behind the eyes.'

Oh, fuck *off*, Max. Poor, sweet little Violet, with her scuffed ballet pumps and her overdraft, come to teach Max and his rich pals the true meaning of Christmas. I take a sip and make a face.

'When money is your greatest source of anxiety, it would be a pleasure to go dead behind the eyes. Honestly, I'd happily go blind if that was a required condition for becoming a millionaire.' My brain catches up with my mouth, and I remember that no matter how condescending he is, I'm a guest in his home. I can fix this by making a joke. 'It would be a weird rule, though.'

Max is pissing me off but I do like his laugh. He puckers his lips and stares at his nose, as if he's trying to trap the sound, and then it bursts out, staccato, a spoken syllabic HA HA HA.

Mimi joins us, still smelling fresh and slightly damp from the shower. She's wearing a pale pink velvet wrap dress, it's a shade that's often described as 'flesh-toned' – and seeing it on Mimi really brings home how misleading that label is, with her own skin rich and gleaming against the pallid, slightly sickly pink. The dress is very fashionable but doesn't quite suit her – her considerable beauty seems to spite it, instead of being accentuated by it. Also, she's wearing high heeled, dark purple satin jewelled mules, in her own house. She reads my expression.

'Is it OK, do you think? It's new, I love the idea of velvet, but ... '

I hear so much unspoken pain in that unfinished sentence. Mimi's beauty and status does not protect her from the hell of womanhood – constantly searching for clues and costumes that will allow us to work out exactly who we should be.

I smile brightly and lie.

'That pink is heaven on you, it's such a pretty shade. I was just thinking about mules, I've never successfully worn any. How do you keep them on your feet?'

Max interrupts.

'Mimi has a collection of what she calls house shoes. Bought to be worn within 2000 square foot of her wardrobe, but unsuitable for pavements. Mimi's shoes are the ultimate symbol of the problem of wealth and decadence.'

Mimi rolls her eyes.

'And owning several thousand records, and playing maybe fifty of them is sheer asceticism, is it?' but she says it warmly and fondly, and she squeezes Max's waist.

I hear a soft noise, then a sharp thump, and the three of us walk to the hall and open the door, where I see Simon and Richard, with Sasha and Lottie standing behind them. Something seems strained and strange. Almost certainly Sasha. She's the one who speaks first.

162

'Thank *God* we're here. I need saving from Lottie's "Common Market For Dummies" nonsense.'

Lottie, seeming unusually serious in a lustrous long black cashmere coat, bristles.

'You're *deliberately* misunderstanding me, I just wanted to make a point about how globally, we need to . . . '

Simon cuts her off with a harsh 'Shhhhh'.

In my head, I compose mean things to say to Sasha. Like, 'It's no wonder that you know all about the common market, that must be where you got those horribly common earrings', even though her earrings look both rare and expensive, Calder-esque suspensions of hammered silver. Or just, 'You're the dummy'.

Mimi is immediately emollient.

'Everyone shut up and come in. I am heating up some tiny M&S beef-filled Yorkshire puddings *as we speak,* and no one is allowed any if they're going to fight. Although, Lottie, you're looking tiny! Is it the Dukan, still? You look so good! Let me sabotage your efforts with delicious, fattening canapés.'

Slightly subdued, everyone troops into the hall. I see Richard touching Sasha's elbow, murmuring something into her ear, before she whips her head away, angrily shrugging him off. I've struggled to make sense of them as a couple, but I still don't like seeing them at odds, prickly and tense.

I walk towards Simon who gives me a perfunctory squeeze, and a 'Hello, you!'

It's *horrible.* I'd been looking forward to seeing him, thinking that there might be a bit of extra intimacy between us, that he'd give me that special look and I could bask in the Readybrek glow of his attention. Now, I'm wondering whether he's forgotten my name.

Lottie is worse, deflecting my hug with her elbows, and not meeting my eye as she says 'Ah, Violet, you came.'

Shit. Perhaps she knows. I hate myself, I absolutely loathe myself. I've betrayed Lottie and her love bombing has turned toxic. Winter is coming, and it's nuclear.

We stand in the centre of the room, making an awkward circle. Max does the drinks – more champagne for the girls, Scotch for the boys – and I wonder whether I should furiously call him out and demand whisky too. I was so looking forward to this, and everyone seems a little too grumpy for it, ruffled and combative. Also, no one is eating the mini Yorkshires, or the prawn dim sum, or the foie gras profiteroles. They're all talking about how someone or other's friend is 'trying to get in with the big boys in Westminster' and I don't know how to join in. I'm so bored and grumpy and hungry that I'm considering walking off with a plateful of canapés and eating them on the toilet.

After twenty minutes of hell, I decide that no one cares whether I'm there or not, so I wander off for another look at the view, and the flat. I'm surprised by the lack of art on the walls. There's a fairly awful blown-up black and white photograph of a young woman lying in a lake, surrounded by bare trees. There's a dull green leaf print collage. There's a *hideous* print of a woman that has been cropped, so you can't see her head, she's mostly torso. There is an empty martini glass positioned between her legs. It looks like a GCSE art project produced by a fourteen-year-old James Bond fanboy, the faint misogyny that characterises the kind of man who hasn't touched a woman who isn't a family member. As I look, and wrinkle my nose, I'm aware of Max's heavy footsteps behind me.

'That's Tatiana Van Wyck, she's a Brooklyn portrait artist, her profile is exploding right now. I bought that last year for three million and it's already worth four point five.'

I turn my face to look up into his, and reply, flatly and obnoxiously.

'I hate it. I don't think it has any creative merit whatso-ever.' *And I hate your stupid flat and your stupid friends, and I want to go home.*

Max puts an arm around my waist, resting a huge hand on my buttock. It feels warm and solid, somehow calming. I take a deep breath and try again.

'It seems a bit reductive. I hate not being able to see her face. I hate that she's being stripped and made consumable, that it's all about the model's body, not her character.'

Max moves his hand to the edge of my buttock, the top of my thigh.

'I think Tatiana would be delighted by your response. The woman in the picture is a cocktail waitress, she was born in Venezuela. This is part of a series about the different ways in which migrant workers are exploited – either through trafficking and forced labour, or in a broader sense. This woman is legally employed, but she goes through all kinds of dehumanising experiences at work, from customers and from her boss, whether it's harassment, racism or worse.'

Now I feel stupid as well as bored. I'm cross with Max, still spoiling for a fight.

'So, the artist has excellent intentions, but why do you need this on the wall of your house?'

Deftly, Max has removed his hand and put it back, only now he's on my naked flesh, inside my dress.

'Surely you of all people know that I can't resist a beautiful woman.'

It's a terrible line. He's a terrible man. He's a middle-aged millionaire touching up a woman half his age, while proudly mansplaining the exposed, exploited nipples on his wall. Yet I can't protest because he is using his thumb to trace and retrace a line of skin that joins my arse to my thigh, almost, *almost* to the point where my pussy starts, and for the first time that night, I am back in my body. I cannot move my feet, because I'm paralysed by rage and lust and convinced that if I shift position, everything will collapse from under me.

Max starts to rub his closed mouth against my neck, my shoulder, the patch of skin behind my left ear. He murmurs, 'I don't know *what's* got into you tonight, but I'm going to fuck it out of you.'

His hand travels between my arse cheeks, and he slowly, forcefully, sinks a finger inside me. He stares at me until I meet his gaze. Then, even more slowly, he removes his finger, delivers a single, stinging slap to my right arse cheek, and walks away, cheerily asking, 'Who wants another drink?'

Lottie looks in my direction, and it might be my imagination, but she seems to sneer. I don't care any more.

Dazedly, I drain my champagne glass, and stumble back into the hall, searching for the bathroom. It seems startlingly white and bright, and there's too much evidence of normal, human things. A gob of toothpaste stuck to the basin, a bright blue box of Tampax visible through a crack in the open cabinet. I lock the door, close the top of the toilet seat and sit down, breathing through my mouth, until my heart rate slows. This is an adventure. I am not out of my depth. I can do this.

I walk back into the room, feeling much calmer. Mimi beckons me over and hands me a fresh glass of champagne.

'Max says you've been slagging off his artistic choices! Honestly, I don't like that print either. We had such a fight about it when he got it home!'

Richard joins her.

'Sorry, Violet, we've all been very boring tonight. An old college buddy is attempting to break into the Cabinet and we're being mean about it.'

Sasha overhears and smiles icily.

'Not mean, just ... realistic.'

Richard laughs.

'Yeah, Sasha has a point. Are we eating soon?'

Mimi gestures to the other end of the room, at a glass topped table, and tells everyone to sit down. The arrangement seems very stark. Shiny cutlery, white lilies, piled up napkins. I ask Mimi if she needs any help in the kitchen, and she smiles gratefully.

'Yes please. Honestly, I haven't cooked anything at all, just heated it through, but it would be great to have a hand getting it out.'

The kitchen is small and windowless, only slightly bigger than the bathroom, the worktop covered in cardboard sleeves which bear words like 'gastro' and 'finest'. Mimi sees me looking and says, 'I used to do proper dinner party stuff, but it seems like such a waste when most of it goes uneaten. Max and I always say that one day we'll be brave and not bother with dinner at all, but then I panic and end up going to Waitrose on my way home.'

I gesture to the kitchen doorway.

'This flat ... somehow, I just imagined you living somewhere different, a bit less minimalist. How did you and Max agree on decor?'

'Oh, darling, this is all Max, it's not me at all. We don't live together, we'd kill each other!'

I turn red. I've got it wrong, again.

'I'm so sorry, I didn't mean to assume ...'

'Don't worry at all, it's a sensible assumption to make! We opened the door together! I have a flat in West London, and Max's away a lot. We keep talking about me moving in here, but I don't want to. I *love* my little place in Westbourne Park, and Max is always on at me to sell it or at least rent it out, but it's cosy and it's mine and I don't know what I'd do with all of my furniture.' Mimi touches my elbow and leans closer. 'This is silly, I know, but I have a very scruffy sofa. It's a sort of green tweed, and I bought it for £250 in 1998. At the time, £250 was the most money I'd ever spent on *anything* and I had to live on luncheon vouchers for two months. Christ, you're probably too young to know what those are.

'Anyway, I'm too sentimental, Max isn't sentimental enough. I'm sitting on a goldmine, but I don't want to live in this big glass mausoleum.' Her voice cracks slightly and she shudders. 'Sorry, bit of a rant. Too much wine already.' She takes my hands in hers and looks straight into my eyes for a little longer than feels comfortable. 'Goodness, Simon's instincts are improving. You're such a good listener. You seem so much more intuitive than the other g—than anyone else I've met lately.'

Puzzled, I pick up a tray of something with cream and potatoes in it. Of course, there have been other girls. Of course, they have all done this before. Why does it bother me? And why does it make me sad that lovely Mimi is so breezy and bright about making a life with lechy Max, with his bad, expensive art? Max cannot conduct a conversation with me without putting his hand up my skirt, yet he's against old, beloved sofas on the grounds of aesthetic propriety. How dare he make the rules?

I'm certain that Lottie knows about the trip to Bristol. I can't bring myself to speak to her. She seems off with everyone. Her cool, cruel mood is so physically palpable it's as if it's an extra guest. It hits me that I really should have explained, or rather, apologised before now. Will she believe that I didn't realise it wasn't OK, until it was too late? Wincing, I silently acknowledge that this is a lie. I definitely knew.

As I'm trying to muster the courage to approach her, I come to and I realise that I'm standing at the centre of a room holding a plastic bowl filled with gourmet meatballs. Everyone is staring at me. I take it to the table and sit down. The only available chair is between Lottie and Sasha. I'm in the middle, and in the way. Sasha sighs audibly when I take my seat. Panic stricken, I smile at her.

'Great,' she says, rolling her eyes, 'It's the Millennial. I'm in for some scintillating conversation. Did you have your avocado on toast today? Have a nice time with your friends on TikTok?'

Oh God, I'm going to cry. I down the white wine that has been placed in front of me, and laugh manically, while blinking at the ceiling, betrayed by my prickly eyes.

To my shock, Lottie gets to her feet and bangs a fist on the table.

'For fuck's sake, Sasha!'

Everyone's eyes travel to the spot she pounded. I'm expecting to see the glass start to splinter.

'Violet is our friend, and everyone else is managing to make her feel welcome, why do you need to be so rude to her?'

Sasha rolls her eyes.

'God, I keep telling you that you're overreacting, I'm only joking.'

Lottie is really shouting now, her skin is flushed, her eyes are flashing, the pale grey mohair dress that she's wearing is rising higher and higher up her thighs as she gesticulates.

'You're fucking not, you're being poisonous. You know when you're being rude, you *know* how to make people feel comfortable, why are you being such a bloody *child*? You're a thirty-nine-year-old woman!'

It's excruciating, but exhilarating. Someone here is on my team! Does this mean I'm forgiven, or that Lottie hasn't found out?

Sasha gasps and reels, as if reacting to an invisible punch. She opens her mouth as though she has plenty to say in reply, but nothing comes out. Everyone who can do so without turning their head stares out of the window. Everyone else looks at their feet.

Mimi catches my eye, and I try to work out what she's thinking. If Sasha's age was supposed to be a secret, it doesn't seem to be a terribly well kept one. I can't quite believe that Lottie is standing up for me, but I'm overcome with gratitude – enough to bring me to my feet. 'Sasha, I know you have a problem with me, and I don't know why, but I wish we could work it out. We both know that you're not joking when you make these little digs, and it doesn't just make me uncomfortable, it's hard for everyone. You don't have to be friends with me, but you can be civil.'

Oh God, oh God, oh God. I can feel the adrenaline surging, and my chest is tight. But I didn't cry. I sit down again and force a grin.

'Besides, I don't know what you're talking about. I haven't eaten avocado toast since 2014. We Millennials barely eat at all now, we just snort lines of chia powder from artisanal marble plinths. Then we make YouTube videos of the inevitable hospital visits when we get pumpkin seeds up our nose.'

Mimi, Richard and Simon all laugh a little too loudly and brightly.

Sasha rejoins, 'I didn't realise that you snowflakes did so well at room temperature,' but she's smiling as she says it, and I think this is going to be OK.

Tentatively, I touch her knee.

'We've got a surprisingly high melting point. How do you think we survive Tinder?'

Max grins.

'Ah, yes, I was hoping you might tell us about some more erotic encounters!'

Simon glances at me warningly.

'Well, I've been busy at work, all spreadsheets and no spread legs, I'm afraid,' I reply, grumpy with myself for the terrible pun. But people giggle, and Mimi talks about a documentary she's just seen about eighties pop, and Lottie mentions bumping into her cleaner in Waitrose and not being able to place her, hugging her and kissing her before she fully processed who she was, and wondering whether she's set a weird precedent, and suddenly it's just like a normal, blissfully boring dinner party, albeit with a size-able food budget, and Barolo instead of Blossom Hill. It's so relaxed that instead of making pudding, Mimi has brought out three different tubs of Häagen-Dazs and dumped them on the table.

What's *weird* is that Sasha has become significantly more tactile, almost warm. She touches my arm to make points, she keeps her hand on my knee, she strokes my thigh. I'm torn between recoiling in fright and genuinely enjoying her attention.

She watches me savour a spoon of salted caramel ice cream and nudges me.

'Lottie said you were a greedy girl.'

'What?'

'You heard me. What you were just doing with your tongue . . . you can do that to me.'

I falter. I had briefly forgotten exactly where I was, what might be expected of me. I'd been delighted by the momen-tary truce with Sasha, but *really*? I bet her pubes are sprayed with Domestos. I bet she will shout at me if I fail to bring her to orgasm in thirty seconds or make some joke about how I shouldn't be licking her pussy because she'd heard all twenty-somethings were vegan. I down my white wine as she stands up, and motions for me to follow her to the other end of the room.

What to do? Excuse myself for the loo, then run out into the night and look for a bus stop? Tell her I'm too full? I've heard many people make whiny jokes about the trouble

172

with extreme Englishness – apologising to shop manne-
quins and lampposts, thanking a waiter for the delicious
soup when there's half a rat torso in a bowl. I don't know of
any other instances where someone has been so awkwardly
English that they had forced cunnilingus with a grumpy
semi-regular *Newsnight* guest instead of staying at the table
for a decaf coffee and a Lindor truffle.

I decide that our *entente* is too delicate for me to risk a
refusal, and I assume that the rules of the orgy don't permit
one. Sasha seems frighteningly forthright and robust – to be
honest, I'd been sure that she had no sexual interest in me
before tonight and would have laughed scornfully if I'd have
tried to broach the subject. But I've seen a chink of light, a
weak spot, some tenderness and vulnerability which makes
her more appealing. Even though she's moved her hand
away, I can still feel the heat from her touch on my knee.

Sasha leads me to a black leather sofa. It looks soft,
weathered and expensive, but it's a horrible thing, and I
feel an additional stab of furious defensiveness for Mimi,
and her lovely green tweed. However, it has a frisson, it
evokes an erotic memory, and I realise it's just a posher
version of the pleather porn sofas I'm so familiar with. To
my surprise, Sasha sits beside me and starts kissing me.
Her lips are shockingly soft, and she's slightly coy, opening
her mouth on mine very slowly, using the tip of her tongue
to tease my lips, without going all the way in. She moans
quietly, a gentle, high sound that I would not have thought
her capable of making, and strokes a spot on the back of
my neck. I want to kiss her harder, deeper, but she's pulling
me back, stopping me from going any further. I groan with
frustration. Eight minutes ago I was desperate to escape

her clutches, now I'm desperate to *have her*. My hips realise this before my brain does; I'm shocked to realise that I'm squirming against her.

She's gripping my skull with her hands, murmuring, unexpectedly, 'You have such soft hair.'

I almost stop and tell her about the blow-dry, but she's shimmying backwards on the sofa, pulling me with her so that my head falls into her lap. I struggle with the tight skirt of her dress, it's thick and unyielding. I don't want to tear it. Ineffectually, I try to roll it up but it keeps unravelling and rolling back.

'Give it here!' she sighs, yanking it up, ignoring my wince when I hear a rip.

At first, I wonder whether Sasha just got a spray tan, and is still wearing her paper knickers. Her underwear is black, a pair of panels connected by strings, and appears to be made of that weird fabric used for those tiny, pointless microfibre towels that people take on their gap years. I can't find any tell-tale lines. Sasha's already so pale that if this is what her skin looks like with a tan, there would be a Farrow and Ball paint named after her. She has the neatest, darkest triangle of pubic hair, tight, careful coils of glossy snakes. She could be a steampunk heroine – I imagine the pubes suddenly sprouting up to surround me, like a forest, with roots and leaves leaving me pinned and pinioned.

I push back the weird pants further, and lick Sasha's lower lips. Surprisingly, she tastes sweet, slightly acrid, something that reminds me of bonfires, toffee, smoke. Sasha has a pumpkin spice pussy! I try not to giggle and start searching for her clit with my right hand. I'm struggling, until she reaches for me and positions me in the right place. It seems to swell beneath my fingers, pulsating slightly. Sasha emits a long, low, sexy moan – and follows it with a low grunt. I try to come up for air for a second and she pushes the back of my neck. I gurgle and she shouts, 'Violet, NOW!'

I feel as though I've been told off until I realise that Sasha is panting and gasping, I can feel her twitch against my cheeks.

I lean forward to kiss her face, but she's kneeling up and pushing me backwards, gripping my hands at the wrist to force my back to the sofa. I'm expecting her to start going down on me, but she says, 'You're going to make yourself come for me.'

Instinctively, I start to touch myself, but she shakes her head and tells me to wrap both of my legs around one of hers and rub myself against her. The skin of her leg feels smooth and cool. Using my thigh muscles to grip and squeeze, I'm aware of a swelling sensation building right inside me, between my legs, within my body, but like a wave that's about to break out of me and break me in two. I shut my eyes and squeeze and squeeze. Somewhere, I register that I must look like a dog humping a chair leg, but I don't care, I don't care at all, I keep squeezing until everything bursts and then I open my eyes, dazed, and realise my slip has concertinaed itself into a strip of silky fabric that rests slightly above my belly button, and that everyone is standing in a circle and looking at me while I'm naked, on the floor. It's like a strange replay of the start of the party, only I'm the centre of attention, post orgasmic and panting.

Max lifts me up with his left hand, while burrowing his right inside my body. He lifts me so high and enters me so deeply that it feels slightly uncomfortable, like a gynaeco-logical exam. As I squeeze my muscles around his hand, he lets go of my legs and drops me to the floor. Now Lottie is in Sasha's old place, sitting directly in front of me on the sofa, her legs wide apart, grey dress pulled up to reveal her bare body underneath. I crawl towards her and she reaches for me, pulling my face between her thighs. As I start to stroke her sticky skin, I realise that my legs are in the air again, and someone – judging by the sounds I can hear and the heft of the hands around my ankles, I think Max – has started to fuck me.

I'm back on the forest floor. I feel like an animal fail-ing to escape capture, and I'm horrified by the pleasure brought about by the sensation of having a predator tear into my flesh. The size and force of Max's penis is such that it's making me question my own anatomy, he's touching a part of my body that I can't reach, something I didn't know was there. I am so shocked by my own helplessness, so complicit in my own surrender, that all I can do is come, come, come.

I can't concentrate on what I'm doing to Lottie, I just moan into her. She moans in an echo. She pulls at my head as if she's trying to make me enter her as deeply as Max enters me. I'm struggling to breathe, and I don't care – I don't notice until Lottie shudders and rolls backwards, and I exhale at last. Opening my eyes, I see that Mimi is on all fours, Sasha's mouth working underneath her, her mouth on Richard, Simon in Sasha. Max spanks me again as I stare at them, and I feel my pussy contract, expand and explode.

I feel a sudden, forceful jet of wetness, and for a second, I think Max is *pissing* on me, until I realise that he's just come all over my arse and he's apologising as though he's just put his arm in a coat sleeve and accidentally knocked over my coffee. I try to say, 'Don't worry, it's fine,' but I'm struggling to form sentences, so it's 'Unurrr-huh!'

I can't get up. It's as if I've used up every single sensation that my body is capable of feeling, and now my nerves are too stunned and pointless to work. This is weirdly familiar. When have I felt like this before? Oh, *I know*, it was after I tried to do a HIIT workout video on YouTube and it was so hard and horrible that I had to wait a full half hour before I could hold a glass of water. Even though it's moments since I had orgasmic thighs of steel, my muscles are barely strong enough to deliver me to a sitting position on the sofa.

Richard and Mimi are making various conclusive noises, and I assume that we're about half an hour away from taxis (or in my case, the dreaded night bus) when Simon moves away from the group, towards me and Lottie.

'Hold on, I want my girls,' he says, sitting beside Lottie, and guiding me up so I'm lying across their knees. Lottie stoops to kiss me, while squeezing my tits and my nipples, occasionally pulling away to suck. She lets her knees slide apart, and I try to reach behind my body to get to hers, but I can't quite touch her, I'm just aware of wetness and warmth. Simon has buried his head between my legs, he's nuzzling and licking with great gentleness. I can't come again, I'm too raw and sore, but he's being so attentive, so infinitely tender, that I feel as though I'm on the brink of another kind of climax. At that moment, everything seems so emotionally charged that there's a real risk of me bursting into noisy, extravagant tears, and then falling asleep. I think Simon is expecting an orgasm from me, so I build up

177

to a sort of heavy sigh, and then roll off their laps. Shakily, I get to my feet, and realise that everyone else is starting to get dressed. As I roll down my slip and shake the chiffon back over my body, I realise how strange it is that putting my clothes back on makes me feel almost normal almost instantly. Violet inviolate once more.

Lottie is rubbing her eyes with her fists. She looks soft and sleepy. Every trace of rancour has vanished from her face.

'Violet, sweetheart, why not come back with us tonight? It's so late for you to go home, the spare room is always made up.'

I find myself feeling strangely relieved. I don't want to go back out into the night alone. I keep taking too many chances, making myself too vulnerable. I've been so lonely – and so ashamed of it. These fleeting moments, when I feel truly included, are enough to make me feel as though I might be able to bear a bit more loneliness later.

I smile gratefully.

'That would be lovely.'

Mimi cuts through my fug of cosiness with a yelped 'Shit!' Everyone turns to look. She is still naked, a scrap of pale pink lace in her right hand. For a moment I worry that she's stepped on an upturned plug. 'Ibiza! We've not talked about it at all! Is everyone still on for it? Are we flying on the nineteenth? Violet, have you booked yet?'

Even though I'd been longing for Ibiza, and dreaming of it, I had wondered whether Lottie is the sort of posh person who invites everyone to everything in a cheery, insincere way. Murmuring 'Darling, you *must* come,' while assuming that the unworthy guest would interpret the code in the spirit that it was offered, an empty gesture of warmth, as meaningful as a post sneeze 'Bless you!' or a 'Merry Christmas!'

Lottie claps my hand over her mouth.

'Oh, God, Violet, I was about to book you a flight and got distracted. Remind me the moment you wake up tomorrow.'

Mimi claps her hands together.

'Yippee! You're going to love it. We've been going for years – it's Simon's mate's place, and he makes loads of money from renting it to pop stars for video shoots, and it's *huge*! We can all have our own bathrooms – which I think is the greatest treat ever, especially after August.'

Everyone laughs. Mimi responds to my puzzled look.

'Me and Max had a few days in France with Richard, his ex and his little monsters. I love those boys, but the gîte only had one bathroom and a separate loo – I don't know how a couple of toddlers could do that to a toilet, but, bloody hell. Never again.'

I'm very curious about what Richard might be like as a parent, how this world is compatible with his family life. Also, whenever anyone mentions their kids I panic and feel obliged to ask a polite question, before I can say what I'm really thinking, which is, How on earth do you cope, and how come you're not constantly crying and covered in sick?

Mercifully, what comes out of my mouth is 'What are your boys called?'

Richard has, while we've been talking, speedily dressed. He's wearing anonymous indigo jeans, and a pale grey, button-down shirt. It reframes him – he's suddenly a nice family man, impervious to his slightly seedy, distasteful

179

surroundings, the patches of bare flesh, discarded underwear, empty wine glasses. I'm glad – I don't think I could ask him about his children while his penis was visible.

'Hugo and Hector. They're twins.'

Ah, yes. Names you could shout in the central aisle of Waitrose without shame. He catches my expression.

'Jen's idea. My ex.'

I don't know how to respond without prying. Well, *obviously* I want to pry, but I know that this is a delicate area, and I have to tread carefully.

'Do you get to spend much time with them? It must be really hard to break up with someone when you're both parents too.'

Richard looks slightly more cheerful.

'To be honest, I know I'm a much better father when I'm not in a relationship with their mother. Jen and I are proper partners now. I was a dick when the boys were born, I wasn't at home enough, I wasn't with her enough – but I think that now, I'm better at doing what's expected of me.'

Sasha cuts him off.

'I know you think you're terribly modern, but we were supposed to raise families in big groups. The boys should thrive in this setting, it's biologically typical.'

'It takes a village,' I offer, without thinking.

Sasha seems to look at me with something akin to respect.

'Indeed!' she says, gracious and remote, even though she's wearing nothing but her weird towel pants.

When someone reveals something personal and intimate, I react as though they have picked up a dinner bill. I feel that I'm obliged to get the next one, even if they're not necessarily expecting it, and you're not sure that you can afford it. So I blurt out some bonus personal information of my own.

'I nearly got married, and I think I'd have a similar story if we'd gone through with it. In fact, the wedding was supposed to be happening just before we go away.'

I have everyone's attention. Mimi moves to hug me.

'Oh, you poor love.'

I assume that she's assumed that I was the jilted party, and nearly shake her off resentfully.

'It was my decision, I knew that it wasn't going to work in the long run. Mark was ... is ... great, but he was quite traditional, and I guess ...'

What do I tell her? That I was so anxious about marrying him that sometimes I'd wake up in the morning and realise I was in the middle of a panic attack? That I needed to be with someone who made me feel like an equal? That Mark had many faults but I miss being with someone who made me feel safe?

'I guess that I didn't know what I wanted. I don't know what I want.'

Lottie is the first to respond.

'That's very brave,' she says, breathily and forcefully, as if she's about to present me with a Pride Of Britain award for refusing to pledge my troth to a man who owns a wall clock which is emblazoned with the slogan 'I do believe it's Beer O'Clock!' She frowns for a second. 'Are you sure you want to come on holiday with us? Would you rather be with your family?'

I wince.

'Honestly, no, that's the last place I want to be. They

haven't really forgiven me. You know, lost deposits and things.'

Max rolls his eyes.

'How bourgeois! As if that's more important than your happiness, ultimately.'

Well, Max, why not give me one of your spare millions, restore my parents' life savings to good health and make them stop hating me again?

I force a smile and say, 'I'm suddenly so, so tired. Would it be all right if we went home?'

I thought I was claiming exhaustion because I couldn't think of anything more to say to Max, but as the words fall out of my mouth they become true. Every bone in my body was taut with tension and anxiety, but now it's drained away I don't have any energy left. If I blink again, I might fall asleep.

Coats are found, and perfunctory pecks are issued to cheeks, and, as if I'm in a dream, I find myself in the lift with Simon and Lottie without fully understanding exactly how I got there. Simon hails a black cab the moment that the door has shut behind us, because that's the sort of man Simon is. I sit between them, and sleep comes suddenly and solidly, and I have to be shaken awake by Lottie when we reach Highbury Corner.

Blearily, not quite consciously, I murmur, 'Are you still angry? I'm sorry. I'm really sorry.'

She shakes her head, saying, 'It's fine. Let's not ...' and then she and Simon start to argue – but I might have dreamed that.

Chapter Fourteen

The trouble started when Mark told my parents that he planned to propose. There was an odd month where Mum kept ringing me up, brightly and breathily enquiring whether I had any 'news'. I struggled for things to tell her. Work had finally got a Nespresso, but it had broken immediately because they would only supply cheap, generic pods to use in it. There had been an outcry because someone in the marketing team had been in Alan's office and noticed that he had his *own* Nespresso on a filing cabinet, a much bigger model than ours, and a large supply of premium pods in unlikely flavours – and Alan didn't so much as offer her a caramel macchiato. Alan had to call a meeting and tell us that he'd been given two identical machines for his birthday, one from his wife and one from his mum, so he'd brought one to work, and he needed it in his office just in case anyone from the parent company popped by for a meeting. Podgate had kept me entertained for ages, especially because the marketeer in question, Suzie, had got drunk in our local Wetherspoons one Friday and tearfully tried to persuade us to form a trade union, muttering, 'But he calls himself a *socialist*!' while gesticulating with a wine glass and pouring Jacob's Creek sauvignon down her jumper.

By her fourth Podgate update, Mum was losing patience.

'No, darling, not the silly coffee thing again, I thought you might have something ... significant to tell us.'

'Er ... I'm not ... pregnant? I don't think so!' I replied.

She paused, sighed, tutted. It wasn't even that she especially loved weddings, she was just desperate for my relationship to have a more respectable label. When I moved in with Mark she told her friends, and my extended family, that we were 'flatmates'. Mum would ring off, saying 'Just keep us posted.' That was when I stopped phoning her and started screening her calls.

The night of the proposal was memorable. Mark had given me instructions to meet him in Covent Garden in a nice dress.

'It's a surprise,' he kept saying.

I should have known. Well, I did know, but I wasn't sure how to process it, so I pretended, to myself, that it was all a great mystery. Strangely, it was easier to imagine his huge face leering at mine through the candlelight, as he said, 'Violet, you're a great girl, but I've met someone else.' I fantasised about taking a week off work, then another, finally turning up and being excused for being teary and useless. Going *home* home for a while, sleeping in a single bed, Mum coming up every hour with a bowl of Heinz Cream Of Tomato, telling me to keep my strength up – an expression I'd never heard her use. At one point, I think my dumpee fantasy became confused with Beth's death scene in the film of *Little Women*, but I luxuriated in pretend pain. What actually happened was much worse.

Mark took me to Clos Maggiore, which is widely feted as one of the most romantic restaurants in London. I'd always wanted to go there, but as I gave up my coat and allowed myself to be led into the fake forest, I had to focus very hard on putting one foot in front of the other, instead of screaming, turning around and running out into the night in search of a KFC. At the time, I didn't know what was wrong with me. Nerves, I thought, or indigestion, or an anxiety triggered by the fact that I was wearing a brand new dress. (Eighty per cent off, almost violet in colour – 'My namesake! A sign!' I'd said in the shop, even though the shade was closer to undiluted Ribena.) My arms were slightly too long for it, forcing a sort of hunched tension to build up in my shoulders.

When we sat at the table, a bottle of champagne was waiting in an ice bucket. A waiter immediately poured it into glasses for us. I wondered whether this was all part of the service, because the restaurant was so fine and fancy that this was all we were expected to drink. I waited for Mark to say, 'No thanks mate, can I just have a pint of Becks?'

Instead, he took my hand.

'Violet, um, you and me. This is the big one, isn't it? You're the girl I'm going to spend the rest of my life with.' He got up, and bent down on his right knee, moaning. 'Woooaaaarghhhh! For fuck's sake, my back. Thompson never should have tackled me, it was only a friendly. Right, Violet, would you do me the honour of becoming my wife.'

That's how he said it. It wasn't a question.

He had the inevitable velvet box in his jacket pocket and showed me a ring. It looked like white gold, a large eye-shaped diamond surrounded by slightly smaller diamonds. The top of the band was raised to meet the central jewel, studded with yet more diamonds. It was a hunchback ring for me, a girl in a hunchback dress. It was hideous.

'It's *beautiful!*' I cried, flinging my arms around him.

'Not bad, eh? You know Harris? His dad has a little shop in Hatton Garden, so ...'

I cut him off, not wanting to hear about how he'd managed to buy this with a wholesale discount, or that one of the actresses who runs the market stall on *EastEnders* has one exactly like it.

'Honestly, you've made me the happiest girl alive!'

Seemingly, I had no control over what was coming out of my mouth. It wasn't exactly a lie. If someone were to pick me up and put me in the middle of a refugee camp, or a tornado, or a graveyard, I would easily be the happiest girl alive in that setting.

Mark slid the ring onto my left hand. I looked down at it, with the raggedy nails, the torn cuticles, the mild but itchy eczema flare-up. It looked hard, alien. What would it be like to run out into the street and wave it into people's faces, take out men's eyes with it, go on a rampage and spend the rest of my life in prison? I could have changed my life that night, altered my destiny, if only I'd been brave enough. I could have responded to the life that was closing in on me by veering off course, driving off the metaphorical cliff. But I've always lacked courage, and that night was no exception. I sat, and smiled at my hand, and tried to work out what was wrong with me, why I was so ungrateful, why I couldn't force myself to make the face that would have come naturally to millions of girls.

Under Mark's gaze, I studied the menu, and brightly suggested that we order the Wagyu beef for two.

Mark ordered for us both, adding, 'And bring some ketchup, yeah?'

The waiter's lip wrinkled with barely perceptible disgust. Our eyes met, and I tried to communicate a silent *I'm sorry*. It might have been my imagination, but I'm sure that he smiled at me, then saw the ring and shuddered.

I remember waking up the next morning with something worse than a hangover, contemplating Mark's lightly sweating, sleeping form and thinking, NO! I hadn't realised I'd been free to leave until I wasn't any more. The world felt smaller. My lungs felt smaller.

As I breathed in through my nose and out through my mouth, counting to ten while surreptitiously wiping mascara from his clammy back, I remember telling myself not to panic. I remember him smiling, his eyes still stuck together with sleep, as he suggested that the future Mrs Barry might like to give Mr Barry a blow job. He looked meaningfully at my left hand, which was nude – I'd left the ring on my bedside table. The future Mrs Barry felt obliged to oblige, even though she had a bout of nausea that signalled either the end of a period of heavy drinking, or the beginnings of an anxiety attack. (She did bring things to a logical conclusion by introducing her hands, clasped in a prayer position, in order to avoid intercourse and the oversubscribed 8.02 train to Cannon Street.)

I remember standing in our old shower, a big shower, surrounded by cylindrical glass doors, with the sort of head that promises great technological cleansing advancement purely because the head is rectangular when you'd expect it to be circular. I remember looking at Mark's array of shampoos and gels, all containing descriptions of their manliness, and how their contents could only enhance and increase the innate masculinity of their user. I remember wondering why every bottle was grey and orange. My life would be grey and orange from then on. I could see myself in a supermarket in five years, picking up something with testosterone and caffeine in it, and adding it to the trolley with a cheery bottle of Matey.

I remember picturing myself bathing our future, faceless child, while something burned in the oven and my phone buzzed with a message from Mark saying he was 'held up in a client meeting'. I remember thinking of Mark's father, winking at his son every time Holly Willoughby was on TV, and the way Mark's mother would look away from these exchanges, so that we never saw a fleeting expression of sadness flickering across her face. I thought of Mark's friends, and how we'd probably see them that evening, and maybe some sort of smart dinner would be planned, but it would inevitably descend into Jaeger-bombs and chaos, and shouty 'hilarious' comments about how I'd 'got' him, and how his life was over. I remember writing 'MY LIFE IS OVER' in the steam and condensation of the shower screen, and then frantically breathing on it, smearing it with my fingertips, so that my cry for help would never be seen again. I remember wondering what was wrong with me, whether I had won some sort of life competition, whether being sad was simply an inevitable tax on being safe, whether I should think myself lucky, lucky, lucky.

*

When I got to work, I did start to think that I was so lucky. It was a bizarre day. When I phoned Mum on the way to work, she simply shrieked 'I knew it!' until Dad had to take over – with astonishing, well-intentioned sweetness, he offered to send me venue deposit money before he said congratulations. I told Nikki on reception out of sheer political terror. If she didn't find out first, straight from me, she would be furious – and that meant that she might stop franking birthday cards and letting me know when my ASOS had reached the post room.

Nikki responded as if I had news of a significant lottery win. *Her* win.

'Oh my God! Oh my God, I can't believe it!' she screamed, in a way which was, in retrospect, unflattering.

Alan opened a bottle of champagne at lunch. Even Connie, forever out of the office, sent a congratulations email promising to take me for a drink on her return. People from other companies on other floors were sending me links to their wedding photographers. ('Kevin did a lovely job for us – he can do all of those nice effects! You could have a tiny Mark sitting on the palm of your hand, framed with a glitter heart! Don't worry about those pictures on his site where the head's cut off, he did it on purpose, to be arty.') My parents sent flowers. Mark's work sent flowers.

There was a predictable dinner where Mark's best man Jonno made a speech, talking about Mark and me for under two minutes, and the 'quality brothels in Tallinn' for twenty. Jamie, Mark's other best man, tried to make me feel better about this.

'I bet you're going to a lovely spa on your hen do, aren't

189

you Violet? Well, this is just like a spa experience, but for the boys.'

We had over a year. A lot could happen in a year. If I'm honest, I started to enjoy it. I liked the fact that I couldn't go drinking with anyone without cries of, 'We simply must have prosecco, because Violet is engaged!' even though I started to worry that my own acidic burps were on the brink of burning a hole in the roof of my mouth. I liked browsing the Kate Spade bridal collection and turned quite quickly from a person who believed that a monogrammed tote decorated with champagne flutes was more tasteless than third-hand chewing gum, to someone who believed that there was no point owning one unless you were going to stump up another £250 for the coordinating wallet. I liked going to restaurants and tasting canapés, although 'tasting' implies a restrained nibble, rather than working one's way through a plate of giant prawns and washing them down with yet more fizzy wine, then sneering, 'You know, I think the pastry was *slightly* more buttery and flaky at the place we tried last week.' Essentially, I embraced the opportunity to behave like a total dick.

It was Nadia who caught me out. Her response to my engagement was possibly the weirdest of all. Without admitting it, I think I'd hoped she'd be the one to grab me by the elbow, drag me back to reality and scream my own name in my face until I woke up. But she'd changed, too. We were eating pizza in her flat one rainy Tuesday, for hen do planning. We'd chosen the date because, as she explained, 'It's literally the only day I'm not training.' While I longed to call her out for her linguistic hyperbole, it was probably true. Nadia had spent her twenties running, and it was all my fault.

After an especially toxic New Year, which, if it were a *Friends* episode, would have been entitled 'The One Where The Very Expensive Coke Turned Out To Be Crystal Meth', I turned to Nadia and said, 'Enough! This is far too studenty for my liking. We left uni nearly three years ago, we're getting far too old to be this ridiculous. It ends now! I am signing us up for a run.'

I stopped drinking for a month, and ate more vegetables, and shuffled about the park on Sundays, complaining every step of the way. I managed to complete the tiny, unimpressive, five-kilometre run in April, and discovered that I was the fourth slowest person to go around the course. I never bothered again.

Nadia *hated* me for suggesting that we do some exercise – her college netball glory long forgotten – and briefly threatened to stop speaking to me. I didn't realise I was unwittingly introducing her to her new best friend. After our first attempt, I was sweaty, angry and achy, and on the point of suggesting we give up and go for a beer.

She turned to me, gleamy of brow and huge of pupil, and breathed, 'That was *amazing*! This is *amazing*!'

She started to ask me if I wanted to go for extra runs. I did not. She started running in secret, setting an alarm and leaving her flat before the sun came up – in my meaner moments, when I saw her leaping about in neon Lycra, I thought, *you can tell that she dresses in the dark*. She made new friends, all eternally bonded in their mutual hatred of bread. She never, ever had cigarettes, but she was always good for an isotonic gel. If only I knew what one was.

Over the next twelve months, it slowly became impossible to get hold of Nadia. If I'd had any spare time at all, I'd spent it with her – and I'd taken it for granted that she was always around to come over for cheap wine and gluey pasta after I'd fought with Mark, or that if a new no-reservation brunch place opened, she'd spend her Sundays braving the queue with me. Slowly but surely, she replaced me with running. I cried the first time I realised that I'd not seen her for nearly a month, and she'd cancelled on me again to go on a park run.

Once, I tried to meet her for a coffee in town, and ended up resentfully sipping a latte and watching as she hopped from limb to limb while rummaging for a Ziploc bag. Then she swallowed cold hard-boiled eggs whole, like a snake. Whenever I messaged her, or tried to spend some time with her, she made me feel she was the President Of The United States and I was, I don't know, someone who had been knocked out of the first round of a reality show. She talked about windows – 'I might have a window that afternoon', 'I could find you a window in November'. It was ironic, because I never saw her.

I became evil. Apropos of nothing, I'd be in pubs, cackling into my cheap white wine and exclaiming, 'Thank God that Nadia isn't here, bumming us out with protein chat! I'd better drink her share!' Other friends, understandably, would defend her, and I'd burst into tears. 'I just miss her so much!' I couldn't quite articulate that I didn't just miss Nadia because she was busy – I missed the version that didn't exist any more. It was easier to be around Mark, and his friends. They liked to 'party', a euphemism for waking up with a pressing need to vomit and an unexpected £150 bar receipt in a trouser pocket. Because I was the only girl-friend in the gang who egged them on, without criticism, they thought I was wild. Their approval made me wilder, although again, this wildness was defined by a willingness to buy and consume drinks that I couldn't really afford.

To all intents and purposes, Nadia was still my 'best' friend, but it was like having my name on the deeds of a dilapidated, condemned house. I didn't dare to give a name to the sensation of loss that I felt when I thought of her. When I woke in the night, silent and alone, she was the one who occupied my thoughts, after a cursory trip through the intertwined hells of my job prospects and unauthorised overdraft charges. Still, people would ask me about her, and I'd tell them about her latest race, her new regime, her personal bests, even though the information had been gleaned impersonally, on Facebook. Yet, when Mark asked me to marry him, I rang her straight after I rang my parents.

Her first response made me realise that things between us had become truly terrible.

'Oh my God, Vi, are you OK? Has something happened? What's going on?'

A relationship has issues that urgently need addressing if you assume that you'll only get in touch with each other on the occasion of very bad news. Suddenly, I felt shy with her.

'Actually, I wanted to let you know that I'm getting married. Mark asked me to marry him.'

The line went dead for a few seconds, and then I heard a sob.

'Oh, Vi, Violet, this is ... wow! This is big news! Good for you! We need to celebrate!' Unexpectedly, I heard myself asking, 'Would you be my maid of honour?'

More sobbing, and then a muffled 'Of course!'

I assumed she was happy for me. Everyone else was.

Nadia treated my wedding like a marathon. She kept lists of lists, maintained a laser-like focus and occasionally became exasperated with me and my growing indifference to cocktail choices and colour schemes. She gave up a lot of her time, even though she kept reminding me that it was a commodity more valuable than ambergris, caviar and looted art. However, Nadia kept surprising me with her soft, sentimental side. I asked her to give a reading during the service, expecting her to pick something bittersweet, perhaps an e.e. cummings poem or some Frank O'Hara. Instead, she selected 'The Owl And The Pussycat'. I bit my lip and did not say that I had heard 'The Owl And The Pussycat' at every other wedding I had attended since university, and the incidence of the poem seemed to correlate with the divorce rate.

The evening with the pizza (ordered by Nadia as 'The ultimate act of love – you're the only one I'll ever eat carbs with') was the night that put the end of my world in motion. Coyly, just as I was dipping a crust in the dregs of the garlic sauce, she asked, 'How did you know that Mark is The One? Before he proposed, I mean? Was there a day when he said something or did something that made you realise he's the love of your life?'

I froze. How hard could it have been to say something, invent something – that he made me laugh, or opened a car door for me before getting in, or bought me tampons without making a big deal out of it. But my mouth wouldn't play ball. I stuttered and stuttered. I had nothing. And Nadia recognised the panic in my eyes.

'You don't love him, do you.'

'I ... well, I think ... I ... SHIT!' I burst into tears. 'I don't know, Nadia, I don't know what I'm going to do! I don't think I can marry him. It's all such ... shit!'

Nadia didn't hug me, or even put a consoling hand on my back. Her eyes were as hard as mine were wet.

'Violet, it's getting too late not to do this. People have spent so much money. Your big hen do is coming – we've all paid for the house ... in fact, I've still not paid *my* parents back, I had to borrow from them for the deposit ... fuck, do you have any idea how many people this wedding actually involves?'

It took me a few seconds to hear her. For a few seconds I was weightless, floating in space, imagining a free future with no wedding in it. I saw myself as a dystopian renegade, my entire life exploding into fire and dust behind me, as I walked away, happy to build a brand new life on the moon, in exile, alone in the desert – any other nightmare would be a lesser nightmare. Then I was back in the room, reacting. When did Nadia get so conventional? She'd never seemed especially invested in this wedding, anyway. Sure, we'd been having a bit of a rough patch, but surely now, when I needed her the most, she'd take my side?

'But surely it would be wrong to go ahead, to do this when I'm not sure? I know it's a headache for everyone, but it has to be better to call it off while I can? People would have to understand, wouldn't they?' I could hear the pleading in my own voice.

'Violet, *everyone* gets cold feet, everyone is nervous, everyone is uncertain. What if you change your mind, and then change it back?'

'I don't think I would change it back.'

'I just want you to think very, very carefully about what you're saying. Before you do anything rash.'

My eyes filled, and I bit my lip.

'Oh, help. What am I going to do?'

My best friend made an expression I knew well – the eye roll, the sigh, the shoulder shake, the barely perceptible movements you only notice when you know someone intimately, when they're always going to be Ollie to your Stan, and I felt relief. Here's another fine mess for Nads to get me out of. And then, in a fraction of a second, I saw something leak from her. The tenderness had gone.

'I don't know what you're going to do.'

My free-floating, loose sense of fear crystallised into something solid, something impossible to ignore. All that money. All that time. All of those people. No way out at all. Strangely, instead of crying, I started to slow my breathing. *In, two, three, four, out, two, three, four.* Nadia was clever. Surely she would help me. There had to be a wickedly brilliant, complicated solution that would release me from the mess, a switch, a loophole.

'Wedding insurance!' I cried excitedly. 'I have wedding insurance! I can claim on that and get some of the money back!'

Nadia shook her head.

'Yeah, that covers you if the venue goes bankrupt, or if there's another ash cloud and you've got guests coming from abroad. Actually, I reckon most have a policy that prevents you from claiming in the event of an ash cloud, since that happened. Insurance is designed to make it really hard for you to claim, they're not going to pay out if you change your mind.'

This was not what I wanted to hear.

'Nadia, please, please listen. Honestly, I've never been sure of this, never been sure of Mark. And I've been waiting for this to make sense, because I know this is what I'm supposed to want, so every day, I've been trying to make my feelings match the feelings that everyone expects me to have. I can't do it. This isn't a wobble, I've been wobbling for ages.'

She sighed heavily and narrowed her eyes.

'Then why, why in the name of fucking buggery, did you say yes?'

'I don't know! I'm weak and silly and I got frightened, because if I said no to Mark, then I'd have to deal with our relationship ending. Finding somewhere to live. I don't think I can afford to rent on my own, and if I moved back home I'd have to quit my job. And the trouble is that I don't have a proper reason not to be with him. Just lots of little reasons. He doesn't make me happy, and I want to be with someone who makes me happy.'

For a moment, Nadia made an expression that she could have copied directly from my mum.

'Violet, do you think anyone's *happy*, all the time? Do you even *know* how shit it is, being single? You don't, because you never, ever ask me! You only ever talk to me when you want me to do some chore for this wedding, which has taken up *months of my life,* and might not even happen now! You treat me as though I'm *lucky* to be your lady in waiting, Princess Violet! Do you want to be me for a week, waiting in Slug and *Fucking* Lettuce for some mouth-breather with adult acne who's probably going to stand me up?' Nadia looked tearful. Even through my fog of fear, I felt ashamed. I had no idea that *Nadia* could feel this way. I'd always assumed Nadia could be with anyone she wanted – and she didn't want to be with anyone. Perhaps I'd never asked her properly. Perhaps, before the running, I secretly liked things as they were because I didn't have to share her with anyone.

'Do you know why I run, every day? Why I get up in the middle of the *actual shitting night?* It's because I'm lonely, I have no one there in the morning to drink coffee with and curl up with and have sex with! So before you complain to *me* because you've been bored for five seconds, remember you're not the expert on unhappiness!'

We had never spoken to each other like this before. We'd been irritating and exasperating and blunt. We'd had a long and stupid fight on our way back from Amsterdam because we'd both blamed each other for getting too stoned to sort out the online flight check-in, but this was different, vicious, cruel. I let rip. And because I loved her, I knew exactly how to hurt her.

'I'm sorry! I'm sorry that you think your life is so shit that you're actually jealous of mine! I'm sorry that I've included you in my wedding, because I thought you might like to have something fun to do that isn't wearing stretchy clothes and hanging out with weirdos! I'm sorry that you won't ever fucking get married, and you'll say it's because of the patriarchy but it's really because when people want to be close to you, you push them away! You never want to see me. You never make time for me, either. I haven't seen you for months, because as soon as I started planning this wedding, you just ran! You *literally* ran away! And when I *do* fall in love, and get married, for real, you won't need to worry about any of this because you won't be invited!'

Provoked, Nadia went for the jugular.

'If you don't marry Mark,' she started hissing, 'you're probably not going to be able to marry anyone. You'd have to do it in some tacky chapel in Vegas, because no one is going to go to all of this effort again. How much money have your parents spent? Probably more than they can afford, right? Doesn't your dad want to retire soon? Will that feel nice, when you announce that you're single and everything is cancelled when they've already blown ten grand they don't really have on canapé deposits? Look, whatever you think you're missing with Mark, I promise you that it's not out there waiting for you. Life is shit, you don't get a prince, you're lucky if you get a joint National Trust membership.'

I stood up.

'FINE. I guess I'll go off and live my shit life, and let you enjoy yours, on your own.'

Then the tears came. I was crying like a child, screaming and screaming. I picked up the biggest slice of pizza in the box and flung it at her face, as hard as I could, like a Shuriken star. It grazed her cheek and left a tomato trail on her lap. I picked up my bag and ran out into the night, leaving my favourite coat behind forever.

Chapter Fifteen

Lottie couldn't get me onto the same plane as everyone else, so I'm flying much later in the day. I arrive at Gatwick early – I've never been alone at an airport before, and I'm prepared to love it. Simon has some sort of special friends and family lounge pass, which he offered me as casually as most people might offer a Polo from the half packet unearthed at the bottom of their coat pocket. I've bought a pair of knock-off Céline sunglasses from Accessorize and now I'm chilling on a pleather banquette, wondering how many free proseccos I can claim before the man at the bar cuts me off. At the snack table, a middle-aged man in a suit is filling his pockets with foil-wrapped chocolate biscuits. Once his jacket has reached full capacity, he continues to pile them inside his trousers.

I am trying to concentrate on page eighteen of *Jacob's Room*. I have been reading *Jacob's Room* for about four months, partly because people keep mentioning it at parties and in their dating profiles when they want to communicate that they define themselves entirely through their passion for obscure literary fiction. It's usually followed by the expression 'neo-feminist retelling' and sometimes 'the structure *is* the theme'.

The theme of *Jacob's Room* is rooms – I know this because I keep flinging it across them in fits of knuckle-gnawing, eye-bleeding boredom. I am hoping that I look clever and sexy and complicated. Well, if I'm honest, I'm hoping that if I keep trying with the book, I will magically become all of these things before the plane lands, and that I won't run out of intellectual conversation two hours into the trip. I feel profoundly nervous. Have I been asked to come on this holiday because I've accidentally given everyone the impression that I'm smart and cool? I keep wondering whether this is a bizarre, gruelling, extended job interview. No one has really mentioned anything about Intuition since that strange lunch with Simon and Richard, and I'm worried. My confidence is wobbling. I'm not sure that I can convince this many people that I'm hot and hireable.

To be fair to Mark, no matter how many problems our relationship had, he always made me feel clever. Once, I scored some last minute, cheap Saturday matinee tickets and took him to see *Who's Afraid Of Virginia Woolf.* We had an argument and he left during the interval – he'd thought it was an adaptation of a children's book featuring a particularly scary wolf named Virginia. He was so cross that he left his ice cream behind. 'If I'd have known it was just a load of people talking, I would have stayed home and watched the football,' were his final furious words before he stormed out into Covent Garden. It's *very* hard to do any sort of serious storming in WC1, there are far too many people milling about and suddenly standing stock still in the middle of the pavement for no reason. He had to settle for a kind of petulant trot.

Thinking of Mark makes me think of marriage. Wouldn't it be funny if my future husband was right here in the lounge with me? I'm still trying to get used to my freedom, testing the idea that I could marry *anyone*, if I get married at all. Disappointingly, all I see are variations on Max – they're all too loud, too large, too sure. One sparks my attention – early thirties, dark hair, hazel eyes, grey cashmere jumper – and our eyes meet for a moment. *Will he ask me over for a drink?* Attempting to turn without attracting his attention, I squint and try to read the upside down title of the well-thumbed book that is splayed open beside him. *For Crying Out Loud* by … Jeremy Clarkson. Ah.

For the last few days, Simon has been visiting my imagination in the capacity of Potential Husband. But I can't make it work. Even after Bristol, the idea makes me feel empty, insufficiently cosy. Quickly, I find myself bringing Lottie back into the picture, lying between them both on the sofa again, helping Lottie in the kitchen while Simon drinks wine on a stool, eating biscuits with them and swapping Sunday supplements. During one unguarded mental wandering, I saw myself visiting a garden centre with them, having a good-natured argument about the importance of buying a Christmas tree that actually smells like a Christmas tree. It's not sexy, but it makes me feel warm and safe.

Max is too old and bossy, and I can't see myself married to Richard, mainly because I have never met anyone less like me than Sasha. Even though we're reaching some sort of amity, I am still slightly alarmed by the prospect of going on holiday with her. I almost bought a travel kettle, in order to make sure that there is no chance of me bumping into her when I'm trying to make coffee in my pyjamas. It's strange. Lottie and Mimi are every bit as glossy as she is. Sasha isn't as symmetrically, conventionally beautiful as they are. Yet I don't feel as though the world would end if I farted in front of Lottie – in fact, I probably have, when I was asleep. I've seen Mimi with what I assume is her worst towel on her head, which is an immediate barrier breaker, an act of intimacy akin to noticing someone's period knickers in their laundry basket.

Sasha is an enigma. I can't work out how to amuse her, or impress her, and sometimes she looks at me as though she wants to put me in detention. Objectively speaking, she is not as beautiful as the others. Yet, I can't stop thinking about how it felt to have sex with her. She was completely different from the way I had imagined her. I was expecting her to be dominant and abrasive, yet she radiated the purest human warmth. She'd smelled like hot sun on wet earth. Even though I thought I would have to perform for her, she made me fully forget everything that was happening in my head and put me back into my body.

Drifting off, I think about the way she touched me, the way she tasted, the heat rising from my skin as I came. Perhaps I could I go somewhere private for a moment or two, and . . . Shit! I need to board! I throw my coat over my arm and gather my stuff, accidentally lassoing my phone charger around my head and nearly knocking something chocolatey from the grubby hand of Biscuit Man before I dash to the gate.

Chewing my lip and tapping my passport against the

palm of my hand, I try, and fail, to concentrate on the announcements as I line up to board. A woman smiles at me sympathetically.

'Nervous flyer, lovely? My youngest is the same.' She gestures to a small girl, maybe five years old, who is clutching her other hand tightly. 'See, Lila? It's OK to be scared! Even grown-ups get nervous!'

I smile distractedly, surprised and delighted that this stranger has granted me adult status. I am not a sexual deviant. I am not. I am just a nice, normal lady who is going on a little holiday to see her friends. Her much older friends who she has sex with, en masse, without knowing all of their surnames.

Forcefully, I try to put all thoughts of Sasha out of my mind, at least until I'm on the plane, in the air, and the seatbelt sign is off. Then I gaze out of the window and think about her mouth on my breasts, her hands in my hair.

Chapter Sixteen

The airport is fairly quiet, and once I've gone through the passport gates I walk at a clip, scanning every sign I see for a taxi icon, bouncing along to the rhythm of the wheels of my wheelie case, a syncopated succession of trundling squeaks and clicks. I'm sure I can hear someone yelling my name. Perhaps there's a Spanish word that sounds similar . . . wait! It's Lottie and Mimi, holding a sign with my name written in purple felt tip and, somewhat improbably, a blue balloon.

'*Violet!* Fuck's sake, you daft cow, get over here! Were you going to ditch us and sneak off to Manumission?' shouts Mimi, pulling me to her for a hug. 'Why do you walk so fast?'

I smile, hard, in order to stop myself from bursting into happy tears. I can't believe they came to pick me up! It's such a sweet gesture – I feel as though I'm being reunited with beloved old friends, even though I've only known them for a couple of weeks. A knot of anxiety that I wasn't even conscious of starts to unfurl in the pit of my stomach.

Lottie hugs me too.

'I think that you should always have someone to meet

you at the airport, and it's especially nice when you're not expecting it, so I decided to surprise you. Hence, the balloon.'

She gestures a little too sharply, and the ribbon becomes free from her grip, the balloon slowly soaring towards the airport rafters. Out of the corner of my eye, I can see a little girl inhale sharply before bursting into tears. It doesn't have to be your balloon to break your heart. I stifle a laugh, giddy with relief. They want me here. It's going to be OK.

Mimi leads us out to the car park, and into a big black SUV, a music video drug dealer's car. She makes a face.

'Awful, isn't it? Max insisted!'

Sitting in the back, on the slippery seats, I search for traces of the owners. Well, the hirers. For some reason I'd wanted to see a battered road map, lipstick rolling out from under the seats, crumbs. I find an old pot of Carmex in a cup holder. It has Snoopy on the lid. I feel a bit better.

Lottie is flicking through the radio stations, muttering.

'Doof doof doof! This is terrible, the music is terrible, what do people – ah, I like this one!'

Lottie busts out her own surprisingly enthusiastic, tune-less interpretation of an old Mariah Carey song, until Mimi turns to her and cuts her off.

'Lottie, we've talked about this. Foreign roads. I don't drive much. I need to concentrate. Hush, now.'

My question about when they all arrived and how their journey was dies on my lips.

We travel up winding hills, and then reach a near vertical drive. I hadn't googled the place, I'd simply assumed it would be a gleaming white stucco iceberg of a villa, a Malibu mansion dropped into the Balearics. I'm slightly disappointed to see that the property has a weird sort of flat, pebbledash cladding – as though some improbably expensive architect has sat down with his sketch pad and thought, How can we evoke the spirit of suburban Bedfordshire here? Without quite knowing why, I'm relieved to see another car in the drive, a silver Prius. Perhaps we shall need more than one escape route.

Still, I can smell bougainvillea, and I know that there's going to be a pool. The sun is high in the bright blue sky, and no matter what the next few days hold, at least I'm going to get a tan.

Lottie offers to show me to my room, which is perfectly plain – a king-size bed, a cool, cream tiled floor, and a bathroom with an actual bath.

'I don't know about you, but I always want to shower after a plane journey,' she suggests, so I do. Alone. I'm a little concerned about the quiet. There's no murmured chatter, no music playing, and even though it seemed trivial at the time, Mimi's snappiness seems to hang in the air. Something Has Happened.

The shower serves to sever my anxiety, slightly – it seems to have just two settings, scalding and chilling, so I focus my attention on turning the dial and then leaping out of the way of the water jet. I rub my entire, naked body with pungent, unctuous Hawaiian Tropic, more for the scent than the sun protection. While I wait for the oil to seep in, I brush my hair, and then I plait two tiny braids, pinning them so that they lie on parallel sides of my skull. I'm not sure if this makes me look like the Queen of Instagram or the lady in *Lord of the Rings*, so I frown at my reflection for a while, almost unplaiting, and then audaciously adding a pink orchid behind my left ear. I say orchid – it has pointy, polyester leaves and cost five pounds from Claire's Accessories.

Sorting out the swimwear for this trip was tricky. Ideally, I wanted to be a starlet in scarlet, something perfectly plain that would trick people into thinking that my old-fashioned body is entirely of its time. Instead, I found ironic nineties high leg one pieces, emblazoned with breakfast cereal slogans. Shorty wetsuits with the arse cut out, like chaps. Metallic bandeau breast cages, with pom poms on the nipples. Eventually I gave up and dug out my own old, tired H&M sets, which were last worn as solutions to laundry day emergencies. I select a stripy navy and white halter neck and have a brief panic when I can't find a single bikini bottom, matching or otherwise. Ah, I remember now, I shoved them in the zipped front pocket of my wheelie case.

There's a mirror on the wall, and I suck my stomach in and try to give myself an honest but generous assessment. I have looked worse. A spray tan has made all of the difference, and my skin looks even and golden. For once, I feel luscious. On a bad, pallid day, I know that the pink tones in my skin conspire to make me look like a forgotten packet of ham, festering in the back of the fridge. Still, I don't quite have it in me to stroll out to the pool in my two-piece, shouting 'Hiya guys! Are there any cold beers?' Partly because, just *oh my God no*, and mostly because I don't want to be nearly naked when I figure out why the grown-ups are fighting. After longingly fingering the crisp, white cotton sundress that still has its tags on, I throw on something old, ivory, a little worn looking but low-cut. Too late, I realise there's the ghost of something that may or may not be sun cream on the hem.

I discover Max in a vast white sitting room, dwarfing a two-seater sofa. He is wearing the most enormous headphones I have ever seen, the sort that look like they have been constructed from the cushion covers of ergonomic office chairs. Max's face is set, furious and unmoving. He looks like an Easter Island figure. He doesn't seem to see me, so I scuttle out, reluctant to draw attention to myself. It's difficult to tell whether it's accidental or deliberate, but I start to sense Max's presence all over the house. Along a low, narrow hallway, I notice a strange framed photograph. It's slightly under two metres long, perhaps less than half a metre wide, and features a naked, glassy-eyed blonde woman reclining on a Perspex sun lounger, one hand pushing black sunglasses back against the bridge of her nose, the other hand splayed so the photographer can capture the finger she's pushed inside herself. I shudder, feeling horny and queasy. Max, I've started to realise, always inspires these twin reactions from me.

The kitchen is bright and sterile. Happily, the fridge looks like a fridge. It's a gleaming iceberg of a Smeg with a vegetable drawer full of glossy green mini Heinekens, and a half-full bottle of Chablis on the shelf inside the door. I open five or six cupboard doors before seeing a row of wine glasses on a dresser. I fill one to the top and take two big gulps before walking through the back door, to the pool. Everyone else is outside.

'Hi!' I say brightly, 'I—'

'SHHHHHH!' hisses Mimi. 'Sasha is asleep!'

I wonder whether Lottie is still getting on her nerves, as Mimi sounds even grumpier than she did in the car. Sure enough, Sasha, in a lime green swimsuit, is snoring, a straw hat tipped over her head, *God Created The Integers* rising and falling on her chest.

I make a note of the point where the pages separate, and I'm delighted to realise that she can't possibly be more than two chapters in. Still, I feel my face flame. Mimi, my ally, has been in a shitty mood since she first saw me. Perhaps I shouldn't have come. Maybe everyone wishes they'd never invited me. I bite my lip very hard, trying not to cry. I could leave. I could go back through the kitchen, take the rest of the wine to my room and try to get an early flight home. I've just paid my Visa bill, there should be enough space on the card.

Instead, I put my wine glass next to an empty sun lounger and pick up a white towel from a wicker basket. Too late, I notice that Mimi and Max aren't the only ones in a mood. There is a palpable sense of scratchiness in the air. Quiet, unspoken rage seems to emanate from every single lounger. Already, my skin feels sticky with it.

Everyone is sitting separately, on little lounger islands, flanked by empty space. Their silence is deafening. There is no murmur of conversation, just the dull hum of the pool filter. This is not a genial quietness. This feels like coming back to the office after lunch, while everyone reads a passive-aggressive email chain about what does and doesn't go in the microwave.

The trouble is that I feel that if I don't know what's going on, it isn't OK to ask. I'm not among equals. Irrationally, I worry that it's my fault. I must have done something wrong.

They're all holding books, but staring at their phones. As quietly as I can, I lift my dress over my head and drop it on the lounger. I kick my flip-flops underneath and make my way to the steps of the pool. Pursing my lips, I blow out, bracing myself for cold. I must not scream. I must not make a sound.

I'm relieved to discover that the water is warm, just a couple of degrees below my preferred temperature for a bath. My lungs relax and expand, the muscles in my shoulders soften, and I start to plod up and down the pool, as quietly as I can. On my fifth length, I start to feel quite philosophical about the situation. Who cares if Mimi's in a shitty mood? I don't have to be! I'm in Ibiza, for free, feeling hot sun on my bare skin at the end of October! These people can be as mean to me as they like, I can simply drink all of their delicious wine and go for walks! I might even finish *Jacob's Room*! As I smile to myself, I'm startled by a laugh. Am I laughing? No, it's Simon, whose discreet snorts are turning into full body convulsions.

'Violet!' he whisper-shouts. 'Violet! What are you doing? Can you actually swim?'

What?

'Er, what do you think I'm doing now?'

'It's ... it's ... you're,' he honks, unable to control his mirth. 'A doggy paddle! I've never seen an adult doing a doggy paddle!'

I doggy paddle to the side of the pool that's nearest to Simon, and hiss indignantly, '*This* is how I swim! Stop ... dog shaming me!' Then, feeling slightly hysterical now that the tension has broken, I start to laugh too. Giggles escape from the side of my mouth as I try not to rouse the sleeping Sasha. Then, I lose control completely and snort. Out of the corner of my eye, I can see Lottie's shoulders shake, and her stomach tremble, until, unfortunately but aptly, she emits a sort of bark. That sets Mimi off.

211

'Oh, Jesus,' she murmurs, widening her eyes until they bulge, as she tries and fails to control herself.

I'm laughing so hard that I'm sobbing into the water. I'm watching Sasha and waiting for her to tell me off, yet she seems to be snoring more loudly than ever. I can hardly breathe. I think some pool water just went up my nose.

Simon follows my eyes.

'I know how to wake her up. Can anyone do an impression of an ice cream truck?'

We're roaring, and Sasha sits up and rubs her eyes.

'Did someone say we're getting ice cream?'

It turns out that Sasha has genuinely woken up with a craving for a Magnum that can't be shifted, so I volunteer to do a shop run. Even though everyone seems slightly more relaxed, I get the sense that it wouldn't hurt to leave the villa and establish an escape route. Also, now that I've thought about it, I want a Magnum too. I'm surprised, and slightly annoyed, that Sasha wants to come with me. Even though I've just arrived, I'm already feeling a little overwhelmed, and desperate for some decompression time. Still, Sasha insists.

'I don't want you to get lost – or worse, get me a weird pink one.'

The sun is fierce, and keeping up with Sasha, who is *not* a dawdler, is making me slightly sweaty. It doesn't help that I'm still damp from the pool. There is something unexpectedly comforting about watching her smooth, pale, long legs marching into the distance. She reminds me of a feeling – I think it's the deep peace of a museum or a gallery when you're the first in, or the last out. Falteringly, I attempt to make conversation.

'So, you said you were having a tricky time at work. Does it get draining? The women that you're supporting must have gone through some of the most painful experiences imaginable. How do you cope, helping them to cope?'

She turns to me and grins. I notice, for the first time, a tiny chip in her left front tooth.

'Violet, I say this with love – fuck off! I'm on holiday! Right now, every teenage girl in London can join the Triads, for all I care, as long as they quit before next Monday.'

I'm surprised, but delighted to hear her sounding so flippant. Maybe we have more in common than I thought.

'But Sasha,' I say, feigning shock. 'Crime never sleeps!'

'No, it never pays! I reckon crime is secretly quite lazy. Crime takes naps. Now, what ice cream are you getting?'

I pretend I haven't given it much thought, even though I've been thinking about it obsessively since I got out of the pool.

'Maybe a Twister, if they've got them.'

'Really?' Sasha looks gratifyingly intrigued. 'I absolutely had you down as a Magnum girl. Maybe a strawberry Cornetto.'

'I don't like to admit this, but I think Magnums are overrated. The chocolate's too thin. The ice cream isn't creamy enough. They'll do if you're desperate, but I've never met a Magnum that didn't leave me feeling slightly underwhelmed. I do like Cornettos, though.'

We've arrived at the shop, a small supermarket called Eroski, which makes me smile.

'It sounds like a late eighties Eastern bloc sex shop.'

Sasha shakes her head at me.

'Don't joke, those were tough times. People queued for

days to get their hand on a single dildo.' She looks very serious for a moment, then she snorts.

I catch myself noticing that her face looks so much softer on holiday. Maybe it shows just how stressful her job is – she seems like a different person when she's away from work.

We forage for ice creams in the freezer – Sasha talks me into trying a caramel Magnum, and, keen to sustain the warmth of our brand new connection, I let myself be persuaded. We decide that the villa needs crisps, so we gather sackfuls. I hear a gasp. Sasha catches my eye and points at a packet emblazoned with the words 'Crusty nuts'. It's the final icebreaker. She pays at the till, nodding and pointing. I'd be surprised if it's down to a lack of linguistic skill, I think she simply can't trust herself to speak.

The moment we're out of the shop, she's doubled over. She takes my hand and *wheezes*.

'Crusty! Fucking! Nuts! Oh, Violet!'

She's so overcome that she can't quite open the wrapper of her Magnum. The remaining lump of tension dissolves in my stomach. I'd forgotten, this is the rule of holidays. Everyone gets completely wound up by security procedures and passport control queues, and the first few hours make you wonder why you bothered to come. Then you all laugh at something really, really stupid, and all is well.

We start to wander back the way we came. Sasha is expansive.

'For me, the great casualty of globalisation is the lack of – HA! – crusty nuts. My favourite thing about holidays used to be the supermarkets, and the product names that got lost in translation. Now I expect there are vast, expensive marketing teams tasked with ensuring that nothing is given a name that is accidentally or internationally hilarious.'

'I think we should have bought some for Max. Has something upset him? He could definitely use a laugh right now.'

'I think Max already has enough crusty nuts of his own to worry about,' says Sasha, with a grimace.

I'm still trying to figure out the group dynamic. It seems pretty clear that certain people are closer than others. While Sasha and Max might have the least in common with each other, I assumed that they must be reasonably friendly. Yet, I'm sure I can detect genuine dislike in Sasha's tone. I'm longing to get her to gossip about the rest of the group, but we've reached the villa. Maybe we can go for another walk later.

We find the rest of the group sitting outside around a big wooden table, eating lunch. Everyone seems much more cheerful, although Max is still in a mysteriously bad mood. Mimi asks him to pass the salad dressing, and he sighs at her and rolls his eyes by way of a response. I panic and leap up to help Mimi, knocking white wine all over Max's navy cargo shorts as I go.

'VIOLET! FUCKING HELL!' he booms, before leaping to his feet and striding away from us, presumably becoming even more furious as he realises that we're outside and there aren't any doors to slam.

'Ignore him,' says Simon. 'Every time he goes away, his bank blocks his credit card, and it's always everyone else's fault. I think the bank has put a note on his account to do it more, because he gets so riled. They block the card if he's at a motorway services in Wales.'

Mimi, who has triumphantly poured half the remaining

dressing onto her salad, presumably only because it is now available, says, 'The trouble with Max's bad moods is that he can only work through them by making sure they destroy everyone else's good moods. He's . . .'

'A dick!' interrupts Richard. 'Sorry Mimi. But he always wrecks the first day by being a total brat. Even Violet is more mature than he is.'

He sounds really dismissive. It stings, and I gasp. Oh, God. I want to go home. I've made a mistake.

'Sorry, Violet, I didn't mean that. I didn't think,' says Richard, apologising quickly.

Somehow, this makes things worse. If it was clumsy, laddish 'banter', an awkward attempt to include me in the group, I could laugh it off, but I think he really meant it.

Sasha interjects.

'He has a point. Look what you're doing with your hair. What are you, twelve?'

I think she might be trying to lighten the mood, but the damage is done. Too late, I notice that I've been anxiously plaiting a small, tight braid out of a loose bit of ponytail. I freeze and drop the braid.

She forces a laugh.

'You're like every woman in my office, they spend all day flicking it and twiddling with it. Why do you all have such extraordinary hair? Millennials, I mean.' Sasha searches the adjacent seats for allies. 'Lottie! Mimi! We had proper haircuts, didn't we, in our twenties? We didn't spend our days cultivating long Disney princess hair?'

Unfortunately, Mimi and Lottie do have stupid, long Disney bloody princess hair. And I'm not entirely sure that Mimi's is all her own.

I wait for Lottie and Mimi to rise to the bait, but they do not take it.

'Yes, yes, we were all skinheads, and there was pirate radio, which was better, and we all read the latest news about penny-farthings, circulated via Caxton's printing press,' mutters Mimi, flicking her skeins of golden silk over her shoulder, and rolling her eyes at me.

I feel a bit better, although I wish I could keep more than one ally in place at a time. Every time I think I have a handle on how this group works, it slides from my grasp. The politics aren't just baffling, they're exhausting.

Strangely, the more time I spend with Sasha, the more she reminds me of Nadia. I feel as though I've got to keep mentally racing to catch up with her mercurial moods. She pushes, and pulls, and pushes again. It's disorientating, this feeling of being drawn in and then frozen out again. But I'm prepared to put myself through anything for a small spark of warmth. Maybe I just need to try harder.

But where does this leave the sex? Sometimes, I'm not sure that I want to be wanted by someone whose attitude towards me is friendly and familiar. I want to be torn apart by wild horses, I need tenderness tempered by destructive energy. Sex with Sasha reminded me of the last time I had sex with Mark. I felt indifferent until I was transported by the pressure of his shoulder against my windpipe. I could have told him I couldn't breathe, he would have moved – but I fantasised that I was in the middle of a mercy killing, and that he was rescuing me from the rest of my life. Desire fought confusion and shame, and won. I came straight away.

Sasha keeps trying to place her wine glass on a section

of a table that isn't there; I realise she is extremely drunk. Richard has noticed too, and he starts to rise from his chair.

'I think I'll have an afternoon nap. Come on, sweetheart,' he says, walking around to the other side of the table, and placing his hands on her shoulders. 'We both woke up very early,' he adds, smoothing her curly hair at the temple.

The tenderness of the gesture makes me feel tearful, a little left out. Perhaps I need a nap, too.

The mood is maudlin. We're in holiday brochure country, surrounded by the bright and blue, but I catch Simon squinting through the sunshine into the middle distance, as he peels the label off his beer bottle.

'Sorry babe,' he says, looking at Lottie. 'I know you hate it when I do that.'

'Do what?' She's gazing into the middle distance, ignoring all of us.

Mimi's eyes are worryingly shiny. I don't want to be intrusive, but I want to ask what's wrong. After all, she has been kind to me.

'Mimi, are you all right? Is it Max?'

Simon stops fiddling with his bottle and frowns at me. Even Lottie stares.

I stumble on, searching for something that might make the group laugh, trying to recreate the mood when I was in the pool.

'My ex used to get horribly moody on holiday, it was awful. Then, when he cheered up, he'd go out and get hammered, and spend hours throwing up in the hotel bathroom. Once he refused to go and look at the Acropolis because he said it was "gay".'

More silence.

'Although, I suppose, he was not wrong.'

Everyone else laughs, but Mimi takes a deep breath.

'Violet, I don't mean to be rude, but you have no fucking idea. You've got decades ahead of you to fall in love and get your heart broken. I've ... not got the luxury of time. I've made too many mistakes.'

'But you and Max seem so good together. I can see how he might be tricky, sometimes, but you understand each other! You're both arty! You're so sophisticated, and ...' The expression I can't bring myself to articulate is 'grown-up'. 'You have that beautiful apartment – well, I know it's Max's apartment ...'

I trail off. I am completely out of my depth, and I'm starting to feel as though I'm trapped in a bad dream. Through the edge of my right eye, I notice a dish of enormous, grass-green olives. Panicking, I pick one up and put it in my mouth, without realising that it isn't pitted. One of my molars hits the stone, and I squeak quietly. Mimi does not notice.

'Violet, the only important thing to do is to try to fall in love with someone kind. Max isn't kind, not really. He's clever, and quick, and he can be very generous when it suits him. But he's difficult.'

Lottie looks thoughtful.

'I think he told me once that he had a bad time, growing up. There wasn't much money, and he had to live with his nan for a bit. Or was he in care?'

It's weird that Lottie's concern sounds rehearsed – it's as though she knows, intellectually, that Max's upbringing was bleak and brutal, but she sounds so detached that she could be describing a film she just saw.

Mimi nods.

'I met one of his exes right at the beginning, in New York, at a party for one of his artists. His most recent wife came over and said something I've never forgotten. "He's a lot of fun, but he can't really love anyone." At the time, I thought she was being jealous and mad, and that I was too cool and careful to fall for him anyway. I was wrong on both counts. But,' Mimi pauses for about four seconds, and then looks at a table leg, 'I know that I don't have any right to complain, really.' Her eyes meet Lottie's. 'I mean, it's not a tragedy, is it? "Woman approaching middle age starts to feel differently about the person she's sleeping with." Film at eleven.'

Simon stops picking at the beer bottle, and asks a question.

'How often does Max see his kids?'

Mimi frowns.

'Honestly, not often enough. Milly, she's from his first marriage to Rosa, apparently has her "own life" now, and she's doing some sort of creative writing course on the East Coast – but she rings all the time, and Max makes me say he's out. She's twenty-four – I think you're still allowed to need your dad when you're twenty-four.'

Max has a daughter who is not much younger than I am. This makes me feel odd.

'Then, he's supposed to see Isaac and Abi once a week, but it's really more like once a month. I've caught him out before – he told me he was with them, he told Sarah he was with me . . .'

Simon frowns.

'Do you think he's seeing someone else?'

'I really don't – and in a way it would be better if he was. He's just working and hiding, I think. Being on his own.'

220

It never occurred to me that Max might be unhappy. Stressed, self-important, struggling with the attendant pressures of an enormous, fragile ego – sure. But he seems too controlled to struggle with his emotions. I can't imagine Max ever doing anything that wasn't his choice, or that didn't please him.

I thought about Max being in care, which is a strange expression. I rarely hear it spoken of without the words being weighed down with sadness and a sense of neglect. If you're in care, it means that the people who should care for you won't or can't do it. It makes me think of my own family, and how I never felt properly cared for when I was growing up. I had a home, I suppose. I was looked after, and fed, and kept clean. But my parents seemed put out by everything I did. I was punished for making messes and noise. If I was good, and didn't do anything they could find fault with, they more or less ignored me, which felt safer.

Lottie takes charge, her confident voice ringing out.

'Bloody hell, guys, look at us! I think we should put this on Instagram. "So blessed – weeping poolside in Ibiza!" Max is fine – he's always fine in the end. We're all cranky because we're sleep-deprived and we've had too much wine! Let's go and have naps, watch some shit on Netflix and we'll cheer up in time for cocktails.'

Simon turns to me.

'Violet, my wife has downloaded five series of *Drag Race* if you want to hang out with us?'

I do. I want to curl up at the bottom of their bed, by their feet, and pretend that I belong to them.

Chapter Seventeen

The combination of wine and stress must have knocked me out. I barely remember getting into bed. When I wake up, it takes me a moment to work out that I'm in Simon and Lottie's room. Even though the blinds are drawn, I can feel the late sun beaming through the French windows that face out towards the pool. I've woken up suddenly, and I'm disorientated. The sound of the air conditioning unit, a noise I hadn't even noticed before, seems to be interfering with some signal at the back of my brain – I feel fuzzy and irritable, unable to slice through the screech of it. My tongue feels thick and bitter in my mouth. Without checking, I know my breath is rancid. Slightly hungover and edgy, I breathe in, trying to induce feelings of calm. *You're OK.* I breathe out. *It's OK.*

Out of habit, I rub my thumb against my right nipple, through the tissue-thin fabric of the pale cream T-shirt I've borrowed from Simon. Simon is wearing a white tee with short sleeves and snoring with his mouth open. Lottie is wearing a soft, grey marl vest with a scoop neck. Her skin looks as if it's within the puddle of the reflected light of a pearl. One nipple has freed itself, and I think about taking it into my mouth, tracing a pattern with my tongue, sucking it, biting it. No. No one wants to be woken up by my white wine breath. I roll onto my side, facing Lottie, and think about going back to sleep, but Simon has woken up.

'I see you, Violet. I know what you're doing. Checking out my wife. You dirty girl.' He whispers into my shoulder while he grinds against me. I'm still wearing bikini briefs, but I can feel the soft, papery crush of his cotton boxers against my skin. Slotting his thumbs into the sides of the briefs he tugs them down, so they're just below my knees. He strokes my buttocks, cupping and sliding and rubbing until his hands are inside my thighs. He's still wearing underwear, but his cock is out, and as he presses it against the cleft of my buttocks, I can feel it getting bigger and hotter.

His hands move up, up, searching for my clit, when I want him to feel my soaking pussy. I'm slippery. I'm worrying and wondering about whether I might wet the bed when I notice a damp patch of drool on Lottie's pillow. Simon finds what he's looking for, and rubs with his thumb, plunging four fingers in and out and in and out again. I moan, and he stops abruptly, and traces a circle around my left nipple very slowly, with a wet finger.

'I think you should make Lottie come.'

'She's asleep! I'm not sure I'm comfortable ...'

I gasp, as Simon starts to massage me again, drawing my wetness out, rubbing it around the tops of my thighs, and below my belly button.

'She's definitely awake. Make her come, or I stop doing this.'

I buck my hips against Simon's body, drawing his hand deep inside me, while I tentatively touch Lottie. She's wearing plain grey cotton knickers, and I put the palm of my hand on her crotch – which is very warm. It's like stroking an animal. I keep touching, through her underwear, until she moans, very faintly, her lip trembling. It's absurdly sexy, guttural, fragile. I moan in response. She opens one eye, smiles at me, then licks her lips, pushing her pussy against my palm. So, just as her husband did to me, I pull her knickers down, lick my middle finger and run it along the fold of skin where her lips meet.

It's very hard to concentrate on Lottie instead of focusing on how badly I want Simon to fuck me. His cock is now back between my buttocks, and he's muttering nonsense – 'You make me so hard, you're so wet, you want this so much, don't you?' – and not for the first time I feel furious with myself, for having such a predictable pussy, for claiming to be a feminist who wishes to be treated with respect when under the right circumstances I'll answer to anyone who calls me a 'dirty girl'.

Lottie's thigh muscles are clamped around my hand. It's a little painful, but I'm aroused by the sensation, the knowledge that I'm giving her pleasure. Wiggling away, I position myself between her legs, hoping Simon will notice the new arrangement and take advantage of it. Lottie's thigh muscles are around my neck, she's rubbing herself against my cheeks, mouth and nose.

Hoarsely, Simon says, 'Make her come. Make her come now.'

Lottie gasps obligingly, and Simon forces his cock inside me, grabbing my body hard. I'm aflame with want, greed.

I wish Lottie had a dick, so she could fuck me too, at the same time. It's thrillingly violent, he's gaining speed, and I'm aware of Lottie under me, softness and sensitivity next to so much hard muscle. I don't want to come, I want to be about to come, forever, but it's all too hot, too much, and after seconds of Simon whispering, fucking, grabbing, biting, I am launched into oblivion. I'm aware of Simon's orgasm, the breeze coming through the open window, cool against the heat of my skin, and I feel a strange throb of sadness. It's as though the ride is over, and I've just been told to get off the merry-go-round.

Simon taps my buttock again, no longer my demon lover, just a suave refugee from Liberty's beauty hall.

'Bloody hell Vi, that was intense. Do you want the shower first?'

Lottie sighs and looks slightly put out.

'She has her own shower. And towels.'

'She's right. I do! And I really need to brush my teeth,' I say, and then panic, worrying that Lottie thinks I'm suggesting her intimate area is not mountain fresh. 'You know what it's like, after a nap, sorry about that.'

It occurs to me that there has been a lot of physical contact but no mouth to mouth kissing. Just like *Pretty Woman*. They never treated me like a prostitute, I think, ironically. This is exactly what I wanted, so why do I feel a little bit . . . used?

Climbing out of the bed, I start looking for my dress, thinking that I might feel better if I had some clothes on. I pull up the sheets and check under the pillows, and Lottie frowns at me, exasperated.

'*Chair*, Violet!'

Sure enough, my dress is carefully folded and hung over the chair in front of the dressing table. I yank it over my head, fluff my hair and smile brightly.

'Are you ... are we ... getting up now? Or ... ?'

Once again, I feel a little lost. It's not just that I don't know the rules, but that I feel as though I can't even ask what they are. I'm expected to use my intuition. This is why Lottie chose that word for the name of her company. That's the one quality she expects in her employees, and I'm failing at it.

Simon answers.

'We'll probably go outside for drinks in about half an hour. Now, brush your bloody teeth, Violet. Or the tooth fairy will stop your pocket money.'

Obediently, I leave. Even though I know I should find Simon's paternal tone creepy, it's deeply comforting.

I stop thinking about it as I pad down the hall and hear a surprisingly tuneful voice. Sasha and Richard have left their door ajar. The sound of running water seeps out, and I see a sliver of Sasha sitting and singing in front of the mirror. She's belting out 'Saving All My Love For You'. Giggling, I head to the kitchen and find Max, with a tea towel over his arm, concentrating on the cutlery drawer and humming 'Mack The Knife'. He sees me and grins. 'Well, well, little Vi! What *have* you been up to all afternoon? You're askew!'

My cheeks flush, I'm aware that my neck and chest have gone very red.

'Do you want some help?'

'God no, nearly done. Don't tell anyone, but I *like* washing up. You don't realise how much time you spend staring

226

at screens until you stop and do something with your hands instead.'

I go redder.

'Is that all you think about? You're incorrigible. Go, and make yourself decent!' He blows me a kiss and resumes his whistling.

Everyone has cheered up.

I think I've finally figured out the shower and located a temperature on the dial that is only slightly too hot. The trick is that you stand outside the cubicle before you turn it on. Then you reach in and fiddle about until you find your desired temperature, which means that only your arms freeze and burn! Next time I will remember to put all of my towels on the bathroom floor first, to prevent sliding, tumbling and almost pulling the sink off the wall.

My skin feels tender, and the area around my abdomen is particularly sore. I wish I'd brought some plain cotton underwear with me, and not just my best 'sexy' knickers. The most comfortable looking pair I can find are made of black mesh and I wince slightly as I pull them up – the gusset feels like a plastic bag against my crotch. I'm going to wear a black dress to dinner, a dress I really like myself in – it's stretchy, long but slit to the knee, with spaghetti straps and a very low back. In this, I feel like a young Liz Hurley – until I look in the mirror. Is my left tit lower than my right? Have my hips always been so *lumpy?* I wish I was thinner. I wish I loved my body, like the adverts told me to. I'd love to embrace body positivity, but it makes me feel as though the rug has been pulled from under me. When I was growing up, every single message I heard about beauty and being a woman made me feel as though I looked all wrong. Now, I'm told that my brain is wrong too – if I can't love my body, I'm failing at feminism.

As I walk out of my room I can hear crickets and the low murmur of voices – Richard and Simon are sat outside, by the pool, talking earnestly. I wonder whether it's about setting up the new company – I'm straining to catch the odd word, but the pool filter buzz means I can't really catch anything. Did Richard just say 'unrealistic projections'? Did Simon just say 'drawing board'? That can't be good. Oh, please don't let this be over before it's started. I'd been so worried that I'd somehow betrayed myself, and scuppered my chances with a stupid, unconscious gaffe. But maybe I didn't really have a chance in the first place.

Out of nowhere, I hear a voice in the back of my head, quiet but defiant. *These people are wasting your time.* For a second, I'm jolted by anger. These people can *afford* to waste my time. They don't know what it's like to have nothing, to be a financial fuck up, to be pursued by an endless, low-level sense of dread that you never get to take a holiday from. Perhaps Lottie and Simon just don't understand that they're dangling a life-changing opportunity in front of me, because they can't imagine how it feels to live a life that needs to be changed so badly.

As I get closer, Simon and Richard stop talking and smile at me. A glossy black box rests on the table between them, and I see three lines of bold white writing. *Cards Against Humanity.* Richard looks up.

'Violet, you're going to love this game! It's . . . '

I smile tightly, and my response sounds a little whinier and bitchier than I mean it to.

'Yeah, yeah, I'm familiar.'

This was a great favourite of Mark's, but it gets old when you're forced to play every time you go to a dinner party. No card combination can shock me when it's played by someone who has just given me a virtual tour of Borough Market in order to explain exactly how they assembled their cheeseboard.

Simon grins.

'We played it at Christmas and my sister got *so offended*. It's pretty dark! It's got a real cult following.'

My eyes bulge with the effort of remaining unrolled. I force a laugh.

'Yeah, it's a cult with hundreds of millions of members! Like Scientology!'

I hear Sasha's voice.

'Oh, I see you've got that out. How *original*. What is it with stupid bloody boys and that stupid bloody game?'

I feel another unexpected wave of fondness for Sasha.

'OK, I'll play,' she says. 'But I want to read the cards out first.'

Richard sits up slightly.

'You mean, you want to be the Card Czar!'

This time I don't hold back and synchronise my grimace with Sasha's.

Lottie arrives, followed by Max and Mimi, who have linked their arms. Sasha disappears to the kitchen, returning with a tray, a bucket and wine glasses. Max starts shuffling and gives us each ten cards. He reads the first question.

'What do old people smell like?'

I select a card that reads 'Dead babies' and put it on the pile, just after Mimi adds hers. Once everyone has selected something, Max shuffles.

'So, old people smell like ... Trying to remember what music was! Uncut Daddy dick! Old people smell like a windmill full of corpses! Dead babies! And father-daughter incest! Old people smell like my collection of high tech sex toys! And the winner is ... Dead babies! Lottie, I assume that was you! I mean, you're always playing the dead baby card!'

Everyone else has gone very, very quiet.

'Um, that was my card!' I say.

Simon's face reddens, then turns icy white.

'What. The. Fuck. Violet! What's wrong with you?'

I don't know how I've done it, but I've ruined the evening, the group, the holiday. My face burns for a moment, and then I feel icy. Once again, I've broken the rules, without knowing what they were.

Very quietly, and deliberately, Lottie speaks.

'Max. You *know* that was a shitty thing to say. You need to apologise.'

I open my mouth and shut it again. I don't understand. Max takes a deep breath.

'Lottie, relax. That was a bad joke. I got carried away. Chill out.'

He's trying to sound relaxed, but his face has taken on a greenish tinge. Simon starts to interrupt him, and then Sasha jumps in.

'Don't shout at Violet. Did you tell her? How could she have known? I can't believe that no one thought to take that card out, you must have known it was in there.'

'Know what?' I ask, even though it's horribly, horribly obvious. I think I'm trying to state my innocence, but as soon as the words come out of my mouth, I realise I'm probably making everything worse. Richard tries to fix things.

'Let's play something else. Does everyone know the Hat Game?'

Lottie gets up.

'I'm going to bed. I don't want to play any more.'

Mimi reaches for her arm.

'Let me come with you.'

'No, I'm … I'm …' Lottie blinks very hard, and wails, briefly and sharply.

I look at Simon, assuming he'll leap up and go with her, but he's staring at a distant point in the sky, his face fixed, expressionless. I get up to comfort Lottie, and Simon snaps back to reality.

'Don't touch her!' he snarls.

Max rolls his eyes. 'Well, thanks for another fucking charming evening, everyone,' he mutters, getting up and shoving his chair with such ferocity that it tips over. It's horrible.

'I'm going for a walk,' I say. No one reacts.

My plan is to pace. I'm going to walk up and down this straight bit of road, and avoid getting lost, and when I'm tired, or when it starts to get darker, whichever happens first, I'll sneak back into the villa and go to bed. First thing tomorrow, I'll go home.

My head aches as I scan every single interaction I've had with Lottie and Simon, looking for information, looking for evidence. Did they tell me about this, in a subtle, adult way, and I totally failed to notice? Dead babies. Two words. A tragedy with a greater weight than I will ever be able to comprehend.

They have always seemed so urbane, so polished. I can't

imagine them ever being mildly inconvenienced, let alone being brought to their knees by tragedy. But maybe it does make sense. They can be so brittle, so inconsistent, so difficult to read. They will never, ever hire me now. As soon as the thought formulates, I feel heavy with shame. How can I be so selfish, after what they have gone through?

Trudging away from the villa, I hear my name being called. Turning around, I'm aware of pale limbs and dark curls coming into focus. Bugger. Sasha. Has she come to have a go at me too? I speed up.

'Violet, wait.' She's slightly out of breath.

I try to sound firm.

'Sasha, I just want to be on my own for a bit.'

'No.' She puts a firm hand on my shoulder – she doesn't grab me, but it's an arresting, strangely soothing gesture. It makes me think that she could be a good vet. 'You didn't know about any of this, did you?'

'Look, I'm sorry, OK! I'm going to leave! I promise I'll be out of here tomorrow morning!' Tears gather and spill, so I bury my forehead into my elbow crease. Why do I think that this means she won't notice that I'm crying? She'll notice it more! I'm like a little kid, 'hiding' by closing my own eyes.

'Love, listen to me. Hush, it's not your fault. None of this is your fault. Lottie and Simon ... they shouldn't have brought you here, into this. They're not ready, it's not right.'

I take a steadying breath. Sasha's kindness is completely unexpected, and it's making me cry even harder. She keeps talking.

'You know – well, I don't think you do know, but you must have guessed by now ... They lost a baby. Almost two years ago. He was ten months old, and he died. It was . . . I can't remember what the proper phrase is, you know, cot death.'

It feels very strange when you suspect that you know something to be true emotionally, and then your brain catches up with you and confirms it. The tears won't stop coming now, a lavish, snotty, honking release. I'm vaguely ashamed – this isn't my loss, this is not my tragedy to participate in – but the strangeness of the day has finally reached a climax, and I want to submit to the storm.

Surprisingly, Sasha takes me in her arms, and holds me very tightly for a moment before releasing me.

'Listen, I don't even know them all that well, really, but I know that they're,' she pauses, and I realise she is attempting to navigate a space between kindness and accuracy. 'Broken. Badly, badly damaged. I think it would break any of us, but they're not dealing with it properly and . . . look, I think they are going to hurt you. Horribly. They've done it before.'

She strokes my hair away from my face. I giggle, in spite of myself.

'Careful! That's my stupid princess hair!'

She cackles – it's an unexpected sound, a coarse, cheery bellow that belies the narrowness of her throat – and then looks stern.

'I'm serious, you're getting in too deep. You know you're not the first?'

I'd half guessed, but I want details.

'What do you mean?'

Sasha wiggles awkwardly.

'Simon and Lottie have . . . form. They're fucked up, and

they fuck up other people. They seduce these young women, wide-eyed girls, and they promise this sort of fabulous package, they know that their lifestyle is hard to resist. They're a powerful double act. Lottie knows exactly how to appeal to girls like you, she knows how to spot the ones who are naive, curious, vulnerable. Then, the novelty wears off for them, and they get bored. Or, they get cruel. It stops being all about the sex. Lottie will psychologically destroy you, purely because she feels angry and trapped and she wants to find someone to hurt. And Simon will watch, and play you off against each other, because he needs a game to distract him from all that pain.'

I squeeze my eyes shut, open them, and pick at a bit of dead skin on my thumb. A century passes. Sasha might be right, and I hate her for it. I despise her for seeing me so clearly, for knowing how pathetic I am. How dare she say I'm a type? I've tried so hard to convince these people that I belong in their sphere – that I'm wild enough *and* worldly enough. But Sasha's description makes me feel as though I've failed. Completely. I can't believe I thought I was special, and that Lottie had seen something unique in me. Girls like me. The phrase breaks my heart.

I don't want to give her any more ammunition, but I can't resist.

'I think you're wrong. Lottie and Simon have a plan for me. They've offered me a job.' My voice sounds small, reedy. Even I don't sound convinced of what I'm saying.

Sasha snorts.

'Seriously? They're worse than I thought.'

I didn't know I had any hope left, but I'm aware of the very last drops draining away.

'But they're starting a new company, aren't they?' I say, pleadingly. The tears come, again. 'I need that job.'

'Those fucking *idiots*,' says Sasha, angrily. 'Honestly, for all I know they might be, but you can't work for Simon and Lottie. They're bullshitters. In fact, they're the worst kind because they completely believe their own bullshit. Every six months, there's some sort of plan or scheme, and then they get a bit scared or a bit bored and give up. But they're always doing this, talking as though they're on the brink of a billion dollar idea, and they take too many fools along for the ride.

Thanks Sasha. I was already feeling sufficiently naive and idiotic before you spelt it out for me.

'Fuck you! You don't know what it's like to be me. I know I've been naive, but I literally cannot afford to be anything else. I'm completely trapped, in my own life. If someone offers me a way out I can't be sceptical or suspicious. And maybe there is a job. Maybe they see my potential. Maybe they like the way my mind works.'

Sasha sighs with great force.

'Violet. I am trying to help you. I am trying to look out for you. This is what they did to Ella. They flattered her. They made her feel special, and they fucked her up.'

The sentence makes no sense to me, but something about Sasha's tone brings me out in goosebumps.

'Who is Ella?'

She won't meet my eyes.

'The last girl.'

All at once, I feel anxious and jealous and confused – or rather, I want to be confused but the information Sasha is giving me is chillingly clear. Vomit rises in my throat, and I swallow it back down.

'What do you mean, the last girl?'

Sasha takes a moment to reply.

'Look, it's not for me to judge how people grieve. Ella was … well, when the worst thing you could possibly imagine happens to you, what's left to make you give a shit about anything? Why not start your own tiny, mad sex cult? I mean, it's not a cult, but … it's not healthy. But then, everyone here is a bit of a disaster.'

'You haven't answered my question. Tell me who Ella is.'

She thinks for a minute.

'Are you sure you want to hear this?'

No, but I probably need to. I nod.

'As I say, I've not known Simon and Lottie for long – the accident happened around the time that I met Richard. We were both in awful shape. We were both broken-hearted, his marriage was ending, and I'd been dumped by the girl that I was going to ask to marry me. We met at a party, slept together, and couldn't really think of a good reason to stop. It was one of those relationships you don't realise you're in, until after a few months someone asks you about your boyfriend, and you think, Oh, I suppose that guy is my boyfriend now.'

It's as if Sasha is dismantling her own scaffolding before my eyes. She isn't defensive, or resentful, or barbed. Just a normal girl, talking about her normal-ish life.

'Anyway, Richard used to brag to me about his "wild" friends, he called them "the swingers". I met Simon and Lottie quite soon after we got together. He made a very big deal about the fact that I mostly date women, which I was a little bit uncomfortable with. As soon as this came up, Lottie was all over me. Touching me up at the dinner table, filthy, full on, making all these comments that were obviously intended to get a rise out of the boys – ha! Pun intended. But I felt so shitty and insecure and miserable about my break up, that I loved the attention. So we had a sort of foursome, mostly Richard and Simon watching me making out with Lottie, and it was *fun*. I felt like someone else, and I really, really needed to feel like someone else for a while. Anyway, Simon and Lottie would have these parties . . . '

Out of curiosity, I interrupt.

'Is that where you met Max and Mimi?'

'I knew them a little bit before, they'd turned up at Richard's work drinks. Between us, I remember thinking Max was punching way above his weight – Mimi is, obviously, *stunning*, but Max's such a blowhard – he's got a *very* high opinion of himself, but I'm not sure that anyone else shares it. I was a bit intimidated by Mimi. She's just *so* beautiful.'

Irrationally, I feel a stab of sorrow. Mimi has never made me feel inadequate or envious before, but there's something about the way that Sasha speaks about her that makes me feel as though I don't measure up. I fight the urge to ask her whether she thinks I'm beautiful.

Sasha continues.

'It was a bigger group of people at first. There were drugs around then, too, a bit of coke. Everyone had an attitude, I think we all thought we were being open-minded and wild. Then, one day, Simon brings this young girl along. As a present. For Lottie. Which was messed up on every level.'

I'm staring at Sasha, open mouthed. She is answering the questions I never dared to ask. Isn't it funny that you can

237

have sex with so many people without ever feeling comfortable enough to say, 'So, when did you all start having sex with each other?'

Sasha gives my hands a look of extreme exasperation and continues.

'Ella was sweet, but far, far too young. In her twenties, just very immature for her age. And Simon and Lottie treated her like a new, naughty puppy. They were obsessed with her. She was all they could talk about. And they would do anything for her. At first I was pissed off because it threw off the balance of the group. Especially because I think Simon liked to use Ella to wind up Lottie, he wasn't above playing them off against each other. And Ella could be ...' Sasha looks as though she's just stopped herself from saying something. 'Well, I think most of us found her hard work. She was a *lot*. Very on, very self-obsessed. But when we got to know her a bit better, she was fine ...'

I sense that Sasha is getting distracted.

'Well, what happened?'

For a moment, she looks ashen. The tiny bit of colour in her pale face disappears.

'Well, I will never forgive myself for this. I should have intervened sooner. She was just a kid, and she wanted to go out and have fun. She didn't want to give up every Friday night for the dinner parties, Ottolenghi and saggy ballsacks. She wanted her own life. And Simon and Lottie – well, she *was* their life and if she went, they knew everything would fall apart. So they punished her.'

This comes as a shock.

'What? They didn't ... *kill* her?'

Sasha splutters.

'Oh, God, no, nothing like that. They just froze her out. They'd be really manipulative. Super sweet one minute and chilly the next, sometimes ignoring her, always making her feel as though she'd done something wrong. Sometimes Simon would be a little too attentive, and then Lottie ... well, I remember being out with Lottie once, and Ella kept calling her. Lottie kept sending her to voicemail, and then she turned her phone off. I mean, yes, it's annoying but for all she knew, there might have been an emergency. Lottie started doing all kinds of mad, mean girl shit. If Ella was eating crisps, she'd slap her hand away and say she was getting fat. If Ella mentioned any detail of her life outside the group, Lottie would roll her eyes.'

This reminds me of Mark. The threats disguised as jokes. The constant, tiny digs whenever I talked about my life outside our relationship. The way he'd become moody and bullying whenever I accidentally made him feel insecure. I shudder.

'Then what happened?'

'She had a breakdown. She'd been doing some modelling, and she stopped working.'

I'm shamefully jealous of my poor, mad photogenic rival, with her broken brain and slender thighs.

Sasha continues.

'Luckily, someone at my work knew someone at a rehab facility, and could get her in quickly, she's not really in touch with her parents. Suddenly she just seemed to disappear, Lottie wouldn't tell me anything, she implied they'd fallen out and weren't speaking.' Now Sasha is the one scrunching her face up, punching a tear back with a knuckle. 'Oh my God, Violet, I found her. I knew the name of her local, and she was with these two sketchy guys, so pissed that she was barely conscious. She was in a terrible state. Lottie and Simon had destroyed her and abandoned her. She had been drinking herself to death, and they didn't care.'

'When was this?'

'A little over a year ago, I think. And after you, there will probably be some other twenty-something. I don't get off on power play. And I don't like watching vulnerable young women being exploited.' She grimaces. 'I get enough of that at work, I don't need it when I'm trying to get laid.'

I weigh up Sasha's words. I can't tell if she's genuinely concerned for me, or simply delighted to have the opportunity to dole out some tough love. Does she want me to leave before I get hurt, or does she just want me to leave? Perhaps it's too much wine and too much sun, but I feel wobbly and weepy. If I fell into her arms again, would she catch me or walk away, leaving me to fall to the ground?

'Lottie and Simon have been very generous with me. And I *trust* them. How do I know any of this is true? Maybe Ella was happy enough. Maybe she wanted to live her life on her terms, and you couldn't resist interfering. Maybe you're jealous of Lottie, and you wanted Ella for yourself.' I know I've gone too far, even before I register the anger flashing in Sasha's eyes.

'Yeah, well, maybe I don't want to help you. Maybe it's just that I don't want you on my conscience, too. This is a good time for you to go. It's only going to get harder, and you're the one who stands to get hurt. It's time for you to go back to ... whatever it is you do and move on. I'll help you, if I can. But you need to be very careful. If it's just sex, that's fine – but you cannot even think about having

240

an emotional relationship with Simon and Lottie.' Her voice softens. 'Love, I know it's hard. I've seen how good they make you feel, how dazzling they are when they're on form. But it's not real. It feels awful now, but it's only going to get worse later. Please, take me seriously. Get out while you can.'

She stretches out her arms, as if she's going to hug me again. As she moves towards me, I push her away.

'Oh, fuck off! At least Simon and Lottie are nice to me most of the time! At least they don't make fun of my hair! You're the one who's been constantly putting me down! You can't bear the idea that I'm ambitious, and I have things to say. I think you're jealous of Lottie, and of me, and you can't even admit how insecure you are.'

Sasha is white with rage.

'How dare you? My entire career is about helping women, making their lives better. I have come to you, *on my holiday,* to help.' She gulps. 'Look, you're upset, now I'm upset – just take it back, we'll move on from this, and I'll help you as much as I can with whatever you want to do next.'

'I meant every word, you stupid, fucking bitch. And I never want to see you again,' I howl. Sasha turns on the heel of her Teva, and walks back to the house, away from me.

I don't believe that Lottie and Simon don't feel anything for me. Surely I'm not so naive that I can't tell the difference between genuine passion and tenderness, and a pair of people playing a game? Maybe this Ella is a cautionary tale – and if I can work out what she did wrong, I can make sure that Lottie and Simon don't go off me. If I can fix my mistake, I can become the girl that Lottie and Simon need me to be. I'm convinced that there is a clue buried within Sasha's words. If I'm very good and try very hard, maybe I can fix them. There has to be a way that I can make everything better – including myself.

Chapter Eighteen

The villa is dark when I return. I can hear the sound of crickets in the garden, and the dull hum of the kitchen fridge, but no human voices at all, even though I was braced to come back and find myself in the middle of another argument.

I'm exhausted but twitching with adrenaline. I lie on my bed in my clothes. I don't remember falling asleep, but I have a wide range of nightmares. Sometimes these are vague and shadowy, difficult to describe, but at one point I'm wide awake, still lying in bed, as the others stand around me, staring. I try to get up, but my own body seems to be pinning me to the mattress. When I'm really awake, I'm clammy and shivering. The sweat has marked the sheet with the shape of my body, I've turned the room into a crime scene.

My brain is burned out, I'm too exhausted to think clearly. I could book a taxi now, pay however much it costs for the next flight home and write this off as more proof that my life is just one long, expensive disaster. But honestly, I'm not sure I have the energy to put on a pair of shoes, never mind go to an airport by myself. My brain won't stop repeating Sasha's words, it's as if a tiny projection of her head is orbiting my own, like the cartoon cliché.

I've been exploited. I've been lied to. I've been hurt. But these people are *grieving*. I try, with my pounding head and dry mouth and sense of fuzzy, panicky paranoia, to imagine how this loss could feel. I wonder what it would be like to lose Mark's child, *any* child. I can't do it. I'm angry, angry, angry. I hate Sasha. I hate myself. I hate the fact that I'm stuck here, and it's horrible, but there's nowhere else for me to go. Nobody wants me.

I'm overwhelmed with self-pity. I cry angrily, desperately, picking up objects, thinking about throwing them against windows and mirrors, and losing my nerve. I cry as though I'm throwing up, wailing until my throat is raw, going beyond the point at which there's still anything left to come out. I howl into a pillow, and howl more when I realise it's made of some kind of odd anti-allergy fabric, and designed to repel liquid, rather than absorb it. There is nowhere for my tears to go, they bounce against my skin like hail, my face is getting redder and pulpier and even more furious looking and I *am* furious, furious with myself for failing to fully understand what true tragedy is, and furious with Sasha for seeing me, and making it impossible for me to pretend.

I'm sure that most girls, better girls than me, would be robbed of their appetite at this point. Only a monster would, in this moment, think of food. But that's what I crave. I need true oblivion, and more wine won't do it. I have to find something to fill me up.

I catch myself thinking, *Simon has fudged the truth*

and suddenly bloody fudge is all I can think about, I need something sweet and dense and filling. I find a robe bunched against a hook on the bathroom door, it's too short, slightly scratchy. When I try to fling it on, I discover that the front barely covers one breast when it should be generously shrouding two. I feel disgusting. I am the fat and the furious, and that thought makes me smile for half a second, and before I'm really aware of where I'm going or what my plan is, I'm in the kitchen. Cereal, I could eat a whole box of cereal, and of course these fucking forty-somethings don't have the bullshit chocolate sugar-coated corn syrup crack nonsense I need, so I make do with sad, sugar-free muesli. I take a bottle of milk from the fridge, a hunk of vivid orange cheese, a block of chocolate. I find an improbably long sleeve of cone-shaped crisps, barbacoa? Does that mean barbecue flavoured? Opening and closing cupboard doors in a panic, I search for a bowl, I've got to find a bowl before someone finds me here. Who am I kidding? I can just tip the muesli directly into my mouth. It wouldn't be the first time. Still, I find something that will do, and grabbing it with a sweaty hand I dash back to my room with my haul.

I pause reverentially for a second.

I think of drug addicts in films, setting up lighters and teaspoons before a big binge. I take a breath and fill the bowl to the brim with muesli, realising it isn't even an eating bowl, it's a big plastic one that you're supposed to use for mixing cakes or washing up. I swallow and swallow, more quickly than I can breathe, I don't taste a thing. I don't touch the cheese, proof that I'm *not* mad, I *do* have some control, but everything else is gone within twenty minutes.

Then I turn on the taps, turn on the shower just in case anyone can hear me. I push the handle of my toothbrush down my throat and vomit. My body is so slick with sweat that it's hard to balance against the toilet, but I keep going, pushing myself, acid leaking from every pore of my body until there isn't even any bile left.

Breathing through my mouth, in jagged little bursts, I rinse the toothbrush so that I can brush my teeth. I'm so tired. I am so fucking tired of myself. Lying down on my sweaty sheets, I pull the covers up to my chin. Then I wrap my arms around myself tightly, hugging myself so hard that my shoulder blades hurt, and I go to sleep.

The next morning, Lottie and Simon have left the villa. After waking up, I wait outside their door, listening to silence for ten minutes before knocking. There is no answer. Pushing the handle and peeping through the crack, I see a mess of crumpled sheets, but that's the only proof they were ever there at all.

From his sofa settlement, Max grudgingly tells me that there is a 'work crisis' that requires their attention, and they've flown home. He retreats back into his enormous headphones, telling me the conversation is over.

Mimi is quiet and red-eyed and seems to be spending a lot of time alone in their bedroom. Still, it feels as though a storm has broken. Because she's the friendliest person left, I ask whether I should stay or go, hoping that she'll say she still wants me around.

'It's up to you,' she says, blankly. Her voice is so flat and remote that it could be coming from another room. 'I don't know what everyone else is doing, to be honest, but you might as well make the most of the pool. We can always tell you how to lock up.'

I swim, up and down, in straight lines, while Richard and Sasha sunbathe in silence. There are healing powers in big bodies of warm water. Five more lengths and I'll figure this out. Ten more and the situation will start to make sense. The atmosphere is odd, part snow day, part . . . well, I wonder whether this is how it feels when you're waiting for someone to tell you that war has broken out.

The strangest thing of all is that I've made up with Sasha. I was ready to be defensive, or to simply ignore her. She started the fight, after all, and I expected her to keep picking at it. But she's made absolutely no reference to it – or even acknowledged the fact that Simon and Lottie have fled. I tried to be as sniffy and prickly as possible – and quickly found it *wasn't* possible. Sasha won't stop being nice to me.

She keeps topping up my wine glass, issuing fierce warnings about sun protection (and offering to spray the tricky bits on my back) and most surprisingly of all, starting an enthusiastic conversation about *Lace* by Shirley Conran. I'd found a slightly stained copy on a bookcase on a landing, fully foxed and appealingly emblazoned with a photo of a shiny slip, abandoned on shiny sheets.

'Oh my God, I *love* that book! Have you got to the goldfish yet?'

I laugh.

'It fell open on that very page!'

Sasha tells me that she read her mother's copy in secret instalments when she was twelve, and that she sometimes wonders whether her mum left it out on purpose, 'hidden in plain sight', to deliver a sentimental sex education and nourish the emotional parts that biology classes couldn't reach. She tells me that she used to imagine she was Pagan, but she had a crush on Lily that made her feel a bit guilty and weird. And that at school, when her friends read it, she'd always talk about how much she liked Prince Abdullah, because she was terrified that anyone might notice that she liked girls. (One of her best friends, Hannah, did exactly the same thing, and when she came out to Sasha on the last day of sixth form, the first thing Sasha said was, 'But what about Prince Abdullah?')

Sasha tells me about her work with women in the most deprived parts of London, women whose lives have been torn apart by gang culture, women who keep being told that it's their fault that they keep making bad choices, when they don't have any real choices at all. She talks about how these women are failed by so many systems, explaining that the people who are supposed to help them keep deserting them because they don't seem grateful enough, and how a big part of her job is to inspire volunteers and case workers to keep showing up, literally and figuratively. When she talks, I find myself forgetting all about the villa, the fights, Lottie's tears. I'm captivated by her passion and sense of purpose.

We steal cigarettes from Max, while he sleeps beside the pool. Sasha teaches me how to blow smoke rings. We giggle until Mimi learns what we're up to, and starts shouting, 'For fuck's sake, he told me he'd stopped!' and Max comes to, and storms off his sun lounger. Well, it's something between a roll and a waddle, and I have to bite my lip hard to stop any laughter from burbling out. Doors are slammed.

Richard seems distracted. I'm having such a surprisingly nice time with Sasha that I start to wonder whether I could

248

pursue something with the two of them. It's a daydream, really, I'm not *that* interested, but I've assumed that they come as a pair. However, he isn't making any effort with either of us. He's either speaking on the phone, or staring at the screen. Whenever I ask him a question, it takes him a little while to reply, as though I'm interviewing him on television via a slow satellite link.

I'm hoping that he might be on business – *Intuition* business – and I wonder whether it's worth trying to resuscitate the corpse of my career. Smiling, summoning a false brightness, I speak.

'Have you had any news about what happens next?'

A little light leaves his eyes, and his voice becomes flat.

'Not really, it's so hard to get anything off the ground at the moment, there's so much uncertainty. Don't quit your day job just yet! Ha! Ha! Ha!'

Experimentally, I put my hand on his forearm, but he shrugs me off.

'Sorry, I've got to go and make a phone call.'

In need of entertainment, and out of anthropological curiosity, I distract myself by watching Max. He is like a children's TV character, an Eeyore if the Hundred Acre Wood was populated by the Viet Cong, Mr Magoo with an anger management problem. He is permanently furious. The sun is always sitting out of place in the sky. The ice isn't cold enough. The sound of a chair leg scraping on the patio, or the jolt-click of the dishwasher finishing its cycle is enough to bring him close to committing an act of homicide. Mimi is sometimes craven and apologetic, sometimes furious with him, and sometimes furious with us for accidentally dropping the metaphorical matches that make Max's fuel tank combust. The atmosphere could not be less sexy. Unusually, I don't even feel like having sex with myself. There's a moment when I'm half dozing on a lounger, and I'm just aware of Sasha tucking a strand of hair behind my ear before balancing a straw hat on my head, and something tender is stirred up inside for a second, but I shift, and it goes away. It's a mental mistake, a bit of faulty wiring confusing one kind of touch for the other. It's a little bit like the never-not-depressing experience of coming home, being bewitched by other people's cooking smells and realising you have to try to make dinner out of some sour milk and half a fluffy lemon. Surely Sasha isn't home, she is just someone steady in a sea of strangeness. I'm tired and bewildered and I can't trust anyone to say what they mean. I can't trust myself to understand them.

So when Max pounces, I am not prepared.

I'm creeping through the cool room where he seems to be sleeping, with the intention of retrieving my copy of *Jacob's Room* for one last go, when he opens his eyes and calls my name.

I smile brightly, falsely, and idiotically, bellowing 'Hello!'

He pats a space on the sofa, beside him, and I plod over, feeling my shoulders droop. I'm wearing a bikini, still damp from the pool. I didn't notice that I wasn't quite dry when I could feel the sun on my skin, but here, with the blinds drawn, I feel chilly and slightly itchy.

'It's been a crappy holiday, hasn't it?' he asks.

It's a trick, says my brain, helpfully. *If you agree with him, he'll blow up again. Be diplomatic.* So I pick my words carefully.

'Um, it hasn't quite been what I was expecting, but it's had its high points!'

'It's been a waste of my fucking time.' His breathing is slightly laboured, as though he's expending extra effort by simply releasing it from his chest. He smells sour, I can detect cheap lager, perhaps some ham. 'I don't know why I bother with any of these people.'

Something feels off. It's as if my body has picked up on a warning signal but my brain is being a bit too slow and stupid about translating it. I shiver, and rub my upper arms, partly to warm myself up and partly to buy myself some thinking time. 'Brrrr!' Oh, Christ, I said that out loud. 'Um, you know, it's weird, isn't it, going away with friends, it can be a bit intense! You think it's going to be so relaxing, and then, I don't know, I think there's always quite a lot of pressure on a holiday! I remember once, at uni, we were all supposed to be going to Marbella, and then . . .'

Max cuts me off.

'Are you going to make this worth my while, Violet?'

His right hand clamps down on my left knee. Why are his hands so enormous? His palm is hot, sweaty, so fleshy it feels as though it has been padded. I notice that the signet ring on his little finger is slightly too small, it could be a tiny cock ring, holding the finger stiff and uncomfortably upright. I imagine taking a tiny chainsaw to the ring, releasing Max's finger and hearing him sigh with relief, having him realise that he's been in a bad mood for ten years because of near constant digital numbness. Max pinches the underside of my thigh, hard, and the pain shocks me. I yelp. In my surprise, I sound a little like Hattie Jacques as Matron, grumpy and shocked to discover Sid James under her bed.

251

Max makes direct, uncomfortable eye contact.

'That didn't hurt,' he says, pinching again, even harder.

I feel sick.

'Max, I'm not sure that this is ...' I really need to find the words to stop this before it goes wrong. I think of hostage negotiators. I picture a tiny me, inside my brain with a megaphone, trying to say the right thing, to be charming, to be diplomatic. Why don't I just stand up? In the slow, slow seconds of uselessness, where I clear my throat and open and close my mouth and remain frozen to the spot, Max gets up so that he's kneeling in front of me – that can't be comfortable for someone of his size, I think – and he pulls my bikini bottoms to my knees.

'Look, Max, I'm really not ...'

He lowers his mouth, closing in on me. I shut my eyes. I must be able to remember a magic word that will stop all this. I think I feel his tongue brushing me, but my whole body feels numb. Some people say that in these situations, they float out of their body and watch it from above. This is more like watching a bad play.

I can feel his tepid, beery breath on my pussy when Mimi walks in. I say her name, desperately, gratefully, guiltily, and it turns out *that's* the safe word, that's the only thing that will make Max stop. Mimi stares at us both.

'Are you *fucking kidding me?*' she growls. Then, to me, not Max, 'How could you? I thought you were my friend! This is a shitty thing to do to your friend.'

I might actually be sick now. The nausea becomes extreme, piercing. The sensation reminds me of falling over in the playground, hitting hard concrete. My stomach is churning as it tries to process current pain and future fear, all at once. This feels bad, and it's going to feel worse.

An indignant little voice pipes up inside my head. It's distant, barely audible through the static of my other, panicked thoughts.

Silently, it says: I didn't know the rules. I didn't know there *were* rules. I didn't know that you're OK with your boyfriend doing this when you're in the room, but not when you're in the next room. I didn't know your boyfriend was capable of doing this even when I tried to tell him that *I* wasn't OK with it.

Sasha and Richard rush in – of course they do. Sasha says calmly, coolly, 'What's happening?' Now, she really could be a hostage negotiator.

Mimi is sobbing, howling violently. It might be the saddest sound I have ever heard.

'They were … they … they,' she keens, unable to finish. There is no trace of smoke or husk in her voice any more, she's shrieking a shrill descant.

Everyone is staring at me, and my bottomlessness. Max is *still* between my legs. I bring my knees together and wriggle away, so that I can pull up my bikini. I hate the sensation of the soggy, clammy fabric against my most sensitive skin. I must not cry. I will not cry.

'Look,' I say, noticing the break in my voice and starting again, attempting to centre myself. 'Look, I think Max misunderstood something.'

Mimi looks at me with a glimmer of hope and I become shrill too, indignant. It's been slow to show up, but fury sets in.

'I tried to tell him that I didn't want to! He wouldn't

listen! He ignored me! I couldn't get away from him, and he wouldn't let me.' I look straight at Max, groping for words that will hurt him. 'You're fucking disgusting, you know that? You're a ... fuck you! How fucking dare you?' I run out of words. That's when I understand that I am completely powerless.

Gratifyingly, Sasha and Richard look concerned, but Mimi keeps shouting through her tears.

'Seriously? You expect me to believe that? *Come on*.'

I look away – Mimi probably thinks she's outed me, that I'm too ashamed to reply, but I'm just desperate for a blanket or a sheet to cover myself with. A really big cushion would do. For a second, I'm hot with anger, inflated with it. The fucking *injustice*! How can she say those things to me? And anyway, how am I supposed to know when it is and isn't OK to fuck her boyfriend? How can her boyfriend, who *must* be pushing sixty, not know when it isn't OK to fuck me? How can he not tell when someone really doesn't want him? No one has told me the rules. This is the feeling I've been fighting for almost all of my life. Everything I say and do is wrong. I don't fit in anywhere. I can't make anyone happy without making someone else unhappy. And no one cares if I'm happy. I'm exhausted.

'I'm going,' I say, and standing up, not waiting for anyone to react, I walk to my room. Through the corridor I can hear that Mimi is still crying. Richard and Sasha are murmuring something to her. I wonder whether they're going to defend me. I wonder whether Max will admit to what he did, or whether he even *knows* what he did. Maybe it is all my fault. Perhaps legally you can't knowingly go on holiday with a bunch of swingers and then complain that one of them tried to assault you. And a thin, tiny voice, a scrappy little animal that lives at the very back of my mind, says, He didn't *try* to assault you, Violet. He *did* assault you. I keep forcing air through my nose and mouth, those sharp staccato exhalations they teach at yoga classes, but I can still smell his breath on my skin.

Chapter Nineteen

Thanks to Google Translate and a dubious looking website, I'm in a taxi and on my way to the airport within an hour. (I'm pretty sure that the booking people are doing something dodgy with everyone's credit card details, but the joke's on them – I have nothing left to take; to be honest, I don't think the charge for the journey should have gone through.) I have a mere fourteen hours to kill, on a budget of thirty euros. I feel a pang of despair, and then I remember that I still have Simon's magic card, and access to the lounge.

When I think about Simon and Lottie, I feel a sharp twinge in my chest. I can't quite bring myself to fully believe Sasha's warning. I *miss* them. Sitting at the bar, I shred paper napkins as I think about what might be happening at the villa. I imagine Mimi ringing Lottie, weeping, calling me names, shouting at her for bringing me into the group, as Lottie murmurs soft apologies. Closing my eyes, I try to picture Sasha's face in detail, so that I can analyse it. Did she look concerned, or disappointed? I don't want to think about Max. I don't know what to think. Even though it only happened a few hours ago, the memory is strange, vague, blurred out of shape and distorted by flashes of all the times he touched me with my full consent, and Mimi's blessing.

I sip my white wine, even though I still feel a bit sick. Before I can stop it, another memory surfaces. I think it happened soon after I got engaged. Mark had been out with work people, and I decided – uncharacteristically – to stay in, I had a meeting at ten the next day and I really wanted it to go well. Alan had asked me to pitch a few ideas for Acquire's development and present them formally to him. I was genuinely excited – I'd been staying late at the office to rehearse, layering notes on notes, exhilarated by my ideas and dreaming in highlighters and Post-its.

I'd been fast asleep when Mark came in and woke me up. He slammed the bedroom door, said 'Shhhh!' and giggled. Sticking my head under my pillow, I curled up and tried to return to unconsciousness. I remember Mark getting into the bed beside me, pushing his bare body against mine, facing the wall, pinching a nipple. I remember turning away, as if moving in my sleep, elbowing him briskly in the chest, accidentally-on-purpose.

I remember Mark pulling down my pyjama bottoms, my plaid, flannel, oversized 'period pyjamas', a Christmas present from my parents that had caused much hilarity. When Mark saw them for the first time, he declared them 'the opposite of sex'.

'It's so they can picture me in them and convince themselves that I'm still a virgin,' I told him. 'These pyjamas are a stop sign. A horn halter. A do-not-disturb. If I'm wearing these, assume something biblical is happening to me and stay away.' They were so cosy, and so comfortable – I'd put them on thinking that they guaranteed a good night's sleep.

In the dark, I could feel Mark's flaccid cock hardening slightly against my bare arse. I should have worn knickers, too. I wiggled away. He wiggled into me. I did not want to open my eyes, I was exhausted.

'Mark, stop, you know I've got a really early morning. You're pissed. I don't want to, I need to sleep.' I reached to pull up the pyjamas, but he gripped my hips.

'Shhhh, shut up, you're asleep.'

I couldn't move. His weight held me in place, he was so heavy. I tried to turn over again. He still wasn't completely hard. I felt something warm and wet on my lower back. Then I heard snoring.

The next morning, I tried to talk about it.

'Mark, do you remember what happened last night?'

He looked unconcerned.

'Oh God, did I vom again? Did I leave my phone in the Uber?' He looked over and saw the rectangle of smeared glass on the bedside table. 'Oh, phew, I didn't think I'd be able to claim another one on insurance.'

I tried again.

'No, after you came to bed. When we ... you ... wanted to have sex.'

He frowned and looked blank.

'Nope, can't remember doing that! Although if you want ...' He started fiddling with the fly of his suit trousers.

'No! Mark! I kept telling you I didn't want to, and you ... did it anyway.'

He stared at me in horror.

'Violet, that definitely didn't happen. I'm sure. I would

never do that to you. I was drunk, remember? I'm pretty sure I got in and was out for the count.' He gestured to my pyjamas. 'You've got your Ultimate Boner Killers on, anyway. I think it must have been a weird dream. Sometimes you have very vivid dreams when your sleep gets interrupted . . .'

After Mark left for work, I spent a long time lying in bed, holding my hands up to the light and staring at them. *Ceci n'est pas un pipe.* Was I going mad?

It didn't make any sense. Sometimes we bickered, sometimes Mark could be infuriating but *I knew him.* It wasn't something I'd imagined he would ever do. But then, why did I feel so twitchy, so dirty, so burned out?

I could smell our bodies on the bedsheets, sweat, moisturiser, shower gel, alcohol, toast, a week's worth of cells and secretions. The light coming in from outside changed, from pale yellow, to bold orange, to purple, shadows from the furniture became distended and distorted. At some point I called the office to tell them I couldn't come in, I had an upset stomach. It was true. Every so often, I'd go to the bathroom and retch and retch. Nothing happened. The next day, Alan told me he was very disappointed that I didn't make the presentation.

Chapter Twenty

The past is a foreign country, they say. Conveniently, the converse also holds true. If something very bad happens to you in a foreign country you can pretend it occurred in the distant past, even if it was only last week. I can file away Ibiza, and pretend it was a bad dream. Sasha asked for my number when I left, and she wants to know whether I got back safely. I don't know how to reply. She wants to know if I'm OK, and I don't think I can give her an honest answer. How do I feel? At the moment, I'm not feeling anything at all. I'm a little numb, a little floaty. Nothing is touching the sides.

Because I have nothing better to do, I throw myself into work. I turn up early, before the cleaners arrive, and stay until they lock up the building and I have to leave through the fire escape. I have nowhere else to go. Essentially, I'm feeling so numb and bored that I actually start doing my job. It's not even because I'm scared that I'll get fired. If that happens, I can either kill myself or take holy orders. There's a tab open on my phone with information about an eco-nunnery in Greece who might have me.

At night, I dream about Lottie and Simon, in vivid detail, and I ache. In my dreams, I'm licking Lottie, my tongue is long, and pink and supple, and the deeper I push it, the more loudly she squeals. I sense Simon, I'm aware of his tender gaze on us both, it feels like sun warming my bare back. My face is slick, Lottie's thighs squeeze my face, Simon's fingers reach between my legs and I'm woken up by my orgasm, sweating so hard that I worry I've wet the bed. For a moment, I experience something close to joy. I feel loved. I feel included. I close my eyes, collapse into the pillows and reach for them before realising they aren't really beside me. Their absence makes me ache. I'm pinned to my mattress, crushed by their absence, the weight of their ghosts.

I miss them. I really miss them. Even though I'm trying to stay busy, to numb myself with pointless tasks and invented chores, they keep creeping back into my head. So I'm all alone in the office, staring at my phone, thinking about them, wishing for them, when Simon calls.

'Violet!' He sounds a little forced, a little falsely jovial, but to be fair, this could be because he's speaking from somewhere windy. 'It's been too long! Super short notice, but can you come to ours? Just me and Lottie! We miss you! Lottie's had a rough day and she needs cheering up!'

I take a breath, to stop myself from replying too quickly, from shouting 'YES PLEASE!' Suddenly, I'm back in my body again. Birds are singing. Flowers are bursting into bloom. An improbable shaft of light is emanating from the stationery cupboard.

Simon senses my hesitation, and gabbles.

'Look, where are you? I can get you a taxi, straight away.

I'm sorry we haven't been in touch, it's been a little … a strange time. Are you still in the office? We can send an Addy Lee.'

'That would be lovely,' I say, meaning it. 'I'm really looking forward to seeing you.'

Almost forty-five minutes later, after rubbing toothpaste on my teeth with my index finger, covering my face with concealer and pinching three squirts of Connie's Calèche, I'm walking up the steps and towards Lottie and Simon's glossy front door. I can see my old self – not that old, really – hesitating before she crossed the threshold for the first time, and I wonder whether I'd warn her off. I'm even more nervous, and more excited, than I was a few weeks ago. In the back of the taxi, anticipation curdled with anxiety. It's definitely going to be a little bit weird. It couldn't not be weird. I attempt to distract myself with sex. I think about Lottie's lips, the scent of her skin, I imagine Simon behind me, fucking me, the thrust of his hips pushing me into her pussy. Then I think about Lottie's tears in Ibiza, the atmosphere around the table. Max. I can't let Max win. I can't let this get to me. I need to kill off these demons and get out of my head and back into my body. Every so often, my head swims with a kind of nameless, paralysing fear – anxiety doesn't do it justice. If I choose to sleep with Lottie and Simon, I'm showing some agency. It might be a bad choice, but it's *my* choice.

Lottie answers the door looking oddly done up. She's wearing a shiny black basque, stockings and suspenders. Her eyes are glittering. I think she's pissed. Something is off. Objectively, she looks amazing, but she doesn't look like herself – where are the expensive, fragile scraps of silk and lace? Vulgar is the word on the tip of my tongue.

'Well, hello stranger!' she coos, taking my hand and pulling me inside the house. (For the record, it's my least favourite greeting of all time. It's just passive-aggressive, isn't it? You might as well say, 'Hello, shit friend! You have two hours to compensate for being absent from my life. Go!')

'You look ...' I don't have the vocabulary for this one, 'really good.'

She puts her hands on her shiny hips, looking satisfied.

'Well, we thought it would be fun if we were ... twins, so ...' She gives me a purple Harmony carrier bag that has been resting at the bottom of the stairs. 'Try this! Hope it fits!' She smacks me on the arse and winks.

We're right back where we started, but it seems hollow. Is Lottie trying to recreate the cheeriness of that first time, before it all went horribly wrong? Is that why she's not even mentioning the trip? Her cheeriness is camp and grating. The bag might as well contain the costume for the back half of a pantomime horse.

Inside the bathroom – my happy place – I inspect the contents of the bag. The basque doesn't have a size – just an ambivalent 'M' on the label – and it looks dauntingly small. I have a polyester satin suspender belt that looks just like Lottie's, but the stockings are hold-ups, not the right sort. Lottie, or Simon, must have been in in a hurry and didn't check the label – but I find this quite comforting. It's extra insurance. No matter what happens over the next few hours, my hosiery will not fall down. I remember to put the shiny knickers on *over* the suspender belt – at the very last minute I remember that this is a very important practical consideration when you're having sex in stockings – and then, I take a look in the full length mirror.

I'm a bit sweaty and scrunched, askew. My forehead is ridged like John C. Reilly's. Mascara has pooled and smeared under my eyes, the middle third of my face is slightly grey. I'm not standing up straight. I'm hunched, and apologetic. I take a deep breath and, vaguely remembering something I read in a magazine in the last ten years, I gently massage the points between my eyes and my cheekbones. I smooth my hair and clean up under my eyes with wet cotton wool. I put my hands on my hips, stare down my reflection, and without really thinking about it, I stroke my satiny torso, and rub my nipples until their outlines press against the stiff, plasticky fabric. I look like I'm here for a good time. I feel like having a good time. I'm ready.

I call out, and Lottie – and presumably Simon – are 'in here'. I follow their voices and get to their bedroom. My first instinct is to laugh. Someone has lit a *lot* of candles. Not the expensive, melted candles in glass jars with burned wicks that I see all over the house, but fat pillars of plain white wax. The sort a harried assistant would be dispatched to collect if Mariah Carey decided to make a music video set in a church. The bedlinen is white. The sheer, voile curtains, billowing against the open sash window, are white. Above the bed, there's a painting of a stylised putty pink orchid shedding its petals, presumably an homage to Georgia O'Keefe. In fact, the orchid is so fleshy and curved and sug-gestive that it makes me wonder whether Georgia O'Keefe was actually painting knees and elbow creases. I hadn't noticed it last time I was here, and it adds to the strange staginess of the set-up. This isn't a room that belongs to real people. It's a construct, it's made for a performance. It looks like a branch of John Lewis. I spot a white wicker laundry basket in the corner – my eyes are drawn to it because one black sock is sticking out of the side and making a bid for freedom.

Simon and Lottie are lying on the bed. He's spooning her, his hands are on her hips and he's kissing her neck, but although she's moaning, she doesn't seem to be reacting to his touch. Simon is wearing black jersey underpants, that are *slightly* too short. Even though his feet are bare, the Photoshop of my imagination has dressed him in black socks identical to the rogue laundry basket one. Lottie is staring at me, and I can't tell whether it's with desire or contempt. It takes a great deal of effort not to laugh. All I can think about is the famous photo of Sting and Trudie Styler, where she's stretching in a leotard and he's topless, with a lute.

'Come here,' says Lottie, huskily.

I don't trust myself to speak. I arrange myself on the bed, facing her – even though it's enormous, there isn't really room for the three of us. Simon is too far over. Tensing my body so that I don't fall off, I bring my mouth to meet Lottie's. She wraps her arms around me, and pulls me close, and I feel myself relaxing, dissolving. It's going to be OK. I haven't made a mistake. There can't be any greater aphrodisiac than being wanted, of having a beautiful person making it clear that they can have anyone, and anything that they like – and they choose you. Kissing Lottie is better than some of the better-than-average sex I've had. Her lips are so, so soft, but she kisses with such hunger. I hear a moan and wonder whether it's another noise from outside before realising with some surprise that I have made it.

I put my hands up to bring Lottie's face closer to mine, just because I want to touch her red-gold, silky hair. I wish I could work out precisely why she smells so good. I know it's perfume, and posh products, and a lifetime of being able to pay other people to do your grubbiest chores, but there's a note beyond that. There's something about the scent of her skin, the warmth of her flesh, a spiciness, a saltiness. I always expect her to smell a little more lacquered, to be one of those obviously expensive, touch-me-not women who lock themselves into olfactory cages of citrus and saffron. Lottie does not hide her ripeness. For a second, I think of Sasha, who smells just as expensive, but crisper, slightly botanical, slightly antiseptic. She smells like someone who doesn't yield her secrets easily, yet strangely, she has turned out to be the most honest, straightforward member of the group. For a moment, I wonder what would happen if she was the one behind Lottie, and then I get a grip on myself. This is definitely what I want, who I want. This is my choice.

Lottie pulls away and sits up on the bed.

'I forgot! Drinks! Simon, can you pour Violet some champagne?'

I look at the foot of the bed, expecting to see (and I'm not quite sure why) an ice bucket, a folded linen napkin, a single red rose – but Simon sits up and locates the open bottle of Mumm on the bedside table, and fills up a slightly smeary looking flute.

'Bottoms up,' he says, handing it to me, and I feel something deep inside me shrivelling and turning to dust. He

266

can't bloody help himself. Is he even a human man, or the script for a promotional video for a leisure centre, in badly fitting underpants? I down the champagne, which is slightly warm, but it's helping. Then Simon and Lottie start twisting and biting and sucking my nipples, and that helps too.

I wiggle and buck, and I wrap both of my legs around one of Lottie's thighs. I can feel her tensing and squeezing her muscles against mine. For a moment, I feel ungainly. Even though my eyes are closed, I'm picturing my thick, dimpled legs against her slender one, but soon the pressure and friction means I can't think at all. Still kissing me, she reaches down, cups my pussy, strokes it for a moment before pulling my knickers aside. She breaks away from my mouth and whispers in my ear, 'You're so wet, I need to feel you,' and between us, slowly, awkwardly, unable to let go of each other, stopping to kiss, we edge the knickers to my knees until I bring my right foot up and hook them off with my toes, taking care not to knee her anywhere it might hurt. She presses her thigh into me hard, against my most tender skin, and I squeeze more forcefully than I've ever dared, knowing that I might be hurting her, but needing to come more than anything. One false move, one stupid comment from Simon and I'll miss this.

I concentrate as hard as I can on the feeling, all of that pleasure and tension, the moments before the explosion. I shut my eyes so tightly that tiny flashes, iridescent green and purple shapes, swirl before my eyelids. And when it happens, I roar. I grunt from my gut. I slide down Lottie's thigh, I have no control of any of the muscles in my legs. I feel like a stuck pig rolling in mud, but I don't care. I feel nourished. Days of fear and anxiety are gone. It's as if I've just been given a very strong tranquilliser.

For a little while, I breathe slowly through my mouth, keeping my eyes closed. I'm not ready to be back in the room just yet. I'm floating through space, not avoiding reality, as such – I just feel liberated from it, as though I've been given the option not to participate. When I let myself come to, Simon is kneeling before us, grinning. He looks exactly how I feel, and he's staring at us as though we've invented an extra element, we're alchemists who have turned ourselves into gold.

It's my turn to say something stupid.

'Wow. Oh my God. Wow.' I start to giggle, and I can't stop.

Lottie strokes a strand of hair out of my sweaty face, kisses me very gently, and then stands up on the bed, steps out of her knickers and then crouches over my face. The trouble with this position is that it doesn't give me much control. I can't see what I'm doing, and now I'm a little bit too relaxed to care as much as I should. It's as though she's just cooked me a delicious, complicated dinner, and I'm too full and I've had too much wine to keep my promise and do the washing-up.

If I hold Lottie's hips, I can manoeuvre her body so that the contours and folds of her flesh fit better against my mouth. I can feel her clit swelling against the tip of my tongue, and I make it tense. The tongue is a muscle. I forget that. I lift myself up slightly, shuffling my shoulder blades under my back so I can go lower, licking, licking, and feeling gratified when she drops out of her crouch, and presses against me harder.

I can hear Lottie's breaths becoming more rapid and shallow, and I can feel the weight of Simon pressing against my legs, then his hair brushing my stomach. Simon is licking and flicking with a rigid tongue, and it feels ... good? I want it to feel good. I want this to be hot. The trouble is, I am suddenly realising, is that average sex can be terrible. If there's a moment when it takes me out of my body, even partly, and returns me to my head, the place I'm constantly trapped in during real life, I feel itchy and grumpy, distracted, resentful. Simon's ministrations feel like an interruption. I'm losing Lottie. There is a barely perceptible shift in her breath, her movement, even her skin seems to cool by a fraction of a degree. Oh, hold on, she's shuddering, she's moving, she seems to be bouncing, riding my face ... she's ... *crying?*

Poor Simon is still there, licking away dutifully. I have a theory that there are some intense men who love going down on women, who have a genuine connoisseur's enthusiasm for it, and even though they might be a little creepy in other situations, they know exactly what they are doing. Then there are the men who will go there, boldly and nobly, as if your pussy is Africa and they are Bob Geldof. Even Mark managed to give head cheerfully and voluntarily, rather than bestowing it. In comparison, Simon is a long-suffering saint. There is nothing less erotic than being earnest.

Lottie has stopped moving, but she's sitting on me so heavily that I can't tell Simon to stop. Pointlessly, I shake my head, before trying to lift Lottie off me gently. I fail, and end up pushing her forward, so that she rolls to the bottom of the bed. Finally, Simon stops and stares at both of us.

Pulling away, I cross my legs. I really, really don't need any more awkward moments in which a horrible drama unfolds while someone's head is quite close to my bare crotch.

'Lottie, what's wrong? Did I do something? I'm so sorry, I . . .'

Simon puts an arm around his wife's shaking back.

'Violet, it's probably best if you leave now.' I *hate* the way he's looking at me, as though I'm ruining his lovely marriage with my bad attitude and cheap underwear. It isn't even my underwear. God, I can't do this in a fucking basque. There must be a robe somewhere. I get up and check the back of the door. Nothing. Desperate, I open the laundry basket and rummage for a T-shirt, a shirt, anything. I find something enormous and dark grey and throw it over my head. I'm overwhelmed with relief when it reaches my knees.

I put my hands on my hips and stand up as straight as I can. I glance down and realise that it is a *Game Of Thrones* T-shirt, bearing the lettering: ALL MEN MUST DIE. My feelings exactly.

'No. I *know* . . . something awful happened, and I'm so, so sorry, but you can't keep shutting me out. You can't keep picking me up and then sending me away when I break a mysterious rule, you can't keep making me feel as though it's my fault. Please, let me be your friend. Let me help. Tell me what's going on.'

Lottie gets off the bed and walks towards me. Even though we were both just as close as two people can get, I flinch as she puts her face next to mine. Then she speaks, slowly and quietly. It's chilling.

'You can't help. No one can. You will never, ever, ever

know how much pain I'm in. You will never be able to understand. You don't – you can't feel as much as I'm feeling. You will never know what it's like to be in hell. You're happy to take, and take, and take from us, and all we ask is that you make us feel better. And nothing works. You don't work.' The pitch of her voice lifts, and her hiss builds to a scream. 'Just fuck off! Fuck off and leave us alone, forever.' Looking around the room wildly, she sees a champagne glass. She drains the dregs and then hurls it over my head, against the wall.

I feel very hot, then very cold. I can't fight the memory, I'm back in the room of pain with Max and Mimi. I must not cry. I will not cry.

Simon goes to her and leads her away from me. He holds her tightly and tenderly, rocking her in his arms, as she wails brokenly into his solid body. I've never, ever heard anyone sound so sad, so desperate, so alone. Simon lowers his voice, and says, with barely any intonation or expression, 'Ben would have been three today. Lottie thought this might ... well. It was a bad idea. Go and get dressed, and I'll order a taxi for you.' It's not a suggestion.

Lottie lifts her head from Simon's shoulder to scowl at me.

'I should have known you'd make it worse. Girls like you always make it worse, eventually. You destroy everything. With your rancid cunts.' She says the last three words slowly, taking extra care to emphasise the sibilants.

Even Simon looks shocked.

'Violet, she didn't ... '

'Don't you apologise for me,' Lottie hisses. 'Don't you ever do that again.'

Shaking, I run out of the room, and head to the

bathroom. I know I should be furious, but all the fight has been knocked out of me. I can't find the energy to put my regular underwear back on. Her words were brutal, but she's right. I destroy *everything*. Everything I touch goes wrong.

Chapter Twenty-One

I don't know what to do with myself, so I sit at the bottom of the stairs, listening for the sound of a car. Simon finds me.

'It's going to be fifteen minutes. Come and wait in the kitchen. You've got time for a glass of wine.'

I follow him, moving as though I'm made of lead. My heavy limbs nearly meet their Waterloo on a kitchen stool. I try to lift myself into the high seat, miss, and bang my calf against a heavy brass pole, while grazing my buttock. I lean on the seat, instead, pretending that was my intention all along. Simon looks as though he might be about to comment and thinks better of it. I sip my wine, which is cold, crisp and has a faint, not unpleasant, taste of clay and copper. I know nothing about wine, but I know this is not part of a Tesco Metro three-for-two deal. I'll miss their nice wine.

Simon speaks.

'I have to apologise. We should never have asked you to come here today.'

Even through my bewildered, emotional haze, I can tell that 'I have to apologise' is not the same as saying

'I'm sorry.' Well, I'm not sorry either. I don't know what I did wrong.

'I didn't mean to make Lottie upset. But she should be saying this, not you.' I gulp down some tears. 'Those are the worst, worst things anyone has ever said to me. Even . . .' I think about my fight with Nadia, because I think about it almost every day. I want to tell Simon all about it. I want to tell him exactly how confused, frustrated and hurt I am. I want to tell him that he can go fuck himself and I don't care about his job any more. I can't find the energy. So because the question is hanging in the air, and over my head, I find myself asking, 'What did Lottie mean by "girls like me"?' Even though I have a horrible feeling that I know exactly what – and who – she meant.

Simon takes a big sip of wine and looks out of the window.

'Just a figure of speech. Just something she said in the heat of the moment.'

I can pretend to believe his dissembling, panicky non-sense, or I can take my life into my own hands and make this awkwardness into pure melodrama. *Don't make it worse,* says my brain. *Stay quiet, suck it up, cry yourself to sleep and never see him again.*

You can't be brave unless you're afraid. Who said that? Muhammad Ali? Simba in *The Lion King*? Fuck it. I'm going to do it. *Simon, I know about Ella?* Far too soapy. *Simon, I know the truth?* That's upped the ante into tele-novela territory.

'Simon,' I say, worried that I have started a sentence I can't finish. 'Simon, I need you to tell me about what hap-pened with Ella.'

'Oh God. Oh God. How did you know? Was it Max?'

274

'It doesn't matter. Just tell me.'

Simon looks away, and talks into the space below his collarbone. His golden glow has turned dull. It's as if someone
has blown him out.

'We'd been seeing girls, I guess. We started, after it
happened. We needed something, a distraction, an ...
Oh, Violet, I know what this looks like. But I'm not that
guy, OK? I've always been, basically, monogamous, I've
never really slept around, I met Lottie in college, I'd only
had a couple of girlfriends before her, and I fell for her
straight away.'

Hurry up Simon, the taxi's nearly here. I don't need your
good guy character reference. It's too late for that, anyway.

'Right. Well, we lost Ben, and it was ... hell. I can't even
tell you. I don't have the words. We'd kind of stopped having
sex, we could barely talk to each other, but before, before
we'd always talked about ... *that*. I never thought we'd do
anything, we used to kind of half joke about threesomes
but logistically,' I wince, 'you know, it was never really ...
then, there was this dark point where anything was worth
a try. And I used to find women online who were into it, get
in touch with them,' I sense Simon is being especially vague
here, 'and it *helped*, you know? It was a hobby, a secret, a
way of sharing something. And I think I'd always been so
good, I'd always followed the rules and tried to do the right
thing and look where that fucking got us.'

'So did you meet Ella on the internet?'

'Not exactly, she'd been an old colleague's intern and I
met her at a party – she was so young. Too young, really.'

I must look as horrified as I feel, because Simon interrupts
himself to clarify this.

'She was twenty-four. But she was quite worldly – she flirted really forcefully. She was so confident! And I *could have* taken advantage of her,' I roll my eyes. I can't help myself. 'OK, perhaps I did. I was flattered, and we had sex, and I felt guilty and I told her that I felt horrible, and I shouldn't have done it, and I was married, and she made it very clear that she wanted to meet Lottie. That she wanted both of us.'

'And I guess it wasn't hard to introduce her to Lottie because you were already finding these women ...'

Simon's phone buzzes, and he ignores it. I panic about running out for the taxi before remembering it's his account, his credit card and not my Uber rating at stake.

'Exactly! And Lottie was really excited, at first. These other women had been really, *really* attractive, but we never had much to say to them. They stopped being interesting after an hour. And Ella was like a little pet. She was sexy, she was charming, she was even compellingly annoying. We loved being able to giggle over the stupid things she said – not that she was stupid, she was exceptionally clever, really well read. But she'd say something adorably earnest about Michel Houellebecq, and then she'd sneak out of bed in the early hours of the morning to order a Kendall Kardashian lip kit.'

'Kylie Jenner,' I correct him, absentmindedly. 'What happened next?'

'Well, Lottie went off her, I guess. You know what it's like, when someone starts being annoying, and then *everything they do* is just unbearable.'

'But – she was twenty-four! My generation is inherently unbearable.'

Simon looks out of the window again.

'We tried to let her down gently.'

'Sasha told me it wasn't gentle at all.'

Simon turns to look at me, and his pupils have a strange, shiny, stainless steel dullness.

'Why were you talking to Sasha about Ella?'

Even though Simon is the one at fault, he has a way of making me feel as though I'm twelve years old and waiting outside the headmaster's office.

'It came up! After everything went weird in Ibiza, I had a lot of questions and Sasha was the only one who tried to tell me what was going on.' Then a jolt of anger surges through me, and I allow myself to feel indignant. 'You left me! You both ran away, and abandoned me, and I was stuck with people I barely knew. Max – your *friend* Max – assaulted me! Sasha was the only one who tried to help.'

Simon's voice has chips of ice in it.

'Max wouldn't assault you. And Ella is none of Sasha's business. Anyway, your taxi is here.'

'Just tell me! Tell me what happened to her.'

'Goodbye, Violet.'

Every one of Simon's movements is fluid and deliberate. So even though everything between us should be awkward, clumsy and too painful to bear, he seems to sweep me out of their house as though he's the doorman of a posh hotel, ejecting a drunk guest and her luggage. He does not slam the front door in my face, but there is a solid finality when it clicks shut. It is cold on the street, and cold in the taxi too.

I don't think I can begin to process what just happened. Even though I want to be furious with Simon, I'm too shocked to know where to start feeling. I can't quite work out how I got from a warm bed, to the kitchen table, to the back of the car. I'm tapping out a text, when the driver turns around.

'We're going south, yeah? Forster Road?'

'Change of plan. Could you take me into Soho?' I ask, before pressing send.

Chapter Twenty-Two

Has he always been so *loud*?

The first thing I think of when I see Mark isn't weddings or heartbreak or pieces of my past, but foaming bathroom bleach. He reminds me of Barry Scott, the extremely shouty, enthusiastic ambassador for cleaning products. He says my name as though he's in the middle of having a fit.

The moment I sent the text, I regretted it. I assumed Mark would ignore it – after all, we haven't spoken in months. But because my life is being cosmically organised by Thomas Hardy at his most heroine punishing, with a little assistance from Harry Hill, Mark replied within seconds. He was free and keen. And I could have backtracked, pretended that the message was sent in error, or that I'd come down with food poisoning in the last twenty seconds, but when I commit to doing something stupid, I like to see it through. Especially when the stupid thing is happening in a place that sells alcohol and is situated within five miles of my flat.

As soon as I saw him, I knew I'd made a mistake. It wasn't that I took one look at his face and felt repulsed. The problem was that I couldn't make myself feel anything at all. I was struggling to pick him out of the crowd, squinting unappealingly at four men in suits with brown hair before finding the man I used to wake up next to every morning. Even Mark's exact height eluded me, I could only describe it as 'average'. I wonder how he knows I'm *me*, or whether I'm just one of a million blurry girls loosely defined by some high-street signifiers. Blonde hair, bland dress, scuffed Primark ballet pumps, neither fashionable nor unfashionable, smart for a broke person, stylish for a scruffy person, an Impressionist painting of unidentifiable stains and loose threads.

Mark's hug is a sharp squeeze and release, business-casual with a bonus grope. Did he just touch my tit or is it simply so crowded in here that we will have fondled everyone's nipples by the end of the night? He keeps talking directly into my ear by cupping his hands around his mouth, creating a makeshift megaphone.

In fairness, it is very difficult to hear anything in this bar. Out of the corner of my eye, I can see people mouthing 'Mo-*jeee*-toe', moving every single muscle in their faces, becoming slower and louder, as though they're on a package holiday in Benidorm, speaking English as a foreign language, for foreigners. The bass of the music is fuzzy, over the speakers I am being told to *bounce, bounce, bounce*, and Mark is bouncing, rolling from the heel of his Russell and Bromley brogues to his tippy toes, explaining 'I LOVE THIS SONG!' in a voice that is somehow both a murmur and a scream.

We're both barely on bar stools, I'm leaning with a quarter of a buttock balanced on the edge of some slightly too high pleather, a mortgage on some nighttime real estate I can't quite afford. Every thirty seconds, someone will push past one of us, pressing our bodies together and forcing me to recognise his scent, his heat. I had wondered what it would be like to touch him again, whether some old muscle memory would take over and I'd throw myself into his arms, finding him as revoltingly irresistible as the smell of fried food.

It isn't like that. Right now, being with Mark feels like seeing an old picture taken during the school holidays. He's a centre parting, a silly hat, a sweet squint and sunburn. I feel affection, confusion, but no real nostalgia. The longing is missing. He leans into my ear and yells something that sounds like 'first night out since the hippopotamus merger' and I nearly say 'What?' but change it to 'Right!' just in time. I'm bored, and I'm lonely. I'm surrounded by people who seem to be having the greatest night of their lives. If you could measure joy in decibels, they have all found enlightenment. Once I would have blamed Mark for being boring, but I think I'm the outlier, the malcontent. Who am I to claim I'm better than sugary alcohol and Ed Sheeran?

'YOU LOOK STUNNING!' says Mark, just as I'm jostled from behind by a very young boy who, stumbling on his return from the bar, pours a little rum and something into my hair. 'WATCH IT! CAREFUL! PRICK!' Mark screams, and I wince, waiting for a confrontation. The boy visibly reddens, even though he is already illuminated by pink neon. He scuttles away, even though the bar is so dense with bodies that scuttling seems impossible. Mark leans closer, and I think he is saying, 'You broke my arm, you know.'

'I broke what? Oh, *heart*.'

'Why? Why did you leave me?' He doesn't sound angry, just confused. He seems a little lost, and a lot softer than I remember him being. I feel something within me yield. My boredom softens into calm, my brittle, cloudy fury becomes something limpid and liquid. He cares about me. He might be the only person who still cares about me. Right now, I can't afford to think about Simon and Lottie, or the fact that my life has become an untenable, unfixable disaster. I'm a hot mess, beyond repair, but right now Mark can see some good in me. I drain my sticky, fizzy drink and lean into him.

'I think we need to go somewhere quieter, where we can talk properly. Maybe your place?'

I'm wondering whether Mark will tell me, in no uncertain terms, that I am not to darken his door again, but he smiles, picks up his phone and orders a taxi.

He's really not so bad. In fact, nothing is as bad as it seems. I'm also smiling fondly at a plastic stirrer with a tiny pineapple on the tip. Perhaps all I needed was a little time, and a lot of alcohol. I just think about everything too much. My life would be so much nicer if I could just learn to stop thinking.

Chapter Twenty-Three

Mark might not have made me happy, but I didn't want to hurt him. And I hurt him badly. No one should ever have to reach into their girlfriend's handbag, looking for chewing gum, and discover a scrappy bit of paper with their name at the top of a long list of reasons not to be with them.

For a week after my fight with Nadia, I kept trying to persuade myself that I *had* to marry Mark. I just had cold feet! It would be weird if I didn't have anxiety attacks when I thought about making a lifelong commitment to him in front of our families and friends. I was being selfish and immature. Feelings weren't facts. I was lucky. I didn't know how lucky I was. But one day, on the bus, I was looking at my notebook – it was lists on lists, an initially colour-coded symphony of administration that had degenerated into a series of scrawls such as 'Do cousins need +1s?' and 'Tiered cakes made of cheese – for veggies? Vegan option? INVESTIGATE!!!' – and I started filling in a new page of pastel coloured daydreams.

Run away to Brighton???

Obscure illness? Get sick and ask for delay?

Cheat on Mark?

And then, a silly, stream of conscious scribble: Trapped trapped trapped unhappy trapped so unhappy so scared so trapped so trapped so trapped.

It was a Saturday morning. I was supposed to be going for a final dress fitting. Mum had transferred some cash to my account to pay for it. She said she wanted to be there to see it, but it clashed with her monthly church choir committee meeting. She was angry with me for booking the fitting for when she was busy – and I was angry with her because she wouldn't consider changing her plans for me.

Mark had offered me a lift, I thought it would be quicker to get the Tube, and we were having a half-hearted argument about it. Outside, the wind whipped the rain against the side of a building. It was unseasonably cold, and we were both looking for excuses to stay inside.

Mark asked for gum seconds after he had his hand in my bag. He was always taking mints and lip balm without asking. I rolled my eyes.

'Didn't you just brush your teeth?'

He pulled out the bit of paper, something had caught his eye.

'Oooh, what's this, Vi? Are you sweeping me off my feet to Brighton? You know, that's not a bad idea, we could probably use a weekend away, before ...' He scanned the list. 'You've cheated on me?'

'No! Oh, Mark, of course not!'

'What's trappedunhap – oh. Oh shit. What does this mean, Violet? Are you breaking up with me? Do you want to break up?'

I hung my head.

'I don't know. Mark, I'm so sorry.'

'But we're getting married!'

I looked at him, hoping desperately that I could find the right feelings in his face. I longed to see something in him that would bring me to my senses and show me that he was right, Nadia was right, and I was wrong. But Mark blurred before me. He could have been a stranger.

The stranger spoke again.

'We're not getting married, are we?'

I tried to speak, to find something comforting and conciliatory for him, but nothing came out.

'I ... we ...'

Mark cut me off.

'No. We can't. Not when you feel like this. I loved you, Violet. I thought you loved me too. I thought I was giving you everything you wanted.'

'I know, Mark. I tried to love you. I only wanted to love you.'

He stayed with friends that weekend, while I scoured the internet for somewhere else to live. He told me to keep the ring, but I left it on the bed. I had my wedding dress money and a payday loan to cover my security deposit. (The woman who ran the dress shop left a series of voicemails, initially chiding, passive-aggressive messages of faux concern, with pockets of anger that became briefer and denser, a kind of aural set of Russian dolls. I deleted them all.)

Honestly, I suspect I knew Mark was going to find the list. But what would I have done if he hadn't? My life might be entirely different if my dress appointment had been scheduled for a sunny day.

Chapter Twenty-Four

The first thing I notice when I wake up is the smell. Everything in Mark's bedroom has a stale, fetid scent. This experience is new to me, even though it smells very, very old. Was it this bad when we lived together, or did I just get used to it and fail to notice how bad it was?

It's nothing that couldn't be fixed in fifteen minutes with a can of Pledge and an opened window, but as soon as I become aware of it, I find it nauseating to the point of over-powering. There's a savoury, meaty miasma of unwashed gym kit, takeaways, and is that ... Oh God. His shin support, a rank piece of stiff fabric that he wore whenever he did any exercise. When we were together, I made two abortive, secret attempts to throw it away because the stench was so foul. The bacteria living on that thing have probably spawned warring sweat dynasties by now. Romeo and Juliet, in germ form. It *definitely* smells as though someone, or something has killed themselves on it.

The smell briefly distracts me from the second thing I become aware of, which is my hangover. Everything contained within my body which should be fluid and moist is now straw. I stare at my hand on the pillow and watch my fingers flicker and flare up. It's as if they're independently trying to broadcast a Morse code SOS, but the only alphabet they have ever known is Wingdings. They are also very, very hot. Everything is hot. I pat myself, looking for something to take off, but it turns out that I'm completely naked. This is infuriating. If there was a glass of water on the bedside table, I'd pour it all over me, but there's nothing but ... Oh, Jesus Christ, a half-full can of Desperados Premium Tequila Lager. What *the fuck?* I didn't even know you could get it in cans. They should be banned from sale. Why won't the government step in and protect me from myself?

For a moment, I panic, aware of a damp patch beneath me, but it seems to be nothing more sinister than sweat. I have not pissed myself in my ex fiancé's bed, and that is the closest thing I can make to a dignified statement at this moment in time. Mark is equally lacking in grace. He snorts, mutters something that sounds like 'llamas' and rolls over.

If I concentrate, I can probably work out what we did. I'm not entirely sure I want to do this. After taking a deep breath, I cautiously pat myself between my legs. The area is definitely tender. I'm aware of a familiar dull ache, a slight swelling. It's not an unpleasant sensation but it means we did it. We definitely did it. Right now, I would cut off one of my little fingers and pop it in a gift bag if I could go back in time and stop this from happening.

I can remember Mark gummily biting my shoulder, covering me in slobber, saying, 'You love this, don't you?' between chews. I can picture Mark's face in close up as he sucks on my nipple, lips pursed to a point as though he expected Capri Sun to come out. And – no, no, no! I can remember him looming over me, saying, 'Come for Mark, good girl, come for Marky, that's right, well done.' No wonder my vagina feels like a grumpy pet.

Mark wakes himself up with a belch. This would be hilarious if I didn't already feel so sick. My stomach flips, contracts and gurgles. He leans over for a kiss, tongue protruding slightly from his mouth, and suddenly my naked, sweaty body is moving of its own accord, I'm a spinning, multi-limbed circle, Vitruvian Puking Girl, rolling towards the bathroom where I start to vomit, before bursting into tears. Weeping and throwing up at the same time is absolutely a low point, but on the plus side, the sound of my sobs is drowned out by the sick noises.

Miraculously, when I creep back into the bedroom Mark has rolled over and gone back to sleep. I'm starting to search for my clothes when my phone rings. Oddly, I've left it face down on the bedside table, and it takes me half a second to panic about whether I lost it last night, recognise the noise, snatch it up with relief and say 'Hello?' before remembering that nothing good ever, ever comes from answering an unexpected phone call. Nadia called it 'Satan's marimba' and made up a special song to sing along to the tune. 'Who-is-calling-YOU, might it BE the-bank-Or-it's your-Mum-she-FOUND condoms-in-your-drawer . . .'

'Hello?' The caller is a woman. I'd guess that she's my age, perhaps a little younger. She sounds confused, and slightly edgy.

'Er, who is it?'

'Who are you? Where's Mark?'

Oh, shit. This isn't my phone. Where is my phone?

Rudely, I say nothing while hunting through piles of dirty clothes and detritus. Breathing and thinking at the same time is almost too difficult to manage. I don't know why I'm still holding this phone. Oh, thank goodness, there's my handbag.

'Where is Mark?' the caller asks again, and I'm so relieved that I've found my stuff, and that I've stopped being sick, that I don't think about who might be calling him, and why.

'He's still asleep at the moment. I can get him to ring when he wakes up?'

'Who are you?' the caller hisses, and I suddenly feel very cold and very sober. I hang up. That's when I notice the picture on the screen of Mark's phone. It's him, with an extremely pretty blonde girl, who is wearing a broderie anglaise top. She's beaming directly at the camera while he kisses her on the mouth, with his eyes closed. It looks like an advert for ice cream, or fancy cider. It evokes sunshine, holidays and happiness. It makes me feel cheap, grubby and pathetic.

I should have known. Mark probably put himself on Bumble half an hour after I called off the engagement. Mark would not let the grass grow under his feet, woman-wise. In my head, I'd tweaked him, and made him into more of a monster. The Mark of my imagination was thrilled that I broke up with him and spared him from a lifetime of boring monogamy. Imaginary Mark was as priapic and promiscuous as a team of twenty young men who have walked out of their last A level exam and boarded a plane to Malia. Real Mark *liked* having a girlfriend. I knew his history. He hadn't been single since he was fourteen, and he was still going out with his first girlfriend when he started at university – a Sally or a Sophie, I think – and they had an intense, tearful break up at the end of the summer term. Mark told me he had been 'a bit of a player' and that he was 'too much for her to handle' until he tearfully and drunkenly revealed that he found out she had been sleeping with her linguistics professor, and it broke his heart.

Mark had painted his own legend so effectively that I still believed in it. He made me think he was one of the lads lads lads, a throwback who was just too hunky and lunky to change his ways to suit the age, a seventies cliché in human form, with a flipped-up collar. But he was vulnerable. He was frightened of being alone. He had been abandoned and betrayed, repeatedly. It made sense for him to pretend to be wild and independent. It was a very simple way for him to ensure he never, ever felt like a victim. I'd made him feel safe, and then I'd betrayed him. Was this his revenge? I want to feel angry with him for lying to me, for moving on with his life while mine fell apart, for *having a new girlfriend and not mentioning it once*. But all my brain can come up with is sadness. It doesn't matter how hard I try, I can never be a broderie anglaise girl, all shining, uncomplicated light.

She was made for men like Mark – I was the big, wobbly aberration of his love life, a mess of spilled dinner, bobbly tights and too many feelings.

If I hadn't been avoiding Facebook, and all of my friends, I might have known that Mark had a new girlfriend. Mark loved Facebook. Sometimes I thought he invested more energy in maintaining the idea of our relationship, online, than he did in actually spending time with me. He turned our engagement into a big Facebook moment. He was the one who announced it, minutes after it happened, posting

'SHE SAID YES!!!!' He was the one who changed our relationship status to engaged. He didn't ask – I had a box pop up on my phone when I was at work, and I had to click to approve it. I felt hot and cold all over again, it seemed so transactional. Relationship status. It's a funny phrase. Being in a relationship gave me status. Having a fiancé, being a fiancée, meant that, according to an algorithm, I had value.

Initially, getting engaged made me feel as though I'd successfully made it to my final destination. A fiancé was a prize I was lucky to win. I didn't know how to answer the thin, whispering inner voice that kept asking me whether I really wanted to play this game at all. If I dared to look down, the game would be over. I'd become tiny, two-dimensional, falling off the face of the earth. When Mark produced the ring, my heart didn't say 'yes' – but 'You'd better. What if no one else ever asks?'

Every one of my friends wanted to get married – or rather, I don't remember anyone else questioning it, interrogating it, rationally trying to decide whether it was worth wanting at all. Once, drunk in the pub, some friend of Mark's was doing the stale, predictable routine, telling him about how miserable he'd be when he'd given up his freedom. Then another guy, a colleague of his that I hadn't met before, joined in and asked what was in it for me. He said that he'd read some research that showed that for men, happiness and wellbeing tended to be boosted by marriage, but for women, everything stayed the same, if they were lucky – or they lost out. Mark was very upset by this and kept pointing out that marriage was about committing to each other 'in sickness or in health', as though that somehow guaranteed a woman's wellbeing.

I remember lying awake while Mark snored beside me – this is what usually happened when we'd been out drinking, and we were *always* out drinking. For most of our relationship, I was too numb to question whether I wanted to be there.

It hit me that I was signing up for a lifetime of sleeplessness, waking up in the middle of the night and turning my head to avoid my beloved's beer breath. Once again, I thought of my mum and dad, and their reaction to our engagement. At the time, I'd badly wanted to believe they were happy for me. Now, I realise that for them it held the same meaning as my A level results day. They were relieved that I hadn't let them down. I was doing my job as a young woman, which meant that no one could accuse them of not doing theirs properly.

Then I would have children, and Mark would be their father, and I'd repeat the process, holding my breath and waiting for everything to go wrong, crossing my fingers that exams were passed, curfews were observed, experiments with drugs and alcohol were kept to a minimum and that teen years were pregnancy-free.

What did I *want*? What would I do if I could do what I liked? What would happen if I let myself dream, instead of simply trying to stay out of trouble? Was there a world in which I didn't become a wife, a mother, my mother? Where I didn't feel guilty about everything from hangovers to coming into the office at ten past nine to not ironing my bed sheets?

Since the break up, after I decided that I'd rather have no relationship status, and no status, I haven't been able to face Facebook. Even though I assume everyone either pities me or wants me dead, I don't spend as much time worrying about the way I exist in their imaginations – or if I exist at all. This is progress. But this has also meant that my version of Mark has been frozen in time. I thought I was fucking the *idea* of Mark, but I've fucked with the universe. I feel heavy with guilt, it sits in the pit of my stomach and radiates right down into my bowels, and all the way up to my neck. But he didn't say that he was seeing someone. He didn't stop me. Round and round go the guilt and shame, filling my lungs and threatening to burst through my ribcage.

What *would* I do if I could do what I liked? I make such a mess of things when I'm trying to be good – if I did what I really wanted, cities would probably fall into the sea.

I think about love. I think about when I've felt it in my heart, not my head, what it means to be with someone who wants you and wants to understand you, someone who makes you feel desperate to do your best, but never too frightened to fail in front of them. I think about when I was last *really* happy, and not just desperately trying to corral my thoughts and feelings into some kind of order, into what I believed everyone wanted. And, feeling as though I might as well be throwing myself out of a seventeenth-storey window, I call Nadia.

She doesn't pick up. I almost end things there, thinking that she clearly doesn't deserve my olive branch, how dare she not respond to an old friend in crisis, how can she leave me this way? Then I think of everything we've been through together. I'm angry because I'm scared. Making this call is more frightening than telling Mark that I don't want to marry him. I've never felt more vulnerable – but then, Nadia is worth it. I need her to know how I really feel about her, even if she never wants to speak to me again. OK. Deep breath.

Whispering, because I really don't want to wake Mark up, I plead my case. 'Nadia, this, this is Violet, and I know it's weird to be ringing but I really, really miss you. I would love to talk to you. Please call me when you get this. I . . .' A sob leaks out of me and I hang up.

When Nadia calls, I've escaped Mark's flat, and I'm underground. She leaves two messages, the first guarded, the second panicked, and she picks up as soon as I call her from the steps of Clapham South.

'Shit! Violet! What's going on? Where are you? Are you in trouble?'

'Everything is fine! I'm so sorry, I didn't mean to make you worry.'

'Oh, thank God,' says Nadia, and bursts into tears. We start doing telephonic, synchronised crying. I have to lean against the grubby shutters of a newsagent, and my shoulders shudder against the slats. Out of the corner of my eye I can see a very drunk man pissing into a phone box. He stares at me and rolls his eyes.

'Sorry . . . sorry . . . I'm . . . I'm sorry . . .' We can't stop apologising to each other, getting one word out before the weeping starts up again. I take a deep breath.

'Where are you?' I want to see her. I can get straight back on the Tube. I can get a train to Scotland if I need to.

'I'm on the common. Are you at home? I can run to you!'

We spend a few minutes wrangling over who should come to who, before Nadia convinces me to go wait in the Avalon and get the beers in. My heart is going to explode. I should be nervous, I should be reserved, bitter even, but *this is Nadia!* I'd forgotten what pure joy felt like. My hangover is gone. I could cartwheel across the bar.

When she arrives, she is a vision. She's wearing leggings covered in a strange swirling pattern. Her face, her navel and her arms are like polished mahogany, slick with sweat. Her glorious bonfire hair is held off her face by a towelling band that I'm sure I recognise from a university pub golf outing. She's a gorgeous, glorious amazon. I hurl myself into her arms, and she picks me up, swings me around and kisses me full on the lips.

'Love! Fuck. FUCK! I was so, so scared!'

'Nadia, I'm so, so sorry. I've been a dick. And I've missed you with all my heart.'

'Violet, you disappeared! *No one* knew what was going on. I have been so, so worried.' For a second, she looks stern. 'You shouldn't have shut us out like that. It wasn't fair.'

'I know. I didn't want to face the music, I suppose, so I ran away. But I want to stop doing that.'

Nadia looks as though she might be about to cry again.

'I wasn't a good friend to you, Violet. I'm so sorry. I'm really sorry. I got very caught up in ...' She gestures to her headband. 'It was hard for me when you got engaged. I was so jealous of you, and I *hated* myself for it. I reached a point where I was going mad, I think. I muted you on social media because I thought I was going to lose my mind every time there was mention of a "tasting" or a "fitting" or "the big day".'

'Hey!' I'm indignant. 'I'm sure I *never* said big day.'

Nadia looks as though she's going to contradict me and stops herself.

'The point is that I hated myself for not being excited

for you. I felt so envious and resentful and I couldn't bear feeling that way, so I had to stop being around you. I'm not proud of myself. I was a crap friend.'

'I just wish you'd told me about this at the time. I wish we'd had an honest conversation before everyone spent all that money on the hen do. Sometimes all I can think about is the amount of money I owe my best friends, and I don't have it. If I came into any money at all, if I got the tiniest pay rise, before I thought about the credit cards and overdraft and moving to a less frightening flat I would want to pay it back.'

'Violet, it's not a big deal.'

'It really is.'

'No, Rachel's cousin had the same thing happen to her – spent money on a hen do, wedding was called off – only she had spent *nine hundred quid* on a weekend in New York. That, I think, put it into perspective for everyone. Honestly, everyone thinks you're really, really brave.'

'Urghhhh, I think that's code for "they feel sorry for me".' Although, this sounded like progress. I longed for some sympathy, but I would happily take pity.

'No, look, I am telling you this in confidence, but you know Izzy?'

I knew Izzy. More Nadia's friend than mine, a very sweet-natured girl with no indoor voice who had founded Pole Dance Soc and had frequently been reduced to drunken tears by some of the more hard-line members of Feminism Soc. Very grand church wedding, rumour has it that the vicar got off with her brother afterwards.

'She swore me to secrecy and told me she felt really envious of what you did, she wishes she was as courageous as you. She wishes she'd never married Theo.'

'But they just had a baby!'

'Yeah, well.'

I felt briefly ashamed of ever finding Izzy's Instagram insufferable, of every laboured sigh I'd released over each #yummymummy caption. Why are we so stupid? Why don't we realise that when people are trying so hard to perform and perfect their lives, it's usually a sign that they don't really like living them?

'Nads, I need to tell you something. I'm jealous of you right now. Or maybe envious, I never quite know the difference.'

Nadia automatically says, 'To be envious is to covet what someone else has, to be jealous is to worry that someone wants what you have and is in a position where they are going to take it away from you.'

I get the distinct impression that Nadia is repeating something she heard in therapy.

'I think I'm definitely envious, then. You seem . . . sorted. Calm. We were both so chaotic and messy, and we didn't know what we were doing, and I thought we were happy enough muddling through, then . . . this. The running. The healthiness. I often thought that if we'd met now, if New Healthy You met me, the boozy, grubby fiancé-dumper, that you wouldn't like me. It made me so sad.'

Nadia looks stricken.

'Vi, love, never say that! I've been annoyed with you, I've been going through some weird stuff of my own but I would never, ever stop liking you.'

I gesture to her trainers.

'You have a whole new life now, it's almost like you've become religious. And I'm a horrible lazy heathen.'

'Dude, religious people don't shun the heathens. We convert them! Anyway, don't laugh but the thing I love about running is actually that it gives me some really good thinking time.'

Already, I feel sceptical, and I think it shows on my face.

'No, hear me out. Do you remember, we started doing it together? That first time I thought I'd manage ten minutes, maybe have a late onset asthma attack and then crawl back to the sofa, forever. But that first tiny run felt amazing! It made me *high*! And when all the wedding stuff got going, I loved having something that was just for me. Do you remember that you wanted to come with me, you said you wanted to get in shape, and I kept making excuses? I think about that all the time, and I feel awful.'

I'd forgotten all about that. The time that Nadia insisted she was only free at six o'clock in the morning, so I got up early and waited for a knock at the door, and then she'd claimed that she'd overslept, or got the day wrong, or something – even though her run was thoroughly documented on Instagram. I'd laughed it off, and pretended that it was my mistake, that I was too overwhelmed with wedding planning to know what day it was – but deep down, I knew with acidic clarity that she had left me behind on purpose.

She had left me behind. The phrase gets into my head and it seems so painfully, holistically true that I think I'm going to start crying again.

'Have we grown too far apart? Can we save our love?' I say. I try to make this sound like a joke and fail.

'When I ran, at first, I thought obsessively about you. Like a crazy person. I suppose I was a bit mad. I was fixated on the idea of looking amazing at your wedding. I kept imagining everyone in the church doing a double take, not recognising me, the bridesmaid's dress being far too big, the woman in the shop comparing our bodies ...'

'But you've always looked great! You've never needed to lose weight, or anything!'

'It's not just about that. Listen! So I kept running and running, and this voice in my head was saying, "You're going to show them all!" and I think that it took about a hundred miles for me to realise how insane I was being. How every single thought wasn't really based on anything smart or sensible or real. I was chronically insecure because I didn't think anyone would ever love me ...'

I release a noisy sob.

'Nadia! I love you!'

'Violet, I know! Let me finish! Anyway, I started to work out what my problem was – I realised that as soon as any relationship in my life started going well, I'd fuck it up on purpose. So I started seeing a counsellor, and yeah, *now* I feel sorted. A bit. Getting there. It's a big mess of boy stuff and eating stuff and daddy issues but I am slowly becoming less terrible at being a human person.'

'Teach me. Because I seem to be getting more and more terrible at it.' I take her hand and tell her about my big mess. About the way that something thrilling and fun has got completely out of control. About the disappearing dream job, and my fear that I've ruined my future by being greedy and horny and reckless. About the hideous trip to Ibiza, the shame and pain of the fight with Lottie, the utter self-destructive pointlessness of sleeping with Mark.

To her enormous credit, Nadia simply listens without interrupting. She does not murmur, or nod, or screw her face up in horror. She simply lets me speak, drinking in my words. Eventually, I run out of steam.

'So, in conclusion, while you have been becoming a fitness influencer, I am now a full-time pervert. I'm sure you're judging me right now. Work away! You can't think any less of me than I think of myself. Only my mother can do that.' I try to laugh, and it sounds like a howl.

Nadia squeezes my hand, rubbing her thumb over mine.

'Firstly, you've been through all of this alone. I wish you'd called me. I wish I'd called you. I can't imagine how scary this has been. I was so angry with you ... '

'Yes,' I interrupt, 'I still feel terrible about the wedding, and everyone going to all that effort ... '

'Violet, no one cares about that. I was angry because you pushed me away. I hated you for it – I needed you to need me. And yes, I had been jealous, and I think I wanted to punish you a little bit because you left me! You got engaged! But also, *are you shitting me?* You've ignored us all in order to transform your life from *Four Weddings* to *Eyes Wide Shut*! You've had this insane, amazing ... adventure – and I know it's wrong but I'm kind of jealous again.'

'You're not judging me? You don't think I'm a weird sex person?'

'Come *on*! I wish my love life was as wild. I've looked on Feeld when I'm pissed. I came quite close to meeting a couple until I had a good look at their profile picture and clocked the "Keep Calm" cushion on their sofa. But it sounds as though it's gone beyond hook-ups. Lottie and Simon sound ... ' Nadia pauses, and I know she is taking real care in choosing her words. ' ... really, really complicated. So, according to this Sasha person, there was a girl before you, they were horrible to her, and she went mad. And they offered you a job, they had sex with you, the job has mysteriously disappeared and they've started to push you away. Violet, this really isn't good. You need to get out while you can.'

'I don't think I can get out. I'm not sure that I want to. I have no idea what I'm going to do,' I gulp back a sob, 'but when I'm with them and they are on form, there is no one better. Lottie is this force, she's dazzling. I feel like I'm lucky to be swept up in her path. It's not just the sex, she has this aura of possibility. Anything could happen with her. Even when it's really bad, it's never as bad as it was with Mark. I don't feel as though there's a heavy weight crushing my chest when I wake up.'

'If my therapist were here,' says Nadia, attempting a Southern California drawl. She sounds slightly Welsh. 'She would say that you already know exactly what you should do, but you're going to keep asking the question until someone tells you what you want to hear.'

'But I think I might be in love with them.'

'It doesn't sound like good love though, does it? You can't be happily in love with someone who doesn't give you any reason to trust them. And what about Sasha?'

'What about her?'

'She sounds really nice.'

A month ago, I would have disagreed completely, or said, 'Sasha is about as nice as a basket of tarantulas.' Now, I choose my words carefully.

'I think she's decent. I think she's very kind, but ... I reckon she thinks I'm an idiot.'

'It sounds like she's really been looking out for you. Why

is she even friends with these people? How is she Richard's girlfriend? I mean, she sounds *especially* sane and the rest sound like a gang of pervy nutters!'

'They have redeeming features. Apart from Max. Does that mean you think I'm a pervy nutter?'

'Violet, I knew that about you the day I laid eyes on you, and I wouldn't want you any other way.'

Chapter Twenty-Five

After a few more beers, and *lots* of happy crying, Nadia left to shower and change her clothes. Now I'm home, sitting on my bed, trying to figure out a plan. I can't stop smiling. Even my gloomy, gritty little box room looks a little lighter and brighter now. I can *do this*. I've got Nadia back. I can do anything.

The trouble is that while I love the idea of a list, I'm paralysed by blank paper. I'm staring at a virgin notebook from the Tate's Dora Maar exhibition, and a bumper pack of sparkly gel pens, leftover hen party supplies. The last time I did this – outside the office, I mean – I detonated my life. I'm not sure list making is the best way to rebuild it.

Apparently the best way to get started is to write down something you've done already, so you can tick if off and feel inspired, or smug. *Make up with Nadia!* I write, in tinfoil letters, underlined with swirly rose gold. I add a giant, flicky tick next to my words, and feel really, really stupid.

Frowning at the page, I think about Lottie and Simon, Simon and Lottie, how to distil the problems they bring up into a list-friendly format – and how to tick them off. So

the next sentence I write surprises me. *Apologise to Sasha.*
I suppose that her intentions have been good. She's stuck up
for me and spoken out against her friends, when she really
doesn't owe me anything. She has been decent. In fact, she's
practically Mr Darcy, if Mr Darcy had frizz control issues
and bought most of his clothes from Millets. My cheeks
burn when I think about it – and my bastard brain plays
me all the greatest hits, every cruel word I screamed at her.
I realise that before our argument, Sasha was starting to feel
like a good friend. A person who cared about me. In fact,
she wasn't just picking a fight and trying to interfere with
my life. She was acting as though she had a duty of care
towards me. It has been a long time since someone went out
of their way to help me.

While I'm thinking about pain and humiliation, I add
another item to my list. *SORT OUT CAREER!* How
has my professional life become such a mess? When this
started, I thought I was about to be offered the opportunity
of a lifetime. Now, I barely have one job. No matter what
happens, I don't think I can stay at Acquire, being belittled
and humiliated by Connie, and only just making enough
to pay the rent. Maybe the Lottie situation will blow over.
I desperately want to believe that I'm being paranoid and
overreacting, and that this time next year, we could be sitting in the same office, laughing about it. I don't yet know,
for sure, that there is no job. Emotionally, I'm clinging to the
idea, even though I can still hear the acid in her voice when
I close my eyes. Every single one of my cells burns with it.

I could block her number and never look back. It's how
I've coped with everything, each faltering friendship, the
marriage that ended before it started.

Yet, in spite of myself, I miss her, and Simon. I don't think I'll never get over them. I could spend months or years trying to be fine, but I'd still be knickerless and in a taxi to North London the second they deigned to summon me. I need help. I know exactly who to ask. Although I don't think they'll be happy to hear from me.

I'm very relieved when Sasha replies straight away, saying she's free to meet on Monday night and suggesting we have a drink at the House of St Barnabas. I was torturing myself with panicky thoughts about where I could take her that was affordable *and* smart and cool, but not so smart and cool that she'd feel obligated to lecture me about the fact that you could find housing for four of her teenage clients for the price of a miniature hamburger. She's given my name to the man on reception, and I feel unusually calm, especially because I'm about to run through an inventory of failure and humiliation, before begging for forgiveness. I'm even wearing a new dress. I'd bought it impulsively, planning to save it for special occasions, and this is the first that has come along. For once, I don't feel insecure about the way it looks. I don't find myself cataloguing the way the dress highlights my flaws, the moment I rip off the price tag. It helps that it's not the B-list version of something fashionable and unaffordable that I've spotted on Instagram. It's timeless, too – letter-box red, fitted, with a knee-length skirt that makes me think of the petals of a softly blooming tulip. I'm even wearing red lipstick, because now I'm a woman who knows where she's heading and has a positive mental attitude. Well, I was wearing red lipstick until I checked it with my phone, decided that I looked like I had a big mad clown mouth, and wiped it off into the crease between my index finger and thumb.

Sasha is sitting on the terrace, under a heater, with what might be two gin and tonics and a woman who is definitely Mimi. Sasha smiles and waves enthusiastically. She looks genuinely pleased to see me. Mimi just manages to meet my eyes. She does not wave. This can't be good.

'Violet! Thank you so much for coming! It's good to see you!'

Oh, God, I could do with some gin too. Deep breaths.

'Sasha, Mimi . . . I think it's time for an apology . . . '

Mimi cuts me off. She appears to be in physical pain.

'Violet, I am so, *so* sorry.'

Eh?

'I've broken up with Max, it had been over for months, really, but what I said to you was unforgivable. I was just in such a state over him – that's no excuse, I know. I'm really, really sorry about what he did to you. And what I did.'

I'm totally thrown. Sasha is beaming at both of us, and I sense she's been instrumental in this apology. I feel a great giddy surge of relief.

'Mimi, I'm sorry too, I know what it must have looked like—'

'Shhhh,' says Sasha. 'You did *nothing* wrong. This is all on Max, and on us for ignoring him.'

Nonetheless, I keep speaking.

'Anyway, I came here because *I* wanted to say sorry. Mimi, everything got so weird when we were away. Obviously, I wasn't doing anything with Max, but I hate the idea that you'd think I'd hurt you on purpose. I don't know how, but I wish I'd handled it all differently. And Sasha . . .

you looked out for me, and you helped me, and you were kind when you didn't have to be, and I threw it all back in your face. I can't apologise enough.'

Sasha frowns for a second, and then starts to roar with laughter.

'Jesus Christ Violet, I'm not your mum! I was trying to be a mate! And I was a bit heavy handed! I've always been terrible for interfering, and I was just upset with myself for getting it wrong. Don't even think about it!'

'But I've been a real brat. I know I have. And I'm sorry.'

'Well, I accept your apology. Even though you've done nothing wrong. But now that you're here, we can get the champagne! I've broken up with Richard!' Sasha reaches out to high five me and Mimi, and then she cackles.

'I'm sorry,' I say, redundantly. 'Are you all right?'

'I'm good. *Really* good. He's a perfectly nice man – well, you know, as far as it goes. He'll be a lovely boyfriend for someone, but not for me. I don't think I'll bother with boys again, to be honest.'

Mimi leans forward.

'I'm so, so sorry about what happened with Max. Please believe me – I honestly didn't know he was capable of it. You must have been so frightened. He was scaring you, and he'd been scaring me for ages. Not in that way, but he was always shouting, finding fault, and then being very sweet, and making me wonder whether I was going mad because I was upset about his moods. And he'd always seemed to attract women very easily. When we met, one of the first things he said to me was, "I hope you're not going to be boring and get upset about my reputation" – that was Max all over. He was all ego, and it was my problem.'

Sasha shakes her head.

'Max's ego has been a problem for *everyone* but Max. Anyway, I had such a surge of joy, and relief, when Mimi told me it was over. I hadn't let myself admit, even secretly, how I felt about that man. I always thought that if Mimi was with him, he couldn't be all that bad. Now I can say it! He's a cunt. No, that word is far too good for him. He's ... mould on a scrotum. The absolute worst.'

'So how did you break up with Richard?' I ask, elbows on the table, leaning forward, not even attempting to conceal my nosiness.

'I realised that being happy for Mimi made me feel sad too. A bit bored, a bit defeated – I thought, Well, it's good that my relationship is jogging along, that everything is so *normal* – and then I felt so pissed off and knackered that I wasn't sure whether to cry or go for a lie-down. I fancy him, in a vague way – he could make a living looking moody in coats for John Lewis – and we have loads of mutual friends. But for as long as we went out, the only time he ever, ever made me laugh was when I watched him at his mum's trying to get up from a bean bag while holding a bowl of trifle.'

Mimi has managed to attract a waiter's attention, and glances at me as she makes the universal symbol for 'three glasses'. I get the sense that she has heard the beanbag story at least twice.

There's an awkward pause, and then Mimi and Sasha exchange a glance I'm familiar with. Once again, they're colluding. They know something I don't. I'm the odd one out.

'Look, Violet ...' says Mimi. 'We've got something to say to you.'

'We've had some thoughts,' adds Sasha.

'We need to talk about your job.'

They look so serious and intense that I start to panic. Which job? Is this to do with Acquire? I don't know why they would be the ones to tell me, if it was, but I'm too anxious to think rationally. Have I let something slip in the office, made a stupid mistake, been caught leaving early too often? I suddenly feel very hot, even though the heater is doing nothing to soften the chill of the winter evening air. My ears seem to swell, everything sounds muffled. Maybe they know someone who knows Connie? Am I getting fired?

Sasha taps the side of her nose.

'We have a hot lead for you! Mimi, you know more than I do.'

'We've been a bit forward with this one. I hope it's OK. Our pal has just won a contract to work on a new educational programme for the Guggenheim. They need someone who knows art, and social – they had someone, but she's run off to Brazil to get married – and you'd be absolutely perfect. They want to meet you this week, but they will definitely hire you unless you tell them that your favourite artist is Andy Warhol, or that you don't think there was a moon landing. It's a six-month contract at first, I think – I asked about money and it's decent but you could probably push them up a bit.'

Mimi tells me the day rate. According to my hasty maths, it's just over three times my current salary. This is life changing. This is the nicest thing anyone has ever, ever done for me.

'Thank you. Thank you so much. I can't tell you what this means.' My eyes start to fill, and Mimi elbows me.

'Shut up! It's just a job! You're doing them a favour, really.

And us. You're *good,* Violet. You know you are. I couldn't think of anyone else who has a strong working knowledge of the tech side, but who really cares and knows about the art. They've seen loads of candidates who could do the job, but it's your passion that sets you apart. Your ... what's that word? Pers ... '

'Perspicacity,' says Sasha, in a tone I can't quite read.

Mimi continues.

'They'd want you to start as soon as you could, but they know you've probably got a notice period – if you don't mind doing some out of hours stuff remotely I think they can be quite flexible.'

'Violet,' Sasha says, sounding as severe as she did when we first met – stern, almost chilly. 'What Mimi said is right. It is *just* a job. And this isn't happening because of kindness, or luck. You have much more to offer than you know. Don't wait for anyone else to tell you that you're talented, that you're worth something. When we were in Ibiza, we could be chatting away about trashy books or crisps or crap telly, and you'd be making all of these insightful comments without realising. You wear your knowledge so lightly, but the depth of it is undeniable. I'd hire you, to be honest. You just need to stop behaving like a Disney orphan with empty dinner plate eyes, hoping someone will discover you. You're giving all your power away. You need to remember that you're in charge.'

This is not what I was expecting to hear. I frown.

'That's easy for you to say, Sasha. I think you were born in charge. I don't feel as though I've got any power to give away.' Although, as the words leave my mouth, I'm aware of a new sensation glimmering in the pit of my stomach, sparking into life. A rebellious force. Maybe I am in charge of myself. Even though I've been doing a lot of stupid, self-destructive things, I've been propelled by a sense of purpose. Nadia and I are speaking again, because I called her, even though it was the most terrifying thing I can think of. Yes, sleeping with Mark was stupid, but I'm glad I did it – because now I'm absolutely sure that I was right to call off the wedding. No matter how complicated my life has become, it's better than being trapped in a bad marriage. Sasha is right. I have been giving all of my power away, on purpose, because the alternative – taking charge – was terrifying, and I was exhausted from running away. But I think I might be ready to acknowledge my power, and use it for good.

Sasha's expression is soft, even tender.

'Violet, your trouble is that your greatest asset is also your biggest liability. You're one of the most passionate, excitable people I've ever met. You don't need to charm or impress or trick anyone into giving you a job. You're already charming and impressive enough. Focus on your passion for the art, but don't confuse your own ambition with the things other people tell you that you're allowed to want. Don't let work define you, don't let it be the force that tells you whether you're a success or a failure.'

It's as if Sasha has entered my brain and switched all the lights on. I've never thought this way before. Growing up, I was told that ambition meant working as hard as you possibly could, no matter how unhappy it made you. I believed that I *was* a failure, because I earned so little, and that must mean my job wasn't as 'good' as anyone else's. I thought it was better to be miserable at a glamorous-sounding start-up than happy in a cafe or a supermarket. Perhaps this is why I fell for Lottie. In her weird way, she was the first person to make me question what I was allowed to want – she showed me that it was OK to be greedy, for sex, success and status. But is that still what I want? Do I want those things on her terms?

Mimi sighs.

'Sasha, you're starting to sound like a Brené Brown TED talk. She has a point though, Violet. After we met for the first time, I couldn't stop thinking about my career mistakes, and the way I poured all of this emotional energy into obsessing over things I had no control over. If you show that you care too much about what people think of you, they take advantage of you *all the time*. Especially if you're a woman. You're supposed to put up with being bored, earning less, doing the tedious stuff that no one else wants to do *while smiling*. I wish I'd cared a lot less and worked smarter – instead of learning the hard way that putting up and shutting up is not a game plan.'

Sasha adds, 'This is about being your own woman. This job should give you the space to do that. Your personality is an asset – don't hide it away, worrying that it's a liability. You'll probably fuck things up. You'll probably have days when you are bored. But it's not *you*. It's something that you do. You're passionate. It's great to be passionate. But if you let that passion control you, you'll burn out.' She exhales, heavily. 'This is the trouble with my office Millennials. They make everything so dramatic! You sound a bit short with them on an email, and they're weeping like Vivien Leigh in *Gone With The* bloody *Wind*.'

It's not a reference I'd expect from Sasha, and it makes me laugh. This woman contains multitudes.

'With God as my witness,' I say, my voice cracking slightly, 'I shall never cry in the toilets again!'

We're on our second bottle of champagne before I can get to my most pressing problem. These women are such fun, gossipy company that I can almost forget why I'm there, and what brought us together in the first place. But every so often I'm seized by an urge to check my phone and see whether Lottie has been in touch to apologise. My chest tightens every time I take a peek. No news is bad news. I'm desperate to ask after them, but the words keep catching in my throat.

Unexpectedly, it's Sasha who brings it up.

'So, assuming all goes well with these Guggenheim people – and I have no doubt it will – you don't need to wait around for Lottie's "job".' She makes air quotes with her fingers. 'You can have a good, clean break from them. Just what you need.'

Oh. I know I should feel relieved, but the idea of a clean break is devastating. Until this moment, I hadn't realised just how much I'd invested emotionally in the idea of working with Lottie. Even when I wasn't having conscious thoughts about the job, I'd sort of been carrying it around in my heart. Lottie had ignited a flare of hope that had been burning since the day I met her in the gallery – and it couldn't be extinguished, no matter what she called me. Yes, they're horribly damaged, and they can be incredibly cruel. But now that I know what they've been through, maybe I can make myself bear it? When things are good, there are no other people in the world that I'd rather be with. They make me feel as though I belong to them. I think about the first party, the pizza, the sofa, the exquisite tenderness with which they treated me. There has to be a way of recreating that feeling, getting back to the way it was.

'Look, I appreciate your help, and maybe I should think about that job. I need some sort of job. But I'm not sure that I want a clean break, I don't think it can be that simple,' I stutter. Two pairs of eyes are rolled in my direction.

Sasha frowns.

'Violet, this is how simple it is. You can get out now, or you can have a breakdown, like Ella.'

'If you're completely against Simon and Lottie, then what are we all doing here? Why are you even friends with these people, if they're so terrible?' I say, before I can stop myself.

'God knows,' Sasha replies. 'To be honest, I'm not sure that we are, or that we will be. Like I told you, Richard was a rebound, I wasn't myself, and I just drifted into it.'

'Same,' says Mimi. 'I wanted to show Max that I could handle him, I suppose. Why does any woman love a bastard? I've bought enough bloody books about it and I've not worked it out yet.'

'It's because they have no self-esteem,' explains Sasha. 'Still, I have plenty of self-esteem so I don't know what went wrong for me. Heartbreak and alcohol, probably.'

I'm curious.

'Do you still miss your ex?' I ask Sasha. 'You know, before Richard?'

She smiles at me. Is it my imagination, or is she a tiny bit flushed?

'I think I'm over her.'

Old Violet would have gone straight to Islington to hammer on the door until the brass knocker fell off. But I go home to my hovel, drink two pints of water and stare at the ceiling. *What do I want?* A second of heaven for every hour of hell? A lifetime of nothing? A career change? An escape route? Closing my eyes, I allow my imagination to walk me down the chilly stairwell, across the frosted car park and into the 24-hour garage on the corner. I think about buying crisps, chocolate, packets of ham, eating until my swollen stomach hurts more than my head, the blissful release of a purge. It doesn't do anything for me.

I turn over onto my stomach, inching my knickers (New Look, blue mesh, ladder in the crotch, shrunk in the wash) down to my ankles. I try to imagine Simon and Lottie, finishing the scene that was interrupted, wanting them both inside me, swallowing me up, impaling me with multiple arms and legs. I can't quite make myself come.

As I start to fall asleep, still touching myself, I imagine a woman. I can't see her, or describe her, but she fills me up, I'm bubbling over with hot, satiny liquid, and I can feel our outlines dissolving, I'm melting, lost in longing, and as I orgasm I feel a deep, profound peace.

Chapter Twenty-Six

When I wake up, I check my phone immediately, certain that a message will have arrived in the night. My wanting and wondering seems so powerful that it should force Simon and Lottie to make contact. Obviously, nothing. I shower, I check again. I put one leg into a pair of tights and check again. I type and retype a message five times, deleting several variations of 'Long time, stranger!' before settling on *I miss you. I would love to see you* to them both. Immediately, I regret everything. Simon replies straight away with *I don't think that's a good idea* – no kiss, no full stop, when all I want is a full stop. I try to finish putting the tights on and burst into tears.

Lottie replies minutes later. *Sounds good. Pub? Saturday 1ish? X.* She doesn't want me in their flat. She's breaking up with me. She wants neutral territory. Daylight hours. I get back under my duvet and spend five minutes trying to breathe in through my nose for five seconds, and then out through my mouth. I hyperventilate. Attempting to make a mental inventory of all the pubs I know around Angel, I struggle to think of somewhere nice enough to be free of vomit and football fans who have been drinking since they got on the train at seven o'clock in the morning, but not so nice that the burgers cost more than twenty quid. For their sake, if not mine, it needs to be somewhere that won't be filled with brunching neighbours – otherwise I'll end up having to pretend to be their niece.

After I suggest one pub, Lottie suggests a different one, while Simon messages asking me to cancel, then phones me. I stare at his name on the display.

'Hello?' I say to myself. I can hear the snot in my voice. I decline the call.

The week begins to get a little bit better. I arrange a meeting with Mimi's friend Agata, who seems genuinely excited about my CV.

'So, you manage all the social media channels at Acquire? And you've grown the audience yourself? Your tone is perfect for us. Intelligence worn lightly. Dignified, yet flippant. And your knowledge of contemporary art easily makes you the best candidate I've seen. There are loads of opportunities for you here. We can give you a free rein. Depending on how things go, we can hire some support staff, so you can concentrate on the big picture stuff. Your ideas are brilliant, really fresh and innovative.'

Still, I think of Sasha. I listen very carefully about the job that Agata is offering, and about whether I want it, instead of desperately rushing to fill silences, or downplaying the successes on my CV. Exciting trips are mentioned, and I ask pertinent questions about what my work will involve – because emailing press releases doesn't magically become more exciting just because you're five thousand miles away – instead of screaming 'ZOMG, *PLEASE* take me to New York!' When Agata offers me the job, and the weekend to think about whether I want it, I tell her I'll call her on Monday and manage not to whoop for joy until I'm four streets away.

Be your own woman. Whenever I feel a little down or daunted, I think about Sasha's words, and I realise that I've spent years of my life trying to be a different woman for everyone I'm with. A slut, a scholar, a smiler. A people pleaser. Who am I, really? Am I doing this for me, or because Sasha told me to?

On Friday night, I go to bed at ten with a valerian tea, a downloaded meditation app and a head full of vague good intentions. On Saturday morning I wake up early, make myself some green tea and go to the shop for fruit. I buy a four-pack of croissants, turn the oven on to warm one gently, then eat all four, cold, before making myself sick.

After showering, I try to cover my body in mango-scented moisturiser. It sits on top of my damp, sweaty skin. I look like bait for a yoghurt fetishist. I spy a rogue hair sprouting from the middle of my neck, a pube tourist that has taken a series of wrong turns. I tweeze it out, and my neck starts bleeding and won't stop. After failing to staunch the wound I pluck my eyebrows until there are barely any left. I try to fix them with a pencil. In a few strokes I go from Cara Delevingne to Bert from Sesame Street.

There's just enough time to wiggle into my red dress, check the laundry basket for some unladdered tights, to brush my teeth again, and just miss covering the front of my dress with foamy white spit, and to breathe into my hand and check that I definitely don't smell of vomit, and then twenty seconds for *keysphonewalletshoesbreathebreathe-breathe*. I'm late, I'm late, and I'm not sure they'll wait.

I spot Lottie first, tucked away in a corner, but waving her arms and semaphoring her presence across the entire bar.

'Gorgeous girl! Get over here!' she screams.

She's in full White Company catalogue drag – dark denim, cream silk shirt rolled up the cuff and unbuttoned to show a camisole and creamy cleavage, but no obvious bra. She smells like the bathroom in the sort of restaurant where you have to dry your hands with a small, fluffy flannel, and you're never sure whether or not you're supposed to put it in the bin. Anyone watching her might think that we met when we were out skiing. She looks as though she's only ever seen the word 'cunt' written down – not some-one who has both intimate knowledge of mine and has screamed it at me.

She hugs me a little too hard and then, instead of simply releasing me, she pushes me away. Nothing about her demeanour says she's sorry – or even, that she's still angry. I feel a little let down, and then indignant. Who wouldn't say sorry, after what she did? I'd rather she called me a cunt again than this.

Simon looks rumpled. He's in his usual casual weekend linens but they look as though they were last washed in the twelfth century, with rocks, in a pond. As does his face. In fact, he's so grey and waxy that the general effect is that of a hospital poster, designed to inform and scare. *ARE YOU AT RISK OF A HEART ATTACK? Know the signs!*

'You came,' he says flatly. I think he really means 'piss off' but he doesn't even have the energy to look annoyed with me. I'm desperately scanning him for a drop of warmth when I realise that Lottie, with powerful sleight of hand, has somehow got me sitting in a chair, holding a glass of white wine, with a hand on her knee. I retract the hand and fiddle with the glass stem.

'So, we were thinking!' Lottie says breathily, eyes sparkling, pure Noel Coward heroine. 'We could all go to Puerto Banús! Before Christmas! It's still quite warm, and our pal has a gorgeous place that's right on the coast . . .'

Have I entered some kind of time slip? I look around the pub, searching for reassurance that something is solid, that the walls are real, that we're not on a sound stage surrounded by friendly ghosts drinking ether. Does Lottie have *amnesia*? Rage blackouts?

Simon exhales sharply through his teeth. He sounds as though his nerves are so frayed, they're tasselled.

'Lottie, we talked about this, and we decided it wasn't. A good. Idea.'

Lottie pouts, which makes her look supernaturally beautiful, and ridiculous.

'You're always spoiling my fun! One little trip. Poor Violet had a rubbish time in Ibiza. Don't worry, Max told us about the misunderstanding. You're not embarrassed, are you? Don't be! It's absolutely fine!'

At first I am so overwhelmed with anger that I think I'm going to be sick. Then, I *am* embarrassed, I'm right back in the villa, clammy, ashamed and frightened. Lottie says it's fine. Why can't I be fine? It's cool, says my brain. Forget about it, it's not a big deal. But another part of me answers back. It's not fine. You were assaulted. You should be really fucking angry. Lottie is manipulating you.

An eternity passes. A lifetime is contained within every

rotation of the second hand of the fake station clock. I could swear that I can hear the ice cubes freezing behind the bar. It feels as though I'm watching myself starring in a bad horror film. Don't open the door! The call is coming from inside the house! Lottie is about to rip her own face off and reveal herself to be a killer lizard! Yet I feel trapped, strange and sticky – and embarrassed. That's the feeling I should follow.

Simon gets up and announces he's going for a cigarette, and Lottie tucks an arm through my elbow. It feels unnatural, cloying and little-girl-ish. She looks at me from under her lashes.

'Violet, we've missed you so much, it's just been so awful without you. I don't expect you to understand what we've been through, but you do make everything so much better for us. You make us feel so much better about ourselves.'

I stiffen, attempting to unhook my arm from hers without touching her. Operation for the socially awkward.

'Lottie, you said awful things to me. Really unforgivable things. It would mean a lot if you said sorry.'

At once the warmth vanishes from her face.

'You know, we've done a lot for you. We've introduced you to some really exciting people.'

I think of Max and shudder, feeling the goose pimples forming on my forearms.

'We've taken you on holiday. We've brought you into our home. And if you're not grateful for that, we can find other girls who are. I'm sorry if I hurt you, but I'm really sensitive. It's just the way I am, and if you can't accept it, we're going to have problems. If you can't,' Oh, please don't say it, 'handle me at my worst, then you don't deserve me at my best.'

321

'Lottie, I think I have real feelings for you. For both of you.' Lottie's smile is triumphant, not tender. 'But at the moment it's too unpredictable for me. I need a bit more equality, I never know where I am with you and I can't bear it.'

For a precious second, I have her full attention.

'I agree. And I've been thinking – well, we've been thinking that we want to make you an offer. We think you should come and live with us, and work on developing the business with us from home, while we're waiting to hear about the next investment cycle. We've got so much room, it's silly not to, really! And we can pay you a monthly salary, and sort of keep an eye on you. I worry about you in Streatham. And obviously we'd love the, ah, company!' She raises her eyebrows.

I cannot work this woman out. And even though I know in my brain, in my bones and in my soul that this is a laughable idea, some tiny, barely visible part of me is tempted. It wants to recreate the early days, pizzas and cuddles and love. It wants to have a home to go to. One where everything is laundered and fresh smelling, piles of books and forty quid candles, soothing as the crockery floor of a department store, a catalogue where everything is pristine and perfect. And if you mess something up, you just throw it away and get a new one.

I imagine myself on their sofa, a safe velvet vessel, the Good Ship Good Taste, navigating the calm parquet waters. I'm curled up, my hands in a prayer position, under my head, listening to that first Goldberg Variations aria, and the rain falling softly into the bushes outside the window. I imagine sitting down to dinner every night with good wine and comforting conversation, then, 'Leave the washing-up, Marta's coming in the morning,' or, 'There's a documentary on BBC4 tonight about Keith Haring, do you want to watch it now or shall we Sky Plus it for you?'

Oh, to belong.

I can put up with a lot of loneliness, a lot of slammed doors and silences, if it means I can briefly belong. My heart aches for a drop of love. It doesn't need much.

Still, there's a reason for saying no and she is staring at me with narrowed eyes, drumming her fingers on the table top and making me feel like a puppy standing in a puddle of its own creation. I start talking, even though I have no idea what to say.

'This is so, so kind of you. You've given me a lot to think about. I mean, I'm not sure it's right for you to pay me, not while there isn't a proper job for me to do, anyway, but living with you – I don't know! Yes! Maybe! I think I should talk to Simon, because I really would need him to want that, too.'

Lottie sips her wine and allows herself a small smile. I search for love in her eyes, but I can only see satisfaction. She looks like a woman who just got exactly what she wanted.

'Of course. Why don't you go outside and have a chat now?'

I do as I'm told. Simon is leaning against a wall, under the restaurant awning. Slumped and colourless, he makes me think of day-old city snow. He's smoking a cigarette as though he's getting through a disappointing main course as quickly as he can, so that he can have another cigarette for pudding.

I don't bother explaining what Lottie has told me.

'Of course, I'd love to live with you, I'm just worried that Lottie is the only one who wants it. I don't want you to think that it's a terrible idea.'

He won't look at me.

'I don't know. I honestly don't know. It isn't you. It's just that I know how this will end. You go mad, or Lottie goes mad. And she leaves me. And then I go mad. But she wants you – and I think she loves you, in her way. That's why she is the way she is. You make her feel vulnerable. And I . . .' he tries to look at me and fails, ' . . . have feelings for you too. And you need someone. You need looking after. In your way, you're just as much of a disaster as we are!' Simon smiles, and giggles, and then produces a proper belly laugh. The snow has melted. The golden man is back. 'Why don't we just give it a go, eh? It can't be worse than what we have now. We'll do it properly, I promise that we'll make sure you're looked after. If the worst comes to the worst, we'll set you up with a flat or something.' He stubs out his cigarette. 'It might even be fun!'

Back inside the pub, Lottie is filling up my wine, even though I've barely sipped at the full glass. It splashes over the sides, and onto my dress as I sit down. She sees my disgruntled expression and waves it away.

'Never mind.'

'Lottie, if we're going to do this, I need to know . . .' I'm not sure what I need to know. I want to reach up into the air and grab words out of the sky, to say what will keep me safe and cocooned. 'I need to know you're truly, properly sorry about what you did. I need to know that you're taking me seriously, that you're not going to do it again. Otherwise I can't see you. Either of you.'

For a moment, I think Lottie is going to throw her wine at me, and then she bursts into tears. Not soft, pretty, performed tears. Lottie is crying like a child. She squeezes my hand, my arm, under my armpit as though it's a beloved old bear. I wince with pain, but I don't move. I can't move.

'Violet, you can't leave us! If you leave me, Simon will too, and I can't, can't ... can't be,' she pushes her head against my chest. Her whole body is shuddering. Her tears soak through my dress and onto my bra. I can just about make out the muffled sentence, as she mouths 'alone' against my collarbone.

I hold on to Lottie tightly, smoothing her hair against her forehead with my left hand. It's a gesture of tenderness, but not an effective one – I know it can't be soothing. It's making my wrist ache. Her shoulder blades shake, the force of her bones against my arms is difficult to bear, straddling the line between discomfort and genuine pain. Then, after two long minutes, she sits up, takes a deep breath, and wipes her eyes with the heel of her hand.

'So, it's decided. You'll come to live with us.'

Without warning, another scene enters my head. I'm lying on the lovely sofa, and Lottie bursts through the door, furious, throwing a wet coat on the floor, demanding to know where dinner is, or why I didn't tell her about the road works on Commercial Road, or why the light in the hall wasn't on. Simon gets home, slams the door and storms up the stairs. I imagine an atmosphere, thick and furious, that is only lightened when they lock themselves in their room for noisy make-up sex, leaving me locked outside on the landing. I think about my new job, and whether they'd be impressed, whether they'd resent it, whether they would miss me when I was on a fabulous trip. My new life could be spectacular. Sex, security, exciting work, plenty of money, a shiny postcode. Why am I filled with an overwhelming sense of dread? Lead me not into temptation. Maybe it's a bit late for that. Maybe this is love. At least, as much love as I'm allowed. Sasha floats into a thought bubble above my head. *Be your own woman. You're worth more than this.* Oh, piss off.

Chapter Twenty-Seven

That night, I lie awake in bed, dazzled by hope and tormented by anxiety. The thought of never again having to lie awake in this particular bed, listening to violent arguments and clashing basslines, is such a pleasing one that it makes me want to leap out and set off for Islington immediately, in my nightie.

Lottie and Simon are so broken that they almost fit together and make a whole. There's a chance that I'm exactly the right shape to fill the gap. After all, I'm broken too. I had my chance at love, and maybe this is my consolation prize.

Lottie is so volatile and damaged. I wonder whether she can truly love anyone, or whether she just uses one strong feeling to distract herself from another. Just like I do. I'm not stupid enough to believe that I could ever usurp her in Simon's affections, but it occurs to me that I only see Simon as an extension of Lottie anyway. She's the one I want badly, and the one who can hurt me hardest. It's Lottie's love I really want to win.

I would spend a lifetime trying to love them both if it

meant that any one of us could be fixed, even though I have a suspicion that three is just as lonely a figure as one. It seems so secure, so sensible, to seek safety in numbers – but maybe it just means there is one more person who can shut you out.

Sometimes I wonder whether I am mourning something that has yet to happen to me. Maybe I'm like them. Maybe I can't love the way the other people love, and I just need to find enough to rescue myself, to protect myself from that which does not nourish me or make me strong.

I used to believe that life was something it was possible to protect yourself from. I thought everyone else knew the rules and if I watched what they did for long enough, I'd be safe. I wouldn't feel left out any more. I would do anything if there was a chance it might have made me feel real, or just included. Now I know that we're all just idiot children in the dark. There is no plan for me. Maybe Simon and Lottie exploited me, manipulated me, compromised my safety – but they showed me love, in their way. They have been crushingly cruel at times, yet they have shown me more care and tenderness than almost anyone else I have ever known. Maybe, once you've lost what they have lost, nothing is dangerous any more. All I could ever be was collateral. Still, perhaps that's true of all relationships, to some extent. We all start off pursuing our own happiness, and we all hurt each other in the process.

Yet I'm consumed by a sense of restlessness. It's as though half of my mind knows something the other half can't hear, or rather, doesn't want to listen to. What do I really want? Is there a way that I could love and be loved that isn't so horribly, crushingly complicated? Am I allowed to be happy?

I imagine a future sunny Sunday morning, drinking coffee in bed with someone I care about. I think about the times when I have happy news or sad news to share, and who it is that I would most like to share it with. The one who drifts into my thoughts when I'm under the cover and my eyelids start to flicker. The person who is usually on my mind when I make myself come. I want them badly, I can only ever think about just how badly when I am half asleep. I miss them in a way that makes my bones feel hollow. When I dare to hope that they might feel something for me, I become, momentarily, solid. For days, I've been settling into the exquisite torture of wanting, but not doing. I've allowed the wanting to become an abstract background noise. I can only allow myself to want them in the way that I want to win the lottery.

I imagine a life filled with their love, and it makes me feel both joyous and deeply peaceful. Perhaps that life doesn't even exist for me, but I want to try. Melodramatically, I decide that I cannot risk declaring myself because I cannot live without them. If they were to reject me, they would break my heart. I would bleed to death on the street, from lack of love. Then I realise that is nonsense. I would be sad, sad for a long time, but then I would get better. And it's better to feel real pain for a moment than to feel nothing forever.

So, with one eye open, trying to make myself believe that I'm dreaming, and my actions have no consequences, I type a message, quickly. I press send before I can think myself out of it. I don't know what's going to happen. I know I might not get what I want. This might lose me a friend. But I have to try. And if I get the answer I expect, or no answer at all, it will hurt and hurt and hurt until it doesn't any more. Eventually, I will be fine.

I don't know what I'm doing, but I'm doing it. This morning, I woke up to a reply, and now I'm on my way to find out the final answer. Perhaps for the first time, I might get what I want. I'm terrified. I'm also very, very wet. My shoes, dress and coat are soaked through. I rubbed some rain off my chin and discovered some mascara had migrated to my jawline.

The rain has stopped, but the street lights gleam against the puddles, tiny pools of light that throw the darkness into greater relief. My instinct is to get out of the elements and into the warmth as fast as I can. Yet, I hesitate when I see the doorman. It's not just that it is so obviously and undeniably a date venue – it is absolutely *not* her natural habitat. Also, the last time I was in this restaurant, I was with Mark, making a big, huge mistake.

But when I see her stretching one long leg against her stool, I feel an unfurling, a bursting. I *know* this is right, or rather, this is the closest I have ever come to knowing. I'm anxious, I'm uncertain – but for the very first time in my life, I'm too buoyed by hope to be crushed by fear. Looking at the back of her neck makes me feel a fizzy sensation in the joints of my knees. My bloodstream runs rainbows and MDMA. I know that neck, I know it smells of quicksilver nothings, crisp cotton and warm sand. I know that the faintest touch of teeth, a gentle breath, will elicit a gasp, a low groan, that her neck is the remote control that switches everything on. Knowing she can't see me, I trace the curve of her jawline from a discreet distance, with a fingertip. I know she will be drinking gin and she will have asked for Schweppes because posh tonic is 'bubble-less bullshit'. I know she'll have ordered the steak tartare, and then she'll order a salad and chips. I know there will be a Tessa Hadley book in her bag, and she'll cry at the end, and she'll murder anyone who shares that information. I know she'll be wearing her strange microfibre triangular travel knickers.

Unless she isn't wearing any knickers at all.

I sit down beside Sasha. She looks at me as though I'm a Scooby Doo villain, and she's just pulled my mask off.

'Here we fucking are. My *coup de foudre*. I always knew about you, you know. That day, that party. I was in such a bad mood, and I was grumpy about having to meet this new girl, and suddenly Marianne Faithfull's funny twin turns up. I never stopped thinking about you. I did everything I could to put you off, everything I could to get you out of my head—'

I cut her off.

'When I finally figured it out, I was so scared that I might be too late. Or that I'd got it wrong, and you weren't really interested at all.'

'Never think that. I was scared. I didn't want to mess you up. I was so worried that you were another girl who was so badly damaged that I wouldn't be able to love you without hurting you. So I tried to stop it before it started.'

She takes me by the hand and looks me in the eyes with an expression I've never seen before – a little uncertain, hopeful, blooming, not brittle. She smiles as though she's asking me a question and she's nervous of the answer. It's yes. I feel like I've come home.

And when she kisses me, it's different from all the other

times. It's not a showy kiss, a ritualistic kiss, a performed kiss. Sasha's tongue is tentative and gentle. She is the first person to kiss me as though simply kissing might be enough for her. I moan into her neck, and I mean it. It's a noise I've made a thousand times in a different context – the sound of getting out of the rain, collapsing onto a pub sofa after a long country walk, finding a lost key.

'Violet,' she says. 'I know we were supposed to have dinner, and I know it's impossible to get a table here, but shall we – can we – go back to my flat?'

Sasha's home is not quite what I was expecting. I only realise how much I'd been thinking about her and wondering where – and how – she lived, when she opens the door of an attic flat by Blackheath Common, and I'm genuinely shocked that it does not look like a live action set from *The Jetsons*. Where I expected glass and steel, I see wood and wool. I thought she might own a few heavy, serious textbooks, or a coffee table with a stack of old copies of *The Economist*. Sasha's back wall is almost completely concealed by three bookcases, which are all so full that the shelves are sagging. Books are piled up on top of books, reaching to the ceiling, forming an extra shelf. I'm surprised to see a lot of poetry, and PG Wodehouse. Sasha follows my gaze.

'Whenever I need cheering up, I always turn to Bertie Wooster. Also, those books are brilliant for greedy people. They are constantly sitting down to something delicious, sometimes I read one and it helps me decide exactly what I want to eat for dinner.'

She also has a proper record player, and a messy vinyl

collection. Nothing is neatly stacked. These records have been heard and loved. She removes Blondie from the turntable and replaces Debbie Harry with Chet Baker. I don't know this song, but when I hear 'I fall in love too easily, I fall in love too fast,' it's so true, so knowing, that I need to grab the back of a chair to steady myself.

Sasha shakes a box of matches and flamboyantly strikes one, lighting a candle in a glass jar on the table. It's blackened and smeared, and it doesn't have a label – it's not even distant cousins with Lottie's Diptyque collection – but it smells, not unpleasantly, of sage and something slightly spicy. I pick up the match and inhale the tip.

'I *love* matches,' I say, which is a rubbish conversational gambit.

'Me too! I'm starting to realise that I only bother with scented candles because I like the match smell.'

I offer the match to Sasha, lifting it to a point just above her lips, and then, greedily and unselfconsciously, I start to look at her face. Sasha's mouth is rarely still, and I'd never noticed how beautiful it is – she has a very full, rounded bottom lip, and the top is a perfect lower case 'm'. Her nose isn't quite aquiline, it starts slightly too high up, and she has a light dusting of freckles on her left cheek which I've never noticed before. Up close, her jaw is softer than I realised. I used to think she was all angles and sharp edges, but then it's always taken me a long time to really see what's right in front of me. This is a face, I realise, that I could never get tired of looking at.

Sasha grins, suddenly – it's a giant, goofy smile that splits her face apart, fracturing her almost classical beauty into something much more animated and joyous. Her eyes dart to the corner of the room, I've never seen her this vulnerable and uncertain. Yet, for once in my life I'm absolutely sure of what I want and how I feel. I know what I'm doing. With the match, I slowly, carefully trace the space under her lower lip, right into the corners of her smile. Then, I let it fall. I cup her chin in my hand and bring my lips down to hers. I slow my movements, because I want to remember this forever. I slide my hands to the back of her neck, to her hair, which feels soft and silky in my hands, not wiry to the touch. Underneath the sharp, expensive citrus, her skin smells of creamy petals, a secret sweetness. I open my mouth, very gently and deliberately, and she moans, again, shattering my expectations and predictions. I've heard her grunt. I've heard her shout. But this is all honey, no acid.

I don't know whether we've been kissing for ten seconds or half an hour. My hands have moved to her back, and hers are on my neck. She finds a patch of skin behind my right ear that's almost too sensitive to touch, and rubs her thumb against it with shuddering, calculated slowness. I've never felt more exposed – it's as if I've been hiding my sensitivity in plain sight, and now she's seen *everything*. We're lying on the sofa, now. I'm on top of her, pressing my body into hers. My blood is stretching my skin to bursting point, every bit of my body is engorged with wanting her, but I daren't start taking her clothes off, or mine, because I don't want to do anything practical or prosaic. I can't break the spell. I can't stop kissing her.

Eventually, Sasha's hands find the strap of my dress. She slides it over my shoulder with special care, as though it might be made of blown glass.

She draws a new, imaginary strap with her finger, while

kissing my collarbone, inhaling the scent of my skin, as I wriggle against her. I don't know what I'm doing, I'm completely disarmed, but I feel safe, no, *calm*. There's a stillness radiating from my solar plexus. With my right hand, I search for the edge of her shirt, and gasp as my flat palm encounters her curved belly. She is so, so beautiful. I cup her roundness, instead of reaching higher, I think of the weirdness of womanhood, the difference between what we think people want to see, and what actually feels good to the touch.

Sasha obligingly moves, and briefly – no! – takes my hands away from her body so that she can hold them above her head. I slide the top over and off, and at this point in time my senses are confused and overwhelmed, I feel so wound up that I can hear colour, yet I can't find the words to describe the colour of the top that Sasha is wearing. I long to pinch and squeeze and suck, to greedily take her whole body in my hands, but instead I stroke the strip of skin where Sasha's tits curve and fold over. I touch her in the ways I have longed to be touched, the ways in which I've never found the courage to ask anyone to touch me.

She has her eyes closed, and she's moaning sweetly – the curve of her eyelids and her straight fine lashes make me think of calligraphy pens, of those perfect, fine ink illustrations on the covers of thick pads of drawing paper – then, as my tongue starts to circle a delicious Jelly Tot nipple she smiles lazily and says 'Violet. Get your frock off.' I reach up to get rid of it as quickly as I possibly can – I'd happily throw it out the window – but she sits up, opens her eyes and tells me to wait.

'I want to see you. I really want to see you.'

So, feeling a little flushed, a little self-conscious, I stand in front of Sasha, and let my dress fall to the floor. I'm not wearing a bra, and suddenly I get an urge to cross my arms in front of my chest.

'Stand up straight! Don't hide yourself away.'

Cringing, I do what she says, and she looks at me. I'm rewarded with an audible gasp.

'You are the Golden Age of Hollywood. In this light you're Veronica Lake. Look.' Sasha stands up and takes my hand. She leads me to an old-fashioned, frameless mirror on the wall next to the door. Standing behind me, she wraps her arms around my waist. I can feel the warmth against mine.

'Violet. Can you see what I see?' says Sasha, before finding that spot on my neck again with her mouth. Her hands reach under my armpits, before spanning my flank, she touches my curves like a sculptor, and suddenly I feel *right*. I am wide where I am supposed to be, narrow where I am supposed to be. Every part of my body is exactly where it should be. I am exactly where I should be. I feel beautiful. Not because she told me to. I came up with it all on my own. And when Sasha sinks down to her knees, when she parts my legs, when she uses her middle finger to draw a vertical line against my most sensitive skin, I know I am. When I push the full weight of my body against her, I don't care whether I know anything at all. I am simply soaring. I close my eyes and feel some dark spirit pour out of me.

Sometimes, when I come, it's like falling into a bottomless black hole. I'm so overwhelmed by pure sensation that I feel nothing, and I revel in the escape, the chance to fully detach from my body and mind, even for less than a second.

But this time, it's pure white light. I've been shot into a galaxy of luminous, trailing stars.

For as long as I can remember, I've been swollen with emptiness, driven mad by a want I could never put into words. But now, I don't feel overwhelmed with hunger any more. My life is full.

Acknowledgements

I did not believe I was capable of writing a novel-length story with an ending. My agent, Diana Beaumont, did. All my love and thanks to her, for her dauntless generosity, support, encouragement and wisdom. Also much love and thanks to her colleagues at Marjacq Scripts – especially Guy, Sandra, Leah, Imogen and Phil (whose *unforgettable* reaction to the earliest draft kept me going when I got stuck!)

Enormous thanks to Maddie West, for her enthusiasm and insight, and to Darcy Nicholson, a true force of nature, for her dazzling ideas and her exceptional ability to make creative dreams come true. Also huge thanks to Lucy Malagoni, Millie Seaward, Brionee Fenlon, Thalia Proctor (and her genius proofreading team) and to Bekki Guyatt, for designing a cover that thrills me every time I see it. Also huge thanks to Julie Plovnick who so kindly allowed me to use the lines from her translation of Bianca Lamblin's memoir, *A Disgraceful Affair*.

Thank you, thank you, thank you to my earliest readers – Grace Plant, Maddy Peden, Lauren Bravo, Ana

Fletcher, Holly Williams, Heloise Wood, Jo West, Emma Jane Unsworth, Dolly Alderton, Sarra Manning, Lucy Vine, Caroline Corcoran, Laura Jane Williams, Amy Jones, Lissa Evans, Cathy Rentzenbrink, Nina Stibbe, Marina O'Loughlin, Julia Raeside and Sarah Bauer. I am more touched and overwhelmed than I will ever be able to tell you by your generosity, patience and the time you have spent reading what is essentially an absolutely enormous Word document. I say this without irony; you all make my heart soar. And I'm so sorry about all the s*x.

As always, thanks to the Jilly Cooper Book Club and the South London Lovers, my favourite people and constant (unwitting) colleagues. Thank you so much to everyone who listens to *You're Booked*, and every guest who lets me poke about their bookshelves. There are no writers without readers like you. Thank you to all my sisters, and to my parents for raising me to believe that books furnish rooms, minds and worlds. (Please don't read this one, though.)

Finally, thank you, Dale. For being the kindest, most constructive cheerleader, for reading this on a train from the moment it was hours old and just a five-thousand-word orgy, for being the greatest writer, reader and friend I will ever know, and for making me so happy that I wasn't scared to write about feeling sad. I could never have written a love story if I hadn't fallen in love with you.